A BRIDE FOR THE ISLAND PRINCE

BY
REBECCA WINTERS

First published in Great Britain 2012
by Mills & Boon, an imprint of Harlequin (UK) Limited,
Eton House, 18-24 Paradise Road, Richmond, Surrey TW9 1SR

© Rebecca Winters 2012

ISBN: 978 0 263 89415 8

23-0312

Harlequin (UK) policy is to use papers that are natural, renewable and recyclable products and made from wood grown in sustainable forests. The logging and manufacturing processes conform to the legal environmental regulations of the country of origin.

Printed and bound in Spain
by Blackprint CPI, Barcelona

Rebecca Winters, whose family of four children has now swelled to include five beautiful grandchildren, lives in Salt Lake City, Utah, in the land of the Rocky Mountains. With canyons and high alpine meadows full of wildflowers, she never runs out of places to explore. They, plus her favourite vacation spots in Europe, often end up as backgrounds for her romance novels, because writing is her passion, along with her family and church. Rebecca loves to hear from readers. If you wish to e-mail her, please visit her website at www.cleanromances.com.

I'd like to dedicate this book to JULIE the speech
therapist at the elementary school. With her sunny
smile and dedication, she helped my children
work through a difficult period for them and
I'll always be grateful.

CHAPTER ONE

PRINCE Alexius Kristof Rudolph Stefano Valleder Constantinides, Duke of Aurum and second in line to the throne of Hellenica, had been working in his office all morning when he heard a rap on the door. "Yes?" he called out.

"Your Highness? If I might have a word with you?"

"What is it, Hector?" The devoted assistant to the crown poked his head in the door. Hector, who'd been the right hand to Alex's father and grandfather, had been part of the palace administrative staff for over fifty years. He knew better than to disturb Alex unless it was urgent. "I'm reading through some important contracts. Can't this wait until after lunch?"

"The national head of the hospital association is here and most eager to thank you for the unprecedented help you've given them to build four new hospitals our country has needed so badly. Would it be possible for you to give him a little of your time?"

Alex didn't have to think about it. Those facilities should have been built long before now. Better health care for everyone was something he felt strongly about. "Yes. Of course. Show him to the dining room and I'll be there shortly."

"He'll be very pleased. And now, one other matter, Your Highness."

"Then come all the way in, Hector."

The substantial-looking man whose salt-and-pepper hair was thinning on top did Alex's bidding. "The queen instructed me to tell you that Princess Zoe has had another of her moments this morning." In other words, a temper tantrum.

He lifted his dark head. His four-year-old daughter meant more to him than life itself. For this reason he was alarmed by the change in her behavior that was making Zoe more and more difficult to deal with.

Unfortunately the queen wasn't well, and Alex had to shoulder his elder brother Stasio's royal responsibilities while he was out of the country. He knew none of this was helping his daughter.

For the past four months her meltdowns had been growing worse. He'd been through three nannies in that period. At the moment Alex was without one for her. In desperation he'd turned to Queen Desma, his autocratic grandmother, who, since the death of his grandfather, King Kristof, was the titular head of Hellenica, a country made up of a cluster of islands in the Aegean and Thracian seas.

She had a soft spot for her great-granddaughter and had asked one of her personal maids, Sofia, to look after her until a new nanny could be found. What his grandmother really wanted was for Alex to take a new wife. Since by royal decree he could only marry another princess, rather than being able to choose a bride from any background, Alex had made the decision never to marry again. One arranged marriage had been enough.

Lately Zoe had been spending most of her time in the

quarters of her great-grandmother, who'd been trying in her unsubtle way to prepare Zoe for a new mother. The queen had been behind the match between Alex and his deceased wife, Teresa. Both women were from the House of Valleder.

Now, with Teresa gone, his grandmother had been negotiating with the House of Helvetia for a marriage between her grandson and the princess Genevieve, but her machinations were wasted on Alex.

"I had breakfast with her earlier this morning and she seemed all right. What happened to set her off with Sofia?"

"Not Sofia," he clarified. "But two new situations *have* arisen. If I may speak frankly."

Only two? Alex ground his teeth in worry and frustration. He'd had hopes this was a phase that would pass, but the situation was growing worse. "You always do."

"Her new American tutor, Dr. Wyman, just handed in his notice, and her Greek tutor, Kyrie Costas, is threatening to resign. As you know, the two have been at odds with each other over the proper curriculum for the princess. Dr. Wyman is out in the hall. Before he leaves the palace, he requests a brief audience with you."

Alex got to his feet. Two weeks ago he'd been forced to withdraw her from the preschool classes she went to three times a week because her teacher couldn't get her to participate. Fearing something was physically wrong with Zoe, he'd asked his personal physician to give her a thorough examination. But the doctor had found nothing wrong.

Now her English tutor had resigned? Alex's wife, who'd spent a portion of her teenage years in America, had died of a serious heart condition. Before passing away she'd made him promise Zoe would grow up to be fluent in English. He'd done everything in his power to honor her wishes, even hiring an American tutor. Alex himself made an effort to speak English with her every day.

He took a fortifying breath. "Show him in."

The forty-year-old American teacher had come highly recommended after leaving the employ of Alex's second cousin, King Alexandre Philippe of Valleder, a principality bordering the Romanche-speaking canton of Switzerland. No longer needing a tutor for his son, the king, who was best friends with Alex's brother, had recommended Dr. Wyman to come to Hellenica and teach Zoe.

"Your Highness." He bowed.

"Dr. Wyman? Hector tells me you've resigned. Is my daughter truly too difficult for you to handle any longer?"

"Lately it's a case of her running away when she sees me," he answered honestly. "It's my opinion she's frightened about something and hardly speaks at all. What comes out I don't understand. Mr. Costas says it's my method, but I disagree. Something's wrong, but I'm only a teacher."

Since Zoe's medical exam, Alex had considered calling in a child psychiatrist for a consultation. Dr. Wyman said she was frightened. Alex agreed. This behavior wasn't normal. So far he'd thought it was a case of arrested development because Zoe had been born premature. But maybe not having a mother had brought on psychological problems that hadn't been recognizable until now.

"If she were your child, what would you do?"

"Well, I think before I took her to a child psychologist, I'd find out if there's a physiological problem that is preventing her from talking as much as she should. If so, maybe that's what is frightening her."

"Where could I go for that kind of expertise?"

"The Stillman Institute in New York City. Their clinic has some of the best speech therapists in the United States. I'd take my child there for an evaluation."

"I'll look into it. Thank you for your suggestion and your help with Princess Zoe, Dr. Wyman. I appreciate your honesty. You leave the palace with my highest recommendation."

"Thank you, Your Highness. I hope you get answers soon. I'm very fond of her."

So am I.

After Dr. Wyman left, Alex checked his watch. By the time he'd had lunch with the head of the hospital association, the clinic in New York would be open. Alex would call and speak to the director.

Dottie Richards had never ridden in a helicopter before. After her jet had touched down in Athens, Greece, she was told it was just a short journey to Hellenica.

The head of the Stillman Speech Institute had picked her to handle an emergency that had arisen. Apparently there was an important little four-year-old girl who needed diagnostic testing done ASAP. A temporary visa had been issued for Dottie to leave the country without having to wait the normal time for a passport.

For security reasons, she hadn't learned the identity of the little girl until she was met at the helicopter pad in Athens by a palace spokesman named Hector. Apparently the child was Princess Zoe, the only daughter of Prince Alexius Constantinides, a widower who was acting ruler of Hellenica.

"Acting ruler, you say?"

"Yes, madame. The heir apparent to the throne, Crown Prince Stasio, is out of the country on business. When he returns, he will be marrying Princess Beatriz. Their wedding is scheduled for July the fifth. At that time the dowager queen Desma, Princess Zoe's great-grandmother, will relinquish the crown and Prince Stasio will become king of Hellenica.

"In the meantime Prince Alexius is handling the daily affairs of state. He has provided his private helicopter so you can be given a sightseeing trip to the palace, located on the biggest island, also called Hellenica."

Dottie realized this was a privilege not many people were granted. "That's very kind of him." She climbed aboard and the helicopter took off, but the second it left the ground she grew dizzy and tried to fight it off. "Could you tell me what exactly is wrong with Princess Zoe?"

"That's a subject for you to discuss with the prince himself."

Uh-oh. "Of course."

Dottie was entering a royal world where silence was the better part of discretion. No doubt that was why Hector had been chosen for this duty. She wouldn't guess the older man was the type to leave the royal household and write a book revealing the dark secrets of the centuries-old Constantinides family. Dottie admired his loyalty and would have told him so, but by then she was starting to experience motion sickness from the helicopter and was too nauseated to talk any more.

Several years earlier, Dottie had seen pictures of

the Constantinides brothers on various television news broadcasts. Both had playboy reputations, like so many royal sons. They'd been dark and attractive enough, but seen in the inside of a limo or aboard a royal yacht, it was difficult to get a real sense of their looks.

Dottie had never been anywhere near a royal and knew nothing about their world except for their exposure in the media, which didn't always reflect positively. But for an accident of birth, she could have been born a princess. Anyone could be. Royals were human beings after all. They entered the world, ate, slept, married and died like the rest of humanity. It was what they did, where they did it and how they did it that separated them from the masses.

Raised by a single aunt, now deceased, who'd never married and had been a practical thinker, Dottie's world hadn't included many fairy tales. Though there'd been moments growing up when Dottie had been curious about being a queen or a princess. Now an unprecedented opportunity had arisen for her to find out what that was like.

Dottie had seen and heard enough about royals involved in escapades and scandals to feel sorry for them. The trials of being an open target to the world had to be worse than those of a celebrity, whose popularity waxed strong for a time in the eyes of public adulation and curiosity, then waned out of sight.

A royal stayed a royal forever and was scrutinized ad nauseum. A prince or princess couldn't even be born or die without a crowd in attendance. But as Dottie had learned during an early period in her life, the trials of an ordinary human were sometimes so bad they drew unwanted attention from the public, too. Like with King

George VI of England, her own severe stuttering problem had been an agony to endure. However, to be human and a royal at the same time placed one in double jeopardy.

At the age of twenty-nine and long since free of her former speech problem, Dottie loved her anonymity. In that sense she felt compassion for the little princess she hadn't even met yet. The poor thing was already under a microscope and would remain there for all the days of life she was granted. Whether she had a speech problem or something that went deeper, word would get out.

One day when the motherless princess was old enough to understand, she'd learn the world was talking about her and would never leave her alone. If she had a physical or a noticeable psychological problem, the press would be merciless. Dottie vowed in her heart she'd do whatever possible to help the little girl, *if* it were in her power.

But at the moment the helicopter trip was playing havoc with her stomach and the lovely sightseeing trip had been wasted on her. The second they landed and she was shown to her quarters in the glistening white royal palace, she lost any food she'd eaten and went straight to bed.

It was embarrassing, but when she was green around the gills and unable to rally, nothing except a good night's sleep would help her to recover. When her business was finished here and she left the country to go back to the States, she would take a flight from Hellenica's airport to Athens before boarding a flight to New York. No more helicopter rides.

* * *

Alex eyed his ailing, widowed grandmother, whose silvery hair was still thick at eighty-five. She tired more easily these days and kept to her apartment. Alex knew she was more than ready for Stasio to come home and officially take the worries of the monarchy from her shoulders.

No one awaited Stasio's return with more eagerness than Alex. When his brother had left on the first of April, he'd promised to be home by mid-May, yet it was already the thirtieth with his wedding only five weeks away. Alex needed out of his temporary responsibilities to spend more time with Zoe. He'd built up his hopes that this speech therapist could give him definitive answers. It would be a step in the right direction; his daughter was growing unhappier with each passing day.

"Thank you for breakfast," he said in Greek. "If you two will excuse me, I have some business, but I'll be back." He kissed his petite daughter, who was playing with her roll instead of eating it. "Be good for *Yiayia*."

Zoe nodded.

After bowing to his grandmother, he left her suite and hurried downstairs to his office in the other part of the palace. He'd wanted to meet this Mrs. Richards last evening, but Hector had told him she'd never ridden in a helicopter before and had become ill during the flight. There'd been nothing he could do but wait until this morning and wonder if her getting sick was already a bad omen.

He knew better than to ask Hector what she was like. His assistant would simply answer, "That's not for me to say, Your Highness." His tendency not to gossip was a sterling quality Alex admired, but at times it drove Stasio insane.

For years his elder brother had barked at Hector that he wasn't quite human. Alex had a theory that the reason why Hector irked Stasio was because Stasio had grown up knowing that one day he'd have to be king. Hector was a permanent reminder that Stasio's greatest duty was to his country, to marry Princess Beatriz and produce heirs to the throne.

Like the queen, who wanted more great-grandchildren for the glory of Hellenica, Alex looked forward to his brother producing some cousins for Zoe. His little girl would love a baby around. She'd asked Alex for a sister, but all he could say was that her uncle Stasi would produce a new heir to the throne before long.

After reaching his office, he scowled when he read the fax sent from Stasio, who was still in Valleder. *Sorry, little brother, but banking business will keep me here another week. Tell Yiayia I'll be home soon. Give Zoe a hug from her uncle. Hang in there. You do great work. Stasi.*

"Your Highness? May I present Mrs. Richards."

He threw his head back. Hector had come in the office without him being aware of it and was now clearing his throat. A very American-looking woman—down to the way she carried herself—had entered with him, taller than average, with her light brown hair swept up in a loose knot. Alex was so disappointed, even angered by his brother's news, he'd forgotten for a moment that Hector was on his way down. Stasio had taken advantage of their bargain.

"One month, little brother," he'd said when he'd left.

"That's all I need to carry out some lucrative banking negotiations. Philippe is helping me." But Stasio had been gone much longer and Alex wasn't happy about it. Neither was the queen, the prime minister or the archbishop, who were getting anxious to confer with him about the coronation and royal nuptials coming up soon.

Pushing his feelings aside, Alex got to his feet. "Welcome to Hellenica, Mrs. Richards."

"Thank you, Your Highness."

She gave an awkward curtsey, no doubt coached by Hector. He hated to admit she looked fresh, appealing even, as she stood there in a pale blue blouse and skirt that tied at her slender waist, drawing his attention to the feminine curves revealed above and below. He hadn't meant to stare, but his eyes seemed to have a will of their own as they took in her long, shapely legs.

Alex quickly shifted his gaze to her face and was caught off guard again by the wide, sculpted mouth and the cornflower-blue of her eyes. They reminded him of the cornflowers growing wild alongside larkspurs on Aurum Island where he normally lived.

He missed his private palace there where he conducted the mining interests for the monarchy, away from Hellenica. The big island drew the tourists in hordes, Aurum not quite so much. He shouldn't mind tourists since they were one of his country's greatest financial resources, but with his daughter in such distress, everything bothered him these days. Especially the woman standing in front of him.

A speech therapist could come in any size and shape. He just hadn't expected *this* woman, period. For one thing, she looked too young for the task ahead of her. No wonder Hector hadn't dropped a clue about her.

"I've been told you suffered on your helicopter ride. I hope you're feeling better."

"Much better, thank you. The view was spectacular."

One dark brow dipped. "What little you saw of it in your condition."

"Little is right," she acknowledged in a forthright manner. "I'm sorry your generous attempt to show me the sights in your helicopter didn't have the desired outcome." Her blunt way of speaking came as a surprise. "Will I be meeting your daughter this morning?"

"Yes." He flicked his glance to Hector. "Would you ask Sofia to bring Zoe to us?"

The older man gave a brief bow and slipped out of the office, leaving the two of them alone. Alex moved closer and invited her to sit down on the love seat. "Would you care for tea or coffee?"

"Nothing for me. I just had some tea. It's settling my stomach, but please have some yourself if you want it."

If *he* wanted it? She was more of a surprise than ever and seemed at ease, which wasn't always the case with strangers meeting him.

"My boss, Dr. Rice, told me your daughter is having trouble communicating, but he didn't give me any details. How long since your wife passed away?"

"Two years ago."

"And now Zoe is four. That means she wouldn't have any memory of her mother except what you've told her, and of course pictures. Did your wife carry Zoe full term?"

"No. She came six weeks early and was in the hospital almost a month. I feared we might lose her, but she finally rallied. I thought that could be the reason why she's been a little slower to make herself understood."

"Was her speech behind from infancy?"

"I don't really know what's normal. Not having been around children before, I had no way to compare her progress. All I know is her speech is difficult to understand. The queen and I are used to her, but over the past few months her behaviour's become so challenging, we've lost her art, English and dance teachers and three nannies. Her Greek tutor has all but given up and she's too much for the teacher to handle at her preschool."

"It's usually the caregiver who first notices if there's a problem. Would that have been your wife?"

"Yes, but a lot of the time she was ill with a bad heart and the nanny had to take over. I took charge in the evenings after my work, but I hadn't been truly alarmed about Zoe until two weeks ago when I had to withdraw her from preschool. As I told you earlier, I'd assumed that being a premature baby, she simply hadn't caught up yet."

"Has she had her normal checkup with the pediatrician?"

"Yes."

"No heart problem with her."

He shook his dark head. "I even took her to my own internist for a second opinion. Neither doctor found anything physically wrong with her, but they gave me the name of a child psychiatrist to find out if something else is going on to make her behind in her speech. Before I did that, I decided to take Dr. Wyman's advice. He recommended I take her to the Stillman Institute for a diagnosis before doing anything else."

"I see. What kind of behavior does she manifest?"

"When it comes time for her lessons lately, Zoe has tantrums and cries hysterically. All she wants to do is hide in her bed or run to her great-grandmother's suite for comfort."

"What about her appetite?"

This morning Zoe had taken only a few nibbles of her breakfast, another thing that had alarmed him. "Not what it should be."

She studied his features as if she were trying to see inside him. "You must be frantic."

Frantic? "Yes," he murmured. That was the perfect word to describe his state of mind. Mrs. Richards was very astute, but unlike everyone else in his presence except the queen and Stasio, she spoke her mind.

"Imagine your daughter feeling that same kind of emotion and then times it by a hundred."

Alex blinked. This woman's observation brought it home that she might just know what she was talking about. While he was deep in contemplation, his daughter appeared, clinging to Sofia's hand. Hector slipped in behind them.

"Zoe?" Alex said in English. "Come forward." She took a tentative step. "This is Mrs. Richards. She's come all the way from New York to see you. Can you say hello to her?"

His daughter took one look at their guest and her face crumpled in pain. He knew that look. She was ready for flight. With his stomach muscles clenched, he switched to Greek and asked her the same question. This time Zoe's response was to say she wanted her *yiayia*, then she burst into tears and ran out of the room. Sofia darted after her.

Alex called her back and started for the door, but Mrs. Richards unexpectedly said, "Let her go."

Her countermand surprised him. Except for his own

deceased father, no one had ever challenged him like that, let alone about his own daughter. It was as if their positions had been reversed and she was giving the orders. The strange irony set his teeth on edge.

"She probably assumes I'm her new nanny," she added in a gentler tone. "I don't blame her for running away. I can see she's at her wit's end. The first thing I'd like you to do is get her in to an ear, nose and throat specialist followed up by an audiologist."

He frowned, having to tamp down his temper. "As I told you a minute ago, Zoe has already been given two checkups."

"Not that kind of exam," she came back, always keeping her voice controlled. "A child or an adult with speech problems could have extra wax buildup not noticeable with a normal check-up because it's deep inside. It's not either doctor's fault. They're not specialists in this area. If there's nothing wrong with her ears and I can't help her, then your daughter needs to see a child psychiatrist to find out why she's regressing.

"For now let's find out if more wax than normal has accumulated recently. If so, it must be cleaned out to help improve her hearing. Otherwise sounds could be blocked or distorted, preventing her from mimicking them."

"Why would there be an abnormal amount of wax?"

"Does she get earaches very often?"

"A few every year."

"It's possible her ear canals are no longer draining as they should."

That made sense. His hands formed fists. Why hadn't he thought of it?

Her well-shaped brows lifted. "Not even a prince

can know everything." She'd read his mind and her comment sent his blood pressure soaring. "Will you arrange it? Sooner would be better than later because I can't get started on my testing until the procedure has been done. That child needs help in a hurry."

As if Alex didn't know... Why else had he sent for *her*?

He didn't like feeling guilty because he'd let the problem go on too long without exploring every avenue. Alex also didn't like being second-guessed or told what to do. But since it was Zoe they were talking about, he decided to let it go for now. "I'll see that a specialist fits her in today."

"Good. Let me know the results and we'll go from there." She turned to leave.

"I haven't excused you yet, Mrs. Richards."

She wheeled back around. "Forgive me, and please call me Dottie." Through the fringe of her dark, silky lashes, her innocent blue gaze eyed him frankly. "I've never worked with a parent who's a monarch. This is a new experience."

Indeed, it was. It appeared Alex was an acquired taste, something he hadn't known could happen. He wasn't a conceited man, but it begged the question whether she had an instant dislike of him.

"Monarch or not, do you always walk away from a conversation before it's over?"

"I thought it was." She stood firm. "I deal with pre-schoolers all the time and your little girl is so adorable, I'm hoping to get to the bottom of her problem right away. I'm afraid I'm too focused on my job. Your Highness," she tacked on, as if she weren't sure whether to say it or not.

She was different from anyone he'd ever met. Not rude exactly, yet definitely the opposite of obsequious. He didn't know what to think of her. But just now she'd sounded sincere enough where his daughter was concerned. Alex needed to take the advice his mother had given him as a boy. Never react on a first impression or you could live to regret it.

"I'm glad you're focused," he said and meant it. "She's the light of my life."

The briefest glint of pain entered her eyes. "You're a lucky man to have her, even if you *are* a prince."

His brows furrowed. "Even if I'm a prince?"

She shook her head. "I'm sorry. I meant— Well, I meant that one assumes a prince has been given everything in life and is very lucky. But to be the father of a darling daughter, too, makes you that much luckier."

Though she smiled, he heard a sadness in her words. Long after he'd excused her and had arranged for the doctor's appointment, the shadow he'd seen in those deep blue eyes stayed with him.

CHAPTER TWO

DOTTIE stayed in her room for part of the day, fussing and fuming over a situation she could do little about. *I haven't excused you yet, Mrs. Richards.*

The mild rebuke had fallen from the lips of a prince who was outrageously handsome. Tall and built like the statue of a Greek god, he possessed the inky-black hair and eyes of his Hellenican ancestry. Everything—his chiseled jaw, his strong male features—set him apart from other men.

Even if he weren't royal, he looked like any woman's idea of a prince. He'd stood there in front of his country's flag, effortlessly masculine and regal in a silky blue shirt and white trousers that molded to his powerful thighs.

He'd smelled good, too. Dottie noticed things like that and wished she hadn't because it reminded her that beneath the royal mantle, he was human.

Already she feared she might not be the right person for this job. Dr. Rice, the head of her department at the Stillman clinic, had said he'd handpicked her for this assignment because of her own personal experiences that gave her more understanding. Fine, but in order to give herself time to get used to the idea, she should have been told she was coming to a royal household before she boarded the jet in New York.

The atmosphere here was different from anything Dottie had known and she needed time to adjust. There was so much to deal with—the stiffness, the protocol, the maids and nannies, the teachers, the tutors, a prince for a father who'd been forced to obey a rigid schedule his whole life, a princess without a mother....

A normal child would have run into the room and hugged her daddy without thinking about it, but royal etiquette had held Zoe back from doing what came naturally. She'd appeared in the doorway and stood at attention like a good soldier.

The whole thing had to be too much for a little girl who just wanted to be a little girl. In the end she'd broken those rules and had taken off down the hall, her dark brown curls bouncing. Despite his calling her name, she'd kept going. The precious child couldn't handle any more.

Dottie's heart ached for Zoe who'd ignored her father's wishes and had run out of his office with tears flowing from those golden-brown eyes. She must have gotten her coloring from her mother, who'd probably been petite. His daughter had inherited her beauty and olive skin from her father, no doubt from her mother, too.

The vague images Dottie had retained of him and his brother through the media had been taken when they were much younger, playboy princes setting hearts afire throughout Europe. In the intervening years, Zoe's father had become a married man who'd lost his wife too soon in life. Tragic for him, and more tragic for a child to lose a parent. Unfortunately it had happened.

Dottie was the enemy of the moment where Zoe was concerned, and she'd would have to be careful how she approached her to do the testing. Soon enough she would discover how much of Zoe's problem was emotional or physical. Probably both.

With a deep sigh she ate the lunch a maid had brought her on a tray. Later another maid offered to unpack for her, but Dottie thanked her before dismissing her. She could do it herself. In fact she didn't want to get completely unpacked in case she'd be leaving the palace right away. If the little princess had a problem outside of Dottie's expertise, then Dottie would soon be flown back to New York from the island.

At five o'clock the phone rang at the side of her queen-size bed. It was Hector. The prince wished to speak to her in his office. He was sending a maid to escort her. It was on the tip of Dottie's tongue to tell him she didn't need help finding the prince's inner sanctum, but she had to remember that when in Rome... Already she'd made a bad impression. It wouldn't do to alienate him further, not when he was so anxious about his daughter.

She thanked Hector and freshened up. In a minute, one of the maids arrived and accompanied her down a different staircase outside her private guest suite to the main floor. The prince was waiting for her.

Out of deference to him, she waited until he spoke first. He stood there with his hands on his hips. By the aura of energy he was giving out with those jet-black eyes playing over her, she sensed he had something of significance to tell her.

"Sit down, please."

She did his bidding, anxious to hear about the result of the examination.

"Once we could get Zoe to cooperate, the doctor found an inordinate amount of wax adhering to her eardrums from residual fluid. She hated every second of it, but after they were cleaned out, she actually smiled when he asked her if she could hear better. The audiologist did tests afterwards and said her hearing is fine."

"Oh, that's wonderful news!" Dottie cried out happily.

"Yes. On the way back to the palace, I could tell she did understand more words being spoken to her. There was understanding in her eyes."

Beneath that formal reserve of his, she knew he was relieved for that much good news. A prince could move mountains and that's what he'd done today by getting her into an ear specialist so fast. In fact, he'd made it possible for Dottie to come to Hellenica instead of the other way around. What greater proof that the man loved his daughter?

"This is an excellent start, Your Highness."

"When do you want to begin testing her?"

"Tomorrow morning. She needs to have a good night's sleep first. After what she's been through today, she doesn't need any more trauma."

"Agreed." She heard a wealth of emotion in that one word. Dottie could imagine the struggle his daughter had put up. "Where would you like to test her?"

Since the prince was still standing, Dottie got to her feet to be on par with him, but she still needed to look up. "If you asked her where her favorite place is to play, what would she tell you?"

After a moment he said, "The patio off my bedroom."

That didn't surprise Dottie. His little girl wanted to be near him without anyone else around. "Does she play there often?"

She heard his sharp intake of breath. "No. It's not allowed unless I'm there, too." Of course not. "My work normally goes past her bedtime."

"And mornings?"

"While we've been at the palace, I've always had breakfast with her in the queen's suite. Zoe's the most comfortable there."

"I'm talking before breakfast."

"That's when I work out and she takes a swimming lesson."

Dottie fought to remain quiet, but her impulse was to cry out in dismay over the strict regimen. "So what times does she get to play with you on your patio?"

He pursed his lips. "Sunday afternoons after chapel and lunch. Why all these questions?"

She needed to be careful she didn't offend him again. "I'm trying to get a sense of her day and her relationship with you. When is her Greek lesson?"

"Before her dinner."

"You don't eat dinner with her, then?"

"No."

Oh. Poor Zoe. "You say she was attending a preschool until two weeks ago?"

"Yes. The sessions went in two-hour segments, three times a week. Monday, Wednesday and Friday. But lately I haven't insisted for the obvious reasons."

"When does she play with friends?"

"You mean outside her school?"

"Yes. Does she have friends here at the palace?"

"No, but we normally live on Aurum where she has several."

"I see. Thank you for giving me that information. Would it be all right with you if I test her out on your patio? I believe she'll be more responsive in a place where she's truly happy and at ease. If you're there, too, it will make her more comfortable. But with your full schedule I don't suppose that's poss—"

"I'll make time for it," he declared, cutting her off.

No matter how she said things, she seemed to be in the wrong. It wasn't her intention to push his buttons, but she was doing a good job of it anyway. "That would be ideal. It's important I watch her interaction with you. Before you come, I'd like to set up out there with a few things I've brought."

His brows lifted. "How much time do you need?"

"A few minutes."

He nodded. "I'll send a maid to escort you at eight. Zoe and I will join you at eight-twenty. Does that meet with your approval?"

Eight-twenty? Not eight-twenty-one? *Stop it, Dottie. You're in a different world now.* "Only if it meets with yours, Your Highness."

This close to him, she could see a tiny nerve throbbing at the corner of his compelling mouth. His lips had grown taut. "If I haven't made it clear before, let me say this again. My daughter is my life. That makes her my top priority." She believed him.

"I know," Dottie murmured. "While I'm here, she's mine, too."

A long silence ensued before he stepped away. "I've instructed Hector to make certain you're comfortable while you're here. Your dinner can be served in the small guest dining room on the second floor, or he'll have it brought to your room. Whatever you prefer. Anything you want or need, you have only to pick up the phone and ask him and he'll see to it."

"Thank you. He's been so perfect, I can hardly believe he's real."

"My brother and I have been saying the same thing about him for years." The first glimmer of an unexpected smile reached his black eyes. He did have his human moments. The proof of it set off waves of sensation through her body she hadn't expected or wanted to feel.

"If you'll eat your eggs, I have a surprise for you." Zoe jerked her head around and eyed Alex in excitement. "I'm going to spend time with you this morning and thought we'd play out on my patio. That's why I told Sofia to let you wear pants."

She made a sound of delight and promptly took several bites. The queen sent him a private glance that said she hoped this testing session with the new speech therapist wasn't going to be a waste of time. Alex hoped not, too. No one wanted constructive feedback more than he did.

After Zoe finished off her juice, she wiggled down from the chair and started to dart away. Alex called her back. "You must ask to be excused."

She turned to her grandmother. "Can I go with daddy, *Yiayia*?"

The queen nodded. "Have a good time."

Alex groaned in silence, remembering the way his daughter had flown out of his office yesterday after one look at Dottie.

Zoe slipped her hand into his and they left for his suite. She skipped along part of the way. When he saw how thrilled she was to be with him, he found himself even more put out with Stasio.

As soon as his brother got back from Vallader, Alex planned to take more time off to be with his daughter. While he'd had to be here at the palace doing his brother's work plus his own, he'd hardly had a minute to spend time with her. Maybe they'd go on a mini vacation together.

The curtains to the patio had been opened. Zoe ran through the bedroom ahead of him, then suddenly stopped at the sight of the woman sitting on the patio tiles in jeans and a pale orange, short-sleeved cotton top.

"Hi, Zoe," she spoke in English with a smile. Dottie had put on sneakers and her hair was loose in a kind of disheveled bob that revealed the light honey tones among the darker swaths. "Do you think your daddy can catch this?" She threw a Ping-Pong ball at him.

When he caught it with his right hand, Zoe cried out in surprise. He threw it back to Dottie who caught it in her left. Their first volley of the day. For no particular reason his pulse rate picked up at the thought of what else awaited him in her presence.

"Good catch. Come on, Daddy." Her dancing blue gaze shot to his. "You and Zoe sit down and spread your legs apart like this and we'll roll some balls to each other." She pulled a larger multicolored plastic ball from a big bag and opened those long, fabulous legs of hers.

Alex could tell his daughter was so shocked by what was going on, she forgot to be scared and sat down to imitate Dottie once he'd complied. Dottie rolled the ball to Zoe, who rolled it back to her. Then it was his turn. They went in a round, drawing Zoe in. Pretty soon their guest pulled out a rubber ball and rolled it to his daughter right after she'd sent her the plastic ball.

Zoe laughed as she hurried to keep both balls going. His clever little girl used her right and left hand at the same time and sent one ball to Dottie and one to him. "Good thinking!" she praised her. "Shall we try three balls?"

"Yes," his daughter said excitedly. Their guest produced the Ping-Pong ball and fired all three balls at both of them, one after the other, until Zoe was giggling hysterically.

"You're so good at this, I think we'll try something else. Shall we see who's better at jumping?" She whipped out a jump rope with red handles and got to her feet. "Come on, Zoe. You take this end and I'll hold on to the other. Your daddy's going to jump first. You'll have to make big circles like I'm doing or the rope will hit him in the head."

"Oh, no—" Zoe cried.

"Don't worry," Dottie inserted. "Your daddy is a big boy. It won't hurt him."

So their visitor *had* noticed. Was that a negative in her eyes, too?

Zoe scrutinized him. "You're a boy?"

"Yes. He's a very big one," Dottie answered for him and his daughter laughed. Soon Zoe was using all her powers of concentration to turn the rope correctly and was doing an amazing job of it. After four times to get it right he heard, "You can jump in anytime now, Daddy."

Alex crouched down and managed to do two jumps

before getting caught around the shoulders. He was actually disappointed when their leader said, "Okay, now it's Zoe's turn. How many can you do?"

She cocked her dark brown head. "Five—"

"Well, that's something I want to see. Watch while we turn the rope. Whenever you think you're ready, jump in. It's okay if it takes you a whole bunch of times to do it, Zoe. Your daddy isn't going anywhere, right?"

She didn't look at him as she said it. He had a feeling it was on purpose.

"We're both in your hands for as long as it takes, Dorothy." He'd read the background information on her and knew it was her legal name.

"I never go by my given name," she said to Zoe without missing a beat while she continued to rotate the rope. "You can call me Dottie."

"That means crazy, doesn't it?" he threw out, curious to see how she'd respond.

"Your English vocabulary is remarkable, Your Highness."

"Is she crazy?" Zoe asked while she stood there, hesitant to try jumping.

"Be careful how you answer that," Dottie warned him. "Little royal pitchers have big ears and hers seem to be working just fine."

Alex couldn't help chuckling. He smiled at his daughter. "She's funny-crazy. Don't you think?"

"Yes." Zoe giggled again.

"Come on and jump." After eight attempts accompanied by a few tears, she finally managed a perfect jump. Dottie clapped her hands. "Good job, Zoe. Next time you'll do more."

She put the rope aside and reached into her bag of

tricks. His daughter wasn't the only one interested to see what she would pull out next. "For this game we have to get on our tummies."

The speech therapist might as well have been a magician. At this point his daughter was entranced and did what was suggested without waiting for Alex. In another minute Dottie had laid twenty-four cards facedown on the floor in four rows. She turned one card over. "Do you know what this is, Zoe?"

His daughter nodded. "Pig."

"Yes, and there's another card just like it. You have to remember where this card is, and then find the other one. When you do, then you make a book of them and put the pile to the side. You get one turn. Go ahead."

Zoe turned over another card.

"What is it?"

"Whale."

"Yes, but it's not a pig. So you have to put the card back. Okay, Daddy. It's your turn."

Alex turned over a card in the corner.

"Tiger, Daddy."

Before he could say anything, he saw their eyes look to the doorway. Alex turned around in frustration to see who had interrupted them.

"Hector?"

"Forgive me, Your Highness. There's a call for you from Argentum on an urgent matter that needs your attention."

Much as Alex hated to admit it, this had to be an emergency, otherwise Bari would have sent him an email. Barisou Jouflas was the head mining engineer on the island of Argentum and Alex's closest friend since college. He always enjoyed talking to him and got to his feet, expecting an outburst from Zoe. To his astonishment, Dottie had her completely engrossed in the matching game.

"I'll be back as soon as I can."

Dottie nodded without looking at him.

"Bye, Daddy," his daughter said, too busy looking for a matching card to turn her head.

Bye, Daddy— Since when? No tantrum because he was leaving?

Out of the corner of her eye Dottie watched the prince disappear and felt a twinge of disappointment for his daughter. They'd all been having fun and it was one time when he hadn't wanted to leave, she felt sure of it. But there were times when the affairs of the kingdom did have to take priority. Dottie understood that and forgave him.

He might be gone some time. Dottie still had other tests to do that she preferred to take place outside the palace. Now would be a good time to carry them out while Zoe was still amenable. Her speech was close to unintelligible, but she was bright as a button and Dottie understood most of what she was trying to say because of her years of training and personal experience.

Once they'd concluded the matching game she said, "Zoe? Do you want to come down to the beach with me?" The little girl clapped her hands in excitement.

"All right, then. Let's do it." Dottie got up and pulled a bag of items out of the bigger bag. "Shall we go down from here?"

"Yes!" Zoe stood up and started down the stairs at the far end of the patio. Dottie followed. The long stairway covering two stories led to the dazzling blue water below.

It was a warm, beautiful day. When they reached the beach, she pulled out a tube of sunscreen and covered both of them. Next she drew floppy sun hats from the bag for them to put on.

"Here's a shovel. Will you show me how you build a castle?"

Zoe got to work and made a large mound.

"That's wonderful. Now where do you think this flag should go?" She handed her a little one.

"Here!" She placed it on the very top.

"Perfect. Make a hole where the front door of the castle is located."

She made a big dent with her finger at the bottom. Dottie rummaged in the bag for a tiny sailboat and gave it to her. "This is your daddy's boat. Where do you think it goes?"

"Here." Zoe placed it at the bottom around the side.

"Good." Again Dottie reached in the bag and pulled out a plastic figure about one inch high. "Let's pretend this is your daddy. Where does he live in the castle?"

Zoe thought about it for a minute, then stuck him in the upper portion of the mound.

"And where do you sleep?" Dottie gave her a little female figure.

"Here." Zoe crawled around and pushed the figure into the mound at approximately the same level as the other.

"Do you sleep by your *Yiayia*?"

"No."

"Can you show me where she sleeps?" Dottie handed her another figure. Zoe moved around a little more and put it in at the same height. Everyone slept on the second floor.

"I like your castle. Let's take off our shoes and walk over to the water. Maybe we can find some pretty stones to decorate the walls. Here's a bucket to carry everything."

They spent the next ten minutes picking up tiny, multicolored stones. When they returned to the mound Dottie said, "Can you pour them on the sand and pick out the different colors? We'll put them in piles."

Zoe nodded, eager to sort everything. She was meticulous.

"Okay. Why don't you start with the pink stones and put them around the middle of the castle." Her little charge got the point in a hurry and did a masterful job. "Now place the orange stones near the top and the brown stones at the bottom."

While Zoe was finishing her masterpiece, Dottie took several pictures at different angles with her phone. "You'll have to show these pictures to your daddy. Now I think it's time to put our shoes on and go back to the palace. I'm hungry and thirsty and I bet you are, too. Here—let me brush the sand off your little piggies."

Zoe looked at her. "What?"

"These." She tugged on Zoe's toes. "These are your little pigs. Piggies. They go *wee wee wee*." She made a squealing sound.

When recognition dawned, laughter poured out of Zoe like tinkling bells. For just a moment it sounded like her little boy's laughter. Emotion caught Dottie by the throat.

"Mrs. Richards?" a male voice spoke out of the blue, startling her.

She jumped to her feet, fighting the tears pricking her eyelids, and looked around. A patrol boat had pulled up on the shore and she hadn't even heard it. Two men had converged on them, obviously guards protecting the palace grounds. "Yes?" She put her arm around Zoe's shoulders. "Is something wrong?"

"Prince Alexius has been looking for you. Stay here. He'll be joining you in a moment."

She'd done something wrong. Again.

No sooner had he said the words than she glimpsed the prince racing down the steps to the beach with the speed of a black panther in pursuit of its prey. The image sent a chill up her spine that raised the hairs on the back of her neck.

When he caught up to them, he gave a grim nod of dismissal to the guards, who got back in the patrol boat and took off.

"Look what I made, Daddy—" His daughter was totally unaware of the byplay.

Dottie could hear his labored breathing and knew it came from fright, not because he was out of shape. Anything but. While Zoe gave him a running commentary of their beach adventure in her inimitable way, Dottie put the bucket and shovel in the bag. When she turned around, she discovered him hunkered down, examining his daughter's work of art.

After listening to her intently, he lifted his dark head and shot Dottie a piercing black glance. Sotto voce, he said, "There are pirates in these waters who wait for an opportunity like this to—"

"I understand," she cut him off, feeling sick to her stomach. She'd figured it out before he'd said anything. "Forgive me. I swear it won't happen again."

"You're right about that."

His words froze the air in her lungs before he gripped his daughter's hand and started for the stairs.

"Come on," Zoe called to her.

Dottie followed, keeping her eyes on his hard-muscled physique clothed in a white polo shirt and dark blue trousers. Halfway up the stairs on those long, powerful legs, he gathered Zoe in his arms and carried her the rest of the way to the patio.

"The queen is waiting for Zoe to have lunch with her," he said when she caught up to him. "A maid is waiting outside my suite to conduct you back to your room. I've asked for a tray to be sent to you. We'll talk later."

Dottie heard Zoe's protests as he walked away. She gathered up the other bag and met the maid who accompanied her back to her own quarters. Once alone, she fled into the en suite bathroom and took a shower to wash off the sand and try to get her emotions under control.

No matter how unwittingly, she'd endangered the life of the princess. What if his little daughter had been kidnapped? It would have been Dottie's fault. All of it. The thought was so horrific, she couldn't bear it. The prince had every right to tell her she was leaving on the next flight to Athens.

This was one problem she didn't know how to fix. Being sorry wasn't enough. She'd wanted to make a difference in Zoe's life. The princess had passed every test with flying colors. Dottie was the one who'd never made the grade.

After drying off, she put on a white linen dress and sandals, prepared to be driven to the airport once the prince had told her he no longer required her services.

As she walked back into the bedroom, there was a knock on the door.

Dottie opened it to a maid who brought her a lunch tray and set it on the table in the alcove. She had no appetite but quenched her thirst with the flask of iced tea provided while she answered some emails from home. As she drained her second glass, there was another knock on the door.

"Hector?" she said after opening it. Somehow she wasn't surprised. He'd met her at the airport in Athens for her helicopter ride, and would deposit her at Hellenica's airport.

"Mrs. Richards. If you've finished your lunch, His Highness has asked me to take you to his office."

She deserved this. "I'm ready now."

By the time they reached it, she'd decided to leave today and would make it easy for the prince. But the room was empty. "Please be seated. His Highness will be with you shortly."

"Thank you." After he left, she sat on the love seat and waited. When the prince walked in, she jumped right back up again. "I'm so sorry for what happened today."

He seemed to have calmed down. "It's my fault for not having warned you earlier. There was a kidnapping attempt on Zoe at her preschool last fall."

"Oh, no—" Dottie cried out, aghast.

"Fortunately it failed. Since then I've tripled the security. It never occurred to me you would take Zoe down that long flight of stairs, even if it is our private beach. We can be grateful the patrol boats were watching you the entire time. You're as much a target as Zoe and you're my responsibility while you're here in Hellenica."

"I understand."

"Please be seated, Mrs. Richards."

"I— I can't," she stammered. Dottie bemoaned the fact that earlier during the testing, he'd called her Dorothy and had shown a teasing side to his nature. It had been unexpected and welcome. Right now those human moments out on the patio might never have been.

He eyed her up and down. "Have you injured yourself in some way?"

"You know I haven't," she murmured. "I wanted to tell you that you don't need to dismiss me because I'm leaving as soon as someone can drive me to the airport."

His black brows knit together in a fierce frown. "Whatever gave you the idea that your services are no longer required?"

She blinked in confusion. "*You* did, on the beach."

"Explain that to me," he demanded.

"When I swore to you that nothing like this would ever happen again, you said I was right about that."

His inky-black eyes had a laserlike quality. "So you jumped to the conclusion that I no longer trusted you with my daughter? Are you always this insecure?"

Dottie swallowed hard. "Only around monarchs who have to worry about pirates and kidnappers. I didn't know about those incidents and can't imagine how terrifying it must have been for you. When you couldn't find us today, it had to have been like déjà vu. I can't bear to think I caused you even a second's worry."

He took a deep breath. "From now on, whether with Zoe or alone, don't do anything without informing me of your intentions first. Then there won't be a problem."

"I agree." He was being much more decent about this than she had any right to expect. A feeling of admiration for his willingness to give her a second chance welled up inside her. When their eyes met again, she felt something almost tangible pass between them she couldn't explain, but it sent a sudden rush of warmth through her body, and she found herself unable to look away.

CHAPTER THREE

THE prince cleared his throat, breaking the spell. "After spending the day with my daughter, tell me what you've learned about her."

Dottie pulled herself together. The fear that she'd alienated the prince beyond salvaging almost made her forget why she'd come to Hellenica in the first place.

"I'll give you the bad news first. She has trouble articulating. Research tells us there are several reasons for it, but none of it matters. The fact is, she struggles with this problem.

"Now for the good news. Zoe is exceptionally intelligent with above-average motor and cognitive skills. Her vocabulary is remarkable. She understands prepositions and uses the right process to solve problems, such as in matching. Playing with her demonstrates her amazing dexterity. You saw her handling the balls and jumping rope. She has excellent coordination and balance.

"She follows directions the first time without problem. If you took a good look at that castle, it proves she sees things spatially. Her little mound had a first floor and a second floor, just like the palace. She understands her physical world and understands what she hears. Zoe only has one problem, as I said, but it's a big one since for the most part she can't make herself understood to anyone but you and the queen and, I presume to some extent, Sofia."

Alex nodded. "So that's why she's withdrawing from other people."

"Yes. You've told me she's been more difficult over the past few months. She's getting older and is losing her confidence around those who don't have her problem. She's smart enough to know she's different and not like everyone else. She wants to avoid situations that illuminate the difference, so she runs away and hides. It's the most natural instinct in the world.

"Zoe wants to make herself understood. The more she can't do it, the angrier she becomes, thus the tantrums. There's nothing wrong with her psychologically that wouldn't clear up immediately once she's free to express herself like everyone else does. She pushes people away and clings to you because you love her without qualification. But she knows the rest of the world doesn't love her, and she's feeling like a misfit."

The prince's sober expression masked a deep fear. She saw it in his eyes. "Can she overcome this?"

"Of course. She needs help saying all her sounds, but particularly the consonants. *H*'s and *T*'s are impossible for her. Few of her words come out right. Her frustration level has to be off the charts. But with constant work, she'll talk as well as I do."

He rubbed the back of his neck absently. "Are you saying you used to have the same problem?"

"I had a worse one. I stuttered so severely, I was the laughingstock of my classes in elementary school.

Children are cruel to other children. I used to pretend to be sick so I wouldn't have to go to school."

"How did you get through it?" He sounded pained for her.

"My aunt raised me. She was a stickler for discipline and sent me to a speech therapist every weekday, who taught me how to breathe, how to pace myself when I talked. After a few years I stuttered less and less. By high school it only showed up once in a while.

"Zoe has a different problem and needs to work on her sounds every day. If you could be the one encouraging her like a coach, she would articulate correct sounds faster. The more creativity, the better. I've brought toys and games you can play with her. While she's interacting with you, she'll learn to model her speech after you. Slowly but surely it will come."

"But you'll be here, too."

"Of course. You and I will work with her one on one, and sometimes the three of us will play together. I can't emphasize enough how much progress she'll make if you're available on a regular basis."

He shifted his weight. "How long do you think this will take?"

"Months to possibly several years. It's a gradual process and requires patience on everyone's part. When you feel confident, then another therapist can come in my place and—"

"I hired *you*," he interrupted her, underlining as never before that she was speaking to a prince.

"Yes, for the initial phase, but I'm a diagnostician and am needed other places."

His eyes narrowed on her face. "Is there a man in New York waiting for you to get back to him?"

No. That was a long time ago, she thought sorrowfully. Since then she'd devoted her time to her career. "Why does my personal life have to enter into this discussion?"

"I thought the point was obvious. You're young and attractive."

"Thank you. For that matter so are you, Your Highness, but you have more serious matters on your mind. So do I."

There she went again, speaking her thoughts out loud, offending him right and left. He studied her for a long time. "If it's money…"

"It's not. The Institute pays me well."

"Then?" He left the word hanging in the air.

"There is no *then*. You have your country to rule over. I have a career. The people with speech problems are *my* country. But for the time I'm here, I'll do everything in my power to get this program going for Zoe."

An odd tension had sprung between them. "Zoe only agreed to stop crying and eat lunch with the queen as long as she could return to the patio to play with you this afternoon," he said. "She had a better time with you this morning than I think she's ever had with anyone else."

Dottie smiled. "You mean besides you. That's because she was given the nonstop attention every child craves without being negatively judged. Would it be all right with you if she comes to my room for her lessons?"

"After the grilling you gave me, will I be welcome, too?" he countered in a silky voice that sent darts of awareness through her body. The prince was asking *her* permission after the outspoken way she'd just addressed him?

"I doubt Zoe will stay if you don't join us. Hopefully in a few days she'll come to my room, even when you can't be there. The alcove with the table makes it especially convenient for the games I've brought. If you'll make out a schedule and rules for me to follow, then there won't have to be so many misunderstandings on my part."

"Anything else?" She had a feeling he was teasing her now. This side of him revealed his charm and added to the depth of the man.

"Where does her Greek tutor teach her?"

"In the library, but she's developed an aversion to it and stays in her bedroom."

"That's what I used to do. It's where you can sleep and have no worries. In that room you can pretend you're normal like everyone else." Maybe it was a trick of light, but she thought she saw a glimmer of compassion radiate from those black depths. "As for your patio, I think it ought to remain your special treat for her."

"So do I. Why don't you go on up to your room. I'll bring Zoe in a few minutes. Later this evening you'll join me in the guest dining room near your suite and we'll discuss how you want to spend your time while you're in Hellenica when you're not with my daughter."

"That's very kind of you," Dottie murmured, but she didn't move because she didn't know if she'd been dismissed or not. When he didn't speak, she said, "Do I need to wait for a maid to escort me back to my room?"

His lips twitched, causing her breath to catch at the sight of such a beautiful man whose human side was doing things to her equilibrium without her consent. "Only if you're afraid you can't find it."

She stared into his eyes. "Thank you for trusting me. With work, Zoe's speech *will* improve."

On that note she left his office, feeling his all-seeing gaze on her retreating back. She hurried along the corridor on trembling legs and found the staircase back to the guest suite. Now that she'd discovered she was still employed by him, she was ravenous and ate the lunch she'd left on the tray.

Before he came with Zoe, she set things up to resemble a mini schoolroom; crayons, scissors, paper, building blocks, beads to string, hide-and-seek games, puzzles, sorting games. Flash cards. She'd brought several sets so he could keep a pack on him. All of it served as a device while she helped his daughter with her sounds.

That's why you're here, Dottie. It's the only reason. Don't ever forget it.

Alex found Dottie already seated in the guest dining room when he joined her that evening. She looked summery in a soft blue crochet top and white skirt that followed the lines and curves of her alluring figure.

He smiled. "May I join you?"

"Of course."

"You're sure?"

"I came from New York to try to be of help."

It wasn't the answer he'd wanted. In truth, he wasn't exactly sure what he wanted, but he felt her reserve around him when she wasn't with Zoe and was determined to get to the bottom of it. He sat down opposite her and within a minute their dinner was served.

Once they were alone again he said, "Whenever you wish to leave the palace, a car and driver will be at your disposal. Hector will arrange it. A bodyguard will always be with you. Hopefully you won't find my security people obtrusive."

"I'm sure I won't. Thank you." She began eating, but the silence stretched between them. Finally she said, "Could I ask you something without you thinking I'm criticizing you or stepping over the line?"

"Because I'm a prince?"

"Because you're a prince, a man and a father." She lifted her fabulous blue eyes to him. "I don't know which of those three people will be irked and maybe even angered."

Alex tried to keep a straight face. "I guess we won't know until I hear your question."

A sigh came out of her. "When did you stop eating dinner with Zoe as part of your natural routine?"

He hadn't seen that question coming. "After my wife died, I had to make up for a lot of missed work in my capacity as overseer of the mining industry of our country. Hellenica couldn't have the high quality of life it enjoys without the revenue paid by other countries needing our resources. It requires constant work and surveillance.

"I spent my weekends with Zoe, but weekdays my hours were long, so she ate dinner with her nannies and my grandmother, who could get around then and spent a lot of her time on Aurum with us. However, I never missed kissing my daughter good-night and putting her to bed. That routine has gradually become the norm.

"With Stasio gone the past six weeks, I've had to be here and have been stretched to the max with monarchy business plus my own work."

"Do you mind if I ask what it is you do for your

brother? I've often wondered what a crown prince's daily routine is really like."

"Let me put it this way. On top of working with the ministers while he runs the complex affairs of our country on a daily basis, Stasio has at least four hundred events to attend or oversee during a year's time. That's more than one a day where he either gives a speech, entertains international dignitaries, attends openings or christens institutions, all while promoting the general welfare of Hellenica."

"It's very clear his life isn't his own. Neither is yours, obviously. Where did you go today after our session with Zoe?"

Alex was surprised and pleased she'd given him that much thought. "I had to fly to one of the islands in the north to witness the installation of the new president of the Thracian college and say a few words in Stasio's place. I should have stayed for the dinner, but I told them I had another engagement I couldn't miss." Alex had wanted to eat dinner with her. He enjoyed her company.

"Do you like your work? I know that probably sounds like an absurd question, but I'm curious."

"Like all work, it has its good and bad moments, but if I were honest I'd have to say that for the most part I enjoy it—very much, in fact, when something good happens that benefits the citizenry. After a lot of work and negotiations, four new hospitals will be under construction shortly. One of them will be a children's hospital. Nothing could please me more."

"Does Zoe know about this hospital? Do you share some of the wonderful things you do when you're with her?"

Her question surprised him. "Probably not as much as I should," he answered honestly.

"The reason I asked is because if she understood what kinds of things take up your time when you're away from her, she'd be so proud of you and might not feel as much separation anxiety when you're apart."

He looked at her through shuttered eyes. "If I didn't know better, I'd think you were a psychiatrist."

She let out a gentle laugh. "Hardly. You appear to have an incredible capacity to carry your brother's load as well as your own and still see to your daughter's needs. I'm so impressed."

"But?"

"I didn't say anything."

"You didn't have to. It's there in your expression. If I ate dinner with my daughter every evening, her speech would come faster."

"Maybe a little, but I can see you're already burning the candle at both ends out of concern for your country and necessity. It would be asking too much of you when you're already making time for her teaching sessions." She sat back. "I'm so sorry you lost your wife, who must have been such a help to you. It must have been a terrible time for you."

"It was, but I had Zoe. Her smiling face made me want to get up in the morning when I didn't think I could."

Moisture filmed her eyes. "I admire you for the wonderful life you're giving her."

"She's worth everything to me. You do what you have to do. Don't forget I've had a lot of help from family and the staff."

"Even so, your little Zoe adores you. It means whatever you're doing is working." She pushed herself away from the table and got to her feet. "Good night, Your Highness. No, no. Don't get up. Enjoy that second cup of coffee in peace.

"What with worrying about your grandmother, too, you deserve a little pampering. From my vantage point, no one seems to be taking care of you. In all the fairy tales I read as a child, they went to the castle and lived happily ever after. Until now I never thought about the prince's welfare."

Her comment stunned him before she walked out of the dining room.

Two nights later, while Alex was going over a new schedule he'd been working out with his internal affairs minister, a maid came into his office with a message. He wasn't surprised when he heard what was wrong. In fact he'd half been expecting it.

"If you'll excuse me."

"Of course, Your Highness."

Pleased that he'd been able to arrange his affairs so he could eat dinner with Zoe and Dottie from now on, he got up from the desk and headed for Zoe's bedroom. He heard crying before he opened the door. Poor Sofia was trying to calm his blotchy-faced daughter, who took one look at him and flung herself against his body.

Alex gathered her in his arms. "What's the matter?" he asked, knowing full well what was wrong. She'd been having the time of her life since Dottie had come to the palace and she didn't want the fun to stop.

Sofia shook her head. "She was asleep, and then suddenly she woke up with a nightmare. I haven't been able to quiet her down, Your Highness. She doesn't want me to help her anymore."

"I understand. It's all right. You can retire now. Thank you."

After she went into the next room, where she'd been sleeping lately, Zoe cried, "I want my mommy."

She'd never asked for her mother before. From time to time they'd talked about Teresa. He'd put pictures around so she would always know what her mother looked like, but this was different. He pulled one of them off the dresser and put it in her hand. To his shock, she pushed the photo away. "I want Dot. She's my mommy."

Alex was aghast. His daughter had shortened Dottie's name, but the sound that came out would make no sense to anyone except Alex, who understood it perfectly. "No, Zoe. Dottie's your teacher."

She had that hysterical look in her eyes. "No—she's my mommy. Where did she go?"

"Your mommy's in heaven."

"No—" She flung her arms around his neck. "Get my mommy!"

"I can't, Zoe."

"Has she gone?" The fright in her voice stunned him.

Alex grabbed the photograph. "This is your mommy. She went to heaven, remember?"

"Is Dot in heaven?"

Obviously his daughter's dreaming had caused her to awaken confused. "Dottie is your teacher and she went to her room, but she's not your mommy."

"Yes, she is." She nodded. "She's my new mommy!" she insisted before breaking down in sobs.

New?

"I want her! Get her, Daddy! Get her!" she begged him hysterically.

Feeling his panic growing, he pulled out his cell phone to call Hector.

"Your Highness?"

"Finds Mrs. Richards and tell her to come to Zoe's suite immediately."

"I'll take care of it now."

Alex could be thankful there was no one more efficient than Hector in an emergency.

When Dottie walked into the room a few minutes later with a book in her hand, his daughter had calmed down somewhat, but was still shuddering in his arms.

"Dot—" Zoe blurted with such joy, Alex was speechless.

"Hi, Zoe. Did you want to say good-night?"

"Yes."

"She thought you were gone," Alex whispered in an aside.

Dottie nodded. "Why don't you get in bed and I'll read you a story. Then *I* have to go to bed, too, because you and I have a big day planned for tomorrow, don't we?"

Zoe's lips turned up in a smile. "Yes."

Like magic, his daughter crawled under the covers. Dottie pulled up a chair next to the bed. "This is the good-night book. See the moon on the cover? When he's up there, everyone goes to sleep. Freddie the frog stops going *ribbbbbit* and says good-night." Zoe laughed.

Dottie turned the page. "Benny the bee stops *buzzzzing* and says good-night." She showed each page to his daughter who was enchanted. "Charlie the cricket stops *chirrrping* and says good-night. Guess who's on the last page?" Zoe didn't know. Dottie showed it to her. There was a mirror. "It's *you!* Now *you* have to say good-night."

Zoe said it.

"Let's say the *g* again. Mr. G is a grumpy letter." Zoe thought that was hilarious. "He gets mad." She made a face. "Let's see if we can get as mad as he does. We have to grit our teeth like this. Watch my mouth and say *grrr.*"

Alex was watching it. To his chagrin he'd been watching it on and off for several days. After half a dozen tries Zoe actually made the *grrr* sound. He couldn't believe it. In his astonishment his gaze darted to Dottie, but she was focused on his daughter.

"You sounded exactly like Mr. G, Zoe. That was perfect. Tomorrow night your father will read it to you again. Now Dot has to go to sleep. I'll leave the book with you." She slipped out of the room, leaving the two of them alone.

Zoe clasped it to her chest as if it were her greatest treasure. Alex's eyes smarted because lying before him was *his* greatest treasure. She fell asleep within minutes. As soon as she was out, he left the room knowing Sofia was sleeping in the adjacent room and would hear her if she woke up.

He strode through the palace, intending to talk to Dottie before she went to bed. Hector met him as he was passing his grandmother's suite on his way to the other wing.

"The queen wants to see you before she retires."

His brows lifted. "You wouldn't by any chance be spying on me for her, would you, Hector?"

"I have never spied on you, Your Highness."

"You've been spying for her since the day Stasi and I were born, but I forgive you. However, Stasi might not be so forgiving once he's crowned, so remember you've been warned. Tell the queen I'll be with her in ten minutes."

He continued on his way to Dottie's apartment. After he knocked, she called out, "Yes?"

"It's Alex."

The silence that followed was understandable. He'd never used his given name with her before, or given his permission for her to use it. But considering the amount of time they'd been spending together since her arrival at the palace, it seemed absurd to say anything else now that they were alone. "Would you be more willing to answer me if I'd said it's Zoe's father, or it's your Royal Highness?"

He thought he heard her chuckle before she opened the door a couple of inches. "I was on the verge of crawling into bed."

Alex could see that. She'd thrown on a pink toweling robe and was clutching the lapels beneath her chin. "I need to talk frankly with you. Zoe has decided you're her new mommy. She got hysterical tonight when I tried to tell her otherwise."

"I know. She's told me on several occasions she wishes I were her mother. This happens with some of my youngest students who don't have one. It's very normal. I just keep telling them I'm their teacher. You need to go on telling her in a matter-of-fact way that Princess Teresa was her mommy."

"I did that."

"I know. I saw the photograph and see a lot of the princess's beauty in Zoe. What's important here is that if you don't fight her on it, she'll finally get the point and the phase will pass after a while."

"That's very wise counsel." He exhaled the breath he'd been holding. "You made a breakthrough with her tonight."

"Yes. I've wanted her to feel confident about one sound and now it has happened."

"How did you know she would do it?"

"I didn't, but I hoped. Every success creates more success."

Talking through the crack in the door added a certain intimacy to their conversation, exciting him. "Her success is going to help me sleep tonight."

"I'm glad. Just remember a total change isn't going to happen overnight. Her vowels are coming, but *G* is only one consonant out of twenty-one. Putting that sound with the rest of a word is the tricky part."

"Tricky or not, she mimicked you perfectly and the way you read that book had her spellbound."

"There was only one thing wrong with it."

"What's that?" He found himself hanging on her every word, just like his daughter.

"It didn't have a page that said the prince stopped *rrrrruling* and said good-night."

Alex broke into full-bodied laughter.

Her eyes smiled. "If you'll forgive me, you should do that more often in front of Zoe, Your Highness."

"What happened to Alex? That is my name."

"I realize that."

"Before I leave, I wanted you to know that I've worked things out with my internal affairs minister so I can eat dinner with my daughter every night. From now on he'll take care of the less important matters for me during that time period."

"Zoe's going to be ecstatic!" she blurted, displaying the bubbly side of her nature that didn't emerge as often as he would have liked to see.

"I hope that means you're happy about it, too, since you'll be joining us for our meals. Good night, Dottie."

"Good night, Alex."

She shut the door on him before he was ready to leave. After being with her, he wasn't in the mood to face his grandmother. As he made his way back to her suite, he thought about his choice of words. The only time he'd ever *faced* the queen was when he'd been a boy and had a reason to feel guilty about something.

Tonight he had a strong hunch what she wanted to discuss with him. After Zoe's nightmare, now he knew why. If she'd told *Yiayia* that Dottie was her new mommy, nothing would have enraged his grandmother more. She would have told Zoe never to speak of it again, but that wouldn't prevent his daughter from thinking it in her heart.

Until the phase passed, Dottie had said.

What if it didn't? That's what disturbed Alex.

Zoe's insistence that Dottie was her new mommy only exacerbated his inner conflict where the speech therapist was concerned. Since he'd peered into a pair of eyes as blue as the flowers fluttering in the breeze around the palace in Aurum, he couldn't get her out of his mind.

In truth he had no business getting physically involved with someone he'd hired. He certainly didn't need the queen reminding him of what he'd already been telling himself—keep the relationship with Mrs.

Richards professional and enjoy the other women he met when he left the country for business or pleasure.

Too bad for his grandmother that he saw through her machinations and had done so from an early age. She always had another agenda going. Since Teresa's funeral, she'd been busy preparing the ground with the House of Helvetia. But until Stasi married, she was biding her time before she insisted Alex take Princess Genevieve of Helvetia to wife for the growth and prosperity of the kingdom.

Lines darkened his face. The queen would have to bide away forever because Stasi would be the only one doing the growing for the Constantinides dynasty. He was the firstborn, Heaven had picked him to rule Hellenica. Ring out the bells.

Alex had a different destiny and a new priority that superseded all else. He wanted to help his daughter feel normal, and that meant coaching her. With Dottie's help, it was already happening. She understood what was going on inside Zoe. Her story about her own stuttering problem had touched him. He admired her strength in overcoming a huge challenge.

His first order of business was to talk to Stasio tonight. His brother needed to come home now! With Alex's work schedule altered, he could spend the maximum amount of time with Zoe and Dottie throughout the day. It was going to work, even though it meant dealing with his ministers in the early morning hours and late at night when necessary.

Once Stasio was home, Alex would move back to the island of Aurum, where he could divide his attention between helping Zoe and doing the work he'd been overseeing for the country since university. With Dottie installed and a palace staff and security waiting on them, Zoe couldn't help but make great strides with her speech and he'd convince Dottie she couldn't leave yet.

CHAPTER FOUR

LIKE pizza dough being tossed in the air, Dottie's heart did its own version of a flip when the prince entered her schoolroom a few days later with Zoe. They must have just come from breakfast with the queen. Zoe was dressed in pink play clothes and sneakers.

Dottie hardly recognized Alex. Rather than hand-tooled leather shoes, he'd worn sneakers, too. She was dazzled by his casual attire of jeans and a yellow, open-necked sport shirt. In the vernacular, he was a hunk. When she looked up and saw the smattering of dark hair on his well-defined chest, her mouth went dry and she averted her eyes. Zoe's daddy was much more man than prince this morning, bringing out longings in her she hadn't experienced in years.

He'd been coming to their teaching sessions and had cleared his calendar to eat dinner with Zoe. Dottie was moved by his love and concern for his daughter, but she feared for him, too. The prince had the greatest expectations for his child, but he might want too much too soon. That worry had kept her tossing and turning during the night because she wanted to be up to the challenge and help Zoe triumph.

But it wasn't just that worry. When she'd told Alex

she'd had other patients who'd called her mommy, it was a lie. Only one other child had expressed the same wish. It was a little boy who had a difficult, unhappy mother. In truth, Zoe was unique. So was the whole situation.

Normally Dottie's students came by bus or private car to the institute throughout the day. Living under the palace roof was an entirely different proposition and invited more intimacy. Zoe was a very intelligent child and should have corrected her own behavior by now, but she chose to keep calling Dottie Mommy. Every time Zoe did that, it blurred the lines for Dottie, who in a short time had allowed the little girl to creep into her heart.

To make matters worse, Dottie was also plagued by guilt because she realized she wanted Alex's approval. That sort of desire bordered on pride. Her aunt had often quoted Gibran. "Generosity is giving more than you can, and pride is taking less than you need." If she wanted his approval, then it was a gift she had to earn.

Did she seek it because he was a prince? She hoped not. Otherwise that put her in the category of those people swayed by a person's station in life. She refused to be a sycophant, the kind of person her aunt had despised. Dottie despised sycophants, too.

"GGGRRRRRR," she said to Zoe, surprising the little girl, who was a quick study and *gggrrrred* back perfectly. Alex gave his daughter a hug before they sat down at the table.

"Wonderful, Zoe." Her gaze flicked to him. "Good morning, Your Highness." Dottie detected the scent of the soap he'd used in the shower. It was the most marvelous smell, reminding her of mornings when her husband—

But the eyes staring at her across the table were a fiery black, not blue. "Aren't you going to *gggrrr* me? I feel left out."

Her pulse raced. "Well, we don't want you to feel like that, do we, Zoe?" The little girl shook her head, causing her shiny brown curls to flounce.

Dottie had a small chalkboard and wrote the word *Bee*. "Go ahead and pronounce this word for us, Your Highness." When he did, she said, "Zoe? Did you hear *bee*?"

"Yes."

"Good. Let's all say *bee* together. One, two three. *Bee*." Zoe couldn't do it, of course. Dottie leaned toward her. "Pretend you're a tiny goldfish looking for food." Pressing her lips together she made the beginning of the *B* sound. "Touch my lips with your index finger." Her daddy helped her. In the process his fingers brushed against Dottie's mouth. She could hardly breathe from the sensation of skin against skin.

"Now feel how it sounds when I say it." Dottie said it a dozen times against Zoe's finger. She giggled. "That tickled, didn't it? Now say the same sound against my finger." She put her finger to Zoe's lips. After five tries she was making the sound.

"Terrific! Now put your lips to your daddy's finger and make the same *B* sound over and over."

As Zoe complied with every ounce of energy in that cute little body, Alex caught Dottie's gaze. The softness, the gratitude she saw in his eyes caused her heart to hammer so hard, she feared he could hear it.

"You're an outstanding pupil, Zoe. Today we're going to work on the *B* sound."

"It's interesting you've brought up the *bee*," Alex interjected.

"They make honey," said Zoe.

"That's right, Zoe. Did you know that just yesterday I met with one of the ministers and we're going to establish beekeeping centers on every island in Hellenica."

"How come?"

"With more bees gathered in hives, we'll have more honey to sell to people here as well as around the world. It's an industry I'd like to see flourish. With all the blossoms and thyme that grow here, it will give jobs to people who don't have one. You know the honey you eat when we're on Aurum?" She nodded. "It comes from two hives Inez and Ari tend on our property."

Zoe's eyes widened. "They do? I've never seen them."

"When we go home, we'll take a look."

Zoe smiled and gave her father a long hug. As he reciprocated, his gaze met Dottie's. He'd taken her suggestion to share more with his daughter and it was paying dividends, thrilling her to pieces.

"I'm going to give your daddy a packet of flash cards, Zoe. Everything on it starts with a *B*. He'll hold up the card and say the word. Then you say it. If you can make three perfect *B* sounds, I have a present for you."

Zoe let out a joyous sound and looked at her daddy with those shiny brown eyes. Dottie sat back in the chair and watched father and daughter at work. Zoe had great incentive to do her best for the man she idolized. The prince took his part seriously and proceeded with care. She marveled to watch them drawing closer together through these teaching moments, forging closer bonds now that he was starting to ease up on his work for the monarchy.

"Bravo!" she said when he'd gone through the pack of thirty. "You said five *B*'s clearly. Do you want your present now or after your lesson?"

Zoe concentrated for a minute. "Now."

Alex laughed that deep male laugh. It resonated through Dottie to parts she'd forgotten were there. Reaching in the bag in the corner, she pulled out one of several gifts she'd brought for rewards. But this one was especially vital because Zoe had been working hard so far and needed a lot of reinforcement.

Dottie handed her the soft, foot-long baby. "This is Baby Betty. She has a *bottle*, a *blanket* and a *bear*."

"Oh—" Zoe cried. Her eyes lit up. She cradled it in her arms, just like a mother. "Thank you, Mommy."

The word slipped out again. Dottie couldn't look at Alex. His daughter had said it again. These days it was coming with more frequency. The moment had become an emotional one for Dottie, who had to fight her own pain over past memories that had been resurrected by being around her new student.

"I'm not your mommy, Zoe. She's in heaven. You know that, don't you."

She finally nodded. "I wish you were my mommy."

"But since I'm not, will you please call me Dot?"

"Yes."

"Good girl. Guess what? Now that you've fed Betty, you have to burp her." Puzzled, Zoe looked up at her. "When a baby drinks milk from a bottle, it drinks in air, too. So you have to pat her back. Then the air will come out and she won't have a tummyache. Your mommy used to pat your back like that when you were a baby, didn't she, Your Highness?"

Dottie had thrown the ball in his court, not knowing what had gone on in their marriage. He'd never discussed his private personal life or asked Dottie about hers.

"Indeed, she did. We took turns walking the floor with you. Sometimes very important people would come in the nursery to see you and you'd just yawn and go to sleep as if you were horribly bored."

At that comment the three of them laughed hard. Dottie realized it provided a release from the tension built up over the last week.

From the corner of her eye she happened to spot Hector, who stood several feet away. He was clearing his throat to get their attention. How long had he been in the room listening?

"Your Highness? The queen has sent for you."

"Is it a medical emergency?"

"No."

"Then I'm afraid she'll have to wait until tonight. After this lesson I'm taking Zoe and Mrs. Richards out on the *boat*," he said emphasizing the B. "We'll work on her *B* sounds while we enjoy a light *buffet* on *board*, won't we, Zoe?" He smiled at his daughter who nodded, still gripping her baby tightly. "But don't worry. I'll be back in time to say good-night to her."

"Very well, Your Highness."

Dottie had to swallow the gasp that almost escaped her throat. Lines bracketed Hector's mouth. She looked at the floor. It really was funny. Alex had a quick, brilliant mind and a surprising imp inside him that made it hard for her to hold back her laughter, but she didn't dare laugh in front of Hector.

After Hector left, Dottie brought out a box containing tubes of blue beads, so Zoe and Alex could make a bracelet together. They counted the beads as they did so, and Dottie was pleased to note that Zoe's *B* sounds were really coming along.

Satisfied with that much progress, Dottie cleaned everything up. "That's the end of our lesson for today." She got up from the chair, suddenly wishing she weren't wearing a T-shirt with a picture of a cartoon bunny on the front. She'd hoped Zoe would ask her about it and they could practice saying the famous rabbit's name. But it was Alex who'd stared at it several times this morning, causing sensual waves to ripple through her.

He swept Zoe in his arms. "I'm very proud of you. Now let's show Dot around the island on the sailboat." His daughter hugged him around the neck. Over her shoulder he stared at Dottie. "Are you ready?"

No. Sailing with him wasn't part of her job. In fact it was out of the question. She didn't want to feel these feelings she had around him. Yearnings…

"That's very kind of you, Your Highness, but I have other things to do this afternoon, including a lot of paperwork to send in to the Institute. In case you don't get back from sailing by dinnertime, I'll see you and Zoe in the morning for her lesson."

He lowered his daughter to the floor. "I insist."

She took a steadying breath. "Did you just give me a command?"

"If I did, would you obey it?"

There was nothing playful about this conversation. The last thing she wanted to do was offend him, but she refused to be anything but Zoe's speech therapist. With his looks and charismatic personality, he could ensnare any woman he wanted. That's what royal playboys did.

Alex might be a widower with a daughter, but as far as she was concerned, he was at the peak of his manhood now and a hundred times more dangerous. She was reminded of that fact when he'd eyed her T-shirt. A little shiver went through her because he was still eyeing her that way and she was too aware of him.

Dottie needed to turn this around and make it right so he wouldn't misunderstand why she was refusing the invitation. Using a different tactic she said, "I gave you that pack of flash cards. You should take your daughter on your sailboat this afternoon and work with her while the lesson is fresh in her mind."

In a lowered voice she added, "I might be her speech therapist, but outside this classroom I can only be a distraction and cause her more confusion over the mommy issue. She wants your undivided attention and will cooperate when you do the cards with her because she'd do anything for you. There's a saying in English. I'm sure you've heard of it. 'Strike while the iron's hot.'"

"There's another saying by the great teacher Plato," he fired back. "'We can easily forgive a child who is afraid of the dark; the real tragedy of life is when men are afraid of the light.'" He turned to his daughter. "Come with me, Zoe."

Dottie trembled as she watched them leave. Alex had her figured out without knowing anything about her. She *was* afraid. Once upon a time her world had been filled with blinding, glorious light. After it had been taken away, she never wanted to feel it or be in it again. One tragedy in life had been too much.

* * *

Alex put his daughter to bed, but he had to face facts. After the outing on the sailboat and all the swimming and fun coaching moments with the flash cards, it still wasn't enough for his little girl. She didn't want Sofia tending to her.

He'd read the good-night book to her six times, but the tears gushed anyway. She was waiting for her favorite person. "Have you forgotten that Dottie had a lot of work to do tonight? You'll see her in the morning. Here's Betty. She's ready to go to sleep with you." He tucked the baby in her arm, but she pushed it away and sat up.

"Tell Dot to come."

Alex groaned because these tears were different. His daughter had found an outlet for her frustration in Dottie who understood her and had become her ally. What child wouldn't want her to be her mommy and stay with her all the time? Alex got it. She made every moment so memorable, no one else could possibly measure up. Dottie was like a force of nature. Her vivacious personality had brought life into the palace.

Earlier, when he'd asked Hector about Dottie's activities, he'd learned she'd refused a car and had left the grounds on foot. Security said that after she'd jogged ten miles in the heat, she'd hiked to the top of Mount Pelos and sat for an hour. After visiting the church, she'd returned to town and jogged back to the palace.

"Zoe? If you'll stay in your bed, I'll go get her."

The tears slowed down. She reached for her baby. "Hurry, Daddy."

Outside the bedroom he called Dottie on his cell phone, something he'd sworn he wouldn't do in order to keep his distance, but this was an emergency. When she picked up, he asked her to come to Zoe's bedroom.

He sensed the hesitation before she said, "I'll be right there."

It pleased him when a minute later he heard footsteps and watched Dottie hurrying towards the suite with another book in her hand.

"Alex—" she cried in surprise as he stepped away from the paneled wall.

He liked it that she'd said his name of her own volition. "I wondered when you would finally break down."

Dottie smoothed the hair away from her flushed cheek. Her eyes searched his. Ignoring his comment she said, "Did Zoe have another nightmare?"

He moved closer. "No. But she's growing more and more upset when you're not with us. Why didn't you come today? I want the truth."

"I told you I had work."

"Then how come it was reported that you went jogging and climbed Mount Pelos, instead of staying in your room? Were you able to see the sail of my boat from the top?"

A hint of pink crept into her cheeks. She *had* been watching for him. "I saw a lot of sailboats."

"The security staff is agog about the way you spent your day. Not one visit to a designer shop. No shopping frenzy. You undoubtedly wore them to a frazzle with your jogging, but it was good for them."

A small laugh escaped her throat. He liked it that she didn't take herself seriously.

"I'll ask the question again. Why didn't you come with us this afternoon?"

"Surely you know why. Because I'm worried over her growing attachment to me."

"So am I, but that's not the only reason you kept your distance from me today. Are you afraid of being on a boat? Don't you know how to swim?"

"Don't be silly," she whispered.

"How else am I to get some honesty out of you? It's apparent you have a problem with me, pure and simple. My earlier reputation in life as Prince Alexius may have prejudiced you against me, but that was a long time ago. I'm a man now and a father the world knows nothing about. Which of those roles alarms you most?"

She folded her arms. "Neither of them," she said in a quiet voice.

His brows met in a frown. "Then what terrible thing do you imagine would have happened to you today if you'd come with us?"

"I'd rather not talk about it, even if you are a prince." She'd said that "even if you are a prince" thing before. After retaining his gaze for a moment, she looked away. "How did your afternoon go with Zoe?"

"Good, but it would have been better if you'd been along. She won't go to sleep until you say good-night. Tonight she fired Sofia."

"What?"

"It's true. She doesn't want a nanny unless it's you. To save poor Hector the trouble of having to summon you every night, why don't you plan to pop in on her at bedtime. In the end it will save my sanity, too."

She slowly nodded. "Since I won't be here much longer, I can do that."

"Let's not talk about your leaving, not when you barely got here."

"I—I'll go in now." Her voice faltered.

"Thank you." For several reasons, he wasn't through with her yet, but it could wait until she'd said good-night to his daughter. Alex followed her into the bedroom. Zoe was sitting up in her bed holding her baby. She glowed after she saw Dottie.

"Hi, Zoe. If I read you a story, will you go to sleep?"

"Yes. Will you sit on the bed?"

"I can read better on this chair." Dottie drew it close to the bed and sat down. Once again Alex was hooked by Dottie's charm as she read the tale about a butterfly that had lost a wing and needed to find it.

She was a master teacher, but it dawned on him she always kept her distance with Zoe. No hugs or kisses. No endearments. Being the total professional, she knew her place. Ironically his daughter didn't want hugs or kisses from her nannies who tried to mother her, but he knew she was waiting for both from Dottie.

Zoe wasn't the only one.

The second she'd gone to sleep, Dottie tiptoed out of the room. Alex caught up to her in the hall. She couldn't seem to get back to her suite fast enough. They walked through the corridors in silence. As she reached out to open the door to her apartment, he grasped her upper arms and turned her around.

They were close enough he could smell her peach fragrance. She was out of breath, but she was in too good a shape for the small exertion of walking to produce that reaction. "Invite me in," he whispered, sensing how withdrawn she'd become with him. "I want an answer from you and prefer that we don't talk out here in the hall where we can be observed."

"I'm sorry, but we have nothing to talk about. I'm very tired."

"Too tired to tell me what has you so frightened, you're trembling?"

A pained expression crossed over her face. "I wish I hadn't come to Hellenica. If I'd known what was awaiting me, I would have refused."

"For the love of heaven, why? If I've done something unforgivable in your eyes, it's only fair you tell me."

"Of course you haven't." She shook her head, but wouldn't look at him. "This has to do with Zoe."

"Because she keeps calling you Mommy?"

"That and much more."

At a total loss, he let go of her with reluctance. "I don't understand."

She eased away from him. "Five years ago my husband and son were killed by a drunk driver in a horrific crash." Tears glistened on her cheeks. "I lost the great loves of my life. Cory was Zoe's age when he died."

Alex was aghast.

"He had an articulation problem like hers, only he couldn't do his vowel sounds. I'd been working with him for a year with the help of a therapist, and he'd just gotten to the point where he could say *Daddy* plainly when—"

Obviously she was too choked up to say the rest. His eyes closed tightly for a moment. He remembered the pain in hers the other day.

"I've worked with all kinds of children, but Zoe is the only one who has ever reminded me of him. The other day when she laughed, it sounded like Cory."

"You didn't let on." His voice grated.

"I'm thankful for that." He thought he heard a little

sob get trapped in her throat. "It's getting harder to be around her without breaking down. That's why I didn't go with you today. I—I thought I'd gotten past my grief," she stammered, "but coming here has proven otherwise."

He sucked in his breath. "You may wish you hadn't come to Hellenica, but keep in mind you're doing something for my daughter only you can do. Watching Zoe respond to your techniques has already caused me to stop grieving over her pain.

"No matter how much you're still mourning your loss, doesn't it make you feel good to be helping her the way you once helped your son? Wouldn't your husband have done anything for your son if your positions were reversed?"

She looked away, moved by his logic. "Yes," came the faint whisper, "but—"

"But what? Tell me everything."

"It's just that I've felt…guilty for not being with them that terrible day."

"You're suffering survivor's guilt."

"Yes."

"In my own way I had the same reaction after Teresa passed away. It took me a long time to convince myself everything possible had been done for her and I had to move on for Zoe's sake."

She nodded.

"Then it's settled. From now on after her morning lessons, we'll have another one during the afternoons in the swimming pool. We'll practice what you've taught her while we play. After finding your strength and solace in furthering your career, don't you see you can make a difference with Zoe and maybe lay those ghosts to rest? It's time to take a risk. With my schedule changed, I can spend as much time as possible with both of you now."

"I've noticed." After a pause, she added, "You're a remarkable man."

"It's because of you, Dottie. You're helping me get close to my daughter in a whole new way. I'll never be able to thank you enough for that."

"You don't need to thank me. I'm just so glad for the two of you." Dottie wiped the moisture from the corners of her eyes. "Tomorrow we'll work on her *W* sounds. Good night, Alex."

CHAPTER FIVE

WHAT luxury! Dottie had never known anything like it until she'd come to the palace ten days ago. After a delicious lunch, it was sheer bliss to lie in the sun on the lounger around the palace pool enjoying an icy fruit drink.

Zoe's morning lesson with her daddy had gone well. Her *B* and G sounds were coming along, but she struggled with the *W*. It might be one of the last sounds she mastered on her long journey to intelligible speech.

Dottie was glad to have the pool to herself. While they were changing into their swimsuits, she was trying to get a grip on her emotions. She'd been doing a lot of thinking, and Alex had been right about one thing. If she'd been the one killed and Cory had been left with his speech problem, then she would have wanted Neil to stop at nothing to find the right person to help their son. At the moment, Dottie was the right person for Zoe.

Deep in her own thoughts, she heard a tremendous splash followed by Zoe's shriek of laughter. Dottie turned her head in time to see Zoe running around the rim of the pool in her red bathing suit, shouting with glee. She was following a giant black whale maybe five feet long skimming the top of the water with a human torpedo propelling it.

Suddenly Alex's dark head emerged, splashing more water everywhere. Zoe got soaked and came flying toward Dottie, who grabbed her own towel and wiped off her shoulders. "You need some sunscreen. Stand still and I'll put it on you." Zoe did her bidding. "I didn't know a whale lived in your pool."

The child giggled. "Come with me." She tugged on Dottie's arm.

"I think I'd rather stay here and watch."

Alex stared at Dottie with a look she couldn't decipher, but didn't say anything. By now Zoe had joined him and was riding on top of the whale while he helped her hold on. The darling little girl was so happy, she seemed to burst with it.

Dottie threw her beach wrap around her to cover her emerald-colored bikini and got up from the lounger. She walked over to the side of the pool and sat down to dangle her legs in the water while she watched their antics.

All of a sudden it occurred to her she was having real fun for the first time in years. This was different than watching from the sidelines of other people's lives. Because of Alex she was an actual participant and was feeling a part of life again. The overpowering sense of oneness with him shook her to the core. So did the desire she felt being near him. That's why she didn't dare get in the water. Her need to touch him was overcoming her good sense.

"I think we need to name Zoe's whale," he called to her.

Dottie nodded. "Preferably a two syllable word starting with *W*."

Both she and Alex suggested a lot of names, laughing into each other's eyes at some of their absurd suggestions. Zoe clapped her hands the minute she heard her daddy say *Wally*. Though it wasn't a name that started with *Wh* like whale, it was the name his daughter wanted. When Zoe pronounced it, the sound came out like *Oye-ee*.

Dottie was secretly impressed when he came up with the idea of Zoe pretending she was a grouper fish. Evidently his daughter knew what one looked like and she formed her mouth in an *O* shape, opening and closing it. After a half hour of playing and practice, the *wa* was starting to make an appearance.

"Well done, Your Highness." Dottie smiled at him. "She wouldn't have made that sound this fast without your help."

He reciprocated with a slow, lazy smile, making jelly of her insides. The afternoon was exhilarating for Dottie, a divine moment out of time. Anyone watching would think they were a happy family. Before she knew it, dinner was served beneath the umbrella of the table on the sun deck. Zoe displayed a healthy appetite, pleasing her father and Dottie.

Toward the end of their meal he said, "Attention, everyone. I have an announcement to make." He looked at Zoe. "Guess who came home today?"

She stopped drinking her juice. "Uncle Stasi?"

"Yes. Your one and only favorite uncle."

"Goody!" she blurted. "He's funny."

"I've missed him, too. Tonight there's going to be a

party to welcome him back. I'm going to take you two
ladies with me."

Zoe squealed in delight.

"After we finish dinner, I want you to go upstairs
and get ready. Put on your prettiest dresses, because
there's going to be dancing. When it's time, I'll come
by for you."

Dancing?

Adrenalin surged through Dottie's body at the
thought of getting that close to him. Heat poured off
her, but she couldn't attribute all of it to the sun. She
suspected his announcement had caused a spike in her
temperature.

Her mind went through a mental search of her ward-
robe. The only thing possibly presentable for such an
affair was her simple black dress with her black high
heels.

"Will it be a large party, Your Highness?"

He darted her a curious glance. "Thirty or so guests,
mostly family friends. If you're both finished with
dinner, let's go upstairs."

After gathering their things, Dottie said she'd see
them later and she hurried back to her bedroom for a
long shower and shampoo. She blowdried her hair and
left it loose with a side part, then put on her black dress
with the cap sleeves and round neck.

While she was applying her coral-frost lipstick, she
thought she heard a noise in the other room. When she
went to investigate, she saw Zoe looking like a vision
in a long white dress with ruffles and a big yellow sash.
But her face was awash in tears. She came running
to her.

Without conscious thought, Dottie knelt down and

drew her into her arms. It was the first hug she'd given her, but she could no longer hold back. Zoe clung to her while she wept, exactly the way Cory had done so many hundreds of times when he'd needed comfort.

"What's wrong, darling?"

"Daddy's going to get married."

Dottie was trying to understand. "Don't you mean your uncle?"

"No—I heard *Yiayia* tell Sofia. My daddy's going to marry Princess Genevieve. But I want *you* to be my new mommy. When I kissed *Yiayia* good-night, she told me Princess Genevieve will be at the party and I had to be good."

A stabbing pain attacked Dottie until she could hardly breathe. "I see. Zoe, this is something you need to talk to your daddy about, but not until you go to bed. Does he know you're here with me?"

"No."

Dottie stood up. "I need to phone Hector so he can tell your daddy you ran to my room."

When that was done, she took Zoe in the bathroom. After wetting a washcloth, she wiped the tears off her face. "There. Now we're ready. When we get to the party, I want you to smile and keep smiling. Can you do that for me?"

After a slight hesitation, Zoe nodded.

Dottie clasped her hand and walked her back in the other room. "Have I told you how pretty you look in your new dress?"

"Both of you look absolutely beautiful," came the sound of a deep, familiar voice.

Alex.

Dottie gasped softly when she saw that he'd entered

the room. Since Zoe had left the door open, he must not have felt the need to knock. The prince, tall and dark, had dressed in a formal, midnight-blue suit and tie, taking her breath. His penetrating black eyes swept over her, missing nothing. The look in them sent a river of heat through her body.

"Zoe wanted to show me how she looked, Your Highness. In her haste, she forgot to tell Sofia."

He looked so handsome when he smiled, Dottie felt light-headed. "That's understandable. This is my daughter's first real party. Are you ready?"

When Zoe nodded, he grasped her other hand and the three of them left the room. He led them down the grand staircase where they could hear music and voices. Though Zoe lacked her usual sparkle, she kept smiling like the princess she was. Her training had served her well. Even at her young age, she moved with the grace and dignity of a royal.

Some of the elegantly dressed guests were dancing, others were eating. The three of them passed through a receiving line of titled people and close friends of the Constantinides family.

"Zoe?" her father said. "I'd like you to meet Princess Genevieve."

For a minute, Dottie reeled. She'd seen the lovely young princess in the news. Zoe was a trooper and handled their first meeting beautifully. One royal princess to another. Dottie loved Zoe for her great show of poise in front of the woman she didn't want for her new mother.

Dottie was trying to see the good. It was natural that Alex would marry again, and Zoe desperately needed a mother's love. Plus their match would give Alex more children and Zoe wouldn't have to be the only child. In that respect it was more necessary than ever that her speech improve enough that when Alex married Princess Genevieve, his daughter could make herself understood. Zoe also needed to be strong in her English speech because she would be tested when French was introduced into their household. Princess Genevieve would expect it. The House of Helvetia was located on the south side of Lake Geneva in the French-speaking region.

Now that she knew of Alex's future plans, Dottie had to focus on the additional goal to pursue for his daughter. She needed to help prepare Zoe for the next phase in her life and—

"My, my. What have we here?"

A male voice Dottie didn't recognize broke in on her thoughts. She turned her head to discover another extremely attractive man with black hair standing at the end of the line. Almost the same height as Alex, he bore a superficial resemblance to him, but his features were less rugged. The brothers could be the same age, which she estimated to be early to mid-thirties.

When she realized it was Crown Prince Stasio, she curtsied. "Welcome home, Your Highness."

He flashed her an infectious smile. "You don't need to do that around me. My little brother told me you're working with Zoe. That makes us all family. Did anyone ever tell you you're very easy on the eyes?" His were black, too. "Alex held back on that pertinent fact."

What a tease he was! "Zoe told me you were funny. I think she's right."

The crown prince laughed. She noticed he had a fabulous tan. "Tell me about yourself. Where have you been hiding all my life?" He was incorrigible and so different from Alex, who was more serious minded. Of the two, Dottie privately thought that Zoe's father seemed much more the natural ruler of their country.

"I'm from New York."

His eyes narrowed. "Coming to Hellenica must feel like you dropped off the edge of the planet, right?"

"It's paradise here."

"It is now that I've got my little Zoe to dance with." He reached over and picked up his niece. After they hugged, he set her down again. "Come on. I'm going to spin you around the ballroom."

Zoe's smile lit up for real as he whirled her away. Dancing lessons hadn't been wasted on her either. She moved like a royal princess who was years older, capturing everyone's attention. People started clapping. Dottie couldn't have been prouder of her if she'd been Zoe's real mother.

While she watched, she felt a strong hand slip around her waist. The next thing she knew Alex had drawn her into his arms. His wonderful, clean male scent and the brush of his legs against hers sent sparks of electricity through her system. In her heels, she was a little taller and felt like their bodies had been made for each other.

"Why won't you look at me?" he whispered. "Everyone's going to think you don't like me."

"I'm trying to concentrate on our dancing. It's been a long time." The soft rock had a hypnotizing effect on her. She could stay like this for hours, almost but not quite embracing him.

"For me, too. I've been waiting ages to get you in my arms like this. If it's in plain sight of our guests, so be it. You feel good to me, Dottie. So damn good you're in danger of being carried off. Only my princely duty keeps me from doing what I feel like doing."

Ah… Before Zoe's revelations in the bedroom tonight, Dottie might have allowed herself to be carried away. The clamorings of her body had come to painful life and only he could assuage them.

"I understand. That's why I'm going to say goodnight after this dance. There are other female guests in the ballroom no doubt waiting for their turn around the floor with you. You're a terrific dancer, by the way."

"There's only one woman I want to be with tonight and she's right here within kissing distance. You could have no idea the willpower it's taking not to taste that tempting mouth of yours." He spoke with an intensity that made her legs go weak. "While we were out at the pool, I would have pulled you in if Zoe hadn't been with us."

"It's a good thing you didn't. Otherwise your daughter will be more confused than ever when she sees you ask Princess Genevieve to dance."

His body stiffened. She'd hit a nerve, but he had no clue it had pierced her to the depths. "I know you well enough to realize you had a deliberate reason for bringing up her name. Why did you do it?"

Dottie's heart died a little because the music had stopped, bringing those thrilling moments in his arms to an end. She lifted her head and looked at him for the first time since they'd entered the ballroom. "When you put Zoe to bed tonight, she'll tell you. Thank you for an enchanting evening, Your Highness. I won't forget. See you in the morning."

She eased out of his arms and walked out of the

ballroom. But the second she reached the staircase, she raced up the steps and ran the rest of the way to her room.

"Dot," Zoe called to her the next morning as she and her father came into the classroom. "Look at this?" She held up a CD.

"What's on it?"

"It's a surprise. Put it in your laptop," said Alex.

After giving him a curious glance, Dottie walked around to the end of the table and put it in. After a moment they could all see last night's events at the party on the screen, complete with the music. There she was enclosed in Alex's arms. Princess Genevieve would not have been happy.

Whoever had taken the video had caught everything, including what went on after Dottie had left the ballroom. Her throat swelled with emotion as she watched Alex dance with his daughter. If he'd asked Princess Genevieve to dance, that portion hadn't been put on the CD.

She smiled at Zoe. "You're so lucky to have a video of your first party. Did you love it?"

"Yes!" There weren't any shadows in the little girl's eyes. Whatever conversation had taken place between father and daughter at bedtime, she looked happy. "Uncle Stasi told me I could stand on his feet while he danced with me. He made me laugh."

"The crown prince is a real character." Her gaze swerved to Alex. "He made me laugh, as well. I've decided you and your brother must have given certain people some nervous moments when you were younger."

Alex's grin turned her heart right over. "Our parents

particularly. My brother was upset you left the party before he could dance with you."

"Maybe that was for the best. My high heels might have hurt the tops of his feet."

At that remark both he and Zoe laughed. Dottie was enjoying this too much and suggested they get started on the morning lesson.

They worked in harmony until Alex said it was time for lunch by the pool. After they'd finished eating, Zoe ran into the cabana to get into her swimsuit. Dottie took advantage of the time they were alone to talk to him.

"I'm glad we're by ourselves for a minute. I want to discuss Zoe's preschool situation and wondered how you'd feel if I went with her to class in the morning. You know, just to prop up her confidence. We'll come back here for lunch and enjoy our afternoon session with her out here. What do you think?"

He sipped his coffee. "That's an excellent suggestion. Otherwise she'll keep putting off wanting to go back."

"Exactly."

Alex released a sigh. "Since our talk about her friends, I've worried about her being away from the other children this long."

Dottie was glad they were on her same wavelength. "Is there any particular child she's close to at school?"

Their gazes held. "Not that she has mentioned. As you know, school hasn't been her best experience."

"Then tell me this. Who goes to the school?"

"Besides those who live in Hellenica, there are a few children of some younger diplomats who attend at the various elementary grade levels."

"From where?"

"The U.K., France, Italy, Bosnia, Germany, the States."

The States? "That's interesting." Dottie started to get excited, but she kept her ideas to herself and finished her coffee.

Alex didn't say anything more, yet she felt a strange new tension growing between them. Her awareness of him was so powerful, she couldn't sit there any longer. "If you'll excuse me, I'll go change into my bathing suit."

"Not yet," he countered. "There's something I need to tell you before Zoe comes out."

Her pulse picked up speed. "If it's about her running to my room last eve—"

"It is," he cut in on her. "After what Zoe told me while I was putting her to bed, I realize this matter needs to be cleared up."

"Your marriage to Princess Genevieve is none of my business. As long as—"

"Dottie," he interrupted her again, this time with an underlying trace of impatience. "There will be no marriage. Believe me when I tell you there was never any question of my marrying her. I impressed that on Zoe before she went to sleep."

Dottie had to fight to prevent Alex from seeing her great relief and joy.

"Since Teresa's death, it has been my grandmother's ambition to join the House of Helvetia to our own. Zoe had the great misfortune of overhearing her tell Sofia about her plans. In her innocence, Zoe has expressed her love for you and has told *Yiayia* she wants *you* to be her new mommy."

"I was afraid of that," she whispered.

"Last night I spoke to my grandmother. She admitted that she arranged last night's party for me, not Stasi. She hoped that by inviting Princess Genevieve, it would put an end to Zoe's foolishness."

"Oh, dear."

"The queen has taken great pains to remind me once again what a wonderful mother Teresa was and that it is time I took another wife. Naturally she's grateful you've identified Zoe's problem, but now she wants you to go back to New York. I learned she's already found another speech therapist to replace you."

Dottie's head reared. "Who?"

"I have no idea, but it's not important. My grandmother is running true to form," he said before Dottie could comment further. "She tried to use all her logic with me by reminding me Zoe will have to be taken care of by a nanny until maturity; therefore it won't be good to allow her to get any more attached to you."

"In that regard, she's right."

Anger rose inside him. "Nevertheless, the queen stepped way out of bounds last night. I told her that I had no plans to marry again. She would have to find another way to strengthen the ties with Helvetia because Zoe's welfare was my only concern and you were staying put."

His dark eyes pierced hers. "I'm sure my words have shocked you, but it's necessary you know the truth so there won't be any more misunderstandings."

"Daddy?" They both turned to see Zoe trying to drag out her five-foot inflated whale from the cabana, but it was stuck. "I need help!"

Before he moved in her direction he said, "My grandmother may still be the ruler of Hellenica, but I rule over my own life and Zoe's. My daughter knows she doesn't have to worry about Princess Genevieve ever again, no matter what her *yiayia* might say."

With that declaration, he took a few steps, then paused. "Just so you know, after I've put Zoe to bed tonight, I'm taking you to the old part of the city, so don't plan on an early night."

Alex stayed with Zoe and read stories to her until she fell asleep. Since she realized he wasn't going to marry Princess Genevieve, his daughter actually seemed at peace for a change. With a nod to Sofia in the next room to keep an eye on her, he left for his own suite.

He showered and shaved before dressing in a sport shirt and trousers. On his way out of the room, he called for an unmarked car with smoked glass to be brought around to his private entrance. With Stasio in the palace, Alex didn't need to worry about anything else tonight. He called security and asked them to escort Dottie to the entrance.

After she climbed in the back with him, he explained that they were driving to the city's ancient amphitheater to see the famous sound and light show. "We're going to visit the site of many archaeological ruins. As we walk around, you'll see evidence of the Cycladic civilization and the Byzantium empire."

Alex had seen the show many times before with visiting dignitaries, but tonight he was with Dottie and he'd never felt so alive. The balmy air caused him to forget everything but the exciting woman who sat next to him.

Throughout the program he could tell by her questions and remarks that she loved it. After it was over he lounged against a temple column while she explored.

The tourists had started leaving, yet all he could see was her beautiful silhouette against the night sky. She'd put her hair back so her distinctive profile was revealed. She was dressed in another skirt and blouse, and he was reminded of the first time he'd seen her in his office.

"Dottie?" he called softly in the fragrant night air as he moved behind her. She let out a slight gasp and swung around.

He caught her to him swiftly and kissed her mouth to stop any other sound from escaping. Her lips were warm and tempting, but he didn't deepen the kiss. "Forgive me for doing that," he whispered against them, "but I didn't want you to say *Your Highness* and draw attention. Come and get in the car. It's late."

He helped her into the backseat with him and shut the door. "I'm not going to apologize for what I did," he murmured against her hot cheek. "If you want to slap me, you have my permission. But if I'm going to be punished for it, I'll take my chances now and give you a proper reason."

Alex's compelling mouth closed over Dottie's with a hunger that set her knees knocking. She'd sensed this moment was inevitable. Since her arrival in Hellenica, they'd been together early in the morning, late at night and most of the hours in between. He possessed a lethal sensuality for which she had no immunity.

Knowing he had no plans to marry Princess Genevieve, Dottie settled deeper into his arms and found herself giving him kiss for kiss. It was time she faced an ironic truth about herself. She wasn't any different than the rest of the female population who found the prince so attractive, they'd give anything to be in her position.

Royal scandal might abound, but she'd just discovered there was a reason for it. Forbidden fruit with this gorgeous male made these moments of physical intimacy exquisite. When a man was as incredibly potent and exciting as Alex, you could blot out everything else, even the fact that the driver ferrying them back to the palace was aware of every sound of ecstasy pouring out of her.

She finally put her hands against his chest and tore her mouth from his so she could ease back enough to look at him. Still trying to catch her breath, she asked, "Do you know what we are, Your Highness?" Her voice sounded less than steady to her own ears. She hated her inability to control that part of her.

"Suppose you tell me," he said in a husky voice.

"We're both a cliché. The prince and the hired help, nipping out for a little pleasure. I've just confirmed everything I've ever read in books and have seen on the news about palace intrigue."

"Who are you more angry at?" he murmured, kissing the tips of her fingers. "Me, for having taken unfair advantage? Or you, for having the right of refusal at any time which you didn't exercise? I'm asking myself if I'm fighting your righteous indignation that served you too late, or the ghost of your dead husband."

She squirmed because he'd hit the mark dead center. "Both," she answered honestly.

"Tell me about your husband. Was it love at first sight with him?"

"I don't know. It just seemed right from the beginning."

"Give me a few details. I really want to know what it would be like to have that kind of freedom."

Dottie stirred restlessly, sensing he meant what he said. "We met in Albany, New York, where I was raised. I went to the local pharmacy to pick up a prescription for my aunt. Neil had just been hired as a new pharmacist. It was late and there weren't any other customers.

"He told me it would take a while to get it ready, so we began talking. The next day he phoned and asked me out with the excuse that he'd just moved there from New York City and didn't know anyone. He was fun and kind and very smart.

"On our first date we went to a movie. After it was over, he told me he was going to marry me and there was nothing I could do about it. Four months later we got married and before we knew it, Cory was on the way. I was incredibly happy."

Alex's arm tightened around her. "I envy you for having those kinds of memories."

"Surely you have some wonderful ones, too."

A troubled sigh escaped his lips. "To quote you on several occasions, even if I am a prince, the one thing I've never had power over was my own personal happiness. Duty to my country came first. My marriage to Teresa was planned years before we got together, so any relationships I had before the wedding couldn't be taken seriously.

"She was beautiful in her own way, very accomplished. Sweet. But it was never an affair of the heart or anything close to it. On his deathbed, my father commanded me to marry her. I couldn't tell him I wouldn't."

Dottie shuddered. "Did you love him?"

"Yes."

"I can't comprehend being in your shoes, but I

admire you for being so devoted to your father and your country. Did Teresa love you?"

He took a steadying breath. "Before she died, she told me she'd fallen in love with me. I told her the same thing, not wanting to hurt her. She told me I was a liar, but she said she loved me for it."

"Oh, Alex… How hard for both of you."

"I wanted to fall in love with her, but we both know you can't force something that's not there. Zoe was my one gift from the gods who brood over Mount Pelos."

Her gaze lifted to his. "Not to be in love and have to marry—that's anathema to me. No wonder you seek relief in the shadows with someone handy like me. I get it, Alex. I really do. And you *didn't* take unfair advantage of me. It's been so long since I've been around an attractive man, my hormones are out of kilter right now."

"Is that what this tension is between us? Hormones?" he said with a twinge of bitterness she felt pierce her where it hurt most.

"I don't have a better word for it." She buried her face in her hands. "I loved Neil more than you can imagine. Thank heaven neither of us had a royal bone in our bodies to prevent us from knowing joy."

He stroked the back of her neck in a way that sent fingers of delight down her spine. "How did you manage after they were killed?"

"My aunt. She reminded me not everyone had been as lucky as I'd been. Her boyfriend got killed when he was deployed overseas in the military, so she never married. In her inimitable way she told me to stop pitying myself and get on with something useful.

"Her advice prompted me to go to graduate school

in New York City and become a speech therapist. After graduation I was hired on by the Stillman Institute. Little did I know that all the time I'd been helping Cory with his speech that last year, I was preparing for a lifetime career."

"Is your aunt still alive?"

"No. She died fourteen months ago."

"I'm sorry. I wish she were still living so I could thank her for her inspired advice. My Zoe is thriving because of you." He pulled her closer. "What about your parents?"

"They died in a car crash when I was just a little girl."

"It saddens me you've had to deal with so much grief."

"It comes to us all. In my aunt's case, it was good she passed away. With her chronic pneumonia, she could never recover and every illness made her worse."

"My mother was like that. She had been so ill that Stasi and I were thankful once she took her last breath."

"What about your father?"

"He developed an aggressive cancer of the thyroid. After he was gone, my grandmother took over to make sure we were raised according to her exacting Valleder standards. She was the power behind my grandfather's throne."

"She's done a wonderful job. I'll tell her that when I leave Hellenica." Dottie took a deep breath and sat back in the seat. "And now, despite her disapproval that I haven't left yet, here I am making out in an unmarked car with Prince Alexius Constantinides. How *could* you have given Zoe such an impossible last name? Nine consonants. *Nine!* And two of them are *T*'s," she half sobbed as the dam broke and she felt tears on her cheeks.

Alex reached over and smoothed the moisture from her face. He put his lips where his hand had been. "I'm glad there are nine. I won't let you go until she can pronounce our last name perfectly. That's going to take a long time."

"You'll have gone through at least half a dozen speech therapists by then."

"Possibly, but you'll be there in the background until she no longer needs your services."

"We've been over this ground before."

"We haven't even started," he declared as if announcing an edict. "Shall we get out of the car? We've been back at the palace for the past ten minutes. My driver probably wants to go to bed, which is where we should be."

She didn't think he meant that the way it came out, but with Alex you couldn't be absolutely sure when his teasing side would suddenly show up. All she knew was that her face was suffused with heat. She flung the car door open and ran into the palace, leaving him in the proverbial royal dust.

The death of her husband had put an end to all fairy tales, and that was the only place a prince could stay. She refused to be in the background of his life. It was time to close the storybook for good.

CHAPTER SIX

AT ELEVEN-FORTY-FIVE the next morning, Alex did something unprecedented and drove to the preschool to pick up Zoe and Dottie himself. He'd decided he'd better wear something more formal for this public visit and chose his dove-grey suit with a white shirt and grey vest. He toned it with a darker grey tie that bore the royal crest of the monarchy in silver, wanting to look his best for the woman who'd already turned his world inside out.

The directress of the school accompanied him to the classroom, where he spotted his daughter sitting in front and Dottie seated in the back. As the woman announced the arrival of Prince Alexius Constantinides, Dottie's blue eyes widened in shock. Her gaze clung to his for a moment.

He heard a collective sound of awe from the children, something he was used to in his capacity as prince. Children were always a delight. He was enjoying this immensely, but it was clear Dottie was stunned that he'd decided to come and get them. He knew in his gut her eyes wouldn't have ignited like that if she hadn't been happy to see him.

The teacher, Mrs. Pappas, urged the roomful of

twelve children to stand and bow. Zoe stood up, but she turned and smiled at Dottie before saying good morning to His Royal Highness along with the others. Alex got a kick out of the whole thing as the children kept looking at Zoe, knowing he was her daddy.

He'd never seen his daughter this happy in his life, and he should have done this before now. It lit up her whole being. Dottie was transforming his life in whole new ways. Because of her influence, Alex wanted to give his struggling preschooler a needed boost this morning. But she wasn't so struggling now that she had Dottie in her court.

He shook hands with everyone, then they returned to the palace. After changing into his swimming trunks, he joined them at the pool for lunch. With Zoe running around, he could finally talk to Dottie in private.

"How did my daughter do in class?"

"She participated without hanging back."

"That's because you've given her the confidence."

"You know it's been a team effort. While I've got you alone for a minute, let me tell you something else that happened this morning."

Alex could tell she was excited. "Go ahead."

"I arranged to talk with the directress about Zoe and was given permission to visit the other preschool class. One of the boys enrolled is an American from Pennsylvania named Mark Varney. He's supposed to be in first grade, but his parents put him back in preschool because he has no knowledge of Greek and needs to start with the basics. The situation has made him unhappy and he's turning into a loner."

"And you've decided that two negatives could make a positive?"

"Maybe." She half laughed. "It's scary how well you read my mind. Here's the thing—if you sanctioned it and Mark's parents allowed him to come back to the palace after school next time, he and Zoe could have some one-on-one time here in the pool, or down on the beach. I'd help them with their lessons, but the rest of the time they could have fun together. A play date is what she needs."

"I couldn't agree more."

"Oh, good! The directress says he's feeling inade-quate. If his parents understood the circumstances and explained to him about Zoe's speech problem, he might be willing to help her and they could become friends in the process. That would help his confidence level, too."

Alex heard the appeal in Dottie's voice. "I'll ask Hector to handle it and we'll see how the first play date goes."

Light filled her blue eyes, dazzling him. "Thank you for being willing."

"That's rather ironic for you to be thanking me. I'm the one who should be down on my knees to you for thinking of it. She's a different child already because of you."

"You keep saying that, but you don't give yourself enough credit, Alex. When she saw you walk into the schoolroom earlier today, her heart was in her eyes. I wish I'd had a camera on me so I could have taken a picture. Every father should have a daughter who loves him that much. The extra time you've spent with her lately is paying huge dividends. I know it's taking time away from your duties, but if you can keep it up, you'll never regret it."

He rubbed his lower lip with the pad of his thumb,

staring at her through shuttered eyes. "That's why I sent for Stasi to come home. With you showing me the way, I'm well aware Zoe needs me and am doing everything in my power to free myself up."

"I know." She suddenly broke away from his gaze to look at Zoe. "She's waiting for us. Today we'll work on the letter *C*. Her preschool teacher brought her own cat to class. The children learned how to take care of one. Zoe got to pet it and couldn't have been more thrilled."

Dottie had inexplicably changed the subject and was talking faster than usual, a sign that something was going on inside her, making her uncomfortable. When she got up from the chair, he followed her over to the edge of the pool and listened as she engaged his daughter in a conversation that was really a teaching moment. She had a remarkable, unique way of communicating. Zoe ate it up. Why wouldn't she? There was no one else like Dottie.

Dottie was more than a speech therapist for his daughter. She was her advocate. Her selfless efforts to help Zoe lead a normal life couldn't be repaid with gifts or perks or money she'd already refused to accept. The woman wanted his daughter to succeed for the purest of reasons. She wanted it for a stranger's child, too. That made Dottie Richards a person of interest to him in ways that went deep beneath the surface.

Alex took off his sandals and dove into the deep end. After doing some underwater laps, he emerged next to his daughter, causing her to shriek with laughter. The day had been idyllic and it wasn't over.

As he did more laps, his thoughts drifted to his conversation with Dottie last night. When he'd turned eighteen, his family had arranged the betrothal to Princess

Teresa. However, until he'd been ready to commit to marriage, he'd known pleasure and desire with various women over the years. Those women had understood nothing long lasting could come of the relationship. No one woman's memory had lingered long in his mind. Forget his heart.

When Zoe came along, their daughter gave them both something new and wonderful to focus on. With Teresa's passing, Zoe had become the joy of his life. There'd been other women in the past two years, but the part of his psyche that had never been touched was still a void.

Enter Dottie Richards, a woman who'd buried a son and husband. He could still hear her saying she'd lost the great loves of her life. She'd experienced the kind of overwhelming love denied him because of his royal roots. He really envied her the freedom to choose the man who'd satisfied her passion at its deepest level and had given her a child.

Though it was an unworthy sentiment, Alex found himself resenting her husband for that same freedom. If Alex had been a commoner and had met her in his early twenties—before she'd met her husband—would she have been as attracted to him as he was to her? Would they have married?

She wasn't indifferent to Alex. The way she'd kissed him back last night convinced him of her strong attraction to him. He'd also sensed her interest at odd times when he noticed her eyes on him. The way she sometimes breathed faster around him for no apparent reason. But he had no way to gauge the true depth of her emotions until he could get her alone again.

As for his feelings, all he knew was that she'd lit a

fire inside him. In two weeks, even without physical intimacy, Dottie affected him more than Teresa had ever done during the three years of their marriage.

For the first time in his life he was suddenly waking up every morning hardly able to breathe until he saw her. For the only time in his existence he was questioning everything about the royal legacy that made him who he was and dictated his destiny.

His jealousy terrified him. He'd seen his brother's interest in her. Stasi's arranged marriage would be happening on his thirty-fifth birthday, in less than three weeks now. Until then it didn't stop him from enjoying and looking at other women. But it had angered Alex, who felt territorial when it came to Dottie. That's why he hadn't let Stasi dance with her. Alex had no right to feel this way, but the situation had gone way beyond rights.

Alex *wanted* his daughter's speech therapist. But as he'd already learned, a command from him meant nothing to her. A way had to be found so she wouldn't leave, but he had to be careful that he didn't frighten her off.

He swam back to Zoe, who hung on to the edge of the pool, practicing the hard *C* sound with Dottie. Without looking him in the eye, Dottie said, "Here's your daddy. Now that your lesson is over, I have to go inside. Zoe, I need to tell you now that I won't be able come to your bedroom to say good-night later. I have plans I can't break, but I'll see you in the morning." She finally glanced at him. "Your Highness."

Alex had no doubts that if she'd dared and if it wouldn't have alarmed Zoe, Dottie would have run away from him as fast as she could. Fortunately one of the positive benefits of being the prince meant he could keep twenty-four-hour surveillance on her.

After she'd left the sun deck, he spent another half hour in the pool with his daughter before they went inside. But once in her room, Zoe told Sofia to go away. When Alex tried to reason with her and get her to apologize, she broke down in tears, begging him to eat dinner with her in her room. She didn't want to be with *Yiayia*.

Dottie's announcement that she wouldn't be coming in to say good-night had sent the sun behind a black cloud. Naturally Dottie had every right to spend her evenings the way she wished. That's what he told Zoe. He had to help his daughter see that, but the idyllic day had suddenly vanished like a curl of smoke in the air.

"Make her come, Daddy."

A harsh laugh escaped his lips. You didn't make Dottie do anything. He didn't have that kind of power. She had to do it herself because she wanted to.

What if she *didn't* want to? What if the memory of life with her husband trapped her in the past and she couldn't, or didn't want to, reach out? On the heels of those questions came an even more important one.

Why would she reach out? What did a prince have to offer a commoner? An affair? A secret life? The answers to that question not only stared him in the face, they kicked him in the gut with enough violence to knock the wind out of him.

Once Zoe was asleep, Alex left for his suite, taking the palace stairs three steps at a time to the next floor. The last person he expected to find in his living room was Stasio with a glass of scotch in his hand.

He tossed back a drink. "It's about time you made an appearance, little brother." For a while now a cross-grain tone of discontent had lain behind Stasi's speech and it had grown stronger over the last few months. No crystal ball was needed here. The bitter subject of arranged marriages still burned like acid on his tongue as it did on Stasi's.

"Did you and *Yiayia* have another row tonight?" Alex started unbuttoning his shirt and took off his shoes.

"What do you mean, another one?" Stasio slammed his half-empty glass on the coffee table, spilling some of it. "It's been the same argument for seventeen years, but tonight I put an end to it."

"Translate for me," Alex rapped out tersely.

Stasio's mouth thinned to a white line. "I told her I broke it off with Beatriz while I was in Valleder. I can't go through with the wedding."

Alex felt the hairs on the back of his neck stand on end. He stared hard at his brother. All the time Stasi had put off coming home, something in the back of Alex's mind had divined the truth, but he hadn't been able to make his brother open up about it.

Since Stasio had been old enough to comprehend life, he'd been forced to bear the burden of knowing he would be king one day. That was hard enough. But to be married for the rest of his life to a woman he didn't love would have kept him in a living hell. No one knew it better than Alex.

"How is Beatriz dealing with it?"

"Not well," he whispered in agony.

"But she's always known how you truly felt. No matter how much this has hurt her, deep down it couldn't have come as a complete surprise. I thought she would have broken it off a long time ago."

"That miracle never happened. She wanted the marriage, just the way Teresa wanted yours." Alex couldn't deny it. "What always astounded me was that you were able to handle going through with your marriage to her."

Alex wheeled around. "The truth?"

"Always."

"It was the last thing I wanted. I wouldn't have married her, but with Father on his deathbed making me promise to follow through with it, I couldn't take the fight with him any longer and caved. The only thing that kept me sane was the fact that I wouldn't be king one day, so I wouldn't have to be in the public eye every second. And then, Zoe came along. Now I can't imagine my life without her."

Stasio paled. "Neither can I. She's the one ray of sunshine around this tomb." He took a deep breath. "Under the circumstances I should be grateful *Yiayia* isn't taking her last breath because there will be no forced wedding with Beatriz. Philippe has backed me in this and he holds a certain sway with our grandmother."

Alex was afraid that was wishful thinking on Stasio's part. Not only was Philippe his best friend, he'd been one of the lucky royals who'd ended up marrying the American girl he'd loved years earlier. They'd had a son together and the strict rules had been waived in his particular case.

But the queen hadn't approved of Philippe's marriage, so it didn't follow she would give an inch when it came to Stasio's decision. In her eyes he'd created a monumental catastrophe that could never be forgiven.

"So what's going to happen now?"

"Beatriz's parents have given a statement to the press. It's probably all over the news as we speak or will be in a matter of hours. Once the story grows legs, I'll be torn apart. I had to tell *Yiayia* tonight to prepare her for what's coming."

"What was our grandmother's reaction?"

"You know her as well as I do. Putting on her stone face, she said the coronation would go ahead as scheduled to save the integrity of the crown. A suitable marriage with another princess will take place within six months maximum. She gave me her short list of five candidates."

Alex felt a chill go through him. "Putting the cart before the horse has never been done."

"The queen is going to have her way no matter what. Let's face it. She's not well and wants me to take over."

"Stasi—"

Sick for his brother, he walked over and hugged him. "I'm here for you always. You know that."

"I *do*. A fine pair we've turned out to be. She told me you're still resisting marriage to Princess Genevieve."

"Like you, I told her no once and for all," he said through clenched teeth. "I sacrificed myself once. Never again."

"She's not going to give up on Genevieve. I heard it in her voice."

"That's too bad because my only duty now is to raise Zoe to be happy."

With the help of Dottie, he intended that to become a reality. Walking over to the table, he poured himself a drink. He lifted his glass to his brother.

"To you, Stasi," he said in a thick-toned voice. "May God help you find a way to cope." *May God help both of us.*

* * *

After a sleep troubled with thoughts of Alex, Dottie felt out of sorts and anxious and only poked at her breakfast. Since he hadn't brought Zoe for her morning session yet, she checked her emails. Among some posts from her friends at the Institute in New York she'd received a response to the email she'd sent Dr. Rice. With a pounding heart, she opened it first.

Dear Dottie:

Thank you for giving me an update on Princess Zoe. I'm very pleased to hear that she's beginning to make progress. If anyone can work miracles, it's you. In reference to your request, I've interviewed several therapists who I believe would work well with her, but the one I think could be the best fit might not be available as soon as you wanted. She's still working with the parent of another child to teach them coaching skills. I'll let you know when she'll be free to come. Give it a few more days.

By the way, it's all over the news about Crown Prince Stasio calling off his wedding to Princess Beatriz. She's here in Manhattan. I saw her on the news walking into the St. Regis Hotel. What a coincidence that you're working for Prince Alexius. Have you ever met his brother? Well, take care. I'll be in touch before long. Dr. Rice.

She rested her elbow on the table, covering her eyes with her hand. Prince Stasio's teasing facade hid a courageous man who'd just done himself and Princess Beatriz a huge favor, even if talk of it and the judgments that would follow saturated the news.

The world had no idea what went on behind the closed doors of a desperately unhappy couple, royal or otherwise. What woman or man would want to be married to someone who'd been chosen for them years earlier? Alex's first marriage had been forced. It boggled the mind, yet it had happened to the royals of the Constantinides family for hundreds of years in order to keep the monarchy alive.

Poor Zoe. To think that dear little girl would have to grow up knowing an arranged marriage was her fate. Dottie cringed at the prospect. Surely Alex wouldn't do that to his own daughter after what he and his brother had been through, would he?

"Dot?" Zoe came running into the alcove and hugged her so hard, she almost fell off the chair.

Without conscious thought Dottie closed her eyes and hugged her back, aching for this family and its archaic rules that had hung like a pall over their lives. When she opened them again, there was Alex standing there in a navy crew neck and jeans looking bigger than life as he watched the two of them interact.

She saw lines and shadows on his striking face that hadn't been there yesterday. But when their eyes met, the black fire in his took her to the backseat of the car where the other night they'd kissed each other with mindless abandon.

"We're here to invite you out for a day on the water," he explained. "The galley's loaded with food and drink. We'll do lessons and have fun at the same time."

As he spoke, Zoe sat down to do one of the puzzles on the table out of hearing distance. It was a good thing, because Alex's invitation had frightened Dottie. Though her mind was warning her this would be a mistake, that vital organ pumping her life's blood enlarged at the prospect.

The other night she'd almost lost control with him and the experience was still too fresh. To go with him would be like watching a moth enticed to a flame fly straight to its death.

"Perhaps it's time you enjoyed one day without me along. It won't hurt Zoe to miss a lesson." She'd said the first thing to come into her mind, frantically searching for an excuse not to be with him.

Lines marred his arresting features. "I'm afraid this is one time I need your cooperation. There's something critically urgent I must discuss with you."

Dottie looked away from the intensity of his gaze. This had to be about his brother. The distinct possibility that Prince Stasio needed Alex to do double duty for him right now, or to spend more time with him, crossed her mind. Of necessity it would cut short the time he'd been spending with Zoe. If that was the case, she could hardly turn him down while he worked out an alternative plan with her.

"All right. Give me a minute to put some things in the bag for our lesson."

"Take all the time you need." His voice seemed to have a deeper timbre this morning, playing havoc with the butterflies fluttering madly in her chest.

After Zoe helped pack some things they'd need, Dottie changed into a sleeveless top and shorts. When she emerged from the bathroom with her hair freshly brushed, the prince took swift inventory of her face and figure, whipping up a storm of heat that stained her cheeks with color. Once she'd stowed her swimsuit in the bag, she put on her sunglasses and declared she was ready to go.

Dottie had assumed they'd be taking his sailboat. But once they left the palace grounds, Alex informed her he had business on one of the other islands so they were going out on the yacht. The news caused a secret thrill to permeate her body.

That first morning when she and Zoe had gone down to the private beach, she'd seen the gleaming white royal yacht moored in the distance. Like any normal tourist, she'd dreamed of touring the Aegean on a boat while she was in Hellenica. Today the dream had become reality as she boarded the fabulous luxury craft containing every amenity known to man.

With the sparkling blue water so calm, Zoe was in heaven. Wearing another swimsuit, this one in lime-and-blue stripes, she ran up and down the length of it with her father's binoculars, looking for groupers and parrot fish with one of the crew.

Alex settled them in side-by-side loungers while the deck steward placed drinks and treats close enough to reach. With Zoe occupied for a few minutes, Dottie felt this would be the best time to approach him about his brother and turned in his direction. But he'd removed his shirt. One look at his chest with its dusting of black hair, in fact his entire masculine physique, and she had to stifle a moan.

The other night she'd been crushed against him and, heaven help her, she longed to repeat the experience. Fortunately the presence of Zoe and the crew prevented anything like that from happening today.

Admit you want it to happen, Dottie.

After losing Neil, she couldn't believe all these feelings to know a man's possession had come back this strongly. For so long she'd been dead inside. She was frightened by this explosion of need Alex had ignited. She had to hope Dr. Rice would email her the good news that her replacement could be here by next week because she could feel herself being sucked into a situation that could only rebound on her.

Not for a moment did she believe Alex was a womanizer. He was a man, and like any single male was free to find temporary satisfaction with a willing woman when the time and opportunity presented itself. With her full cooperation he'd acted on one of those opportunities and she'd lost her head.

It wasn't his fault. It was *hers*. She'd been an idiot.

Unless she wanted a new form of heartache to plague her for the rest of her life, she couldn't afford another foolish moment because of overwhelming desire for Alex. There was no future in it. She'd be gone from this assignment before long. Nothing but pain could come from indulging in a passionate interlude with a prince. *Nothing*.

"Alex. The head of my department at Stillman's responded to one of my emails this morning."

He removed his sunglasses and shifted his hard-muscled body on the lounger so he faced her. "Was that the one asking him to find another therapist for Zoe?" he inquired in a dangerously silky voice. An underlying tone of ice sent a tremor through her body.

"Yes. He says he'll probably have someone to replace me within another week. By then Zoe ought to have more confidence in herself and will work well with the new speech teacher."

Paralyzing tension stretched between them before

eyes of jet impaled her. "You don't believe that piece of fiction any more than I do. In any event, there can't be a question about you leaving, not with the coronation almost upon us."

She sat up in surprise. "You mean there's still going to be one?"

Like lightning he levered himself from the lounger. "Why would you ask that question?"

"At the end of Dr. Rice's email, he told me there were headlines about Prince Stasio calling off his wedding to Princess Beatriz."

"So it's already today's news in New York." He sounded far away. She watched him rub the back of his neck, something he did when he was pondering a grave problem.

Growing more uneasy, Dottie stood up. "Forgive me if I've upset you."

He eyed her frankly. "Forgiveness doesn't come into it. They were never suited, but I didn't know he'd made the break official until he told me last night."

She rubbed her arms in reaction. "What a traumatic night it must have been for all of you and your grandmother."

"I won't lie to you about that." His pain was palpable.

Dottie bit her lip. "For both their sakes I'm glad he couldn't go through with it, but you'll probably think I'm horrible for saying it."

"On the contrary," Alex ground out. "I'd think something serious was wrong with you if you hadn't. His life has been a living hell. He should have ended the betrothal years ago."

Alex... She heard the love for his brother.

"Does it mean the queen will go on ruling?" she

asked quietly. "I'm probably overstepping my bounds to talk to you like this, but after meeting your brother, I can't help but feel terrible for what he must be suffering right now, even if he didn't want the marriage."

"Between us, he's in bad shape," he confided, "but the coronation is still on. Our grandmother is failing in small ways and can't keep up her former pace as sovereign, but she's still in charge. She has given him six months to marry one of the eligible royals on her list."

"But—"

"There are no buts," he cut her off, but she knew his anger wasn't directed at her. "I just have to pray he'll find some common ground with one of the women." His voice throbbed. Again Dottie was horrified by Prince Stasio's untenable situation. "Since there's nothing I can do except stand by him, I'd rather concentrate on Zoe's lesson. What do you have planned for today?"

Heartsick as Dottie felt, she'd been sent to Hellenica to do a job and she wanted desperately to lift his spirits if she could. "Since we're on the yacht, I thought we'd work on the *Y* sound. She can already say *Yiayia* pretty well."

"That's where her Greek ought to help."

"Why don't you say hello to her in Greek and we'll see what happens."

Together they walked toward the railing at the far end. Zoe saw them coming and trained the binoculars on them.

"Yasoo," her father called to her. The cute little girl answered back in a sad facsimile of the greeting.

Dottie smiled. "Do you like being on this boat?"

"Yes."

Today they'd work on *ya*. Another day they'd work

on *yes*. "Do you know what kind of a boat this is?" Zoe shook her head. "It's called a yacht. Say *yasoo* again." Zoe responded. "Now say *ya*." She tried, but the sound was off with both words.

"I can't."

Dottie felt her frustration.

Alex handed Dottie the binoculars and picked up his daughter. "Try it once more." He wanted her to make a good sound for him. Dottie wanted it, too, more than anything. But this was a game of infinite patience. "Be a parrot for daddy, like one of those parrot fish you were watching with its birdlike beak. Parrots can talk. Talk to me. Say *ya*."

"Ya."

"Open your mouth wider like your daddy is doing," Dottie urged her. "Pretend he's the doctor looking down your throat with a stick. He wants to hear you. Can you say *ya* for him?"

She giggled. "Daddy's not a doctor."

The prince sent Dottie a look of defeat. "You're right." He kissed Zoe's cheek. "Come on. Let's have a lemonade." As soon as he put her down, she ran back to the table by the loungers to drink hers.

Clearly Zoe wasn't in the mood for a lesson. Who would be on a beautiful day like this? The translucent blue water was dotted with islands that made Dottie itch to get out and explore everything. She put the binoculars to her eyes to see what was coming next. "What's the name of that island in the distance?"

"Argentum."

"You mine silver there?"

"How did you figure that out?"

"You told me you lived on Aurum. Both islands have Latin names for gold and silver."

His eyes met hers. "You're not only intelligent, but knowledgeable. We'll anchor out in the bay. The head mining engineer is coming aboard for a business lunch. He's also my closest friend."

"Where did you meet?"

"We were getting our mining engineering degrees at the same time, both here and in Colorado at the school of mines."

"That's why your English is amazing. Is your friend married?"

"Yes. He has a new baby."

"That's nice for him."

"Very nice. He's in love with his wife and she with him."

Dottie couldn't bear to talk about that subject. "Tell me about the tall island beyond Argentum with the green patches?"

"That's Aurum, where Zoe and I normally live." He hadn't put on his shirt yet. She could feel his body radiating heat. "As you guessed correctly, rich gold deposits on the other side of the mountain were discovered there centuries ago. Bari and I are both passionate about our work. There are many more mining projects to be explored. I'm anxious to get back to them."

By now she was trembling from their close proximity. Needing a reason to move away from him, she put the binoculars on the table and picked up her lemonade. "Do you miss Aurum?"

"Yes." His dark gaze wandered over her, sending her pulse rate off the charts. "Zoe and I prefer it to Hellenica. The palace there is much smaller with more trees and vegetation that keep it cooler. We'll take you next week so Zoe can show you the garden off her room."

Dottie let the comment pass because if she were still here by then, she had no intention of going there with him. It wouldn't be a good idea. Not a good idea at all. "Do you get her to preschool by helicopter, then?"

He nodded. "Once she's in kindergarten, she'll go to a school on Aurum, but nothing is going to happen until after the coronation." After swallowing the contents of his drink without taking a breath, he reached for his shirt. "Shall we go below and freshen up before Bari comes on board?"

She followed the two of them down the steps of the elegant yacht to the luxurious cabins. "Come with us." Zoe pulled on her hand.

Dottie bent over. "I have my own cabin down the hallway."

"How come?"

"Because I'm a guest."

She looked at her daddy. "Make her come."

"Zoe? We have our room, and she has hers," he said in his princely parental voice as Dottie thought of it.

To the surprise of both of them, Zoe kept hold of Dottie's hand. "I want to be with you."

"It's all right, Your Highness," Dottie said before he could protest. "Zoe and I will freshen up together and meet you on deck in a little while." Their family was going through deep turmoil. The burden of what his brother had done had set off enormous ramifications and Alex was feeling them.

For that matter, so was Zoe, who'd behaved differently today. With the advent of Prince Stasio's stunning news, she couldn't have helped but pick up on the tension radiating from the queen and her father during breakfast. She might not understand all that was going on, but she sensed upheaval. That's why she'd given up on her lesson so easily.

His eyes narrowed in what she assumed was speculation. "You're sure?"

"Do you even have to ask?" Dottie had meant what she'd told him last week about his needing some pampering. He had work to do with Mr. Jouflas, but no one else was there to help him with Zoe the way he needed it. Dottie found she wanted to ease his burden. He'd made sacrifices for the love of his country. Now it was her turn, no matter how small.

"You're operating under an abnormal amount of strain right now. You could use a little help. I don't know how you've been doing this balancing act for such a long time." She smiled at Zoe. "Come on."

Dottie saw the relief on his face and knew she'd said the right thing. "In that case I'll send the steward to your cabin with a fresh change of clothes for her."

"That would be perfect."

CHAPTER SEVEN

DOTTIE felt Alex staring at her before they disappeared inside. Since she'd been trying so hard to keep a professional distance with his daughter, he knew this was an about-face for her. But no one could have foreseen this monarchial disaster.

Alex was being torn apart by his love for his brother, his grandmother and the future of the crown itself. He was Atlas holding up the world with no help in sight. This was a day like no other. If Dottie could ease a little of his burden where Zoe was concerned, then she wanted to.

"I've got an idea, Zoe. After you shower, we'll take a little nap on the beds. The heat has made me sleepy."

"Me, too."

There were two queen beds. Before long she'd tucked Zoe under the covers.

"Dot? Will you please stay with Daddy and me forever? I know you're not my mommy, but Daddy said you were once a mommy."

She struggled for breath. "Yes. I had a little boy named Cory who had to work on his speech, just like you."

"What happened to him?"

"He died in a car accident with my husband."

"So you're all alone."

"Yes," she murmured, but for the first time it wasn't hard to talk about. The conversation with Alex last night had been cathartic.

"My mommy died and now Daddy and I are all alone."

"Except that you have your great-grandmother and your uncle."

"But I want you."

Dottie wanted to be with Zoe all the time, too. Somehow she'd gotten beyond her deep sadness and would love to care permanently for this child. But it was impossible in too many ways to even consider.

"Let's be happy we're together right now, shall we?" she said in a shaky voice.

"Yes." Zoe finally closed her eyes and fell asleep.

Dotti took her own shower and dressed in a clean pair of jeans and a blouse. When she came out of the bathroom, the other bed looked inviting. She thought she'd lie down on top while she waited for Zoe to wake up.

The next thing she knew, she heard a familiar male voice whispering her name. Slightly disoriented, she rolled over and discovered Alex sitting on the side of the bed. She'd been dreaming about him, but to see his gorgeous self in the flesh this close to her gave her heart a serious workout. His eyes were like black fires. They trapped hers, making it impossible for her to look away.

"Thank you for stepping in."

She studied his features. "I wanted to."

"With your help I was able to conclude our business lunch in record time and came in to bring Zoe a change of clothes. Do you have any idea how beautiful you are lying there?"

Dottie couldn't swallow. She tried to move away, but he put an arm across her body so she was tethered to him. "Please let me go," she begged. "Zoe will be awake any minute now."

He leaned over her, running a hand up her arm. The feel of skin against hot skin brought every nerve ending alive. "I'll take any minute I can steal. Being alone with you is all I've been able to think about."

"Alex—" she cried as his dark head descended.

"I love it when you say my name in that husky voice." He covered her mouth with his own in an exploratory kiss as if this were their first time and they were in no hurry whatsoever. He took things slow in the beginning, tantalizing her until it wasn't enough. Then their kiss grew deeper and more sensuous. His restless lips traveled over every centimeter of her face and throat before capturing her mouth again and again.

The other night he'd kindled a fire in her that had never died down. Now his mastery conjured the flames licking through her body with the speed of a forest fire in full conflagration.

Out of breath, he buried his face in the side of her neck. "I want you, Dottie. I've never wanted any woman so much, and I know you want me."

"I think that's been established," she admitted against his jaw that hadn't seen a razor since early morning. She delighted in every masculine line and angle of his well-honed body. With legs and arms entwined, their mouths clung as their passion grew more frenzied. They tried to appease their hunger, but no kiss was long enough or deep enough to satisfy the desire building.

He'd taken them to a new level. She felt cherished. Like the wedding vow repeated by the groom, it seemed as if Alex was worshipping her with his body. But in the midst of this rapture only he could have created, she heard the blare of a ship's horn. With it came the realization that this was no wedding night and a groan escaped her throat.

She'd actually been making out with Prince Alexius of Hellenica on his royal yacht! Never mind that it was the middle of the day and his daughter was asleep in the next bed. What if Zoe had awakened and had been watching them?

Horrified to have gotten this carried away, Dottie wrenched her mouth from his and slipped out of his arms. So deep was his entrancement, she'd caught him off guard. Thankfully she was able to get to her feet before he could prevent it, but in her weakened state she almost fell over.

"Dottie?" he called her name in longing, but she didn't dare stay in here and be seduced by the spell he'd cast over her. On the way out of the cabin she grabbed her purse and hurried down the corridor to the stairs.

At the top of the gangway the deck steward smiled at her. "Mrs. Richards? We've docked on Hellenica. You're welcome to go ashore whenever you please."

Could he tell she'd been kissed breathless by the prince? The sun she'd picked up couldn't account for mussed hair and swollen lips, too.

The queen didn't deserve to hear this bit of gossip on top of Prince Stasio's shocking news. Every second Dottie stayed on board, she was contributing to more court intrigue. She couldn't bear it. In fact she couldn't believe they were back at the main island already. She'd been in such a completely different world with Alex, she'd lost track of everything including her wits.

"Th-thank you," her voice faltered. Without hesitation, she left the yacht and got in the waiting limousine. While she was still alone, she brushed her hair and applied some lipstick, trying to make herself presentable.

A few minutes later Alex approached the car with Zoe. "Dot!" she cried and climbed in next to her.

"Did you just wake up?" Dottie concentrated on Zoe, studiously avoiding his eyes. "You were a sleepyhead."

Zoe thought that was funny. She chatted happily with her daddy until they reached the palace where Hector stood outside the entry.

"Welcome back, Your Highness. The queen is waiting for you and the princess to join her and Prince Stasio in her suite."

A royal summons. It didn't surprise Dottie. She'd had visions of the queen herself waiting for them as they drove up to the entrance. For an instant she caught Alex's enigmatic glance before he alighted from the car. All their lives he and Stasio had been forced to obey that summons. A lesser person would have broken long before now.

She might be an outsider, yet she couldn't help but want to rebel against this antiquated system she'd only read about in history books. Unbelievable that it was still going on in the twenty-first century!

Alex helped them out of the backseat. "Come on, Dot." Zoe's hand had slipped into hers. She had to harden herself against Zoe's plea. The child's emotional hold on her was growing stronger with every passing day.

"I'm sorry. The queen has asked for you and your

daddy to come, and I have to speak to my director in New York." Aware Alex's eyes were on her she said, "You have to go with him. I'll see you tomorrow when we leave for your preschool."

Gripping the bag tighter, Dottie hurried inside the palace doors and raced up the stairs. She fled to her suite pursued by demons she'd been fighting from the beginning. Since this afternoon when she'd fallen into Alex's arms like a ripe plum, those demons had gained a foothold, making her situation precarious.

Her instincts told her to pack her bags and fly back to New York tonight. But if she were to just up and leave Hellenica, it would only exacerbate an already volatile situation with Zoe, who'd poured her heart out to her earlier.

Without hesitation she marched over to the bed and reached for the house phone. "This is Mrs. Richards. Could you bring a car around for me? I'm going into the city." She'd eat dinner somewhere and do some more sightseeing. After the nap she'd had, it might take hours before she was ready for bed again.

Alex waited for Hector to alert him on the phone. When the call came, he learned Dottie had just returned to the palace. He checked his watch. Ten to ten.

He left Zoe's bedroom and waited for Dottie at the top of the stairs leading to her suite. This time he didn't step out of the shadows. He stood there in full view. Halfway up she caught sight of him and slowed her steps. Alarm was written all over her beautiful face. She'd picked up some sun earlier in the day, adding appealing color.

"Alex? What's wrong?"

Anyone watching them would never know what had gone on between them on the yacht. He'd nearly made love to her and her passion had equalled his. Her breathtaking response had changed his life today.

"Let's just say there's a lot wrong around here. Since your arrival in Hellenica, you've got me skulking in every conceivable place in order to find time alone with you. At this point you'd have reason to think I'm your personal phantom of the opera." He drew in a harsh breath. "We have to talk, but not here." When he saw her stiffen he said, "I know you can't be commanded, but I'm asking you to come with me as a personal favor." He'd constructed his words carefully.

Tension sizzled between them as he started down the stairs toward her. To his relief she didn't fight him. Slowly she followed him to the main floor. They went down the hallway and out a side door where he'd asked that his sports car be brought around.

Alex saw the question in her eyes. "I bought this ten years ago. It's my getaway car when I need to be alone to think." He intentionally let her get in by herself because he didn't trust himself not to touch her. After leaving the grounds, he headed for the road leading to an isolated portion of the coast with rocky terrain.

"But you're *not* alone," she said in a haunted whisper.

"If you mean the bodyguards, you're right." He felt her nervousness. "Relax. If I had seduction in mind, we wouldn't be in this. I purposely chose it in order to keep my hands off you tonight."

"Alex—"

"Let me finish," he interrupted. "Whatever you may think about me, I'm not in the habit of luring available women to my bed when the mood strikes me. You came to Hellenica at my request in order to test Zoe. Neither of us could have predicted what would happen after you arrived.

"I can't speak for you, but I know for a fact that even if your husband's memory will always be in your heart, the chemistry between us is more powerful than anything I've ever felt in my life. We both know it's not going to go away."

She lowered her head.

"One night with you could never be enough for me." He gripped the steering wheel tighter. "I know you would never consent to be my mistress, and I would never ask you. But until the coronation is over, I'm requesting your help with Zoe."

She shifted in the seat. "In what way?"

"Stasio and my daughter both need me desperately, but I can't be in two places at the same time and still manage the daily affairs of the crown. My brother is going through the blackest period of his life. He's clinging to me and shutting out our grandmother. She's beside herself."

"I can only imagine."

"I'm worried about both of them and asked the doctor to come. He's with them now, seeing what can be done to get them through this nightmare. He says I need to be there for Stasio 24/7. I've asked our cousin Philippe to fly here and stay for a few days so my brother has someone to talk to he trusts."

"I'm so sorry, Alex."

"So am I," he muttered morosely. "This situation is something that's been coming on for years. Unfortunately it's had a negative impact on Zoe. When we got back to the palace today, it took me an hour to settle her down. She wanted to go to your room with you. Tonight she begged me to let you become her official nanny."

Alex heard a half-smothered moan come out of Dottie. The sound tore him up because any kind of connection to keep her with him was fading fast. "It wouldn't work."

"You think I don't know that?" he bit out. "But as a temporary solution, would you be willing to stay at the palace on Aurum with her until the coronation? She loves it there, especially the garden. One of the staff has grandchildren she plays with. I'd fly over each evening in the helicopter to say good-night.

"When the coronation is over, I'll be moving back to Aurum with Zoe, and you can return to New York. Hector will see to your flight arrangements. I assume your replacement will arrive soon after that, if not before. But until then, can I rely on your help?"

She nodded without looking at him. "Of course."

The bands constricting his breathing loosened a little. "Thank you. On Saturday I'll run you and Zoe over in the cruiser. We'll skip her preschool next week."

"Are you still going to go ahead with the arrangements for the Varney boy to come home with Zoe after class tomorrow?"

"Yes," he murmured. "Any distraction would be better than her being around my grandmother, who's not in a good way right now. She's always been a rock, but she never saw this coming with Stasio."

"You sound exhausted, Alex. Tomorrow will be here before we know it. Let's go back to the palace."

She sounded like Hector. *Go back. Do your duty. Forget you're a man with a man's needs.*

Full of rage, he made a sharp U-turn and sped toward the palace tight-lipped, but by the time they reached the entry, he'd turned into one aching entity of pain He watched the only person who could take it away for good rush away on her gorgeous legs.

Dottie could tell Zoe felt shy around Mark Varney. She stuck close to her daddy at the shallow end of the pool.

They'd just returned home from the preschool. Mark was a cute, dark blond first grader who sported a marine haircut and was a good little swimmer already. He didn't appear to be nervous as he floated on an inner tube at the deep end, kicking his strong legs. Dottie sat on the edge by him.

"My mom told me she talks funny. How come?" he said quietly.

"Sometimes a child can't make sounds come out the way they want. But I'm working on them with her. One day she'll sound like you, but for now I'm hoping to get your help."

He blinked. "How? She's a princess."

She looked at his boyish face with its smattering of freckles. "Forget about that. She's a girl. Just be friends with her. In a way, you can be her best teacher."

His sunny blue eyes widened. "I can?"

"Yes. You're older and you're an American who speaks English very well. If you'll play with her, she'll listen to you when you talk and she'll try to sound like you. You're a guy, and guys like to dare each other, right?"

He grinned. "Yeah."

"Well, start daring her. You know. Tell her you bet she can't say *bat*."

"Bat?" He laughed.

"She's working on her *B*'s and *T*'s. Make a game out of it. Tell her that if she can say *bat* right, you'll show her your MP3 player. I saw you playing with it in the limo on the drive to the palace."

"Don't tell my dad. I'm not supposed to take it to school."

She studied him for a minute. "If he finds out, I'll tell him you're using it to help Zoe. She's never seen one of those. There's an application on it that makes those animal sounds."

"Oh, yeah—"

"It'll fascinate her."

"Cool."

"See if you can get her to say *cool*, too."

"Okay. This is fun."

Dottie was glad he thought so. After trying to learn Greek at school and home, it had to be a big release for him to speak English. "Let's go have a war with her and her daddy." She took off her beach coat and slipped into the water. "You get on the whale. I'll push you over to them and we'll start splashing."

"Won't the prince get mad?"

"Yes." Dottie smiled. "Real mad."

His face lit up and they took off.

Hopefully Alex would get mad enough to forget his own problems for a little while. She'd suffered for him and his family all night. No matter her misgivings about spending full days with Zoe until the coronation, she couldn't have turned Alex down last night. The look in his expression had been a study in anguish, aging him.

Once they reached their destination, the happy shrieks coming out of Zoe were just the thing to get their war started. For a good ten minutes they battled as if their lives depended on it. The best sound of all was Alex's full-bodied laughter. After knowing how deeply he'd been affected by his family's problems, Dottie hadn't expected to hear it again.

When she came up for air after Alex's last powerful dunk, his eyes were leveled on her features. "You've been holding out on me. All this time I thought maybe you couldn't swim well. I was going to offer to teach you, but I was afraid you'd think I was a lecherous old man wanting to get my hands on you. After I showed up in your cabin on the yacht, now you know it's true."

She was thankful for the water that cooled her instantly hot cheeks. In the periphery she noticed Mark pushing Zoe around on the whale. He was talking a blue streak and had captured her full attention. The ice had been broken and they were oblivious to everyone else. Dottie couldn't have been more pleased.

Alex followed her gaze. "Your experiment is working. She's so excited by his attention, she hasn't once called for either of us."

"I've asked him to help her. He's a darling boy." In the next few minutes she told Alex about their conversation. "If all goes well today, how would you feel about Mark coming home with us from school on Friday?"

"I'm open to anything that will help her speech improve and make her happy."

"Mark seems to be doing both. I've learned he's been unhappy, so I was thinking maybe he could even come to Aurum with us on Saturday. Naturally you'd have to talk to his parents. If they're willing, maybe he could make a visit to the island next week. You know, after his morning class at preschool. Zoe would have something exciting to look forward to and I know it would be good for him, too."

His eyes glinted with an emotion she couldn't read. "I can see where you're going with this. If you think his being there will prevent her attachment to you from growing deeper, you couldn't be more wrong. But as a plan to entertain them and help her, I like the idea."

"Honestly?"

He ran suntanned hands through his wet black hair. Adonis couldn't possibly have been as attractive. "I wouldn't have said so otherwise."

She expelled the breath she'd been holding. "Thank you. I was thinking Zoe and I could ride the ferry to Hellenica and meet him at the dock after he's out of class. He could ride back with us and we could eat lunch on board. Mark can help her pronounce the names of foods, and she can teach him some more Greek words."

Alex nodded. "I'll fly him back with me in the helicopter in the evening."

"You'd be willing to do that?"

He frowned. "By now I thought it was clear to you I'd do anything to help my daughter. In order to ensure that you stay with her until her uncle Stasi has been proclaimed king, I've even gone so far as to promise I won't touch you again."

She knew that and already felt the cost of it.

If he had any comprehension of how hard this was for her, too… They had no future together, but that didn't mean she found it easy to keep her distance. She'd come alive in his arms. Because she was unable to assuage these yearnings, the pleasure had turned on her so she was in continual pain. This was the precise reason she didn't want to have feelings for any man, not ever again, but it was far too late for that.

"Your Highness?"

Hector's voice intruded, producing a grimace from Alex. Dottie hadn't realized he'd come out to the pool. It seemed like every time she found herself in a private conversation with Alex, some force was afoot that kept wedging them further apart. At this point she was a mass of contradictions. Her head told her the interruption was for the best, but her heart—oh, her heart. It hammered mercilessly.

"King Alexandre-Philippe has arrived from Valleder and your presence is requested in the queen's drawing room. The ministers have been assembled."

Hearing that news, Alex's face became an inscrutable mask. "Thank you, Hector. Tell her I'll be there shortly."

His gaze shot to Dottie's. "I'm afraid this will be a long night. I'd better slip away now while Zoe's having fun."

"I think that's a good idea. We'll walk Mark out to his parents' car before dinner. She can eat with me. Later I'll take her to her bedroom and put her down."

"You couldn't have any comprehension of what it means to me to know you're taking care of my daughter. Sofia will be there to help. I'll try to get away long enough to kiss her good-night, but I can't promise."

"I understand."

"If I don't make it, I'll see you at nine in the morning. After I've talked to Mark's parents, we'll see if he wants to join us on Saturday. I thought we'd take the cruiser to Aurum. Sofia will know what to pack for Zoe."

"We'll be ready."

She heard his sharp intake of breath. "Zoe trusts you and loves being with you. Under the circumstances, it's an enormous relief to me."

"I'm glad. As for me, she's a joy to be with, Your Highness." She had to keep calling him by his title to remind herself of the great gulf between them no ordinary human could bridge. If she were a princess…

But she wasn't! And if she'd been born a royal, he would have run in the other direction.

For him, any attraction to her stemmed from forbidden fruit. She was a commoner. It was the nature of a man or woman to desire what they couldn't or shouldn't have. In that regard they were both cursed!

Fathoms deep in turmoil, she noticed his eyes lingering on the curve of her mouth for a moment. She glimpsed banked fires in those incredibly dark recesses. He was remembering those moments on the yacht, too. Dottie could feel it and the look he was giving her ignited her senses to a feverish pitch.

With effortless male agility he suddenly levered himself from the pool and disappeared inside the palace. When he was gone, the loss she felt was staggering.

CHAPTER EIGHT

"HI, MARK!"

"Hi!"

He got out of his father's limo and hurried along the dock to get in the cruiser. Zoe's brown eyes lit up when she saw him. The two fathers spoke for a minute longer before Alex joined them and made sure everyone put on a life preserver.

The prince piloted the boat himself and they took off. Excitement suffused Dottie, crowding out any misgivings for the moment. She found the day was too wonderful. It seemed the children did, too. Both wore a perpetual smile on their animated faces. Zoe pointed out more fish and birds as they drew closer to their destination. While they were communicating, Alex darted Dottie an amused glance.

She wondered if he was thinking what she'd been thinking. What if his daughter and Mark were to share a friendship that took them through childhood to the teenage years? What if… But she forced her mind to turn off and think only happy thoughts. The island of Aurum was coming up fast. She'd concentrate on it.

Somehow she'd assumed it shared many of the characteristics of Hellenica, but the mountains were higher and woodier. As they pulled up to the royal dock, Dottie had to admit her adrenaline had been surging in anticipation of seeing where they lived. When Alex talked about Aurum, she noticed his voice dropped to a deeper level because he loved it here.

He'd explained that the mountainous part of the island where the palace was located had been walled off from the public. This had been his private residence from the age of eighteen and would continue to be for as long as he retained the title of Duke of Aurum. She'd learned it had its own game preserve, a wildlife sanctuary, a bird refuge and a stable.

Somehow she'd expected this palace to resemble the white Cycladic style of that on Hellenica. Nothing could have been further from the truth. Through the heavy foliage she glimpsed a small gem of Moorish architecture in the form of a square, all on one level.

"Oh!" she cried out in instant delight the second she saw it from the open limo window.

Alex heard her. "This area of the Aegean has known many civilizations. If you'll notice, the other palace leaves the stairs and patios open. Everything tumbles to the sea. You'll see the reverse is true here. The Moors liked their treasures hidden within the walls."

"Whoa!" Mark exclaimed. His eyes widened in amazement. He'd stopped talking to Zoe. *Whoa* was the perfect word, all right.

Dottie marveled over the exterior, a weathered yellow and pale orange combination of seamless blocks delineated by stylized horizontal stripes, exquisite in detail. The limo passed a woman who looked about fifty standing at the arched entry into a courtyard laid out in ancient tiles surrounding a pool and an exquisite garden. At its center stood a latticed gazebo. This was the garden Alex had referred to last week.

As he helped them from the car, a peacock peered from behind some fronds and unexpectedly opened its plumage. The whirring sound startled Dottie and Mark, but Zoe only laughed. It walked slowly, displaying its glorious fan.

"Whoa," their guest said again, incredulous over what he was seeing. It *was* hard to believe.

Dottie eyed Alex. "We're definitely going to have to work on the *P* sound."

One corner of his mouth curved upward. He ran a hand over his chest covered by a cream-colored polo shirt. "Don't look now," he said quietly, "but there's a partridge in the peach tree behind you."

Slowly she turned around, thinking he was teasing her while he made the *P* sounds. But he'd told the truth!

Transfixed, she shook her head, examining everything in sight. A profusion of pink and orange flowers grew against the gazebo. She walked through the scrolling pathway toward it. Inside she discovered a lacy looking set of chairs and a table inlaid with mother-of-pearl. Dottie felt as if she'd just walked inside the pages of a rare first-edition history book of the Ottoman empire. This couldn't possibly be real.

Alex must have understood what she was feeling because he flashed her a white smile. But this one was different because it was carefree. For a brief moment she'd been given a glimpse of what he might have looked like years ago, before he'd had a true understanding that he was Prince Alexius Constantinides with obligations and serious responsibilities he would have to shoulder for the rest of his life.

There was a sweetness in his expression, the same sweetness she saw in Zoe when she was really happy about something, like right now. But the moment was bittersweet for Dottie when she thought of the pain waiting for him back on Hellenica. A myriad of emotions tightened her chest because her pain was mixed up in there, too.

"Do you want to see my room?" Zoe asked Mark.

"I want to follow the peacock first."

"Okay." She tagged along with her new friend, still managing to carry Baby Betty in her hands.

Alex spread his strong arms. "Guys and girls. Human nature doesn't change." Dottie laughed gently, sharing this electric moment with him.

Porticos with bougainvillea and passion flowers joined one section of the palace to the other. The alcoved rooms were hidden behind. Zoe's was a dream of Moorish tiles and unique pieces of furniture with gold leaf carved years ago by a master palace craftsman of that earlier civilization.

A silky, pale pink fabric formed the canopy and covering of her bed. Near a tall hutch filled with her treasures stood an exquisite pink rose tree. When Dottie looked all the way up, she gasped at the sheer beauty of the carved ceiling with hand-painted roses and birds.

Alex had been watching her reaction. "Your room is next door. Would you like to see it?"

Speechless, she nodded and followed him through an alcove to another masterpiece of design similar to Zoe's except for the color scheme. "Whoever painted the cornflowers in this room must have had your eyes in mind, Dottie. They grow wild on the hillsides. You'll see them when you and Zoe go hiking or horseback riding."

She was spellbound. Her eyes fell to the bed canopied with blue silk. "Was this the room you and your wife used? It's breathtaking."

In a flash his facial muscles tensed up. "Teresa never lived here with me. Like my grandmother, she preferred the palace on Hellenica. She thought this place too exotic and isolated, the mountains too savage. This room was used during my mother's time for guests. Since Teresa's death, Zoe's string of nannies have lived in here."

Dottie couldn't help but speculate on how much time he and his wife must have spent apart—that is, when they didn't have to perform certain civic duties together. Separation went on in unhappy marriages all over the planet, but this was different. He'd been born into a family where duty dictated his choice of bride. Even cocooned in this kind of luxury only a few people would ever know, the onlooker could expect such an arrangement to fail.

As Dottie's aunt had often told her, "You're a romantic, Dottie. For that reason you can be hurt the worst. Why set yourself up, honey?" Good question. Dottie's heart ached for Alex and Stasio, for Teresa and Beatriz, for Genevieve, for every royal who had a role and couldn't deviate from it.

"My apartment is through the next alcove. The last section houses two more guest rooms plus the kitchen and dining room. There's a den where I do my work. It has television and a computer. All of it is at your disposal for the time you're here."

"I've never seen anything so unusual and beautiful."

"Those are my sentiments, too. You saw Inez when we drove in. She and her husband, Ari, head the staff here. There's the gamekeeper, of course, and Thomas who runs the stable. All you have to do is pick up the phone and Inez will direct one of the maids to help you."

"Thank you. I didn't expect to find paradise when I came to Hellenica. I don't think your brother believed me when I told him it really does exists here."

"Paradise implies marital bliss. You'll have to forgive him for being cynical over your naïveté."

Alex's comment bordered on mockery, revealing emotions too raw for him to hide. She shuddered and turned away, not wanting to see the bleakness she often saw in his eyes when he didn't know she was looking.

"I'd better go check on Zoe." She hurried through to the other bedroom, but there was still no sign of her.

Alex came up behind Dottie, close enough for her to feel the warmth of his breath on her neck. "I'll give you one guess where she's gone."

"Well, Mark is pretty cute. She doesn't know she's playing with fire yet." The words came out too fast for her to stop them.

"That's true," Alex said in a gravelly voice before she was spun around and crushed against him. "But I do, and right now I don't give a damn. I want you so badly I'm shaking." He put her hand on his chest. "Feel that thundering? It's my heart. That's what you do to me. I know I promised not to touch you, but I'm not strong enough to keep it. You're going to have to give me help."

The moment had caught her unaware. He had a slumberous look in his eyes. His mouth was too close. She couldn't think, couldn't breathe. Dottie tried to remove her hand, but found her limbs had grown weak with longings that had taken over.

"Alex—" She half groaned his name before taking the initiative to kiss him. When she realized she'd been the one to make it happen, it was too late to change her mind. Their mouths met in mutual hunger. She wrapped her arms around his neck, wanting to merge with him.

With one hand cupping the back of her head, his other wandered over her spine and hips, drawing her closer. The kiss she'd started went on and on. She desired him too terribly to do anything that would cut off the divine experience of giving and taking pleasure like this.

In the background she heard the children's muffled laughter. She didn't know if they'd peeked in this room and had seen them or not, but the sound was too close for comfort. Much as she never wanted to leave Alex's arms, she slid her hands back down his chest and tried to ease away from him so he would relinquish her mouth.

"I heard them," he whispered before she could say anything. Alex had the uncanny ability to read her mind.

"I hope Zoe didn't see us."

He sucked in his breath and cupped her face in his hands. "I hate to break this to you, but she woke at the last minute on the yacht."

Guilt swept through her, making her whole body go white-hot.

"Every little four-year-old girl has seen the movie of *Snow White*. My Zoe knows that when Prince Charming kissed the princess awake, it was true love that worked the charm."

What he was telling her now caused Dottie's body to shake with fright. "You don't think she really sees us that way—"

His handsome features hardened. "Who's to say? In her eyes you're her mommy. Zoe has never seen me kiss another woman. I *have* brought you to my castle. The way you and I were devouring each other just now has probably set the seal in her mind."

Aghast, Dottie propelled herself away from him. "Then you have to unset it, Alex."

"I'm afraid it's too late. You might as well know the rest."

She folded her arms to her waist to stay calm. "What more is there?"

"Sofia had a private word with me this morning before I left the palace. Just as Hector spies for my grandmother, Sofia is my eyes and ears where Zoe is concerned. It seems my daughter told her grandmother that you and I were leaving for Aurum today. But she told her not to cry. When we have the baby, we'll bring it to see *Yiayia*."

Dottie didn't know whether to laugh or cry, but the tears won out. The sound that escaped her lips was probably as unintelligible as Zoe's word for Hector. Four consonants. All difficult. "Your grandmother's world truly has come crashing down on her."

She saw his body tauten before he caught her in his arms once more. He shook her gently. "What has happened between you and me wasn't planned. For two years I've been telling the queen I'll never marry again, so it's absurd for you to be feeling guilt of any kind over Genevieve." He kissed her wet eyelids, then her whole face.

"It's not so much guilt as the *fear* I feel for Zoe. She's attached herself to me because of her speech problem. I won't be here much longer, but every day that I stay, it's going to make the ultimate separation that much harder."

A shudder passed through his body she could feel. "You think I'm not aware of that?"

She broke free of him. "I know you are, but we've got to lay down some ground rules. I don't ever want her to see us together like we are now. We can't be alone again. This has to be the end so she won't fantasize about us, Alex. It's no good. I'm going to my room to unpack and settle in. Go be with her and Mark right now. Please."

Blind with pain, she left him standing there ashen-faced.

On Wednesday evening of the following week, Alex's mood was as foul as Stasio's. Five days ago Dottie had virtually told him goodbye on the island, but he couldn't handle it any longer and needed to see her. Something had to be done or he was going to go out of his mind.

Philippe had just left to fly home to Vallader, but he would be coming back with his family to attend the coronation on Saturday just a week off now. Until then Alex and his brother were alone.

Stasio cast him a probing glance. "I do believe you're as restless as I am."

Alex gritted his teeth. "You're right." He shot to his feet. "Alert security and come with me. I'm leaving for Aurum to say good-night to Zoe."

"*And* Dottie?"

"I don't want to talk about her. After Zoe's asleep we'll do some riding and camp out in the mountains."

At least that was what he was telling himself now. Wild with pain, he spun around.

"When it comes to a woman, I can't have what I really want. Even if I could, she wouldn't want me. She adored her husband. Why do you think she's still single? No man measures up. The day after your coronation, she'll be leaving the country whether the new speech therapist replacing her has arrived or not."

"Zoe won't stand for it."

"She'll *have* to," he said in a hoarse whisper. "We're all going to have to go on doing our duty. You've never been able to have what you really wanted. You think I don't know what's been going on inside of you? It's killing me."

Stasio stopped midstride. His tormented expression said it all. "What do you want to do, little brother?"

Alex's brows had formed a black bar above his eyes. "Let's get out of here. Gather anything you need and I'll meet you at the helipad."

Before long they were winging their way to Aurum. Once they'd landed, Zoe came running with a couple of the other children who lived on the estate. Inez chatted with him for a minute.

Alex picked up his daughter and hugged her hard. "I've missed you."

"I've been waiting for you, Daddy. I missed you, too."

He kissed her curls. "Where's Dottie?"

"In town." Tears crept down her cheeks. "She said I couldn't go with her."

Naturally Zoe hadn't been happy about that. Though Alex couldn't argue with Dottie's decision, the news sent his heart plunging to his feet. She'd warned him that she would never be alone with him again and she'd meant it.

"How about a hug for me!" Stasio drew her into his arms to give Alex a chance to pull himself together.

Inez gathered up the other children, leaving the men alone with Zoe. They talked about Mark. "I'm sorry he had a cold and couldn't come today."

"Do you think he can come tomorrow?"

"I'll find out."

"I know he wants to come. Dot told us that after our lesson she'd take us out to look for ducks. He can't wait!"

Of course he couldn't. Any time spent with Dottie was pure enchantment.

"Will you ask his mommy?"

"You know I will."

Stasio put a hand on his shoulder. "I'll be at the stable getting the horses ready."

He nodded. "Come on, my little princess. It's getting late. Time to go to bed."

As she chatted with him, he realized he was starting to hear true sounds coming out of her and she was doing a lot more talking. In a month's time Dottie had already made a profound difference in her. All the thanks in the world would never be able to express his gratitude adequately to her.

For the next half hour he read stories to Zoe, then it was time for her prayers. At the end she said, "Bless my daddy and my Dot."

He blinked. She'd said *Dot* distinctly! He'd heard the *D* and the *T*, plus the *ah* in the middle.

Tears sprang to his eyes. This was Dottie's doing. She'd been trying to get her to say *Dot* instead of *mommy*. Just now the word had passed Zoe's lips naturally. A miracle had happened. He wanted to shout his elation, but he didn't dare because she was ready to go to sleep.

The sudden realization hit Alex hard. He loved Dottie Richards. He loved her to the depth of his being. He wanted her in his life forever and needed to tell her so she wouldn't leave him or Zoe. There had to be a way to keep her here and he was going to find it.

Once his daughter was dead to the world, he stole out of her room and raced to the stable to tell his brother there'd been a major breakthrough with Zoe. It was providential he and Stasio were going riding. Alex did his best thinking on the back of a horse. Tonight he would need all his powers of reasoning to come up with a solution.

But as he approached his brother, Stasio's phone rang. One look at his face after he'd picked up and Alex knew there was trouble.

"That was Hector," he said after ringing off. "*Yiayia* isn't well. The doctor is with her, but he thinks we should come home." They stared at each other. With the queen ill, their best-laid plans would have to wait.

Alex informed Inez. By tacit agreement they left for the helipad. Tonight's shining moment with Zoe had been swallowed up in this new crisis with their grandmother. When they arrived back on Hellenica, Hector was waiting for them in their grandmother's suite.

"The doctor has already left. He says the queen's ulcer is acting up again. He gave her medicine for it and now she's sleeping comfortably. I'm sorry to have bothered you."

Stasio eyed Alex in relief. "Thanks for letting us

know, Hector. It could have been much more serious. We're glad you told us."

"Thank you for your understanding, Your Highness."

"You've been with our grandmother much longer than we have. No one's been more devoted." Stasio's glance rested on Alex. "Shall we go to my suite?"

He nodded at his brother. Both of them needed a good stiff drink about now. As he turned to leave, Hector cleared his throat. "Prince Alexius? If I may have a private word with you first."

Something strange was going on for Hector to address him so formally. Alex eyed his brother who looked equally baffled. "I'll be with you in a minute, Stasi."

After he walked off, Hector said, "Could we talk in your suite, Your Highness?"

"Of course." But the request was unprecedented. As they headed to his apartment, Alex had an unpleasant foreboding. Their grandmother was probably sicker than Hector had let on, but he didn't want to burden Stasio, who walked around with enough guilt for a defeated army. The decision to call off his wedding to Beatriz had dealt a near-lethal blow to their grandmother, and poor Hector had been caught in the fallout.

Once they'd entered the living room, Alex invited the older man to sit down, but he insisted on remaining standing, so they faced each other.

"You have my complete attention, Hector. What is it?"

"When's my daddy coming?"

Dottie had been swimming in the pool on Aurum with Zoe while they waited for Alex. "Last night he told you he would be here after your lesson, didn't he?"

"Yes. I want him to hurry. I hope Mark's still not sick."

"We'll find out soon enough, because I can hear your daddy's helicopter." They both looked up.

When Dottie saw it, the realization that Alex would be walking out here in a few minutes almost put her into cardiac arrest. No mere hormones or physical attraction to a man could cause these feelings that made her world light up just to hear his name or know he was in the vicinity.

She was in love. She knew that now. She was in love again, for the second time in her life, and she cried out at the injustice. Her first love and son had been struck down so cruelly, she'd wondered how she could ever build another life for herself.

Now here she was carrying on with her career and doomed to love again, only this man was a prince who was off-limits to her. By the time of the coronation, Zoe would be snatched from her, too, and she'd be left a totally empty vessel. Blackness weighed her down. *What am I going to do?*

While Zoe shouted with excitement and hurried across the tiles to meet her father, who'd be striding through the entry any second, Dottie got out of the pool and raced to her own room. To be with him would only succeed in pouring acid on a newly opened wound that would never heal.

Knowing Alex needed time alone with his daughter, Dottie would give it to him. Quickly she showered and changed into denims and a top before checking her emails. Dr. Rice had sent her another message.

Dear Mrs. Richards,
Success at last. Your replacement's name is Mrs.
Miriam Hawes. She'll be arriving in Athens to-
morrow. All the arrangements have been made.
When you return to New York, I have a new three-
year-old girl who needs testing. We'll enjoy hav-
ing you back. Good luck and keep me posted.
Dr. Rice.

Dottie read the words again before burying her face in her hands. While she was sobbing, a little princess came running into her room and caught her in the act.

"Why are you crying?" She put her face right up against Dottie's. "Do you have a boo-boo?"

Zoe could say boo-boo well enough to be understood. Nothing could have pleased Dottie more, but right now pain consumed her. Yes. Dottie had a big boo-boo, one that had crumbled her heart into tiny pieces.

She sniffed and wiped the moisture off her face. "I hurt myself getting out of the pool." It wasn't a lie. In her haste she'd scraped her thigh on the side, but she would live. "Did Mark come?"

"Yes. He's running after the peacock." Dottie laughed through the tears. "Can he pull out one of its big feathers?"

"No, darling. That would hurt it."

"Oh." Obviously she hadn't thought about that aspect. "Daddy wants you to come."

Dottie had wondered when the bell would toll. She had no choice but to walk out and say hello to Alex and Mark, who were already in the pool whooping it up. Zoe ran to join them.

"Good afternoon, Your Highness."

His all-encompassing black gaze swept over her. "Good afternoon," he said in his deep, sensuous voice. Her body quickened at the change in him from last Saturday when there'd been nothing but painful tension between them.

"I'm glad you brought Mark with you. How are you feeling today, Mark?"

"Good. I didn't have a temperature, so my mom said I could come."

Dottie took her usual place on the edge and dangled her bare feet in the water. "Well we're very happy you're here, aren't we, Zoe?" She nodded while she hung on to her daddy's neck. "Zoe tells me you'd like to take a peacock feather home for a souvenir."

"Yeah. Could I?"

The sudden glance Alex flashed Dottie was filled with mirth. He wasn't the same man of a few days ago. She hardly recognized him. "What do you say about that, Prince Alexius?"

By now he'd put Zoe up on his powerful shoulders. He looked like a god come to life. "Tell you what, Mark. That peacock is going to moult in another month. When he does, he'll shed his tail feathers. You and Zoe can follow him around. When he drops them, you can take home as many as he leaves."

"Thanks!"

"Cool, Daddy."

Alex burst into laughter. "What did you just say to me?"

"'Cool,'" Mark answered for her.

"That's what I thought she said."

"I've been teaching her."

Zoe patted her daddy's head. "Can Mark come to Uncle Stasi's coronation?"

Alex's black eyes pinned Dottie's body to the tiles at the edge of the pool. The day after she was leaving Hellenica. "His family has already been invited."

"*My* family?" Mark's eyes had rounded like blue marbles.

"*Yiayia* says we have to be quiet," Zoe warned him.

"I won't talk."

"It's going to be a very great occasion in the cathedral," Dottie explained to him. "Hellenica is going to get a new king. You'll be able to see the crown put on his head."

She nodded. "It gave my *pappou* a headache."

Dottie broke down laughing. Despite the fact that part of her was dying inside, she couldn't hold it back.

"Hey—that's not funny!" Stasio's voice broke in. "Do you know the imperial crown of Hellenica weighs over five pounds? I'll have to wear a five-pound sack of flour on my head the whole day before to get used to it."

"Uncle Stasi!" Zoe called to him in delight and clapped her hands. Dottie hadn't realized he'd come with Alex.

"That's my name." He grinned before doing a belly flop in the pool. The splash got everyone wet. When he came up for air, he looked at the children. "You'd better watch out. I heard there was a shark in here."

"Uh-oh." While the children shrieked, Dottie jumped up. "This is where I opt out."

Without looking back she walked across the tiles to her room. She thought she was alone *until* she saw Alex. He'd followed her dressed in nothing more than his wet black swimming trunks. Dottie's heartbeat switched to hyperspeed. "You're not supposed to be in here. That was our agreement."

He stood there with his hands on his hips. "Last night that agreement was rendered null and void."

"Why?" she whispered in nervous bewilderment.

His eyes narrowed on her features. "You may well ask, but now isn't the time to answer that question. The queen has been sick, but she's starting to feel better and is missing Zoe. I promised to take her back to Hellenica. Stasi has volunteered to babysit the children on the flight while you and I take the cruiser. We'll leave here as soon as you're ready. Pack what you want to take for overnight." On that note, he disappeared.

Dottie gathered up some things, not surprised the queen wanted to see Zoe. It would lift her spirits. Before long they were ready and left with Alex for the dock in the limo. Once on board, he maneuvered the cruiser out of the small bay at a wakeless speed, then opened the throttle and the boat shot ahead.

The helicopter dipped low and circled above them so the children could wave to them. Dottie waved back. She could tell they were having the time of their lives. Alex beeped the horn three times before the helicopter flew on.

"That's precious cargo up there," she told him. "The two little sad sacks of a month ago have undergone a big transformation. I had no idea if the experiment would work, but I honestly think they like each other."

He squinted at her. "You only think?"

"Well, I don't know for sure. Mark might be pretending because he wants to haul off some of those peacock feathers."

Alex's shoulders shook in silent laughter. While his spirits seemed so much improved, she decided to tell him about the email from Dr. Rice.

He nodded. "I was already informed by him."

Naturally he was. She cleared her throat. "Under the circumstances I thought the new therapist could come to Aurum and stay in one of the guest rooms. We'll let Zoe get used to her and I'll involve her in our games."

When Alex didn't respond she got nervous and said, "Mrs. Hawes will have her own techniques to try out on your daughter, of course. By the time of the coronation, they'll be used to each other. I know it will be difficult for Zoe to say goodbye to me, so we need to handle that carefully."

"I agree." He sounded remote. "I'll think on it."

With those few words, Alex remained quiet, but she didn't mind because his mellow mood was so different from the way he'd been, she was able to relax. For a little while she could pretend they were a normal couple out enjoying each other on this glorious blue sea with the same color of sky above them. Despite her aunt's warnings, Dottie still had a tendency to dream forbidden thoughts, if only for the few minutes they had until they reached the shore.

In this halcyon state she noticed him turn his dark head toward her. "After we dock, you're free until this evening. At eight-thirty I'll send for you. In light of Mrs. Hawes's imminent arrival, we'll finalize the termination of your contract tonight. For Zoe's sake it will be best if you don't drop by her suite to say good-night."

The trip between islands hadn't taken long. Dottie

had been given her few minutes of dreaming, but that was all. With one royal pronouncement, even that brief time had been dashed to smithereens.

CHAPTER NINE

TONIGHT was different from all the other nights in Alex's life. As he'd told Dottie last week, he couldn't be in two places at once. In order to help his brother, he'd sent her and Zoe to Aurum. But this night he needed to be alone with the woman who'd turned the lights on for him. Only Dottie had known the location of the secret switch. Through her magic, she'd found it and now no power could turn it off.

After eating dinner with Zoe and putting her to bed, Alex asked his brother to read her some stories until she fell asleep. While he did that, Alex slipped away to shower and dress in a black silk shirt and trousers, just formal enough to let Dottie know what this night meant to him.

He flicked his gaze around the private dining room of his own jet. It was one of the few places where they could have privacy and be secure away from the palace. The steward had set up the preparations for their intimate dinner, complete with flickering candlelight.

Alex had never used his plane for anything but transportation and business meetings. Tonight it would serve as his portal to a future he'd never dared dream about. Now that he could, his body throbbed at every pulse point. When he pulled the phone from his pocket to answer it, his hand trembled.

Hector was outside. He'd brought Dottie to the airport in the limousine. "Tell her to come aboard."

He moved to the entrance of the plane. When she saw him, she paused midway up the steps in a pink-and-white-print dress he hadn't seen before. She looked breathtaking. Her honey blond-hair had been swept into a knot.

Though she'd picked up a golden tan over the past month, she had a noticeable pallor. He hoped to heaven it was because the thought of leaving him was killing her. Maybe it had been cruel to set her up this way, but he'd wanted proof that she couldn't live without him either. If he'd misread the radar...

"Come all the way in, Dottie. I've got dinner waiting for us."

She bit her lower lip. "I couldn't possibly eat, Alex. I'm sorry for any trouble you've gone to. We could have taken care of business in your office."

He lounged against the opening, half surprised at that response. "We could have, but the office is too public a place for the proposal I have in mind."

By the look in her blue eyes, she acted as if she'd just had a dagger plunged into her heart. "There can't be anything but indecent proposals between you and me." Her wintry comment might have frozen him if he didn't know certain things she wasn't aware of yet.

His black brows lifted. "If you'll finish that long walk into the plane, I'll enlighten you about a very decent one you wouldn't have thought of."

She remained where she was. "If you've decided to abandon your family and the monarchy and hide away in some distant place for the rest of your life, then you're not the prince I imagined you to be."

Her answer thrilled him because it meant she'd not only thought of every possibility for finding a way the two of them could be together, she'd actually put voice to it.

"Then you like it that I'm Prince Alexius?"

He could tell she was struggling to pretend her breath hadn't almost left her lungs. "That's an absurd question. You couldn't be anyone else. It's who you are."

"In other words I'm *your* highness, and you're *my* lowness."

She averted her eyes. "Don't joke about serious matters like this."

"Joking is how I've gotten through life this far."

Her head flew back. "That's very tragic. Why did you have me driven here?" she cried. "The truth!"

"Can you stand to hear it?" he fired back in a quiet voice.

"Alex—" She'd dispensed with his title. That was progress.

"I have a plan I want to talk over with you."

He could see her throat working. "What plan? There can be no plan."

"If you'll come aboard, I'll tell you. In case you think I'm going to kidnap you, I swear this jet won't leave the ground. But since I'm a target for the press, who have their Telephoto lenses focused on us as we speak, I'd prefer we talked in private."

He felt her hesitation before she took one step, then another, until she'd entered the plane. His steward closed the door behind them.

"This way." Alex refrained from touching her. The

time wasn't right. As soon as they entered the dining room, he heard her soft cry. She looked at everything as if she was in some sort of daze. He'd been in one since last night.

"Why did you go to all this trouble?"

"Because it occurred to me you've done all the work since you came to Hellenica. I thought you deserved a little fuss to be made over *you* for a change." He held out a chair for her, but she didn't budge.

"Alex—it's *me* you're talking to. Mrs. Richards, the speech therapist. If there are lies between us, then this meeting is pointless. Please stop dancing around the subject. What's the purpose in my coming here?"

"More than you know."

"You're being cryptic. I can't do this." She turned away from him but he caught her arm.

"All I ask is that you hear me out."

The beautiful line of her jaw hardened. "What if I don't want to listen?"

They stood there like adversaries. "I thought that after everything we've been through together, you trusted me. I think you know I trust you with my life, but apparently I've made a mistake about you." Alex took a calculated risk and let go of her hand. "If you don't want anything more to do with me, then you're free to leave now."

Dottie stayed planted to the same spot. Her breathing sounded labored. "Is this about Zoe?"

"About Zoe. About you. About me. If you'll sit down, Hector will explain."

Her eyes widened. "Hector—"

"Yes. I'll phone him now."

The older man had a certain gravitas even Dottie recognized. While she continued to stand where she was, he rang the older man. Within a minute, Hector joined them.

"Your Highness?" He bowed.

"Would you please tell Mrs. Richards what you told me last night?"

"Certainly." Hector cleared his throat and proceeded to explain what Stasio had jokingly said earlier was Alex's get-out-of-jail-free card. "Before Prince Alexius married, his father, King Stefano, knew of Princess Teresa's heart condition and worried about it. Eventually he made a legal proviso that cannot be broken.

"Simply stated, it reads that should she precede him in death and he wishes to marry again, he—who is second in line to the crown—would have the constitutional right to choose his own wife whether she be of royal blood or a commoner. However, any children born of that union would have no claim to the throne."

Alex watched Dottie slowly sink to the chair he'd pulled out for her. When the older man had finished, he thanked him.

"I'm happy to be of service, Your Highness. If you need me, I'll be out in the limo." He exited the plane while Dottie rubbed her arms with her hands, as if she were chilly.

"The gods on Mount Pelos have heard me," Alex began. "Until I met you, Dottie, I never wanted to marry again. And now, thanks to my father, I'm now able to ask you to marry me." He stared at her for a long moment. "I'm making you an honorable, legally binding offer of marriage."

She finally looked at him. The pupils of her eyes had grown so large, she was obviously in shock. "I couldn't be happier that because of your father's intervention, you've suddenly been given your free agency to choose your own wife. For him to think that far ahead for your welfare shows he really did love you. What I don't understand is why didn't Hector come forward ages ago so you could have found someone else by now?"

Alex was thunderstruck by her question. Had his proposal of marriage meant nothing to her?

"Hector didn't tell me why, but I suspect it's because he secretly loves Zoe like his own granddaughter. He never married or had children. I'm convinced that seeing her so happy with you and so unhappy at the prospect of becoming the stepdaughter of Princess Genevieve prompted him to come forward. The queen may have his allegiance, but Zoe has his heart. Hector has seen the three of us together and knows I'll always put my daughter first."

"But you've only known me for a month, Alex! You're *young!* You've got years to find the kind of relationship you've dreamed of having."

He leaned forward. "I've already had years of relationships that filled the loneliness from time to time, but now I have a daughter who's as precious to me as your son was to you. If I'd searched the world over, I couldn't have found the more perfect mother for her than you."

"So that's all you want? A mother?"

"After what we've shared, you know better than to ask me that. I'm in love with you and you know it, but even though you've responded to me physically, I'm aware your heart died when you lost your husband and son. I live in the hope that one day you'll come to love me with the same intensity. As for Zoe, she loves you so much, she was calling you mommy almost from the beginning."

"Yes, but—"

"It would be a second chance for both of us to find happiness," he spoke over her. "We could make a home anywhere you want. If you prefer to stay in New York and further your career, we'll buy a house there. Our home will be our castle."

An incredulous expression broke out on her face. "What are you talking about?"

"What all normal couples talk about when they're discussing marriage. I want you to be happy."

"But your place is here in Hellenica!"

"Listen to me, Dottie. I'll always be Prince Alexius, but I don't have to live here. Not now. Thanks to technology, it won't matter where we settle down because I can do my mining engineering work anywhere."

"Be serious—your family and friends are here!"

"Yes, and we'll come for visits."

"I'm talking about your life!"

"My life will be with my own little family. You have no idea how much I want to take care of you. I love you. You'll be my first priority."

"You think the queen is going to stand for that?" She sounded frightened.

"She has no say in this matter."

"You're really serious, aren't you?"

"Of course."

In the quiet that followed, Dottie stared into the candle flames. "I feel like I'm in some kind of strange dream. What if I didn't exist?" she cried out. "What would you be planning to do with this new freedom?"

It appeared he was wrong about her feelings. The

knowledge that they could be together legitimately hadn't changed anything for her.

"It's a moot point. You *do* exist, and you've won Hector around, otherwise he would never have come forward with that document." At this point Alex couldn't comprehend life without her, but maybe he'd been mistaken in thinking there was a future for them. "After the coronation, I plan to live with Zoe on Aurum as always. Shall I consider this your answer?"

When she didn't say anything, Alex's burgeoning hopes disintegrated into blackness. He pushed himself away from the table and got to his feet. "If you're ready to leave, I'll walk you out to the limo and Hector will see you get back to the palace."

Once she'd said good-night to Hector, Dottie hurried to her room so torn up inside she didn't know how she was going to make it through the night. Alex's marriage proposal had turned her world upside down.

He'd told her he'd fallen in love with her, but that had to be his desire talking. She knew he desired her, but feared it would eventually wear off now that she was no longer forbidden fruit. If they married and then he grew tired of her, she couldn't bear it.

She still couldn't comprehend that one minute he was doomed to the life he'd been born into, and the next minute he was free to take a commoner for his wife. It was too convenient. If she hadn't heard it from his own lips—from Hector's—she wouldn't have believed it, not in a million years.

Didn't he realize he could marry any woman he wanted? The idea that he'd move to New York for her was a pipe dream. You didn't take the prince out of the man no matter how hard you tried. She didn't want to do that to him. She loved Alex for who he was, but she wasn't about to ruin his life by condemning him to another prison.

Dottie was painfully in love with him, but she wasn't his grand passion. Once his gratitude to her wore off, he'd want his freedom. She couldn't handle that. It was better to remain single and just do her job. The time had come for her to watch out for herself and what she wanted.

Full of adrenaline, she went to the closet for her luggage and started packing. Mrs. Hawes would be on the job in the morning. Zoe wouldn't be happy about it, but in time she'd adjust. Her speech was improving every day. She was already getting some self-confidence. Alex would keep working with her.

As Dottie cleaned out the schoolroom, she kept telling herself Zoe was going to be fine. She and her daddy had each other. That was the important thing. After another hour she had everything packed and finally crawled into bed, praying for sleep to come. But her pillow was wet before oblivion took over.

The next time she had cognizance of her surroundings, she heard a child crying. The sound tugged at her deepest emotions.

"Cory?" she murmured. Her eyes opened.

"Dot," a voice called out her name clearly in the early morning light. It was Zoe! "Dot?"

"I'm right here."

"Mommy," she cried her other name for her and climbed onto the bed.

Dottie pulled her close and rocked her in her arms. "Did you have a bad dream?"

"No. *Yiayia* says a new teacher has come to help me. Don't go, Mommy. Don't go." Her little body shook from her tears. She clung to Dottie.

"Shh. It's all right." Dottie kissed her wet eyes and cheeks. Her dear little face was flushed. She sang some songs she used to sing to Cory. After a few minutes Zoe started to quiet down. Just when it appeared she'd fallen asleep and Dottie could alert the staff, the palace phone rang, startling both of them.

Zoe lifted her head. "I want to stay here."

Dottie reached for the receiver and said hello.

"Dottie—" The anxiety in Alex's voice was that of any frantic parent who couldn't find his child.

"Zoe's with me. I was just going to let you know."

"Thank heaven. I'll be right there."

Alex must have broken the speed record. By the time she'd thrown on her robe, he'd entered her bedroom out of breath and looking so pale it worried her. He was still dressed in the stunning black silk shirt and trousers he'd worn on the jet. It meant he'd been up all night, which made her feel so guilty she wanted to die.

Zoe stood up in the bed. "Don't be mad, Daddy."

A sound of anguish escaped his throat as he reached for her and hugged her tight. "I went to your room to kiss you good morning, but you weren't there."

"I know. I came to see Dot."

"How did you get past the guards?"

"I ran when they didn't see me."

Dottie heard his groan. "You gave me a fright."

"*Yiayia* said I have a new teacher and Dot is leaving. I don't want a new teacher. Please don't let Dot leave—" The pain in her voice was too much for Dottie, who couldn't stop her own tears.

"I can't make Dottie stay, Zoe." The sound that came out of him seeped from a new level of sadness and despair, finding a responding chord in her.

"Yes, you can," Zoe fought her father.

He shook his dark head and kissed her curls. "You're going to learn you can't force people to do things they don't want to do. Come on. Let's take a walk on the beach and then we'll have breakfast."

"No—" she screamed as he started to carry her out. Still in his arms, Zoe turned her head to look at Dottie. "Don't leave, Mommy. I don't want to go. Stop, Daddy—"

Dottie had a vision of them walking out that door. What if she never saw them again? The day of the car accident Neil had grabbed Cory to take him on an errand. Both of them were smiling as he carried their son out the front door. Dottie never saw them alive again.

The thought of never seeing Alex or Zoe again was unthinkable.

"Wait, Alex—"

He'd already started out the door. The momentum caused him to take a few more steps before he swung around. His haunted expression tore her heart to shreds.

"You really want to marry me?" she whispered shakily.

He slowly lowered Zoe to the marble floor and started toward her. "Would I have asked, otherwise?"

It was the moment of truth. She had to have faith that their marriage could work. He'd told her he loved her. He was willing to move to New York, willing to give her the opportunity of loving his wonderful daughter. What more could a woman ask?

But she'd been thinking about it all night. Her deepest fear was that this royal prince, who'd been denied the possibility of a happy marriage the first time, was jumping impulsively into another marriage he'd regret down the road. He was a free man. If he chose to, he could go where he wanted and live like a commoner with another woman.

After what had happened to Neil and Cory, Dottie wanted a guarantee of happiness. But as her aunt had told her, there were no guarantees. *You're a romantic, Dottie. For that reason you can be hurt the worst. Why set yourself up, honey?*

Her aunt's advice had come too late. For better or worse, Dottie *had* set herself up.

She closed the distance between them. "I love you, Alex. So much, you have no idea." Emotion was almost choking her. "I want to be your wife more than anything in the world."

"Darling—" He crushed her to him, wrapping his arms all the way around her. "I adore you, Dottie. I was up all night plotting how to get you to love me," he whispered against her lips before kissing her long and hard. "We need to get married right away."

"I agree," she cried, kissing him back hungrily. "I think we'd better tell Zoe."

"You think?" His smile lit up her insides before he said, "Why don't we do it right here in the alcove."

His arms reluctantly let her go before he drew Zoe over to the table where they'd spent so many delightful times together. Still trembling from the look he'd just given her, Dottie took her place across from them, her usual teacher position. She checked her watch. It was ten to seven in the morning.

Zoe eyed both of them curiously. She'd seen them

kissing and knew something was going on. "Are we going to have school *now*?"

Alex's lips twitched that way they sometimes did when he was trying to hold back his laughter. When he did that, Dottie thought there could be no more attractive man on earth.

"No," he answered. "This morning is a very special morning and we have plans to make because Dottie has just said she would marry me."

The sweetest smile broke out on Zoe's face. "Then you're going to be my real mommy, like Mark's?"

"Yes." Dottie reached across the table to squeeze her hands.

"They're going to have a baby. Mark told me."

"I didn't know that," he answered, trying to keep a deadpan face. Dottie wasn't as successful.

"Can we have one, too?"

Dottie laughed through the tears. "For now you have Baby Betty."

Alex's dark eyes swerved to hers. The look of desire in them took her breath. "If the gods on Mount Pelos are kind, maybe a new baby will come."

Zoe beamed. "A big boy like you, Daddy!"

He trapped Dottie's gaze midair. Her soon-to-be daughter was precocious to a fault, just like her father. Both of them were remembering the jump-rope game. It was the day she fell so hard for Prince Alexius, she hadn't been the same since. She didn't know which moment was the most surreal. But one thing was absolutely certain. She'd committed herself and there was no going back now.

"I tell you what," Alex said. "Let's all get dressed

and have breakfast in my suite while we make plans. After that we'll tell the family."

Zoe stared at her father before giving him a huge kiss. Then she got down and ran around the table to hug Dottie. "I love you, Mommy."

"I love you, too." Over her brown curls she looked at the man she'd just told she was going to marry. "I love you both beyond belief."

Dottie had been to Alex's apartment once before, but her thoughts had been so focused on her diagnostic session with Zoe, she hadn't really looked around and appreciated the magnificence of her surroundings.

During their fabulous breakfast out on the patio, a delivery came for Dottie. She opened the long florist box and discovered two dozen long-stemmed red roses with the most heavenly fragrance. The little card said, *For the first time in my life, I feel like a king whose every wish has come true.* Coming from Alex, those words had unique significance.

After kissing Dottie hungrily, he excused himself to go visit his grandmother and make sure she was up. He told Dottie and Zoe he'd be coming by for them in a few minutes, at which point they would go to the queen's drawing room and tell her their news.

After Stasio had refused to marry Princess Beatriz, Alex's announcement was going to be another terrible disappointment. Dottie feared it might be too much for Zoe's *yiayia* and she would suffer from something worse than ulcers. In a way Dottie had it in her heart to feel sorry for the dowager whose world was crumbling before her very eyes.

The older woman had grown up knowing nothing

but her duty. Somehow she had made her own marriage work, and so had Alex's parents. Deep down it had to be very hard on her to see her two wonderful grandsons so terribly unhappy up to now.

Dottie played with Zoe out on the patio, but she kept waiting for Alex to appear. A maid brought them some much-appreciated refreshments. Dottie asked for a vase so she could put the gorgeous roses in water. The gesture from Alex was one of the reasons she loved him so much.

After being in the apartment for two hours with no word from him, she started to get nervous. Perhaps his grandmother had suffered a setback from the news. He and Stasio were probably sequestered with her because Alex's news had shattered another dream. Twice Dottie started to pick up the palace phone and ask to speak to him, then thought the better of it.

Zoe seemed perfectly content to play with her toys, but Dottie was turning into a mass of nerves. Another hour went by, still no word about anything. When 7:00 p.m. rolled around, their dinner was brought in, but no news from Alex. When she didn't think she could stand it a second longer, Hector appeared on the patio where they'd started to eat.

"If I might speak to you in private."

Thank goodness. "I'll be right back, Zoe. I'm just going to the living room."

"Okay."

Dottie followed him into the other room. "Obviously something's wrong. It's been ten hours since Alex told me he'd be back."

"He had to fly to Zurich today and might not return until morning."

She blinked. "As in Switzerland?"

"Yes. He asked me to assure you that he would never have left you and the little princess unless it was an emergency. He would like you to stay in his suite."

No doubt Alex had told him they were getting married. "Then we will."

Hector knew what the emergency was, but he would never tell Dottie. Whatever was going on had to be serious for Alex to go away today. She rubbed her arms nervously. "Is he all right?"

The slight hesitation before he said, "Of course," spoke volumes. "If there's anything else you need, you only have to ask."

"We're fine, Hector. Thank you for telling me. Good night."

"Good night."

Hector was always perfectly correct. He'd served the monarchy all his adult life. Like the queen, he didn't deviate from his role. It would be too much to ask of anyone. She thought of Alex who'd told her he would live in New York if she wanted. She had no doubt he could do it and make the most of it, but he'd been raised a prince. That would never change.

Full of musings, she walked out to the patio. "Zoe?"

"Did Daddy come?"

"Not yet. Something came up."

"I know. It's business."

Dottie smiled. Just then Zoe sounded a hundred years old. "Why don't we get you in the tub for a nice bath, then I'll read you some stories."

"Are we going to sleep in Daddy's bed?"

"Yes. At least until he calls or comes."

A little sound of happiness escaped the little girl's lips.

Dottie rang for a maid to bring them some things from their rooms. Within the hour both of them were ready for bed. Zoe picked out the stories she wanted and they climbed under the covers. Dottie looked around the sumptuous room, hardly able to believe she would be marrying the man who slept in this royal bedchamber when he was on Hellenica.

Though she was filled with anxiety over the reason for Alex's absence, the feel of the warm little body nestled against her brought a comfort to her heart she hadn't known in years. When they read the last book, she kissed her. "I'm so thankful you're going to be my daughter soon. I love you, Zoe."

"I love you. Good night, Mommy."

No one slept more peacefully than a child who wasn't worried about anything. Zoe had her new mommy-to-be, her daddy and her Baby Betty. Her world was complete. Dottie wished she could say the same for herself, but without Alex here to tell her what was going on, she was too anxious to sleep.

Instead of lying there tortured by fears she couldn't even identify, she slid out of bed and threw on her robe. Zoe preferred the patio to any other place in the palace. Dottie was drawn to it, too, and wandered out there where she wouldn't disturb Zoe with her restlessness.

CHAPTER TEN

A T ONE in the morning, Alex stepped off his jet into the limo and headed for the palace. He'd been prepared to stay all night in Valleder with Philippe and Stasio, but both men urged him to go back to Hellenica and be with Dottie and Zoe.

There was nothing Alex wanted so much in this life, but since the last time he'd seen Dottie, his entire world had changed. He couldn't reverse time and put it back to the way it was before he'd gone to his grandmother's apartment to let her know he'd returned from Aurum.

He said good-night to Hector, then entered the palace and went straight to his apartment. But he was so torn up in his soul by the events of the past fifteen hours, the burden of what he had to tell Dottie made his limbs heavy. He felt like an old man as he continued up the steps and down the hall to his suite.

No lights had been left on. The place was quiet as a tomb. He tiptoed to the bedroom and was surprised to see Zoe asleep alone. Instinct told him Dottie was out on the patio and he headed for it.

His thoughts flew back to that first day. He'd walked Zoe out there to be tested. When Dottie had thrown him that Ping-Pong ball, she'd set an energy in motion that had turned him into a different man. Now all the dynamics were different because Mrs. Dottie Richards had agreed to become Mrs. Dottie Constantinides. Or so she'd thought.

This happened to be his favorite time of night, when the moon was on the rise over the Aegean. It was the time when the heat of the day released the perfume from the jasmine, filling the warm air with its heavenly scent. Instead of it being day, this was the night of his engagement. It was a singular irony that his daughter occupied his bed.

He stepped out on the patio and glimpsed his bride-to-be at the other end. His pounding heart almost suffocated him as he moved toward her. She stood at the wall and had put her hands on either side of the ledge, taking in the unparalleled view etched in his mind from childhood. With her standing there, a new softly rounded, feminine sculpture had been added to the landscape.

"Dottie?" he murmured. A cry escaped her lips. She turned toward him in surprise. "Enjoying the view?"

"This kind of beauty goes beyond perfection."

He sucked in his breath. "It does now." She looked gorgeous yet maidenlike standing there in the moonlight in her simple pink robe. Alex found it hard to believe she'd given birth to a child in another time and place.

"Hector said you might not be home before morning."

"I thought I might have to stay in Valleder until tomorrow, but my brother and Philippe sent me back."

Her eyes searched his. "Why did you have to go to Philippe's? What's happened?"

"You deserve a full explanation and you're going to

get one, but it's going to take a while. Maybe you should sit down."

"That sounded ominous." Her voice trembled. "I think I'd prefer to stand."

"The bottom line is, Stasio submitted papers to the ministers and has taken the steps to abdicate from the monarchy."

In the silence that followed, he watched her face pale. "*What* did you say?"

"Apparently he's been planning it for a long time. When you suggested that I might have decided to abdicate in order to marry you, the idea wasn't so far-fetched after all. You just happened to apply it to the wrong prince."

A hand went to her throat. "He's really stepping down?"

"Yes. After Stasi called off his betrothal, I should have guessed this would be the next step, but I've been so caught up in my feelings for you, I'm not the same person anymore."

"Darling…"

"It's true, Dottie. The reason he was out of the country so long was because he had to work things out with Philippe."

"What things?"

"Stasi has persuaded our second cousin to rule as king over Hellenica."

She shook her head. "I don't believe it."

"Philippe will be able to reign over both countries without problem. The Houses of Valleder and Constantinides are intrinsically entwined. He's well loved in Valleder. It will be the same here."

She looked shellshocked. "Aren't *you* the second in line to the throne?"

"Yes. But Stasio knows how I feel and would never put me in that position, especially now that I'm going to marry you and move to New York. Zoe is third in line and, if she wishes, will rule one day when Philippe is no longer king."

"So does that mean the coronation has been called off?"

"Yes. The announcement will go out on the news to-morrow evening. My grandmother will continue to be the head of the monarchy until Philippe is installed."

Dottie stared out at the sea. "I'm surprised the queen isn't in the hospital by now."

"She may end up there, but she hasn't given up the fight yet. This change to install Philippe has to be voted on by the ministers of the parliament. She has power-ful friends there. So does Stasi. I believe the votes for Philippe will prevail. She's calling for an emergency assembly."

"What if they vote against installing your cousin?"

"Then she'll continue to reign until her death, issu-ing her edicts through the head of parliament."

"And after that?"

"The parliament will convene to find an heir from the Constantinides line. We have a fourth cousin living on the island of Cuprum in the Thracian Sea. He's in his sixties and could be brought up for consideration. However, we have no idea how long my grandmother will live. She has a strong constitution and could out-live him."

"This is all so unbelievable. Your poor grandmother.

Poor Stasio," she whispered, wringing her hands. "To be so desperate for his freedom, he'd give up everything…"

"Actually, I never saw anyone happier than he was when I left him. He's been in love with a woman from Norway for the past ten years and had to make a choice. In the end he chose Solveig. He's a different man now."

"I can only imagine. The second you said abdicate, I thought there had to be a woman. Only a powerful love could cause him to make a break with your family."

"I told him he was insane if he ever wasted another moment feeling guilty about what he's done."

"You're a wonderful brother to say that to him."

"Stasi would do the same for me. Fortunately our father provided that escape clause for me in his will. Otherwise there would have been two abdications."

"You don't really mean that." Her voice shook.

He gave an elegant shrug of his shoulders. "After Teresa died, I put the idea of marriage completely out of my mind. Much later I realized I wanted to marry you, and knew I would have to have papers drawn up for my abdication because there was no way I was going to let you get away from me. I loved you from the moment I saw you. When Hector heard you were leaving, he acted on my father's wishes and told me about the codicil to his will. As you said, it takes a powerful love."

Her breathing had changed. "You loved me from the beginning?"

"I realize now that I fell for you the moment you walked into my office and treated me like an ordinary man. You had no idea what that did to me. My world changed and I knew I had to have you, even if it meant turning my back on my heritage."

"Alex—

"I love you desperately. When we reach New York, I plan to show you what you mean to me. I'll do whatever I have to in order to make our marriage work."

"So will I," she declared. "Don't you know I'm so crazy about you, I'd do anything for you, too? At first I feared the only reason you wanted to marry me was because I was forbidden fruit and able to be a mother figure for Zoe. But I took the risk and said yes to you anyway because I'm so in love with you, nothing else matters."

"Do you have any concept of what those words mean to me, Dottie? I raced back here from Valleder fearing maybe all this was a fantastic dream. It's so hard to believe that I've found the only woman for me, and she loves me, too."

"Then believe this—I don't want to go back to New York with you. I don't want to live there."

"Of course you do. It's your home."

"It was once, but then I came to your world and I've grown to love it here. *You're* here. I would never expect you to cast aside your whole way of life for me. Being Zoe's therapist has brought me smack-dab into the heart of your world. I've learned so much and I'm still learning."

The blood was pounding in his ears. "You're just saying this because it's what you think I want to hear."

"Well, isn't it? Besides the fact that what I'm telling you is true, what do you think those wedding vows are going to be about? I plan to love, honor and serve you through the good and the bad. This is a bad time for your family. Without Stasio, you need me to help you keep the monarchy together.

"Your grandmother needs you. Even though I haven't

met her, I like her, Alex. I really do. She has tried to do her duty the way she's seen fit and Zoe adores her. Why should King Philippe or any other royal family member have to be brought in when you're the son meant to take up the reins? I believe your father knew that."

Alex couldn't believe what he was hearing.

"Alex, you've already been carrying a lot of the load your whole life. Stasio tried his best to shield you by turning to Philippe. He did everything in his power to help you, but you don't need his help.

"I've watched and listened. Your marriage to Teresa proves to me you cared more for the kingdom than you know, or like Stasio you would have abdicated a long time ago. To my mind, you were born to be king. Your country means everything to you, otherwise you wouldn't have agreed to serve in Stasio's place while he's been away. I love you, Alex. I revere you for wanting to do the noble thing and I love the idea of helping you."

Her brilliant blue eyes flashed like the sapphire of the ring he hadn't given her yet. It was still in his suite on Aurum. Those eyes let him know the truth. It was pouring from her soul. "All you have to do is turn around and accept the crown, my love."

There was a swelling in his chest that felt as though it might be a heart attack.

"You and I will always have each other and you and Stasio will be able to live without any guilt. He can marry the woman he loves. They can come and visit, have children, give Zoe a cousin or two. Hector will be thrilled. The queen can take a well-earned rest and Zoe will always be our darling girl. It's the best of all worlds."

Her logic moved him to tears, but he shook his head. "You don't understand. I can't rule with a commoner for a wife, and I refuse to give you up."

"Who says you can't?" she shot back. "I didn't hear about that when Hector explained the contents of your father's codicil to me. It only said that if we have a child or children together, they won't have claim to the throne. That will be Zoe's privilege."

Alex rubbed the back of his neck. "Everything you've said makes perfect sense, but it's never been done."

"That still doesn't make it impossible. Let's go to the queen right now. Wake her up if you have to and tell her you're willing to rule Hellenica with me at your side. Since your father broke the rules when he made that extension to his will, it stands to reason his mother could be moved to convince the ministers to vote in our favor for the good of the monarchy.

"There's no one who can do greater good for the country than you, Alex. You've already been running everything singlehandedly and doing a brilliant job. Maybe it was a presentiment on my part, but the night of the party I watched you and thought you should be king, not Stasio."

In the next instant he reached blindly for her. "You don't know what you're saying."

"I think I do." She clutched his arms. "All I need to know is one thing. Look me in the eye and tell me you don't want to salvage the House of Constantinides. If you're not truthful with me now, then the marriage we're about to enter into is a sham and won't last."

He crushed her in his arms, rocking her long and hard. With his face buried in her hair he whispered, "What have I ever done to deserve you?"

"It'll take me a lifetime to tell you everything, but first we have to tell the queen. Phone your grandmother now. She needs help. Who better than the father of her beloved Zoe?"

Alex kissed the side of her neck. "Whether or not I become king—whether or not my grandmother decides she wants us to have a public wedding here on Hellenica at the time of the coronation—it doesn't matter as long as for once in my life I do get to do the thing I thought I'd never be able to do."

"What's that?" Dottie asked breathlessly.

He cupped her face in his hands. "Marry the woman of my dreams in the chapel on Aurum tomorrow."

"Alex—"

"It will be a very private ceremony just for us. The tiny church located on the palace grounds isn't open to the public. It was erected for the family's use. Father Gregorius will marry us. I'll ask him to perform the ceremony in English."

"He doesn't have to go to that trouble."

"Yes, he does. I'm marrying the bride of my heart and want to say my vows in English for your sake. My friend Bari will be our witness along with Inez and Ari. And, of course, Zoe."

Dottie clung to Alex's hand as he escorted her and Zoe inside the dark interior of the church that smelled strongly of beeswax candles and incense. She wore her white dress with the yellow sash. Dottie had dressed in the pink print and had left her hair down because Zoe had told her earlier that her daddy loved her hair like that.

Inez stepped forward. She handed Dottie a bouquet

of cornflowers. Against Dottie's ear Alex whispered, "I asked her to gather these this morning. They match the incredible blue of your eyes."

She felt tears start and soon saw that another, smaller bouquet had been picked for Zoe to hold. Alex was wearing a light blue summer suit. After putting two cornflowers inside his lapel, he led her and Zoe to the front where the priest stood at the altar. Inez beckoned Zoe to stand by her.

Despite the fact that Alex would always be a prince, Dottie realized he'd dispensed with all artifice for their wedding. She knew the last thing he wanted was for her to feel overwhelmed. Her heart quivered with her love for him as the ceremony began.

"Do you, Prince Alexius Kristof Rudolph Stefano Valleder Constantinides, Duke of Aurum, take Dorothy Giles Richards to be thy wedded wife? To love, honor and serve her unto death?"

"I do."

Dottie trembled.

"Do you, Dorothy Giles Richards, take Prince Alexius to be thy wedded husband? To love, honor and serve him unto death?"

"I do," she whispered, scarcely able to believe this was really happening.

"Then by the power invested in me, I proclaim you husband and wife from this day forth. What God has blessed, let no man put asunder. In the name of the Trinity, Amen."

"Amen," Alex declared after Dottie spoke.

"You wish to bestow tokens?"

"I do, Father." He reached for Dottie's left hand and slid the one-carat sapphire onto her ring finger.

"You may kiss your bride."

The significance of this moment shook Dottie to her very roots. Alex was her husband now. Her life! Without caring about anything else, she raised her mouth to his, needing his kiss like she needed the sun on her face and air to breathe.

While they stood locked together, Zoe ran over to them and hugged their legs. She felt her little arms, reminding her she and Alex were probably giving Father Gregorius a coronary for letting their kiss go on so long. No doubt she was blushing, but the others wouldn't be able to tell until they went outside.

"Are you married now, Daddy?"

Alex relinquished Dottie's mouth and picked up his daughter to kiss her. "We're very, very married."

She giggled and turned to reach for Dottie, who hugged her.

Bari stepped forward and gave Alex a bear hug before bestowing a kiss on Dottie's cheek.

"Congratulations, Your Highness." Inez and Ari curtsied to him and Dottie, then handed her the bouquet. "Your Highness."

"Thank you," Dottie answered.

Alex shook their hands. "We appreciate all your help."

"It's been our pleasure."

"Let's go outside for some pictures," Bari suggested.

The priest stayed long enough for a group photo in front of the ancient doors, then he had to be on his way to the city. Alex invited Bari to have a drink with them. At Zoe's suggestion they celebrated in the gazebo. Bari drank to their health and happiness. After one more picture, he left to get back to work.

Inez brought out a tray of salad, sandwiches and a pitcher of iced tea. By now they were all hungry, including Zoe. A month ago her appetite had diminished to the point they'd both worried about it, but no longer.

The peacock happened to walk past the gazebo just then. Zoe scrambled out of her chair and went after it, leaving them alone for a minute. Alex caught her in his arms. "Alone at last. Happy wedding day, Mrs. Constantinides."

"I love you, darling," she blurted. "Thank you for the simple, beautiful ceremony. I loved it. I love my ring. I'll treasure this day forever. I'm only sorry I didn't have a ring for you."

He kissed her passionately on the mouth. "I didn't want one. I don't like rings and would prefer not to wear one. Yet I have seven of them, all with precious gems encrusted. The only one that doesn't have stones is this one." He flexed his right hand where he wore the gold ducal crest. "Since I have to wear it, I'll take it off and let you put it on the ring finger of my left hand."

He removed it and handed it to her.

At first she was all thumbs. Finally she took hold of his hand and slid it home. "Did you wear it on this hand when you were married to Zoe's mother?" she asked without looking at him.

"No. She gave me a ring from the House of Valleder. I took it off after she died and put it with the other rings that Zoe will inherit one day."

As she stared into his eyes, she sensed something else was on his mind. "You have news. I can tell."

"Yes. For one thing, Hector explained the situation to Mrs. Hawes and she's been given a free two-week vacation here if she wants. Now you don't have to worry about her needless trip."

"Oh, thank you, darling. That's so generous of you."

"After meeting you, I realized how hard-working and dedicated you therapists are. She deserves every perk we can offer."

Dottie bit her lip. "What else were you going to tell me?"

His expression grew more solemn. She saw the slightest look of vulnerability in his eyes. "Before we left Hellenica this morning, my grandmother told me the vote from the parliament was unanimous. They want me to be king. So does she."

His news was so wonderful, she threw her arms around his neck. "You're going to be the greatest king this country ever had. I'm the luckiest woman in the world because I'm your wife. I promise to help make your life easier. I swear it."

"Dottie—" He pulled her tightly against him. "You realize what this means. The day after tomorrow will be my coronation. The queen wants us to come to the palace immediately to discuss the arrangements for our wedding. We're going to have to go through another ceremony, and then I will be crowned king. She wants to meet the commoner who stole the hearts of her great-granddaughter and grandson."

This time tears rolled down Dottie's cheeks. She grasped his handsome face in her hands. "I can't wait to meet her. I can't wait to say my vows again. I love you," she cried, covering his face with kisses.

The archbishop of Hellenica closed the coronation ceremony with "God Save the King." Dottie adored this great man she'd just married for the second time. He'd now been crowned king in this magnificent cathedral and was so handsome and splendid in his dark blue ceremonial suit and red sash, it hurt to look at him.

Zoe, dressed in a tiara and frilly white floor-length dress, sat on a velvet chair like a perfect little princess between Dottie and her great-grandmother, who'd come in a wheelchair. Stasio sat opposite them in his ceremonial dress. Solveig, the woman he loved, had come and was seated in the crowd. Dottie liked her already and imagined there'd be a wedding soon.

King Philippe and his pregnant American wife sat next to Stasio. Over the past few days Dottie had gotten to know her and couldn't wait to spend more time with her.

When the archbishop bid Princess Dorothy rise to join Alex for the processional out of the church, Dottie realized it was *she* he meant and blushed like mad. Her husband noticed she'd been caught off guard and his black eyes flashed fire as she walked toward him to grasp his hand. Zoe followed to carry the train.

In an intimate appraisal, his gaze swept from the tiara on top of her white lace mantilla, down her white princess-style wedding gown to her satin slippers. He'd given her that same look as she'd started to get out of bed this morning. When she reminded him they should have been up an hour ago, he'd pulled her back on top of him and made love to her again with insatiable hunger.

It was embarrassing how much time they'd spent in the bedroom when there was so much to get done in preparation for the coronation. But obviously not embarrassing enough, because she was the one who always moaned in protest when Hector finally managed to convince Alex he was needed in the office or the queen's drawing room immediately.

Her husband kept squeezing her hand as they slowly made their way toward the great doors. In her heart she knew that if Neil and Cory were looking on, they would be happy for her.

She smiled at the guests standing on either side of the aisle. Everyone looked wonderful in their hats and wedding finery. Halfway down she caught sight of Mark and his parents. He made a little wave to Dottie and Zoe with his hand. It warmed her heart. Next she smiled at Bari and his family. Near the doors she spotted Hector, who beamed back at her.

When she and Alex emerged from the cathedral, a huge roar went up from the crowd in the ancient agora. Alex helped her into the open-air carriage, then assisted Zoe, who sat opposite them. Once he'd climbed inside and closed the door, the bells began to ring throughout the city.

Almost at once a chant went through the crowd for King Alexius to kiss Princess Dot. Somehow word had gotten out that Princess Zoe called her new mother Dot.

"Don't mind if I do," Alex said with a wicked smile before he kissed her so thoroughly her tiara slipped off. The crowd went wild with excitement. The horses began moving.

While Alex fit it back on her, taking his time about it as he stared at her, Zoe said, "Was the crown heavy, Daddy?"

"Very. Your Uncle Stasi wasn't kidding."

"Could Mark ride with us, Mommy?"

"Not today, but you'll see him tomorrow. There are hundreds of children lining the streets with their families. They'd all love to ride in this carriage with you, so wave to them. They're very excited to see you."

"They are?"

"Yes. Just think—today your country got a new king and he's *your* daddy. We need to start working on your K sounds."

Alex's chuckle turned into a deep rumble. He leaned over to give her another kiss that stirred her senses clear down to her toenails. It was a kiss that told her he couldn't wait until they were alone again. As they reached the palace and climbed out of the carriage, the limo carrying the queen and Stasio pulled up behind them.

As they all entered the palace together, Alex's grandmother said, "Really, Alex. Did you have to kiss Dottie like that in front of thousands of people? And you kept doing it! You realize it'll be all over the news."

He grinned at Stasio. "I don't know how to kiss her any other way, *Yiayia*. Worse, I can't seem to stop."

"Are we going to have a baby now?" piped up a little voice.

"Oh, really, Zoe!" her great-grandmother cried out. "You don't ask questions like that in front of people. There's going to be a reception in the grand dining hall and I expect you to behave like the princess you are."

Unabashed, Zoe turned to Hector. "Can Mark sit by me?"

While they were sorting it out, Alex pulled Dottie away from the others and led her to a deserted alcove. Before she could breathe, he kissed her long and deeply. "I needed that," he murmured after lifting his head a few minutes later. "You looked like a vision in the cathedral. Promise me you're not a figment of my imagination. I couldn't take it."

She kissed his hard jaw. "I'll convince you tonight when we're finally alone. I'm so glad I married royalty. I love the idea of going to bed with my husband and *my liege*. It sounds positively decadent and wicked, don't you think?"

"Dottie—"

* * * * *

THE LAST GOODBYE

BY

SARAH MAYBERRY

First published in Great Britain 2012
by Mills & Boon, an imprint of Harlequin (UK) Limited,
Eton House, 18-24 Paradise Road, Richmond, Surrey TW9 1SR

© Small Cow Productions Pty Ltd. 2011

ISBN: 978 0 263 89415 8

23-0312

Harlequin (UK) policy is to use papers that are natural, renewable and recyclable products and made from wood grown in sustainable forests. The logging and manufacturing processes conform to the legal environmental regulations of the country of origin.

Printed and bound in Spain
by Blackprint CPI, Barcelona

Dear Reader,

I have always been fascinated by advice columns. A really good one can keep me in its thrall for years, eagerly awaiting new editions of whichever magazine or newspaper it appears in. It's not so much the solutions that fascinate me—although I am a big fan of common sense!—but the problems that people are dealing with. Believe me, after years of being an assiduous (some might say obsessive) online reader of the Dear Prudence column at *Slate* magazine, truth is definitely stranger than fiction. Definitely.

Given my little obsession, it's probably not a huge surprise that it would make its way into my writing—my heroine in *The Last Goodbye*, Ally, is an advice columnist. Interested and bright and accepting, Ally does her best to respond to readers looking for compassion, a slap on the wrist or instruction on how to navigate the waters of wedding etiquette. The ironic thing is, Ally's own life is far from perfect. She's a born gypsy, travelling from place to place, living out of her suitcase. She's convinced she'll never settle down—that she can't, in fact—until she meets Tyler. As we all know, falling in love is the ultimate game changer.

I hope you enjoy this book. I love to hear from readers—you can contact me via my website at www.sarahmayberry.com.

Until next time,

Sarah Mayberry

Sarah Mayberry lives in Melbourne in a house that needs much renovating, and she's praying for the day when someone invents self-stripping wallpaper. When she's not writing romance novels or stripping wallpaper, she works as a freelance script writer and story consultant for the Australian and New Zealand TV industries. She loves reading, movies, cooking and sleeping. And not necessarily in that order…

This one is definitely for Chris.
Thank you for holding my hand,
for work shopping scenes,
and for setting me straight on more than one
occasion. You are the best friend, mentor, partner,
lover and sidekick a woman could ever ask for.
Thanks also to Wanda, who trims my excesses
and reminds me of all the things I thought I'd
learned absolutely with the last book. Bless you!
I'd also like to acknowledge my father—
Dad, I love you very much.
Thank you from the bottom of my heart
for being one of the good ones.

CHAPTER ONE

TYLER ADAMSON SMOOTHED his hand over the surface of the newly sanded tabletop. The mahogany was warm and smooth as silk and by the time one of his team had rubbed several layers of shellac into it, the wood grain beneath his fingers would glow with a deep red luster. Amazing to think that mere weeks ago this finely honed piece of furniture had been nothing but a pile of roughly hewn wood and an idea on his drawing board.

"When is this scheduled for delivery?" he asked as he stepped back from the table.

His senior cabinetmaker, Dino, rolled his eyes. "Relax. It's on schedule. Go away and design something." He made a shooing motion with his hands.

Tyler ignored him, his gaze sweeping the crowded workshop. A Georgian sideboard was awaiting final sanding and a desk was in the process of having leather inlaid into its surface. A dozen balloon-back rosewood chairs were stacked to one side, ready to be upholstered, while no less than three dining tables were at various stages of assembly.

"Let Gabby know if you need another pair of hands," he said as he turned away.

He'd put too much time and effort into building the business to blow it by letting customers down with long delays now that business was booming.

"She'll hear about it, don't worry," Dino said.

Tyler didn't doubt it. Dino had never been shy about voicing his opinion in the past, after all. Tyler started toward the stairs to his mezzanine workspace, only to change direction when he remembered he'd left the notes from his recent client meeting in his truck. He passed the administration office, where he could see Gabby talking on the phone, then cut across the plush carpeted showroom to the front entrance.

The parking lot was baking in the late-afternoon sun, heat shimmering on the tarmac. He crossed to his truck, grabbed the folder off the rear seat, then headed for the coolness of the building.

"Tyler Adamson?"

He glanced over his shoulder to see a small, dark-haired woman bearing down on him.

"That's me. How can I help you?" he asked.

"My name's Ally Bishop."

She looked at him expectantly, clearly waiting for him to recognize her. He frowned. Her face was round, her eyes big and brown and her hair cut close to her head. She looked like she should be wearing an elf costume as part of Santa's Kingdom at the mall.

Definitely he'd never met her before.

"I'm sorry, but if this is about an order, you're better off speaking to Gabby. I'm a little out of the loop on where we're at with lead times right now."

He offered her a smile, inviting her to be amused by his administrative incompetence.

She crossed her arms over her chest and glared at him as though he'd clubbed a baby seal to death in front of a class of preschoolers.

"I called you yesterday. I'm the one who left the message about your father being in hospital," she said.

Tyler stilled. "What?"

"He didn't want me to call you. He said you didn't have time for him, but I thought you might find room in your busy schedule to visit. Clearly, I was wrong."

She was starting to get red in the face and he got the feeling she was only warming up.

He held up a hand. "Hold on a minute—my father's in hospital?"

"Didn't you get my message?" She sounded suspicious. As though she thought he was lying to make himself look better.

"We had some water damage here a few weeks ago when that big storm came through. The answering machine's been on the blink ever since."

"Right." She frowned. He could practically hear her trying to change gears as she reassessed her opinion of him.

"What's wrong with him?" he asked.

He wanted to take the words back as soon as they'd left his mouth. He'd decided long ago to draw a line under his relationship with his father. Him being sick didn't change that.

"He collapsed in the backyard with stomach pains. They rushed him into surgery. He had a blockage in his bowel."

She stopped, but he knew there was more.

"What is it? Cancer?" He was aware that he sounded abrupt and harsh but was unable to do anything about it.

"Yes. The doctors said there was nothing they could do except make him comfortable."

He stared at her for a moment, then dropped his gaze to the scuffed toes of his boots.

So. The old man was finally on his way out. He was seventy-eight, so it was hardly surprising news. In fact, Tyler had been surprised he hadn't had a visit like this sooner—although he'd expected a lawyer, not a self-righteous elf.

He lifted his head. She was watching him, waiting for his response.

"Thanks for letting me know. I appreciate it." He walked past her, heading for the door to the showroom.

"Don't you want to know where he is so you can see him?" she called after him.

He kept walking. "No."

His father dying didn't change anything. Didn't even come close.

"You don't care that he's going to die alone? That there's no one to look after him? That he's living in a house filled with stacked-up newspapers and eating canned food?"

He stopped and turned to face her. She looked appalled. Shocked that anyone could be so cold. He almost smiled. Almost. His father had obviously done a great job convincing her he was a harmless, little old man. And who knew, maybe age had genuinely mellowed him.

Good for him.

"I said goodbye to my father years ago." He pushed the door open and walked into the showroom.

He half expected her to follow him. She'd been so full of fire and brimstone that he wouldn't have put it past her. He waited, muscles tense, but no one came through the door.

Good.

He strode through the showroom to the office. Gabby was going over a supplies manifest, one elbow on the desk, a fluorescent marker between her teeth.

"I thought you disconnected the old answering machine because it wasn't working?" he asked.

She blinked and he realized he'd barked the question instead of asking it like a normal person.

"Sorry," he muttered.

"What's wrong?"

"Nothing."

She gave him a long look. That was the problem with having his ex-girlfriend as his business manager—she knew him too well to let him get away with anything.

"Is there something wrong with the Crestwell account?" she asked.

"Everything's fine. Where's the old answering machine?"

"I told Dino to disconnect it. But if he didn't, it's where it always is."

She gestured to the far corner where a pile of boxes and files were stacked on a small coffee table, waiting to be returned to order after the flooding from the storm. Tyler hefted boxes out of the way until he'd unearthed the machine.

"It's still connected," he reported.

Gabby made a rude noise. "Bloody Dino. Talk about hopeless."

He pressed the blinking red light. "You have twenty new messages," an electronic voice told him.

"Shit," Gabby said.

He knew from experience that the machine only recorded twenty messages before it reached capacity. He wondered how many important calls they'd missed over the past few weeks.

The first three messages were customers with queries that he knew had long since been handled. He pressed the fast-forward button.

"Hey," Gabby said.

He saw she had a pen in hand and had been jotting down names and numbers as the messages played.

"You can go over them all later," he said.

"What's wrong with doing it now?"

He ignored her, letting the machine hit the end of the tape before rewinding to the last message.

"Hi. I'm calling for Tyler Adamson. My name's Ally Bishop. I'm living next door to his father, Bob, up here in Woodend. I thought Tyler would like to know that his father is in hospital. I think…I think it's pretty serious.…"

He hit the Stop button. Gabby was uncharacteristically silent behind him.

"Can you make sure we replace this thing today?" Tyler said, not turning around.

"Are you okay?"

He nodded.

"Do you want me to make some calls…?" Gabby offered.

"No."

"You don't want to go to him?"

He glanced at her over his shoulder. He and Gabby had gone out for three years, so she knew he never saw his father. But he'd never told her why.

"No."

"But—"

"Leave it, Gab."

He left the office and walked out into the workshop. Dino was on the lathe and Wes was sanding a tabletop, his face hidden behind safety goggles and a dust mask. Paul and Carl were marking up some wood. Kelly would be out the back somewhere, no doubt, checking on inventory or spraying something in the booth. Tyler breathed in the familiar smell of fresh-cut wood and varnish, then headed straight to the mezzanine where his work space was located. He sat in front of his drawing board and tried to lose himself in the design for a sideboard, but his head was full of old memories and feelings he'd thought long forgotten.

His father, red in the face, spittle flying from his mouth as he raged at Tyler for being insubordinate and useless.

His brother cowering beneath the lash of his father's belt while Tyler watched, filled with a mix of horror and shameful relief that this time it wasn't him on the receiving end of his father's wrath.

His mother, thin-lipped, telling him that he'd brought it on himself for being cheeky and rebellious.

Happy times, indeed.

Was it any wonder Tyler had escaped as soon as he could, following his brother's lead and bailing on school and home when he was barely seventeen? He'd left with nothing but a bag full of clothes and his father's angry "good riddance to bad rubbish," ringing in his ears—and he'd never looked back. Not once.

Sure, he'd visited when his mother was still alive, driven by guilt and obligation. But when she died ten years ago, he'd made a promise to himself to never go back, to put it all behind himself and never dredge it up again.

I think...I think it's serious.

Tyler swore beneath his breath. So what if his father was sick? So what if he was dying? Being closer to the grave didn't make him less of a bully and a coward, and it certainly didn't expunge seventeen years of violence and anger.

I think...I think it's serious.

"I can take care of those client briefings tomorrow if you need time off," Gabby said from the doorway.

Tyler glanced at her. She leaned against the door frame, her arms crossed beneath her small breasts, her brown eyes steady on him. She wore her hair short, like Ally Bishop, but it was straight instead of curly so she looked more boyish than puckish.

"I'm not going anywhere."

Gabby studied his face for a beat. "You never told me why you hate him so much."

"I don't hate him." That would give the old man too much power. "I don't want him in my life."

"I don't suppose there's any point in me offering an ear if you need to talk?" Gabby's tone was resigned and sad.

His refusal to talk about his childhood had been one of the major hurdles of their failed relationship. One of her favorite accusations had been that he was "emotionally withholding." Whatever that meant. Just because he wanted to leave the past in the past didn't mean he was holding anything back. It was simply irrelevant.

"There's nothing to talk about."

Gabby sighed. "Well. The offer stands if you want it."

"I appreciate it."

She pushed away from the door frame. "Just remember, you're only going to get this chance once, Tyler."

He nodded tightly. He'd had his fill of short, dark-haired women telling him what to do today.

"Gotcha."

He worked at his drawing board for the rest of the afternoon. By the time he descended from the mezzanine, the workshop was silent and the light was off in Gabby's office.

He did a quick lap of the building, checking doors, inspecting the pieces that had been put to one side ready for delivery, ensuring the machinery was all switched off.

Last year, T.A. Furniture Designs had turned over nearly four million dollars. This year, they were on track to increase that by 20 percent—despite the global economic downturn, despite a general slowdown in spending across the board. Years of hard work and commitment to quality craftsmanship and design were, at last, paying off and if things kept going the way they were, the company would outgrow their current premises in the next few years.

Not so useless, after all, hey, Dad?

He stopped in his tracks, hand poised to flick off the master light switch.

Everything in him wanted to deny that proving himself to his domineering father had been part of his motivation for building this business. It seemed such a childish, petty admission—as though his whole life had been one big "Look, Pa, no hands!"

But the truth was that whether Tyler liked it or not, there would always be a voice in his head telling him that he wasn't good enough and that he'd never amount to anything—and that voice was his father's.

He reached for his phone and hit the speed dial for Gabby.

"I need you to cover for me tomorrow," he said the moment she picked up.

To her credit, she didn't make a smug remark or say I told you so. She simply told him she'd make sure things were taken care of while he did what he had to do.

He stood for a long moment after he'd ended the call, thinking about what it would mean. Going home. Seeing his father again after ten years of silence.

He sighed. Then he flicked the light off and headed for the door.

WHAT AM I GOING TO TELL BOB?

The thought circled Ally Bishop's mind the entire drive to the small rural Victorian town of Woodend. True, she also spared a little time to fume over what a cold, unfeeling jerk Tyler Adamson was. But most of her thoughts were for the old man she was about to disappoint.

She was the one who had insisted Bob think about making contact with his estranged sons. She was the one who'd encouraged him to give his sons a chance to prove themselves, even though Bob had insisted they wouldn't care. And now she was the one who would have to deliver the cruel news that the one son she'd been able to track down wanted nothing to do with him, as Bob had so heartbreakingly predicted.

She still couldn't believe that Tyler had walked away from the news that his father was dying. That he didn't care. That it meant nothing to him that any last chance to reconcile or make his peace with his parent was about to disappear for good.

It wasn't as though she was one of those eternally optimistic people who only saw the best in people— her work as an advice columnist for Melbourne's most popular daily newspaper ensured that she was exposed to pretty much every peccadillo, flaw, pe-culiarity and weakness of human nature possible. In fact, she'd thought she was impossible to shock—until Tyler had coolly thanked her and walked away.

She glanced out the window as she passed the first houses on the outskirts of town. The turnoff to her friend Wendy's house came up on her left but Ally kept driving. Ten minutes later, she steered her car into a parking spot at the Kyneton District Hospital.

She didn't get out immediately. She needed a moment to gather herself for the task ahead.

According to Bob's doctors, his cancer was so widespread, so invasive, he had months, perhaps only weeks, to live. And she'd offered him hope. Now she was about to snatch that hope away from him.

She sighed heavily and scrubbed her face with her hands.

Not for the first time, she wondered how she had become so entangled so quickly in the concerns of an old man who, to all intents and purposes, was a stranger. After all, she'd only been living in Wood-end for four weeks, house-sitting for Wendy. Prior to Bob's collapse, they'd only shared a couple of brief chats across the fence that separated the two properties. She hadn't even known his last name before he'd been admitted to hospital. And yet she'd taken on his cause as though it was her own.

Feeling about a million years old, she climbed out of the car and walked toward the hospital. Bob was dozing when she entered his ward, his face slack. She guessed he'd once been a strapping man—big boned, muscular—but age and illness had whittled him away, reducing him to little more than skin and bone and sinew. As always, his frailty made her chest squeeze with sympathy and she couldn't help flashing back to the awful, terrifying moment when she'd glanced over the fence and seen him sprawled unconscious on the grass. The twenty minutes she'd sat beside his too-still body, holding his hand while she waited for the ambulance to arrive had been the longest of her life.

Bob's eyelids flickered as she sank into the visitor's chair. His eyes opened and he blinked a few times before focusing on her. She smiled.

"Hello. How are you feeling?"

"I'll do."

Not once in all the turmoil and anxiety and uncertainty of the past few days had Bob let on that he was afraid of what his future held.

"Have you seen the doctor today?"

"He came by again. Wanted to make sure he'd given me enough of those little white pills to keep me well and truly off my rocker."

"Good. Because you don't need to be in pain."

Bob pulled a face. She was well aware that he came from a generation of Australian men who'd chop off an arm before they admitted a weakness.

"How are you doing with your crossword-puzzle books? Do you want me to get some more for you?"

"I'm fine for the moment, thanks, love."

Tell him. Tell him and get it over with.

Ally shifted to the edge of her seat. Took a steadying breath. "I spoke to Tyler today," she said.

Bob stilled. It was a moment before he responded. "Lazy bugger finally found the time to call, did he?"

Ally opened her mouth to explain that she'd confronted Tyler in person after he hadn't responded to her phone message, then thought better of it. Bob didn't need to know all the details, only the important ones. She could spare him that, at least.

"I don't think he's going to come, Bob," she said gently.

Bob's hands found each other on top of the sheet. Then he nodded. "No surprises there, I guess. Never did have time for the old man."

Only the muscle working at his jaw gave any hint that he was grappling with strong emotion.

She wondered again what had gone so wrong between Bob and his children, what words and deeds had been said and done to put so much distance between them. One thing was clear—Bob certainly wasn't about to volunteer the details. Which meant that Ally had done all she could to help him on that front.

"I'm sorry, Bob."

"Not your fault, love."

He asked about her column then and she pulled her latest letters from her bag and read him the juiciest problems. After fifteen minutes of offering her his pithy take on her readers' issues, Bob started to slur his words a little and she knew he was getting tired.

"I'll let you get some rest now. But I'll see you again tomorrow, okay?"

"You don't have to come in here every day. You've got your own things to do, all those letters to answer," Bob said.

"I'll see you tomorrow," Ally repeated with a small smile.

She kissed him on the cheek before exiting the room. She let the smile fade when she was in the corridor.

Feeling sad and heavy, she drove to Wendy's house. Mr. Whiskers wound himself around her ankles the moment she opened the front door and she took the hint and fed him immediately. Then she tried to settle down to get a start on tomorrow's column. Her mind kept drifting to Bob, however, unable to let go. She told herself over and over that Bob was not her responsibility, that she'd done all she could do. It didn't make any difference.

Ironic, really, since she'd spent practically all her adult life and much of her childhood ensuring she was as self-sufficient as possible. At thirty-three, she was a master at forming friendships that encompassed favors but not obligations, and relationships that offered companionship and passion without commitment or promises.

Yet here she was, worried and anxious over an old man she barely knew.

It's because he's so alone.

But at the end of the day, everyone was alone.

Shaking off her somber mood, Ally reapplied herself to solving other people's problems.

IT TOOK TYLER JUST OVER an hour to reach the outskirts of Woodend the following morning. He drove into Main Street, taking in the changes that ten years had wrought, a little surprised by how prosperous and lively it all seemed. There was fresh paint on shopfronts, more bustle along the sidewalks, new planter boxes and paving and a brand-spanking-new supermarket complex.

He frowned, struggling to reconcile the present with his memories of a town that had always seemed too grim and too small and too isolated. A town he couldn't wait to escape.

He drove farther north until he found the hospital. The morning sun was warm on his back as he strode toward the front entrance.

He had no idea what to expect. What to say to his father. How he would feel when he saw him for the first time in over a decade.

He'd told Gabby that he didn't hate his father, but he wasn't sure it was true. Once, he'd wanted his father's love and approval as much as any little boy. It had taken him a long time to accept that he would never hear the words of support and unconditional love that he craved. And longer than that again to understand that the fault wasn't with him, but with his father and, to a certain extent, his mother.

Just do it. See him. Listen to whatever he wants to say. Say your bit. Then it's over, once and for all.

He approached the reception desk, breathing in the medicinal smell shared by hospitals the world over, thinking about the phone conversation he'd had with Jon last night.

They weren't the closest of brothers. Even as kids they'd never discussed what went on within the four walls of their home. There had never seemed much point—their parents ruled their world, and there was nowhere else to go. So they'd endured, until one day when Jon was barely fourteen years old. He'd taken a hit from their father, but instead of curling into a ball to brace himself and endure the next inevitable blow, he'd gotten off the floor and squared up to the old man, both fists raised, his whole body trembling with rage. Tyler could still remember the shock and fear in his father's face as he'd realized his eldest son was taller than him. And the dawning anger as he understood that his days of ruling the roost with a casual cuff or kick were over.

Robert Adamson had never dared raise a hand to Jon after that and he was always careful to ensure his eldest son was out of the house before he laid into Tyler. A part of Tyler had wanted to hide behind his brother's newly found strength, to run to him and tell him what was still going on when he wasn't around. But the bulk of him had been too ashamed. Watching his brother stand his own ground had made him feel even smaller and less powerful and more trapped than he had before. It had taken Tyler many secretive sessions on the bench press at his friend Jimmy's house and hours of shadowboxing before he'd gotten the courage to stand his ground in the same way when he was thirteen years old. The beatings had stopped, but not the verbal abuse.

So perhaps it wasn't so surprising that Jon had sounded more cautious than pleased when he'd heard Tyler's voice over the phone last night. Family had never been associated with happiness for either of them. And when Tyler had revealed why he was calling, Jon had laughed outright.

"If that old bastard thinks I'm getting on a plane to play the dutiful son by his deathbed, he can think again," he'd said.

Tyler hadn't tried to talk him around. He'd done his bit, passed on the information. Jon had chosen his route, and Tyler his own. As always.

The woman behind the reception counter directed him to his father's ward. Tyler followed the signs and started counting off numbers as he looked for his father's room.

"Excuse me. Visiting hours don't start until ten."

He turned to find a gray-haired nurse walking toward him.

"I've driven up from Melbourne. I won't be long." It wouldn't take five minutes to say what he needed to say, after all.

"Who are you visiting?" the woman asked.

"Robert Adamson. My father." His throat closed around the unfamiliar word.

The nurse's expression softened. "Of course you are. I can see the family resemblance now. I'm Sister Kemp. Before you go in, can I grab some contact details from you? We don't seem to have them on file."

Tyler hesitated a moment. "Sure."

He followed her to the nurses' station then handed over his cell and home numbers.

"Lovely. I know our social worker will be pleased to know Bob has family looking out for him. You can go in to see him now, but keep it short. He's had major surgery and you'll find he tires very easily." She gave him a small smile before turning to take care of a ringing phone.

Tyler glanced toward the open doorway of his father's room. Then he realized he was hovering like an uncertain schoolboy and made himself move.

The moment he stepped over the threshold, he knew there had been some kind of a mistake. The small, white-haired figure sleeping in the hospital bed was not his father. Robert Adamson was broad shouldered and robust, with a full head of salt-and-pepper hair, not pallid and frail-looking, his features sunken, the pink of his skull showing through a thin covering of white hair.

Tyler took a step backward. Then the man in the bed stirred, his hands flexing briefly before relaxing again on the blanket. Tyler stilled. He knew those hands. Big, broad. Powerful.

Bloody hell.

He moved closer to the bed. How could this shrunken, diminished figure be his father, the man who loomed large and angry in all of Tyler's memories of his childhood? How could so much overbearing energy be reduced to this...?

Tyler eyed the tube snaking into the crook of his father's elbow and the oxygen prongs taped to his upper lip. There were more tubes disappearing beneath the blankets and a heart monitor kept up a steady *beep-beep* at the head of the bed.

How long had his father been so thin, the muscles of his arms so wasted? How long had his collarbone poked so obviously through his skin? What had happened to the square certainty of his jaw? The determined line of his brow?

Tyler swallowed against a wash of emotion. Amazing that after so many years and so much ill feeling he could feel anything, any tug of affection or sentiment at all. But this man was a part of him, a part of his marrow and blood and flesh and bone. He'd taught Tyler how to kick a football and hammer a nail. He'd sat at the head of the table every Sunday and carved the lamb roast. Even in his absence, he'd been the most influential person in Tyler's life.

His father.

"Tyler."

Tyler's gaze snapped to his father's face and he saw that he was awake, his pale blue eyes defiant and proud as he stared at his son.

"That's right."

"Thought you were too busy down there in the city with your little furniture business to have time for your old man."

Typical of his father to come out fighting. It was a painless jab, but it was enough to give Tyler some much-needed perspective. This man—this old, frail man—was not his mentor or his friend. Never had been, never would be.

"We're flat out, actually. So I can't stay long."

"Nobody asked you to." His parent smoothed a hand over his hair. "Did you talk to Jon?"

"I did." He didn't say anything more and his father was the first to look away.

"Well, it's a long way to come from Canada. I assume he's still over there, freezing his nuts off every winter?"

"That's right."

"Wife and kids?" his father asked hopefully.

"No."

"How about you?"

"No."

His father looked disappointed. Tyler glanced around the room, trying to think of something else to say. There were no cards or flowers on the bed stand, but someone had brought his father some crossword-puzzle books. His father shifted in the bed, then winced and subsided back on his pillows.

"You okay?"

"Does it look like I'm okay?" In the old days, his father's words would have been delivered with scathing contempt, just in case Tyler hadn't got the message over the past thirty-seven years that his father found him lacking on almost every front. There was no weight or vehemence behind today's utterance, however—it was simply a reflex, the last remnant of a lifelong habit.

"What are your plans?" Tyler asked.

His father glared at him. "What do you mean, what are my plans? I've got a handful of weeks left. I wasn't planning on a fishing expedition."

Tyler regarded him for a long, silent moment. It was hard to get angry or even irritated when he could see how much effort it was taking his father to maintain his usual brusque demeanor. Robert Adamson was a toothless tiger, a declawed lion, a gelded stallion. Whatever power he once wielded in the world was long gone.

"What have the doctors said?"

"Why? Wondering how soon you can get your hands on the house?"

"I don't need your money, Dad," Tyler said, then cursed himself for rising to the bait.

He took a deep breath. He hadn't come here to fight. He'd come to say his piece, and the sooner he did that, the sooner he could get back to his life.

He opened his mouth to deliver the speech he'd prepared in the small hours of the morning—sharp, brutal words designed to severe the ties between them at last. Then he looked into his father's watery blue eyes and saw past the surface pride to the well of fear and uncertainty beneath.

The words he'd waited years to say died in his throat.

The man lying before him had only weeks, maybe

a handful of months left. No matter how much he deserved it, no matter how many times Tyler had imagined himself looking his father in the eye and listing his father's failures as a parent and a man, he could not make himself say the words sitting like lead in his belly.

He simply couldn't.

Some of the tension eased out of his shoulders.

So. That was that, then. He'd say his goodbyes and walk away and leave the big issues between them unexplored, as they always had been. Let the old man slip away without nailing him with the questions he'd always wanted answers to.

What did we do wrong?

Did you ever love us?

Why even have children if you resented them so deeply?

"I need to go," Tyler said. He dug his car keys from his pocket. "Is there anything you need before I head off? Anything from home? Something from the shop?"

"I'm all covered. Ally brought me my things."

Right. Ally, the next-door neighbor. It sounded like the kind of thing a self-righteous elf would do.

"Then I'd best be getting back to it," Tyler said.

His father nodded as though he'd expected nothing less. "Appreciate you dropping by."

Tyler headed for the door, an odd, sick feeling in his gut.

He'd just said goodbye to his father for the last

time. Once he returned to Melbourne, that would be it. It would all be over.

Impossible to untangle all the thoughts and feelings racing through his mind. Regret, anger, grief, frustration. And, yes, pity.

He strode through the corridors, dodging patients and medical staff. Then he exited the hospital—and almost walked straight into a small, dark-haired woman.

They both stopped in their tracks. For a moment, Ally Bishop simply stared at him. Then a wide smile curved her mouth.

"You came," she said. "I'm so glad. I know he really wanted to see you. He's so proud and stubborn, but the moment I mentioned calling you I could see he wanted it, he simply didn't know how to ask for it."

She was delighted he'd come. Overjoyed by the family reunion she'd effected. No doubt she had visions of him and his father staying up late into the night, exchanging memories, sharing their innermost thoughts. Telling each other how proud they were and how much they loved each other.

He laughed. Couldn't help himself.

"Lady, you have no idea," he said.

He left her standing in front of the hospital, her face pale with shock.

He made it to the safety of his truck before it all caught up with him. He pinched the bridge of his nose but was powerless to stop the tears burning the back of his eyes.

They're not for him. They're not.

He wasn't sure who he was crying for. Definitely not his old man, and certainly not himself. He'd never cried for himself, and he wasn't about to start now.

CHAPTER TWO

I'VE MADE A TERRIBLE mistake.

Ally's hand curled around the strap of her handbag as she watched Tyler Adamson duck his head and brush his forearm across his eyes.

She'd followed him to his truck, determined to make the most of his change of heart despite his less-than-welcoming demeanor. After all, he'd come when he said he wouldn't—that had to mean there was a chance of father and son reconciling.

But now Tyler was hunched in his truck, choking back tears as though they caused him physical pain.

At first she'd thought it was simple grief she was witnessing, that Tyler had seen his father and learned the prognosis and was now experiencing the first wash of sorrow and regret. But there was something about the way he curled into himself that spoke of emotions more complex and uglier than grief alone.

She took a step backward, then another, then another, until there was a tree between herself and Tyler's shiny red pickup. She turned and walked until she was safely inside the hospital foyer, well out of Tyler's sight.

With the abruptness of a camera changing focus, she suddenly understood that she should never have made contact with him. Should never have pushed Bob, should never have pried into what was clearly a very complicated, painful situation. She'd thought she was helping, that if there were issues between Bob and his children, they would all appreciate the opportunity to talk them out before it was too late.

But some scars ran too deep and she'd been hopelessly, childishly naive to dive headfirst into something that was clearly none of her business. She'd been behaving like the worst sort of interfering do-gooder, lumbering in with her hobnail boots on, causing everyone more pain.

She wrapped her arms across herself as she glanced toward the parking lot, feeling cold despite the warmth of the summer's day. She couldn't get the picture of Tyler hunched over his steering wheel out of her mind. She knew instinctively that he would hate for her—for anyone—to have seen him in such a vulnerable state.

The worst of it was, there was nothing she could do to fix the mess she'd made. She'd meddled, and there was no way she could take it back.

And now Ally was uncertain if she should go ahead with her visit or not, unsure what she might find when she entered Bob's room. If he was as upset as his son, she knew absolutely that he would not want anyone to see him break down.

She bit her lip. Then she gave herself a mental shake. She was here. If Bob didn't want to see her, she'd go. And if he was upset, she'd do her best to comfort him—provided he allowed her to. It was the least she could do.

Bob was talking to a nurse when she arrived. Or, more accurately, arguing, judging by the raised voices.

"Fine, Mr. Adamson, I'll go find someone in charge," the nurse said darkly, brushing past Ally as she exited the room.

Bob was scowling as Ally approached the bed. "She'd better be going to find someone to make this TV work, or there's going to be hell to pay."

"What's the problem, Bob?"

"They want to stiff me to watch my TV shows. Twenty bucks a day!"

"It's been like that for a while. Do you want me to arrange it for you?"

"No, I do not. It's an outrage to charge a man to watch what should be free." He was flushed, agitated—far more so than the argument warranted.

Ally reached for one of the gnarled hands fisted on the sheets. "Bob, you need to take a deep breath. Getting upset like this isn't going to help you get better."

He didn't quite meet her eyes but his hand gripped hers tightly, almost painfully.

"I guess you probably think I'm a stupid old bugger, getting upset over a TV." His voice was low, thick with emotion. She returned the pressure on his hand.

"Actually, I don't."

Then she set herself to the task of distracting him, telling him a story about Wendy's cat, Mr. Whiskers. She waited for him to mention his son's visit, but he didn't. And neither did she.

She'd learned her lesson, well and truly.

TYLER HESITATED ON THE rear doorstep of his father's house, the spare key gritty with dirt and cool in his hand. It had been hidden beneath the old brick beside the steps for as long as he could remember, but he'd still been surprised when he'd lifted the brick and found it there. For some reason he'd thought his father would have changed the hiding spot after he and Jon had left.

He rubbed his thumb over the ridges on the key, staring at the peeling paint of the door.

He didn't know why he was here. He'd been driving through town on his way to the freeway, keen to get back to the business, his head busy with all the things he needed to do between now and the weekend. Then he'd seen the sign for his parents' street and signaled to turn.

Like his father, the house hadn't aged well. The paint was peeling, and the trim around several of the window frames was rotten. The garden was overgrown, the gutters sagging along one side of the house.

The key slid easily into the lock. The door swung open and a rush of hot, stale air hit him. He walked into the short hallway, stopping when he saw the boxes stacked against the wall. More than a dozen of them, filled with what looked like newspapers. He took a step closer and inspected the topmost one.

Yep, newspapers. So old they were yellow with age. Frowning, he made his way past the cartons and into the kitchen.

It was dark and he reached for the light switch. Even after twenty years he found it unerringly, some subconscious part of his brain leading his hand to the right point on the kitchen wall. The fluorescent light flickered to life and he surveyed the room, his frown deepening as he took note of yet more newspapers stacked against the wall, the dirty dishes in the sink, the food-encrusted stove.

When his mother had been alive, this room had been pristine, every surface clear, every pot gleaming. It had been his and Jon's responsibility to wash and dry and put away the dishes every night, then his mother would set the table for tomorrow's breakfast, everything neatly lined up.

He glanced toward the crowded sink and a memory hit—him and Jon fooling around while doing the dishes, flicking each other with their damp tea towels. He'd been holding one of his mother's prized Royal Doulton teacups when he'd slipped on the wet floor and instinctively flailed to save himself, dropping the cup in the process. The sound of porcelain shattering had sounded like a gunshot through the house. Tyler could still remember the thrill of panic that had rocketed up his spine.

His mother had appeared in the doorway first, her face twisted with dismay and grief, then his father. One look at his wife's tear-streaked face as she'd knelt to collect the remains of one of her treasured teacups had been enough to seal Tyler's fate.

Tyler walked away from the memory and into the living room. The curtains were drawn, the room dark, and he flicked on more lights. Apart from the cartons of newspapers stacked along the far wall, nothing had changed in here since he'd last seen it, down to his mother's knitting basket sitting beside her favorite chair by the fire.

He crossed to the mantle and picked up a tiny porcelain mouse peering out of a piece of cheese. His mother had loved her menagerie, as she'd called it. He and Jon had selected a new animal for her birthday every year, bought from the jeweler in town and paid for with their hard-earned pocket money. She'd always acted surprised when she'd opened her present, even though she must have known she'd be getting yet another creature to add to her collection.

Tyler traced the line of the mouse's back, remembering how proud he'd always been of the fact that he'd made her happy, even for a moment.

He put down the mouse and glanced toward the

bedrooms. He walked slowly across the threadbare carpet and stepped into the empty hallway. Closed doors lined the right side, the first leading to his parents' room, the next to Jon's, the last to his. At the far end of the hall was the door to the bathroom.

Tyler reached out to flick on the light switch and another memory flashed into his mind. Jon, naked and still wet from the shower, cowering on the carpet as their father lit into him with an old belt. Jon had tried to escape to his room and their father had stalked him up the hallway, raining blows on his exposed back. Tyler had stood in his bedroom door, too afraid to intervene, too afraid to retreat.

Tyler couldn't remember what his brother's crime had been. Perhaps he'd been in their father's toolbox without permission. Maybe he'd sat in their father's car, pretending he could drive, a favorite fantasy for both him and Jon. Or maybe he'd genuinely done something wrong—lied or stolen or cheated at school.

Tyler could feel his heart beating against his rib cage. He glanced around, feeling overwhelmed by the gloom and the smell of old papers and the memories. So much ugliness and sadness.

He'd intended to check out his old room, but instead he turned and grabbed the nearest carton of newspapers. Hefting it, he strode to the entrance and balanced the box on his knee while he opened the front door. Then he strode down the steps and dumped the box by the curb.

He stared at the yellowed newspaper for a beat, then he turned on his heel and went into the house. He crossed into the living room and jerked the curtains open, letting in bright, clean light. He slid the catches free and pushed the window open. He did the same thing with the other window, then he walked into the kitchen and wound the blinds up and pushed that window wide, too.

He returned to the hall, grabbed another box and headed for the curb.

ALLY STOPPED BY THE supermarket on the way home. She was just adding the latest edition of *Country Living* magazine to her shopping basket when she glanced up and saw a familiar blonde head.

"Daniel," she said automatically, taking a step forward.

Immediately she felt ridiculous, because Daniel was in London, thousands of miles away.

The man looked over his shoulder and she murmured an apology. Ducking her head, she made her way to the checkout.

It wasn't the first time she'd thought she'd seen Daniel on the street or in the supermarket. She understood it was guilt, that she still hadn't forgiven herself for leaving and hurting him the way she had. As she paid for her groceries and made her way to her car, she told herself the same thing she always did—she'd done him a kindness in the long-term.

She wondered if he understood that yet.

It's been five years, Bishop. You're probably a faded memory, if that. He's probably married with three kids and a huge mortgage by now.

Strange that the thought made her throat tight when it was everything she knew she didn't want.

She drove home, drowning her thoughts with the car radio. She slowed when she turned onto her street and saw a shiny red pickup parked in her usual spot under the tree.

Tyler's truck, unless she was wildly mistaken. She parked behind him, glancing toward Bob's place. For the first time since she'd been living next door, the curtains were all open, the windows thrown wide. Out the front, half a dozen cardboard boxes were stacked along the curb.

She'd only been in Bob's house twice, once to call the ambulance when he'd collapsed, the second to collect his pajamas and crossword puzzles to make him more comfortable in hospital. Both times she'd been dismayed by the dark rooms and stacks of newspaper and the evidence that he'd been living off canned food and little else. She'd literally itched to do something about all of it—but it hadn't been her place and she'd satisfied herself with disposing of any perishables in the fridge and taking out the garbage.

She gathered her groceries, locked the car and started toward Wendy's front gate. She was fumbling with the latch when she heard heavy footsteps drum on the ancient planks of Bob's porch. Seconds later,

Tyler appeared, a box of newspapers in his arms as he strode up the garden path. He was frowning and his dark hair was ruffled as though he'd been running his fingers through it. He pushed Bob's gate open with his knee, then crossed to the curb. His big biceps muscles bulged as he dropped the box on top of the others. He turned and registered her for the first time.

She felt an odd thud in the pit of her stomach when she met his gaze. She'd been preoccupied during their previous meetings, but in the clear midday light she was struck by the unusual color and clarity of his cool silver-gray eyes.

"Hi," she said.

He nodded his head in silent acknowledgment. Then he headed into the house.

"Wait!"

He paused, one hand on the gate, eyebrows raised, his body angled only slightly toward her.

Not exactly welcoming or encouraging. But she probably deserved not to be welcomed or encouraged, the way she'd lumbered into his life with her preconceived judgments and inexcusable meddling.

"I just wanted to say I was sorry. For yesterday, I mean. I made a lot of judgments based on not a lot of information and it was really out of line for me to read you the riot act the way I did." Her words came out a little rushed, but at least she'd said them.

It took him a moment to respond, and she realized she'd surprised him.

"Don't worry about it."

"But—"

"You were being a good neighbor. I get it."

"Well, yes, but I was also being a horrible busy-body. I get about a hundred letters a week from people making exactly the same mistake, so you'd think I'd know better, but apparently I don't. Apparently I'm as susceptible to do-gooder syndrome as the next person." She offered him a small, self-deprecating smile.

His gaze slid down her body briefly before coming back to her face.

"You're a psychologist?"

She wasn't sure if she should be insulted by the skepticism in his tone or not.

"I'm an advice columnist. I write the Dear Gertrude column in the *Melbourne Herald*."

"Right." He didn't seem very impressed with her profession.

"I see you're having a bit of a clear out," she said, gesturing toward the stacks near the curb.

"Those newspapers are a fire hazard."

There was a preemptive defensiveness to his tone and she guessed that Bob had no idea he was about to lose his newspaper collection.

"Well. Good luck with it," she said. "I hope everything works out okay." She offered him another smile before pushing Wendy's gate open. Once she was safely inside the house, she closed her eyes and groaned.

I hope everything works out okay.

There was only one way things were going to work out. Bob was dying. There was no miracle happy ending to this story.

Rolling her eyes at herself, she carried the groceries to the kitchen and started putting them away.

She'd handled that really well. Not.

She tried to concentrate on work for the rest of the afternoon but it was almost impossible to ignore all the activity next door. Now that the curtains and blinds were open at Bob's house, she had a ringside view into both the kitchen and living room from her customary perch at Wendy's desk in the study. She saw Tyler moving back and forth and back and forth as he worked at clearing Bob's hoard of newspapers. She heard him swear a few times, heard him talking on his phone, his deep voice drifting through the window in indecipherable snatches.

By three, she'd chosen only one letter for her next column and she shut the letters file on her computer with a frustrated sigh. Clearly she was too distracted—unsettled—to work properly. She might as well call it quits for the day.

She logged on to the internet instead and spent the next few hours checking out the latest offerings on her favorite house-sitting site.

She'd been house-sitting for nearly three years now and had a solid history to offer prospective clients, so there was a pretty good chance she had a shot at any job she applied for. Typically, no actual money changed hands—the homeowners provided the accommodation, she ensured their properties and gardens and pets remained in good order. A you-scratch-my-back-and-I'll-scratch-yours kind of deal. To date, the longest span she'd had between jobs was three weeks, and a serviced apartment had provided the necessary stopgap. As far as she was concerned, it was the perfect lifestyle choice, a great solution for a born-and-bred gypsy.

She bookmarked two options that had possibilities—one in Sydney, the other in Brisbane—then shut down the computer and went into the kitchen to stuff and baste the chicken she'd bought for dinner. She could see Tyler moving around Bob's kitchen on the other side of the fence. She watched out of the corner of her eye as he tackled the dishes before turning his attention to the stovetop and oven. Clearly, he was as appalled as she'd been by the way his father had been living.

She frowned as she slid the chicken into the oven. She couldn't work Tyler out. When she'd first accosted him in Melbourne, she'd gained the impression that there was no love lost between father and son. Then he'd shown up at the hospital, and there had been that moment in the parking lot. And now he was clearing out his father's house…

Did we or did we not decide that this was absolutely none of our business and that we'd already grossly overstepped the line with our interfering?

Tearing her gaze from Bob's window, she turned to

grab the tray of potatoes and added them to the oven. Then she settled down to kill an hour with *Country Living* magazine and lots of lovely house interiors.

By seven, the house was filled with the smell of chicken and garlic potatoes. Her stomach rumbled as she put on greens to cook and whisked up some gravy. A bead of sweat trickled down her back and she used her forearm to push her damp hair off her forehead. Roasting a chicken probably hadn't been the smartest choice for such a warm day. She flipped on the air conditioner, then moved to the oven.

Her hands in oven mitts, she grasped the hot pan and pulled the chicken toward herself. The top was golden brown and crispy and she could smell the sage in the stuffing.

"Yum," she murmured.

Suddenly the world went dark.

Ally blinked, aware of the absolute silence around her—no hum from the fridge, no quiet whir from the oven or the air conditioner.

She'd blown a fuse. Damn.

The heat from the roasting pan was starting to burn through the mitts. She pushed the pan forward carefully until she felt it slide into the oven.

She had no idea if Wendy had a flashlight or not, but there was no way she was going to find it in the pitch-black. Arms extended in front of her, she fumbled to the study, where she'd left her phone. The screen came to life when she touched it and she used the light to guide her to the front door. She was pretty sure she'd seen a fuse box on the porch beside the door, the old-fashioned kind with a hinged wooden cover…

And there it was. *Phew.*

She found the catch and opened the cover, squinting in the feeble light from her phone as she tried to read the writing on the various fuses. This wasn't like the more modern trip-switch fuse boxes she was used to in the city. This was old school, with big ceramic plugs and what looked like fuse wire.

"Problem?" a voice asked out of nowhere.

She let out a little yelp and started so violently she nearly dropped the phone.

She pressed her free hand to her chest as she glanced over her shoulder. Tyler stood at the front gate, his face a study in shadows in the dim streetlight.

"You scared me," she said stupidly.

"No kidding." His tone was very dry. He gestured toward the fuse box. "Looks like you've blown something."

"I think I overloaded it having the air conditioner and oven on at the same time."

"Happens sometimes with these old places."

"I don't suppose you have a flashlight I could borrow?" she asked hopefully.

He didn't respond, simply turned on his heel and walked toward his pickup. Twenty seconds later, he pushed open Wendy's gate, a strong flashlight beam bouncing along the path in front of him.

Maybe it was because it was dark, but he seemed much bigger than she remembered as he climbed the two steps to the porch and stopped in front of her. She fought a ridiculous urge to take a step backward.

"Thanks for this. I really appreciate it," she said, holding out her hand for the flashlight.

He ignored her, brushing past her to aim the flashlight beam at the fuses.

She frowned. "I don't want to take up your time."

She made a policy of trying to solve her own problems without relying on the kindness of strangers. It was something she'd learned early in life.

"This fuse box is pretty old," he said.

"I'm sure I can work it out."

He glanced at her, his expression unreadable. "Don't tell me you're one of those feminists."

"'Fraid so. I'm happy to borrow a flashlight, but I'm not a damsel in distress."

He regarded her a moment, then he shrugged and passed her the flashlight. She waited for him to leave, but he simply stood to one side and waved a hand, inviting her into the prime position in front of the box.

"Thank you," she said, not feeling very grateful. She didn't particularly want to fumble around in front of him. Especially when she'd made such a big deal about fending for herself.

She aimed the flashlight, trying to appear as though she knew what she was doing. According to her sketchy memory of how these old systems worked, she was supposed to pull the fuses out to check which one had a broken wire. She reached to check the first one.

"It won't be that one. That's your lighting."

He had a shoulder against the house, his arms crossed over his chest. He looked as though he was enjoying himself.

"It's worth checking them all," she said stubbornly.

"If it makes you feel better."

She grit her teeth and pulled the fuse out. The wire was noticeably still intact and she plugged it in without comment.

"All good?"

"Yes," she said grudgingly. Maybe she would have been better off fumbling around for a candle and going to bed early after all.

"Only five more to go," he said encouragingly.

She shone the flashlight in his face.

"Smugness is really not an attractive trait, you know."

He pushed her hand down so that the beam was angled toward his chest.

"Neither is stubbornness."

They stared at each other a moment, neither giving an inch. Then she sighed and passed him the flashlight.

"Okay. Help me if you must."

"Only because you asked so nicely."

Instantly she felt rude and stupid. He'd come to

her aid, and instead of thanking him she was coming across as a prickly ingrate.

"Sorry. I guess I'm used to fending for myself."

"I can tell. Excuse me."

He moved closer to the fuse box and she took a hasty step backward, but not before she'd bumped against his hard shoulder. He'd been working all afternoon in the heat and he smelled of deodorant and clean sweat. Intensely masculine.

She crossed her arms over her chest. "What do you think it is?" she asked.

"There's a main fuse in here, usually it takes a higher gauge wire than the others…" He pulled a fuse out and inspected it. "Yeah."

"It's that one?"

"Yeah. You've overloaded the main."

"Stupid roasted chicken."

"It was probably the air conditioner."

"Can you fix it?"

"Depends."

He shone the flashlight around the fuse box, then ran his hand along the top shelf. He came away with nothing but dust and cobwebs.

"No spare fuse wire."

"Right." She thought for a minute. "The shops are probably already closed. So I guess that means I'm having an early night."

She spared a thought for the food in Wendy's freezer. Maybe if she didn't disturb it overnight, it wouldn't spoil.

"Hang on a moment."

She was left blinking in the darkness as Tyler left the porch and headed next door. She guessed he was checking his father's place for spare wire and she crossed her fingers. She watched Tyler expectantly as he climbed the steps to rejoin her. He didn't say a word, simply held up a small piece of card with fine wire wrapped around it.

"Bless you, Bob," she said fervently.

"Yeah." There was a dry undertone to the single word and she was reminded of the scene she'd witnessed this morning at the hospital.

Hard to imagine this big, capable man reduced to tears. But he had been. He'd been profoundly affected by his visit to his father.

"Can you hold the light steady for me?"

She trained the beam on his hands as he threaded new wire into the fuse. She took the opportunity to study his profile. He had a bump in his nose as though maybe he'd broken it at some stage, and a strong, square jaw. His dark hair was short and rumpled, and whiskers shadowed the lower half of his face. She could discern a thin scar on his cheekbone, below the corner of his left eye. She wondered how he'd gotten it. Fighting? A car accident?

She'd thought he was focused on the fuse, but he glanced up suddenly and his gaze locked with hers. She looked away quickly, feeling her face heat with embarrassment.

Busted, big-time.

"You might want to turn the air-conditioning off before I turn the power back on. Just in case," he said.

"Right. Of course."

She slipped into the house, feeling her way along the wall with one arm extended. She was only steps from the kitchen when her shin connected with something hard and heavy.

"Shit!" she hissed, bending to rub her aching shin.

"All right in there?" Tyler called.

"Yeah."

She reached out a hand and felt the lumpy metal outline of Wendy's umbrella stand. She stepped around it and entered the kitchen. She found the wall switch to turn off the air-conditioning, then crossed to the oven and turned that off for good measure. Then she made her way back to the porch.

"Houston, we are cleared to launch."

"Roger that." He plugged in the fuse and flipped the switch. She gave a little cheer as Wendy's cottage came back to life.

"Just like magic."

"Something like that."

He switched off the flashlight and collected his father's wire before shutting the fuse box.

"You should probably get an electrician in to update this setup," he said. "With a modern fuse, you'd only have to flip a switch to reset the power."

"I'll get on to it." She made a mental note to

mention it to Wendy during their next Skype chat. "I really appreciate your help."

"No worries." He started down the porch steps.

She watched his broad shoulders as he walked toward the gate, wondering if he ever waxed eloquent about anything.

Probably not. He struck her as being the strong, silent type.

"Have you eaten?" she called after him.

For the second time that day, he stopped and glanced over his shoulder at her.

"Sorry?"

"Have you eaten? I have a whole roast chicken inside and, even at my piggiest, I couldn't possibly eat it all…"

He hesitated, a slight frown forming between his eyebrows.

"Think of it as a barter, a drumstick in return for the loan of your flashlight and expertise," she said. "There are potatoes, too, and gravy."

She wasn't sure why she trying so hard to convince him. If he wasn't hungry, he wasn't hungry.

"Chicken sounds good. Give me a moment to wash up."

He disappeared through the front gate before she could say anything.

She returned to the kitchen and grabbed a second plate. The chicken hadn't had time to cool, but she set the heat beneath the greens on high to bring them back to the boil. The water was starting to bubble when she heard footsteps on the porch.

"Come in," she called.

His hair was damp and he was holding a six-pack of beer in one hand when he appeared in the doorway.

"Dad doesn't run to wine, I'm afraid."

"Beer's perfect. Although I have wine if you want it."

"I'll stick with the beer, thanks. Got to drive to Melbourne tonight."

"Sure."

She served the meal, very aware of him watching her every move. She paused when she was about to pour the gravy. Being a gravy lover, she liked it everywhere, but some people weren't so fond. "You like a little or a lot?" she asked.

"A lot. Can't have too much of a good thing."

A very vivid, very earthy image popped into her mind. She concentrated on pouring the sauce over his chicken and vegetables but she could feel heat climbing into her cheeks again.

Two blushes in twenty minutes. Apparently she was turning into a born-again virgin in her old age.

Get a grip, Bishop. Anyone would think you'd never had a meal with a man before.

"We can eat outside or in here."

"It'll be cooler outside," he said.

"Outside it is, then."

She led the way through the French doors and

onto the deck. They settled on opposite sides of the table. He twisted the top off a beer and placed it in front of her, then did the same for himself while she distributed the cutlery.

"Well," she said. "Enjoy."

She sliced off some chicken and potato and took a bite. He did the same and there was a short silence as they both chewed.

"You're a pretty good cook for a feminist."

She choked on her mouthful.

He gave her an innocent look. "Sorry. Was that politically incorrect?"

She reached for her beer and took a big swallow. Then she pointed the neck of her bottle at him.

"You're lucky I'm not one of those gun-toting members of the sisterhood or you'd be in big trouble right now."

"Would I?" His eyes crinkled at the corners as he looked at her.

Apparently Tyler found her amusing. Which was a little disconcerting, since she'd just made a rather startling discovery—he was a very attractive man. Somehow she'd managed to overlook that fact until now. With his dark hair and unusual silver-gray eyes, that bump in his nose and the decisive shape of his jaw and forehead, he was easily the best-looking man she'd shared a meal with in a long time.

Then there was his body.

Broad, hard, lean, with the kind of muscles that

came from doing things in the real world rather than pumping iron in the gym.

She dragged her gaze from him and concentrated on her meal, suddenly very aware of the fact that she'd pulled on her cowboy-and-Indian pajama pants when she came home from the supermarket and that she wasn't wearing a scrap of makeup.

Not exactly femme-fatale material.

Not that she was in the market to slay any man with her charms, such as they were, but a woman had her pride.

"So, how does a person become an advice columnist?" he asked.

"By accident. I was doing a column on travel destinations and they needed someone to fill in for Dear Gertrude when the writer who'd been doing it for years got sick. I did it for a couple of weeks, she decided to retire and they offered me the gig."

"You said your column's in the *Herald,* right?" he asked.

"Yup." It was also syndicated to a bunch of other papers, but he didn't need to know that.

"So people write in and tell you about all their problems and you solve them?"

"People write in with *a* problem and I attempt to offer them my objective opinion. Sometimes an outsider's point of view gives people a new perspective."

"I suppose you tell all your women readers to change their own tires and tote their own luggage?"

"You know, I do. I happen to be a big believer in personal responsibility. How about you?"

A slow grin spread across his face and she realized he'd risen to his bait without blinking. "Enjoying urself?" she asked.

He made a show of stopping to think about it. "The ken is good."

hank you."

e beer is cold."

os to Bob."

you do rise to the bait pretty quickly."

rowed her eyes. "You're one of those people nk practical jokes are funny, aren't you?"

Guilty as charged, Your Honor."

She couldn't hide her smile. No way would she have ever guessed that the man she'd confronted yesterday and run into this morning was capable of lighthearted teasing.

"So how does a person become a furniture designer?"

He shrugged and took a mouthful of his beer. "He's crap at math and English and science and he wants to leave school as quickly as possible."

She blinked at the harshness of his self-assessment. "Well, you clearly did something right."

"I know how to work hard. And I was lucky enough to have a great boss when I finally scored an apprenticeship. Taught me everything I know."

She studied the man sitting across from her. He was modest almost to the point of self-denigration, yet he was clearly a driven person. She'd seen his workshop in Melbourne—no one could build a business the size of T.A. Furniture Design without having a fire in their belly and the smarts to harness it. She was confused by the apparent contradiction. All t self-made, driven men she'd met had been ego niacs, more than happy to shove their achievem down the throat of anyone who was stupid e to inquire.

It made her wonder, which in turn made l about Bob and all she knew, and didn't kn her neighbor and his son.

None of your business, Bishop. Remembe

"Do you want another beer?" she asked, notic his bottle was empty.

"No, thanks."

She went to collect a second bottle for herself, bringing him a glass of water.

"Thanks."

She racked her brain for a safe topic of conversation. Obviously, Bob was out. Too many pitfalls and unknowns there.

"There's ice cream for dessert," she said after a short silence.

Not exactly a sparkling conversational gambit, but a nice neutral topic nonetheless.

"Yeah?" There was an arrested look in Tyler's eyes. "What flavor?"

"Honey macadamia and New York Cheesecake."

"That's got to be Charmaine's," he said, naming

one of Melbourne's smaller boutique ice cream manufacturers.

She was impressed. "You know your ice creams."

The reason she knew this was because she, too, knew her ice creams. In fact, she had what her friends commonly referred to as a substance-abuse problem where the stuff was concerned.

"Have you tried their chili chocolate?" he asked.

"Yes. Have you tried the Peanut Nutter at Trampoline?" she asked, naming another ice cream parlor.

"Of course. But it's not as good as the cookies-and-cream gelati at this little place—"

"Near the corner of Rathdowne and Lygon streets in Carlton," she finished for him.

He sat back in his chair. "You know about Rafael's."

"I do."

"So if I say the words *almond biscotti…*"

"I'd know you were talking about Antica Gelateria del Corso, flagship store on Collins Street in the city."

They eyed each other for a speculative beat, then spoke simultaneously.

"Favorite flavor ever?"

They both laughed. Ally felt a little pinch low in her belly as she looked into his smiling face. Brooding and taciturn, this man was attractive. Laughing, he about took her breath away.

"You first," he said.

"Hmm…" She propped an elbow on the table while she pondered, very aware of her pulse tripping away at a faster than normal rate. "I'm going to go small and exclusive and homemade. My friend Craig made chocolate-and-lavender ice cream for my birthday last year. I swear, it was a religious experience."

"Full cream?"

"Double cream. Couverture chocolate. French lavender. I ate so much I was sick. The kicker is that he didn't write down the recipe, just threw stuff into the ice cream maker."

"It was a one-off?"

"For one night only." She sat back and crossed her legs. "Your turn."

His gaze drifted beyond her shoulder as he thought it over. She took a mouthful of beer. A warm breeze tickled the back of her neck and the cicadas sang to each other, their music a constant in the background.

"There's this place in Florence," he said after a short silence.

"Italy? You're pulling out the big guns. Going international on me."

His mouth quirked at the corner. "I am. This place is down a little cobbled street, hard to find. They only use fresh ingredients, so their sorbets are seasonal."

"I love a good sorbet."

"The sorbets are good, but they make this amazing

orange cake gelati… It's like eating a piece of orange poppy seed cake. Only better."

"Because it's ice cream."

"Yes."

There was a moment of contemplative, reverential silence. Then Ally laughed and fanned herself with her hand.

"Wow. I almost need a cigarette after that."

A slow grin curled his mouth. For a moment she forgot how and why they'd met, forgot that he'd spent the day clearing out his father's house, and that she'd held his father's hand at the hospital this morning. It was a warm, balmy night and she had alcohol warming the pit of her stomach and the world seemed ripe with possibilities.

It was just her, and him.

The sound of a phone ringing cut through the loaded silence. She blinked, and Tyler reached for his hip pocket.

"Sorry. It's probably work."

He flipped his phone open and took the call.

"Tyler speaking."

It was impossible to miss the way his face and body tensed as he listened to his caller.

"But he's okay now?"

She stilled. It had to be the hospital.

"I understand. Do you need me to come down there?"

She gripped the edge of the table. Surely Bob hadn't…?

"So he'll probably sleep through the night now?"

She relaxed a notch. Bob was alive, then. But clearly something was going on.

Tyler half turned away from her and she stacked their plates, then took them inside to give him some privacy.

She fussed in the kitchen, banging dishes and roasting pans to let him know she wasn't eavesdropping. She was taking the lids off the ice cream tubs when Tyler entered. His gaze took in the bowls on the counter as he slid his phone into his hip pocket.

"I might take a pass on dessert, if you don't mind. There are some things I need to take care of. Thanks for the meal, I appreciate it."

"Not a problem. And it was a barter, not a favor, remember?"

He didn't so much as twitch his lips at her small joke.

"Is everything okay?" she asked quietly. "Is Bob okay?"

"He's fine. He got a little wound up about something, and they had to give him a sedative."

She bit her tongue before she could ask more. Clearly, he didn't want to talk about it. And she'd already overstepped.

"I can make your ice cream to go if you'd like."

"Thanks, but I don't want to cut into your stash."

Let it go, Bishop. The man clearly wants to get out of here.

She followed him to the door. They faced each other across the threshold.

He looked tired all of a sudden, the lines around his mouth and eyes more deeply etched. A small frown wrinkled the skin between his eyebrows.

"Thanks for helping with the fuse."

"It was no big deal."

"Those of us who are once again experiencing the joys of electricity beg to differ."

He mustered a small, distracted smile. "I'll see you around."

She stood in the doorway until he'd disappeared next door. Then she went back to the kitchen. The ice cream had gone soft around the edges. She put the lids on and returned both tubs to the freezer.

She went out to the deck and collected their empty bottles, pulling the French doors shut behind herself when she entered the house. She put the dishes in the dishwasher, packed away the leftovers.

And still she felt restless and edgy and itchy and scratchy.

Relax. You'll probably never see him again, Bishop.

Which was a good thing, because instinct told her that Tyler Adamson wasn't the easy-come-easy-go kind of lover she'd been limiting herself to the past few years. In fact, instinct told her that there was nothing easy or forgettable about the man at all.

She considered that moment toward the end of their dinner when she'd made the joke about needing a cigarette and he'd looked into her eyes and she'd known, absolutely, that they were both thinking about things a lot hotter than ice cream.

Definitely it would be a good thing if she never saw him again.

Crossing to the French doors, she called Mr. Whiskers in from the garden. Then she took herself to bed.

CHAPTER THREE

TYLER THREW THE PILLOW on the couch and sat to untie the laces on his work boots. Despite the fact that the windows had been open all day and he'd cleared out all the moldering newspapers, the room still smelled faintly of must and dust.

Awesome.

By rights, he should be halfway to Melbourne by now. Halfway to his own place and his own bed and his own life. Instead, he was preparing to spend the night on the couch in his parents' house.

He could have bunked in his old room, of course. He'd pushed open the door this afternoon and seen that his single bed was still shoved up against the wall in the corner, even though every other trace of his presence had been eradicated, down to the initials he'd carved in the window ledge.

His father would have had to fill and sand and paint the ledge to remove those initials. Several hours work, no small thing.

The house was still warm after the heat of the day and he stripped down to his boxer-briefs and stretched out on the couch. His feet hung over the arm and something hard pressed into his back.

He rolled onto his side. The couch might be uncomfortable, but it was better than being in that little closet of a room, fighting off too many bad memories.

About a million times better.

He closed his eyes, but his mind was full of the phone conversation he'd just had with the nurse on his father's ward.

"Your father has expressed himself quite vehemently, Mr. Adamson," Sister Kemp said. "He wants to go home to die."

Apparently they'd sicced the social worker on his father this afternoon to talk about his plans for the future and at the first mention of a hospice his father had started raising hell and hadn't stopped until they'd fed something into his I.V. to calm him down.

"We'll be having a meeting to discuss his situation tomorrow morning and it would be helpful if a member of the family could be present," Sister Kemp had explained.

It wasn't as though Tyler had had any option except to agree to be there, hence the necessity to stay the night. Like it or not, Robert Adamson was his father. His responsibility. Even if they were as distant as strangers.

The phone call had destroyed the small oasis of pleasure he'd found in the evening. Talking with Ally Bishop, laughing with her, had been the highlight of his day. Hands down.

He thought about the way she'd bristled when he stepped in to fix her fuse box and despite everything—the shitty couch, the knowledge that staying overnight would put him even further behind at work, the fact that he could feel himself getting sucked into a situation he wanted nothing to do with—he smiled. She was a feisty piece of work, that was for sure. Pretty funny, since she barely came up to his armpit and looked about as fierce as a puppy.

She was a smart lady. Straight-up, too. He appreciated the way she'd seized the bull by the horns and apologized to him this afternoon. She'd looked him in the eye and humbled herself with no excuses.

Hard not to admire that.

Or the way she'd diplomatically steered clear of the subject of his father all evening. He didn't know what his father had told her about their relationship—didn't want to know, either—but he appreciated the way she'd given him some breathing room.

Why don't you go ahead and admit how much you appreciated the way she filled out her tank top, too?

It was true. He'd noticed that his father's next-door neighbor had nice breasts. Full, but not too big. A good, firm handful, if he was any judge. He'd also noticed that she had the sort of mouth that was used to smiling and a round, curvy little behind that bounced ever so slightly when she walked.

So, not so much a righteous elf, then. More a sexy,

cute one. With feminist leanings and a love of ice cream.

His smile faded as his thoughts circled to his father again. He'd committed himself to tomorrow's meeting, and he could distract himself all he wanted but it wasn't going to make any difference to the decision that lay ahead.

He rolled onto his back and folded his arms behind his head. It was going to be a long night.

Ten hours later, Tyler exited the Kyneton District Hospital family meeting room and glanced around to get his bearings. He had a pocketful of paperwork and business cards and what felt like the weight of the world on his shoulders.

Spotting a sign indicating reception was to his right, he started walking. A few minutes later, he stopped outside his father's room.

He'd just listened to two nurses, a doctor and the social worker explain the likely progression of his father's disease. They'd talked about palliative care and the facilities available locally, and they'd talked about the kind of support his father would need if he was to go home to die, as he'd requested.

The reality was, while the government could provide some support for at-home care, they couldn't cover it all. If his father was to go home, Tyler would need to get involved. He'd need to hire a private nurse, sort out his father's cooking-and-cleaning requirements, manage his medical treatment. And if that was a task he wasn't prepared to take on, Robert Adamson would be forced into a hospice against his will.

It would be the ultimate revenge. Walking away and letting his father reap what he had sown—a faceless, nameless death in a state institution, the ideal punishment for a man who had withheld affection and compassion and understanding from his own children. If ever Tyler had wanted to pay back his father for the beatings, the denigration, the lack of interest, the small-mindedness, this was his moment.

Tyler took the final step through his father's doorway. Robert was sleeping and Tyler walked quietly to his side. His father's complexion was pale and his breathing seemed labored. His eyelids flickered as he slept.

Tyler wondered what his father dreamed about, if he dreamed at all. Tyler preferred not to dream, although usually it wasn't a matter of choice. His least-favorite recurring nightmare was the one where his father tortured his and Jon's dog, Astro, to teach Tyler a lesson.

Tyler had been late getting home for dinner, an offense that usually led to a dressing down and a cuff over the ear or a few hits with the belt. But this time his father had simply given him a long, hard look before resuming eating his meal. At first Tyler had been relieved that his father had said nothing. Then he'd been scared.

The next day, his father waited until Tyler was

about to head off to school before backing the car very deliberately over Astro's tail as the dog lay sleeping in a sunny spot beside the driveway.

The dog had yelped with pain, its cries high-pitched and disturbing. His father only rolled the car forward after Tyler had tearfully begged for forgiveness and promised never to be late again.

As usual, there had been precious little sympathy from his mother. "Every action has a consequence," she'd said. "Perhaps now you won't be so quick to be inconsiderate of others."

Tyler had waited a week, then he'd smuggled the dog out of the yard and given him to one of his friends from school. He'd told his parents that he'd left the gate open. He'd been punished for being careless, and Jon had hated him for taking away the one source of love and comfort in their lives, but it was the only way he'd seen to protect his beloved pet.

He'd been eight years old.

Familiar anger and outrage burned in Tyler's gut. As an adult, he could appreciate how masterful his father's choice of punishment had been. What he couldn't understand was the cold calculation that had been behind the act. What kind of man invested time and energy in devising ways to torture his children?

Tyler's hands fisted.

Tell me why I should do this for you, old man. Give me one good reason why I should turn my life upside down so that you can have some peace.

His father stirred in his sleep. The heart monitor kept up its steady rhythm.

Tyler tried to dredge up one good memory. One moment that wasn't infused with fear or disappointment or anger.

A Christmas came to him, hazy, tinted in sepia tones. Wrapping paper everywhere, his mother smiling indulgently for once instead of worrying about keeping everything clean and tidy. There'd been a present, a big one, a combined gift for him and Jon. They'd torn the paper off to find a ride-on wooden train, complete with coal truck and two carriages. The engine had been a shiny cherry-red, the coal truck glossy black, the wheels tricked out in yellow. His father had watched, an expectant light in his eye, soaking up their delight as they ran their hands over their prize and started arguing over who would have the first ride.

"Your father's been putting that together in the shed for the past month," their mother had explained.

Tyler couldn't remember what had happened next. Had they thanked their father? Had they been surprised by such generosity from a man they'd already learned to regard with caution?

He had no idea.

His father stirred again, shifting on the pillow. His face creased with pain and he murmured something beneath his breath. His eyes opened and Tyler met his cloudy gaze.

"I thought you went back to town," his father said.

"The hospital called me last night."

His father's gaze slid over Tyler's shoulder. He was embarrassed, Tyler realized.

"It's my life. Should be my death, too. Anybody would have gotten upset."

"You want to go home."

"They said they wouldn't let me. That they'd get in trouble if they sent me home alone. But I don't need anybody. Been looking after myself for years. Anyway, it's none of their business."

Tyler could hear the desperation in his father's voice. It made his gut tight. Funny, but he'd almost prefer his father yell at him. Seeing him scared like this, beaten... It messed with his vision of the world too much.

"I've got some stuff to sort out in Melbourne, but I'll be back to make arrangements for you. Someone to come in to cook for you and look after the cleaning. And a nurse to manage your medical care. The hospital wants to assess the house, too. Make sure there's good access and that the bathroom's safe for you to use. But if we can cover off the other stuff, they say you're good to go."

"You mean, I can go home? They won't make me stay here?" His father sounded as though he was afraid to hope.

"Yeah, Dad. You can go home."

Tyler waited for him to say something—anything— but he didn't. He simply stared at Tyler for a long moment. Then he blinked and a single tear slid from the corner of his eye and down his cheek onto the pillow.

Tyler looked away.

"The nurses have my number. Call me if you need anything. I'll be back on Monday."

He didn't wait for a reply, simply headed for the door.

There was nothing more to say, after all. He was doing the right thing. Being a dutiful son.

Three cheers for him.

"HERE HE IS. STILL ALIVE and purring. Still shedding on the couch and licking his privates at every opportunity," Ally said.

The large tabby cat in her arms squirmed, trying to escape, but Ally kept him positioned in front of the built-in camera on her laptop. Wendy smiled and waved from inside the frame on the computer screen.

"There's my baby. How you doin', little guy? You missing your mommy? You missing me, buddy?"

Ally cleared her throat. "Um. Do you want me to leave you two alone for a minute…?"

"Shut up. Just because I love my pet."

"You should go the whole hog and have a baby. Stop kidding yourself," Ally said.

"A cat is not a baby substitute," Wendy said.

"You're right. A baby would be less trouble. And he wouldn't leave fur everywhere."

"Says the footloose and fancy-free Ms. Bishop."

The doorbell rang, echoing down the hallway. Ally wheeled the chair back from the desk.

"There's someone at the front door," she said. "It might be the postman with that parcel you're waiting on. Give me a tick to check…"

She left the study, her bare feet padding softly on the wide, worn floorboards. She pulled the door open, expecting to see a blue uniform and a clipboard for her to sign. Instead, she found herself staring at a broad, muscular chest covered in a black cotton T-shirt.

"You're back," she said as she lifted her gaze to Tyler's face.

"It's a long story." He offered her a tight smile, his silver-gray eyes unreadable. "Do you have a minute?"

"I do. At least, I will have. I'm just finishing up a Skype call. But I won't be a sec." She gestured for him to come inside, then hustled down the hallway. She was aware of him shutting the door and following her before she ducked into the study.

"Wendy, gotta go. I'll catch you later, okay?"

"All right, but don't forget to give Mr. Whiskers his flea stuff. And he's due for his worming tablet. You might have to hide it in his dinner to get him to eat it."

"I can handle it, don't worry," Ally said. After three years of wrangling other people's pets, she was an expert at stroking throats and hiding pills in food.

"Speak soon, okay?" she said.

She clicked the mouse to end the call and turned to find Tyler standing in the doorway, a slight frown on his face as he scanned the spines of the many accounting and finance manuals on her friend's bookshelf.

"Sorry about that," she said.

Tyler shifted his attention to her. "You've got a lot of business books for an advice columnist."

She laughed. "They're not mine. God, no. I can barely add two and two. They're Wendy's. I'm house-sitting for her while she's away."

"So this isn't your place?"

"Nope."

His frown deepened.

"Would you like a coffee?" she asked.

"That'd be great, thanks."

She led him into the kitchen and filled the kettle at the sink. She hadn't expected to see him again. Or at least not so soon. She told herself that was why she was feeling a little skittish and self-conscious.

"Did you see Bob this morning? How's he doing?"

"He's good. A little slow to shake off whatever they gave him last night, but otherwise he seemed okay."

"Oh, good. Do you think he'll be up for a visit again this afternoon?" She grabbed two mugs and opened the fridge, searching for the milk.

"Sure."

She studied him over the open fridge door, noting the way he was standing so stiffly. Like a customer in a coffee shop. He'd indicated he wanted to talk, but she had the feeling that she might be waiting all day if she let him work his way around to the purpose of his visit.

She shut the fridge and regarded him frankly.

"Would it help any if I said that whatever it is, I'm happy to help?"

He looked a little taken aback for a moment. Then he rubbed the back of his neck self-consciously. "I'm that obvious, am I?"

"Let's just say you should never play high-stakes poker."

"Thanks for the tip."

"Is it something to do with Bob? Please don't tell me you want me to break it to him that his newspaper collection is gone."

"Dad wants to come home."

She swallowed as the implications inherent in that one small statement hit home.

"I told him I'd arrange things to make it happen, and I can sort out a nurse and someone to handle his meals and things from Melbourne. But the social worker wants to assess the house before she'll agree to discharge him. I've got commitments I can't get out of in town, so…" He pulled a key from the hip pocket of his jeans. "I wondered if you would mind letting her in so she can check the place out and give me her recommendations?"

Ally guessed from the mention of various support staff that Tyler did not plan on nursing his father himself. From what she'd seen of the distance between father and son, she wasn't surprised. In fact, after what she'd seen in the parking lot yesterday, she was surprised Tyler was here at all.

"I can take care of that for you. Not a problem."

"Thanks. I appreciate it."

She held out her hand and he dropped the key into it. The brass was warm from his body and she closed her fingers around it. "Is that all? You don't want to borrow money or ask me to perjure myself on your behalf or bury a body in my backyard?"

It took him a moment to understand she was joking.

"No."

"The way you were looking, I was sure you were about to ask for a vital organ."

"I guess you could say I'm not in the habit of asking favors," he said slowly.

"No kidding. For future reference, I like your father, I'm here during the day and I'm happy to help out in any way I can. Okay?"

He nodded.

"Does that mean you'll ask if there's anything else you or Bob need?"

"Sure," he said, although his posture and the tension in his face told her otherwise.

She shook her head. "Seriously. You should never play cards for money."

His mouth kicked up at the corner. At last. A little more schtick and she might even squeeze a full smile out of him. Why that seemed so important all of a sudden she didn't know, but it did.

"Milk? Sugar?" The kettle was boiling and she poured water into the coffee press.

"Black, thanks."

"Ah, a purist."

"More a pragmatist. The guys at work go through milk like it's going out of fashion, so I figured life would be a lot less disappointing if I got used to having my coffee black."

"That *is* very pragmatic of you. Me, I'd throw a hissy fit until they learned to leave some milk for the boss."

"It's kind of hard for anyone over six foot to pull off a hissy fit. In my experience, anyway."

"True. I hadn't thought of that."

She slid his coffee across the counter toward him. Their fingers brushed briefly as the mug changed hands. She looked up—and got caught in the clear, bright silver of his eyes.

"Has anyone ever told you you have wolf's eyes?" she said before she could stop herself.

He lifted his eyebrows. "Wolf's eyes?"

"The color, I mean," she said, feeling incredibly transparent. "Obviously they're not really hairy or anything."

He took a sip of his coffee. "Can't say that I've heard that before, no."

"Well, now you know."

"Yeah."

His gaze dropped from her face to her chest, then her hips, taking in her Penelope Pitstop pajama pants and matching pink tank top.

"What happened to the cowboys and Indians?"

"Oh, they're after-five wear only. I like to go a little more low-key during the day."

"Ah."

She looked at him over the rim of her mug and her eyes met his and suddenly it was last night all over again, the room crackling with tension and potential. Except this time he wasn't here by accident, and she knew she would definitely be seeing him again.

"Cookies. We need cookies." She crossed to the cupboard, making a big deal out of opening a package of cookies. She didn't quite meet his eyes when she slid the container across the counter toward him.

"I'm good, thanks."

She picked up the tea towel and wiped the counter.

It was just a look, Bishop. Get over it. Hot men have looked at you before. You'll survive.

But none of them had been as…compelling as Tyler.

"Any idea when the hospital people might want to come by?" she asked.

They talked about the appointment and exchanged phone numbers, then Tyler checked his watch and put down his mug.

"I need to go. I've got a client meeting I have to make this afternoon."

She followed him to the front door.

"I should be here again by Monday at the latest," he said.

"Okay. Like I said, call me if you need anything."

He raised his hand in farewell. She told herself to go inside but she remained in the doorway, watching his broad shoulders and firm, round backside as he walked away. He glanced over his shoulder as he passed through the gate, catching her watching him.

Again, their gazes locked and held for a long, sticky beat. Then he kept walking.

Okay, that's going to be a problem.

Last night, the attraction she'd felt for Tyler had been a slightly titillating surprise—a diversion from the mundanity of life, an unexpected blip on her radar. They'd been ships passing in the night, the frisson between them a possibility that had come to nothing. Today...

Today the attraction between them seemed more complicated than titillating.

What's the problem? Nothing is going to happen if you don't want it to.

She knew it was true. And yet, somehow, it wasn't as comforting a thought as it should be.

TYLER ARRIVED AT THE workshop in time to make his client meeting. Afterward, he went straight to his office and checked his schedule for the following week. His diary was full—client meetings, a marketing seminar, a catch-up with one of his major lumber suppliers. For the life of him he didn't see how he could free up enough time to sort out his father's situation. He had an elbow on his desk, his fingers kneading his forehead when Gabby rapped on the door and entered.

"You forgot these," she said, holding up the rolled blueprints from their meeting.

"Thanks," he said. "You were great in the meeting, too, by the way."

She shrugged. "You'd be surprised how much I've picked up being around you guys. I think I could practically make a table myself now."

She turned to leave. Tyler looked at the schedule he'd massacred with red pen and pencil strikes and arrows. He'd been trying to find a way to free up some time, hadn't he?

"Gabby. Before you go."

She gave him an inquiring look.

"How would you feel about taking on more client meetings? Stepping into sales more?"

She looked surprised. "What's brought this on?"

"I need some time off. At least from the day-to-day stuff. I can take the briefs with me, keep working on the designs, but I can't keep driving back and forth all the time."

Gabby frowned, confused. "Sorry?"

Tyler realized he'd skipped an important beat.

"My father wants to be home to die. I told him I'd organize things so that could happen, but I need to be in Woodend to do that in the short-term—"

"Oh, Tyler. That's so sad. I didn't realize things were that serious. Are you okay?"

He shrugged. "Of course."

"There's no *of course* about it. He's your father."

Tyler made a pointless mark on the page in front of him. "In name only."

Gabby shook her head. "You drive me crazy, you know that?"

She rounded the desk and put her arms around him, resting her cheek against his. For a moment he was enveloped in her scent, still familiar despite the fact that it had been two years since they'd been lovers.

His thoughts shifted to Ally. He'd caught a trace of her scent when she'd brushed past him this morning. Vanilla and spice. Completely different from Gabby's lemon freshness.

This wasn't the first time his thoughts had drifted to his father's next-door neighbor today. He'd thought about her on and off during the drive to Melbourne. The way her eyes lit when she laughed. The round fullness of her breasts. The look they'd shared when he'd glanced over his shoulder as he was leaving and caught her watching him.

"It's not a crime to accept a little comfort, Tyler," Gabby said as she stepped back from him.

"I don't need comfort. I need time. Do you think you can do it or not?"

"I might have to juggle some of the admin stuff, but I don't see why not. How many weeks do you need?"

"I only need a few days."

Gabby looked stricken. "He's that bad?"

"They don't know. It could be weeks, it could be months."

"Then maybe we should think more long-term than a week so—"

"I'm getting him a nurse. I just need some time to get things organized, that's all." How many times did he have to say this to people?

"You're not staying with him yourself?" He could hear the censure in her tone.

"No."

Gabby looked as though she wanted to say more, but after a long moment she simply nodded, her lips thin. "It's your life, Tyler. Tell me what you need me to do and I'll do it."

"Thanks. I'll draw up a list of appointments for you."

She nodded, then exited his office.

He knew what she was thinking—that he was cold because he planned on hiring people to nurse his father in his final days.

Maybe he *was* cold. Why not? He'd been taught by a master. Why should he know the first thing about being kind when all he'd been fed as a child was intolerance, impatience and rage?

For the first time it occurred to him that there had been no judgment in Ally's face or voice when he'd told her his plans this morning. She'd simply heard him out and offered her help.

She was an interesting woman. Generous, too—he'd been surprised when he'd learned she'd been living beside his father for only a few weeks. She'd been so fired up on his father's behalf, he'd simply assumed their relationship was one of long standing.

He frowned as he registered what he was doing—thinking about his father's neighbor again.

He couldn't decide if it was a good thing or a bad thing. Obviously he was attracted to her. But he wasn't exactly in a position to get involved with anyone or anything right now. Thanks to his father, his cup was about to runneth over.

Which probably meant he should stop thinking about her. And that he should keep his distance when he returned to Woodend.

He returned his attention to his diary. Reality check—he didn't have the time to be thinking about a woman. Even one as interesting and attractive as Ally Bishop.

CHAPTER FOUR

THE SOCIAL WORKER CAME the following day. Ally showed the woman around Bob's house, took note of her recommendations, then made a couple of quick phone calls before pulling Tyler's business card from where she'd stuck it behind a magnet on the fridge door.

She ran her fingertips over the embossed lettering on the card, thinking about his silver-gray eyes and broad shoulders, then she punched his number into her phone.

"Tyler speaking."

His voice sounded incredibly deep and low over the phone.

"It's me, Ally. The social worker's just been."

"That was quick."

"She said she didn't want to hold things up at her end."

A weary sigh came down the line. "Which means Dad's probably been throwing his weight around again."

"He seemed okay when I saw him this morning. I think he understands he can't go home until the doctors are happy with his recovery from the surgery, so he's been making an effort to eat more and he's been paying attention to his physiotherapist."

"Listen, thanks, Ally. I appreciate you helping out like this."

Ally glanced down at the notes she'd taken. "I've got a list of her recommendations, if you want to hear them?"

"Sure. Thanks."

"She's suggested safety rails at both the front and rear steps as well as in the shower. And she would like to see a handheld showerhead in the bathroom and a bath chair for your father to sit on if he's feeling weak."

"Okay." He sounded as though he was making notes. "Anything else?"

"She said the bedroom doorways were wide enough to allow them to install a hospital bed, if one is required at a later date, but that Bob's own bed would be fine for now."

"That's good to know."

"I wasn't sure if you wanted to do the work yourself, being handy and everything, but she's recommended a local guy and I took the liberty of making a quick call. He can take care of everything on Friday, if you want him to, or the following Monday."

There was a short pause. "Friday, you said?"

"Yeah. He said he could fit you in in the afternoon. If it's a problem for you to get here, I can let him into the house, since I've still got your spare key. It's no big deal."

There was another short silence. "That's very generous of you."

"It really isn't. It'll take two seconds to let him in. And you've got enough on your plate."

She waited for him to tell her to butt out. Or to ask why she kept inserting herself into his and Bob's lives. Usually she confined her do-gooding to her advice column, but for some reason she couldn't seem to stop herself where Bob and Tyler were concerned.

"I read your column today," Tyler said instead.

It was so not what she'd expected him to say that it took her a moment to respond. "Did you?"

"Yeah. The bit about the guy who dresses as a woman."

"Right."

"Turns out that all my staff read you, too."

"That's nice. I think. What did they say about the cross-dressing guy?" She could imagine the comments that must have been flying around. Especially in a very macho environment like a workshop.

"Turns out my senior cabinetmaker has a cousin who works as a drag queen."

"Well, there you go."

"You must get some pretty weird letters."

"I get some very weird letters. But underneath the weirdness, it's amazing how much the same we all are."

"How so?" Tyler asked.

"Everyone wants to be accepted. Everyone wants

to belong. Everyone wants to love and be loved. To feel valued."

"Is that what you want?"

Ally thought about the way she'd taken it upon herself to call the handyman today, and the way she'd thrust herself into Bob's affairs. "I think everyone wants to feel connected, in some small way," she said quietly.

"I guess."

She heard the rustle of paper at the other end of the phone, as though he was shifting things around on his desk.

"So, do you want me to let this guy in?" she asked.

"If you don't mind. It'd be one less thing on my list. We're snowed under at the moment—"

"Then don't think about it again. I'll get the guy to bill you at your factory address, okay?"

"That'd be great."

She told herself to hang up before the conversation strayed any further than it already had.

"You still think you'll be here on Monday?" She winced. Could she sound more obvious and hopeful?

"I'm planning for Sunday at this point. The hospital said Dad might be able to come home Monday, so I wanted to get some food in, that kind of thing."

"I guess I'll see you then, then."

"You will."

There was something in the way he said it that

made her sit holding the phone for a good sixty seconds after she'd ended the call.

It had almost sounded like a promise.

TYLER PULLED UP IN FRONT of his father's house at dusk on Sunday night. He'd spent the past few days working late at the workshop, clearing his desk as much as possible, covering things off with Gabby to ensure she had all she needed to take over his client meetings.

Ally had called him once more to let him know the safety rails and new bathroom fittings had been installed. He'd never been big on talking on the phone, but he'd caught himself attempting to stretch their conversation into more than an update on his father's house remodeling. She'd answered his questions and teased him and asked some of her own, then she'd suddenly clammed up and the conversation had ended.

He glanced at her place as he grabbed his bags from the bed of the truck. Maybe he was misreading things. For all he knew, she could have a boyfriend. Maybe that was why she'd suddenly backed off. He knew nothing about her or her situation—all he had to go on was his gut and those few loaded moments when he'd been intensely aware of her as a woman. But maybe that was all one-sided.

And maybe he was simply looking for something—anything—to distract himself from the grim reality of his situation. Over the past few days he'd become aware of a reluctance within himself to think beyond the nuts and bolts of arranging for his father's respite care. Nurses and social workers he could handle, but the prospect of standing by his father's graveside left him unsettled and uneasy. Not because he cared. He refused to care—although he couldn't explain his reluctance to acknowledge his father's mortality in any other way.

He dumped all but one of his burdens on the front porch of his father's house before making his way next door. Ally still had the spare key, and he had a gift to thank her for her help with the house.

Plus he wanted to see her, distraction or not.

The hall light was on inside the house and the stained-glass panels of the door glowed with rich color as he raised his hand to knock. He saw a shadow approach, then the door opened and she was standing there, cuter and fresher and sexier than he'd remembered. His gaze automatically dropped below her waist and he didn't try to hide the smile tugging at his mouth as he saw today's pajama pants.

"Scooby-Doo. Nice choice," he said.

"I thought so," she said. "Not too dressy, not too informal. A smart-casual kind of a pajama pant."

He held up the small ice chest in his hand. "For you."

Her eyebrows rose as she reached out to take the chest. "For me?"

"To say thank-you."

"For letting a couple of people in next door?" Her

expression told him she considered it the smallest of favors.

"For giving a shit when you didn't have to. If you'll excuse my French. You barely know my father, yet you've bent over backward for him. Not many people put themselves out like that anymore."

"You make me want to find a mirror to check my halo's on straight."

But her cheeks were pink and he could see that she was pleased.

He gestured toward the cooler. "You might want to get that in the freezer."

There was plenty of ice in the chest, but the sooner the contents were below zero the better.

She cracked the lid on the chest. "You bought me ice cream?"

"Dairy Bell Nuts About Chocolate. You mentioned you like it."

"I do. I love it." She seemed thrown. As though no one had ever bought her ice cream before. "You should come in."

"I don't want to get in your hair. I just wanted to pick up the key."

"You mean, you don't want any of this ice cream?" A smile curled the corner of her mouth.

"I do. But I don't want to outstay my welcome."

"As long as you don't hog the lion's share, you're safe."

She gestured for him to follow her into the kitchen.

"You know, I was just wondering what to have for dinner," she said.

"You mean, dessert."

She gave him a cheeky look. "I mean, dinner."

He laughed.

"Big bowl or little bowl?" she asked.

"What kind of question is that?"

"Big bowl it is, then."

She served up two generous portions then led him out onto the side deck.

"This is my favorite ice cream eating spot." She walked to the three stairs leading into the garden and sat on the top step, shooting a glance up at him.

The outside light cast a golden sheen over her hair and face. He looked at her for a long beat, trying to understand why he found her so appealing. She was cute, yes, but not beautiful. And her baggy pajama pants should have been an antidote to sexual desire. But all he could think about were the curves hidden beneath the bright fabric.

"You want to sit at the table?" she asked, starting to rise.

"Here is fine."

He sat beside her, forcing himself to gaze out at the dark garden rather than watch as she licked her spoon.

"Your friend has a nice place here. Good garden."

"Tell me about it. I'm living in fear that I'll kill

everything with my black thumb before she gets back."

He swallowed a mouthful of creamy chocolate and pecans. "So where do you hang out when you're not house-sitting?"

"I'm always house-sitting."

He raised an eyebrow and she shrugged a shoulder.

"I do this on a semiprofessional basis. There are a bunch of house-sitting websites out there, and I look around for jobs that suit me, then apply to look after peoples' homes for them while they're away. I get free room and board, they get to know their pets and gardens and valuables are being looked after."

He paused with his spoon halfway to his mouth, processing what she'd said.

"So you don't have a place of your own, a base?"

"Nope." She closed her eyes as she ate another mouthful. "God, I love the way they mix that chocolate fudge stuff all through it. I wonder what they put in it to keep it all gooey like that?"

Tyler was still trying to get his head around what she'd told him. "What about your stuff? You must have a storage locker somewhere."

"Nope."

"What about your mail?"

"The *Herald* forwards it to me with the Dear Gertrude letters." She laughed. "You should see your face. Nesters always freak out when I tell them I live out of a suitcase."

Tyler frowned. "I'm not a nester."

She smiled mysteriously.

"I'm not. Guys don't nest," he said.

"Do you own your own home?"

"Yes."

"Thought so. It's an old one, too, isn't it?"

"Early Victorian."

"And I bet you've renovated it. Stripped back the floors, restored the fireplaces…?"

She had to be guessing, but it was uncanny how close to the mark she was.

She pointed her spoon at him. "You're a nester. Nothing to be ashamed of. I, on the other hand, am not. Can't stand to be pinned down. Hate staying in one spot for too long. Don't see the point of owning a bunch of stuff. Well, except for pajama pants, but they pack light."

"You must have had a place of your own at some point."

"Sure. Before I decided to stop fighting genetics."

"There's a gene for nomadism?"

"Might as well be. My mother was an artist. I spent my childhood either traveling with her or living with my aunt Phyllis or my grandmother. My mom was a gypsy, and so am I, and it's much easier to go with the flow than fight against it. Believe me." Her gaze grew distant, as though she was remembering something hard or painful.

He studied her profile, wondering. The lifestyle she described sounded free and easy—and lonely. He couldn't imagine not having a place to come home to. A sanctuary that was all his. A circle of friends who knew him intimately, who understood his history and his moods and his sense of humor. As a furniture designer, he had a strong appreciation of history and place. Every time he put pen to paper or chisel to wood, he aimed to create family heirlooms, pieces that would be well-loved and well-used. One of the most satisfying aspects of his work was the idea that his furniture became an integral part of his customers' lives and homes.

But Ally had no home. No place to call her own. No sanctuary. No treasured window seat or favorite corner of the garden or sentimental piece of crockery or glassware.

"And you're never tempted to stop and stay?"

She chased a pecan around her bowl for a few beats before replying. "A few times. But you can't fight nature, and it usually means I end up letting someone down. That's why I do the house-sitting thing now. It suits me, and I suit it, and the rest takes care of itself."

"So when your friend comes back, whenever that is, you'll just pack up your duffel and hit the road again?"

"Absolutely. When Wendy finishes her training course in another six weeks' time, I'll pack up my suitcase and go to Sydney, or maybe Brisbane. I haven't decided yet."

She inspected her empty bowl, scraping the spoon

against the surface to capture the last traces of ice cream. "It would be wrong to have a second serving, wouldn't it? An invitation to Type 2 diabetes," she said wistfully.

"Sometimes it pays to live dangerously."

"Says the man with the six-pack abs."

She blushed as soon as she said it. He felt a smile tug at his mouth. Nice to have the reassurance that she was as aware of him as he was of her.

"I don't have a six-pack."

"Okay, a four-pack. And if I go back for seconds, it won't be long before I have a keg."

She fussed around, stacking the bowls. Then she shot him a quick look from beneath her lashes. He didn't bother trying to hide his grin. Her expression became rueful.

"No need to look so pleased with yourself."

"I'm not. You just answered a question I've been asking myself, that's all."

A crease appeared between her eyebrows. "What question?"

"This one." He leaned across the space that separated them and pressed his mouth to hers.

Her lips were warm and soft and they opened on a surprised inhalation as he kissed her. He waited, keeping the kiss light, even though he'd been wanting to taste her for a long time. After a torturous beat, her mouth moved beneath his and she returned the pressure of his kiss. He palmed the nape of her neck and slid his tongue into her mouth.

She tasted like chocolate, hot and dark and mysterious. Her tongue slid along his, tentatively at first, then with more confidence. He angled his body toward her, leaning closer, wanting more. She gave an encouraging little moan, her hands sliding to his shoulders.

Heat fired in his belly as he felt the weight of her breasts against his chest and inhaled her scent. Vanilla and cloves, sweet and exotic. Their tongues slid and teased, her hunger matching his.

He hadn't been with a woman for months. And he'd been thinking about Ally all week. Wondering. Fantasizing.

He slid his hand from the nape of her neck, down her arm and onto her rib cage, just beneath the swell of her breasts. He was as hard as a rock, his breath coming fast even though they'd barely started. She clenched her hands in his T-shirt and pulled him even closer, her mouth avid on his.

She was so hot, so sexy, so warm and giving. He slid his hand onto her breast, reveling in the warm, resilient weight of her in his palm, his thumb sweeping across the curve in search of her nipple. She was already hard, the peak straining for his attention and he ran his thumb back and forth over it, smiling against her lips as he felt her shudder in response. He squeezed her nipple between thumb and forefinger and she moaned again and pressed herself into his hand.

He'd known it would be like this between them.

Ever since that moment over their impromptu dinner when she'd made a joke about needing a cigarette after their ice cream discussion. She was earthy and human and real, and he wanted her beneath him, wanted to slide his hands inside her ridiculous, sexless cartoon pajama pants and discover the warm curves of her hips and backside and thighs.

But first he wanted to taste her breasts. Wrapping his arms around her, he hauled her into his lap. He wanted to make her shudder some more, wanted to explore the soft, scented skin of her neck and breasts and belly, wanted to tease her with his mouth and his tongue and his teeth until neither of them could take it a moment longer.

He moved his hand to the hem of her tank top and lifted it, sliding his hand onto the warm skin of her belly as he kissed her deeply. He slid his hand higher, up her rib cage, already imagining the silk of her breasts against his hands, the way her—

"Wait."

She said the word against his mouth as he was about to cup her breast. He stilled, even though he was hard and desperate to be inside her.

She pulled away from him. He let his hand slide down her rib cage to rest on her hip. She felt so good. So warm and soft and alive.

"This is a bad idea." It would have sounded a hell of a lot more convincing if she hadn't been breathing as heavily as he was.

"Why?" He felt like a teenager voicing the

question. It had been a long time since a woman said no to him.

"Because it won't work."

She slid from his lap, and even though it had been a hot day and a warm night, he felt the loss of her body heat.

"Unless things have changed drastically since I last did this, I think we were doing okay."

She straightened her tank top, then took a deep breath. "I'm leaving in six weeks. And your father is dying."

"I'm not sure what either of those things has to do with us having sex." He could hear the frustration in his own voice.

"Let me ask you this, then. When was the last time you had a one-night stand?"

He raised his eyebrows, a little taken aback by her question. "I can't remember."

"Exactly." She stood and dusted off the seat of her pajama pants.

He stared up at her, affronted. "So, what, because I usually like to know more than a woman's name before I sleep with her you're kicking me to the curb?"

"I'm kicking you to the curb because I like you, Tyler Adamson. Us getting involved would be a mistake. You're the kind of man who wants more than sex and a few laughs, and I'm the kind of girl who leaves."

"You're making a lot of assumptions."

She gave him a level, knowing, very adult look. Then she reached out and took his hand, pressing her fingers to the pulse point at his wrist. He knew what she could feel there—his heart, still pounding away like a tom-tom, demanding more, wanting more. Wordless, she reversed their grips, pressing her own wrist against his fingertips. He felt an answering rhythm beating through her body, just as wild, just as demanding.

"I don't know about you, but that doesn't happen for me every day," she said quietly.

"All the more reason to do something about it."

He told himself to stop before he begged or reduced himself to the old blue-balls gambit, but everything in him resisted the way she was closing the door on the possibilities between them.

He liked her. He wanted to get to know her. Since when had that been a deal-breaker when it came to sex?

"I'm doing you a favor." There was finality in her voice. And regardless of the frustration he felt, he wasn't about to try to importune her into bed.

"Your call," he said, standing.

They were both silent as they walked to the door.

She handed him the spare key on the threshold. "Thanks for the ice cream."

"Like I said, I appreciate your time." He sounded stiff, formal. Pissed off.

Because he hadn't gotten his way? He didn't like

the idea that he was so petty. That his goodwill toward her depended on her bowing to his sexual will. He liked a hell of a lot more about her than her body.

He tried again.

"Thanks for sharing it with me."

"It seemed only fair."

His gaze slid to her mouth. Her bottom lip was slightly swollen, very pink. He remembered the soft, warm press of it against his.

If she hadn't called a halt, he'd be inside her right now, driving them both a little bit crazy.

"Good night, Ally."

"Good night, Tyler."

He heard the door close behind him. His bags were where he'd left them on the porch and he let himself in then dumped them beside the couch in the living room.

The house wasn't as musty as he'd remembered, and he saw that someone had left a vase of wildflowers on the mantle and that one of the windows was open a few inches, letting in the fresh night air.

Ally, of course.

He walked to the bathroom to inspect the safety rails that had been installed. He'd been so eager to see her that he hadn't paused to inspect the set beside the front steps.

A waterproof chair was in the shower stall, ready for his father's return, and a handheld showerhead was fitted alongside the regular one. The safety rails were good-quality chrome, their surface cross-hatched for grip. He noted with approval that the installer had fixed them into the stud instead of relying on plaster fasteners. Over all, a good job. He made a mental note to send a thank-you email to the contractor.

He returned to the living room, feeling restless, and yes, frustrated.

He'd driven to Woodend this evening with an idea in his mind about the way the immediate future might pan out. Useless to pretend that Ally hadn't featured prominently. He'd anticipated getting to know her. He'd hoped to sleep with her, to act on the tension and attraction that crackled between them every time they met. He hadn't gone much beyond that in his mind, but there'd been a sense of potential around his feelings for her.

But Ally wasn't interested. What had she said again? *I like you. Us getting involved would be a mistake.* Then she'd held his fingers to her pulse so he understood that she was as aroused and fired up as he was.

Yet she'd turned him away. Because—and he still couldn't quite get his head around it—he couldn't remember the last time he'd had a one-night stand.

What did that mean? That she only slept with "slam, bam, thank you, ma'am," kind of guys? That she wasn't interested in liking or getting to know the person she was naked with?

He collected his toothbrush and toothpaste from his bag. He thought about the other thing Ally had said as he returned to the bathroom to brush his teeth.

I don't know about you, but that doesn't happen for me every day.

It hadn't happened that way for him for years. Not since he'd been a teenager, wild and horny and needy. One touch of her, one taste and he'd been on fire, game for anything. The odds were good that if she hadn't called a halt he'd have gotten her naked right there on the deck, he'd been so carried away.

And now he was hard all over again, simply from thinking about her.

Better get over that quickly, mate, because it's not going to happen.

He was disappointed. More so than the situation probably warranted. Rationally, the world wasn't going to end tomorrow because a woman he'd met a few times didn't want to explore the attraction between them. Life was full of small missed opportunities.

Suck it up, big guy.

He spat toothpaste into the basin, rinsed his mouth and dried his face. Then he took himself back to the couch and another bad night's sleep.

AFTER TOSSING AND TURNING for nearly two hours, Ally got out of bed and had a cold shower. Embarrassing to admit to herself how unsettled and aroused she was after a few hot and heavy moments in Tyler's arms. They'd pressed against each other and kissed for no more than five minutes, ten tops—and hours later her body was still humming with need.

This is why he's dangerous. You're always attracted to men you can't have.

She let the cold water hammer the back of her neck, the place where she could still feel the imprint of Tyler's hand against her skin.

The way he'd kissed her…

The extraordinary thrill of need and desire that had rippled through her when he'd slid his hand onto her breast…

In that small breathless moment her imagination had rampaged ahead. She'd seen Tyler peeling off her clothes. Seen herself stripping him of his. She'd imagined him on top of her, big and strong, her legs around his hips. The welcome, masculine weight of him pressing her down. Then, the push of him as he slid inside her, filling her…

She'd wanted it all so badly. Too badly. Too much. An alarm had sounded in the back of her mind, a warning that this was too intense, that he was too much. That if they took this to the inevitable conclusion, it would be much more than a quick roll in the hay with the sexy guy from next door.

Ten years ago, when she'd been in her early twenties, Ally would have thrown caution to the wind and dived headfirst into whatever developed between her and Tyler. Sex, or more than sex, or something in between—her younger self would have been up for anything and everything, heedless of the consequences.

She'd prided herself on being a bohemian like her wild, freewheeling artist mother, on being open to experience. And yet it was experience—bitter, sad, shameful experience—that had taught her that some things were not for her.

Daniel had been broken when she'd left him. He'd dreamed of a future for the two of them, and she'd let him. And then, as always, she'd started to feel suffocated and smothered and she'd chipped away at their happiness until Daniel had finally told her to go if she wanted to. And, God help her, she had.

Daniel hadn't been the first man she'd walked away from, but she'd promised herself he would be the last. Unlike her mother, she wasn't willing to toy with other people's emotions in exchange for temporary happiness. And if that meant she was destined to be essentially alone, then so be it.

For the past five years, she'd done her damnedest to stay away from men who made her feel and think and want too much. Men who had the potential to become important in her life. Men, like Tyler, who she sensed she could care for, and who might come to care for her. Men she could hurt and disappoint when she inevitably packed her bags and left. As she always, always did.

She'd had two lovers in those five years, both of them younger than her, both fellow nomads. Good, safe choices, lovers who had offered her the comfort of human contact for a few weeks without the risk of strings.

Not very emotionally satisfying, perhaps. Some might even say empty. But it was better than letting people down.

She turned off the water and stepped onto the bath mat. For a moment she simply stood in the quiet darkness, letting the water roll down her body.

Absurd, but standing here like this, the memory of what had almost happened tonight still resonating within her, she felt an echo of the panic that had dogged her in the last days of her relationship with Daniel.

The need to go. To put him and the mess she'd made of them behind her.

She took a deep breath, then another. She needed to rein herself in. Get a grip—and some much-needed perspective.

She'd kissed Tyler. Pressed herself against him. Fantasized about doing more. And then she'd called a halt.

They'd had four encounters altogether—five, if she counted the time in front of the hospital when she'd seen him break down in his truck. That was it, the sum total of their interactions to date.

So what if the man had brought her ice cream all the way from Melbourne? In an ice chest no less? So what if she found him magnetic and compelling in the extreme? There was absolutely no reason for her to be carrying on like an overwrought and histrionic damsel in distress.

Nothing had happened. Nothing was going to

happen. She'd made that clear, and she knew Tyler had heard her.

She combed her fingers through her hair, scattering droplets. Then she grabbed a towel and blotted away the last of the water from her arms and breasts and belly and legs.

Naked, she walked through the silent house and back to bed.

CHAPTER FIVE

HIS FATHER WAS SITTING on the edge of the bed when Tyler arrived at the hospital the following morning. He was dressed in a wrinkled white shirt and a pair of track pants, and his good black leather loafers sat beside the bed. His hair had been combed flat across his head. A small overnight bag was at the ready on the visitor's chair.

"You're on time," his father said.

"I said I'd be here."

Tyler had been calling the hospital every other day during the week to stay informed on his father's progress, but he hadn't once spoken to his father, and his father had made no effort to contact him.

No surprises there.

Now, they eyed each other silently before his father dipped his head in a small, grudging nod.

Tyler glanced at the overnight bag. "Is this yours?"

"Who else would it belong to?"

Tyler ignored the goad and hefted the bag. "Do we need to sign you out or anything?"

"The head nurse, the gray-haired one, said she had some instructions for you."

"Right."

He left the bag on the bed and exited the room. Sister Kemp was working at the computer when he approached the nurses' station.

"Mr. Adamson," she said as he approached. "You're here bright and early."

"My father is pretty keen to get home. He said you had some instructions for me."

"Yes. The doctor wanted us to be sure to go over your father's medication with you."

They spent the next few minutes reviewing his father's medication, then she handed him some information sheets and a list of numbers.

"If you have any questions or feel out of your depth, call."

"Thanks, Sister."

"It's Carrie. And I mean it about calling. It can be a daunting business, taking care of a loved one."

He didn't bother explaining that he'd hired a nurse for the task. "Thanks for looking after him," he said instead.

"It was a pleasure," Carrie said. "He's a gruff old character, but once you get him chatting he's got a lovely sense of humor. He's had us all in stitches more than once."

"Yeah, he's a real old charmer."

It had always been that way. The teachers at school, his friends' parents, they'd all thought his father was an affable, easygoing guy. When he wanted to, his father knew how to lay on the charm.

He'd simply never bothered to expend any of it on his sons.

Tyler walked back to his father's room.

"Let's go," he said, as he collected the bag.

His father shifted to the edge of the bed, wincing a little. Tyler watched as his father slid his right foot into the loafer, only to frown impatiently as his heel got caught on the back of the shoe. He tried again, but succeeded only in depressing the leather beneath his heel.

"Stupid bloody thing," his father muttered. Then he stuffed his left foot into the other shoe until he'd achieved the same half-assed result and slowly stood.

"You can't walk out like that. You'll trip," Tyler said.

"I'm fine." His father took a couple of shuffling steps to prove his point.

Tyler put down the overnight bag and dropped to one knee in front of his father. "Lift your foot."

"I said I'm fine."

"Do you want to go home or not?"

"You know I do."

"Then lift your foot so I can fix your shoes and we can walk out of here safely."

Probably there were better ways to handle the situation, kinder things to say. His father's pride was clearly stinging at the idea of appearing so helpless in front of the son he once dwarfed. But Tyler wasn't about to pander to him. Not now, not ever. It was enough that he was here. More than enough.

His father muttered under his breath, but he lifted his left foot out of the shoe. Tyler unfolded the leather, then held the shoe at the correct angle to allow his father's foot to slide inside. He repeated the move with the second shoe.

Despite his irritation, it was impossible not to be aware of how profoundly the small act reflected the reversal of their roles.

He pushed himself upright, avoiding his father's eyes. "Let's go."

He knew from his consultations with the nursing staff that his father had been walking the corridors each day in a bid to recover his strength, but his father's steps were still slow. Tyler hovered at his side, one hand at the ready in case his father faltered. When they reached the entrance, he turned to his father.

"Wait here. I'll go grab the truck."

"I can walk."

"Wait here," Tyler repeated.

It wasn't until he was unlocking the door that he noticed his father had ignored him and was slowly shuffling his way across the parking lot.

Stubborn old bastard.

Tyler had a premonition of how the next few days were going to pan out—his father belligerently trying to do everything as though he hadn't had major surgery and a life-changing diagnosis, Tyler playing umpire and trying to curtail his excesses.

Fun and games, to be sure.

By way of rounding off the experience, his father attempted to get into the truck on his own when Tyler pulled up alongside him, ignoring Tyler's order to wait for assistance. By the time they were on the road, Tyler was grinding his teeth with frustration.

"I've arranged for a nurse to visit you twice a day, starting tomorrow," he explained as they drove into town. "She'll check your wound and your medication and help you shower. And there's a meal service I've organized to bring you your meals."

"Don't need a meal service. I can still cook. I'm not dead yet."

"You can't live on canned food."

"What do you think I've been living on?"

Tyler bit his tongue on the observation that his father's current situation was hardly an advertisement for his dietary choices.

"Canned food is full of sodium and additives. The stuff I've arranged for you is fresh."

His father set his jaw. In the old days, it would have meant a flare-up was in the offing, and Tyler and Jon would have made themselves scarce in the hope of avoiding the inevitable fallout. Today, his father merely crossed his arms over his chest and sulked.

When they pulled up in front of the house, his father peered through the windshield, frowning as he spotted the shiny new handrails on either side of the steps.

"Where did those ugly things come from?"

"The hospital wanted them installed before they'd let you come home."

"Nobody asked me."

Tyler threw his hands in the air. "Fine. I'll rip the handrails out and you can go into the hospice."

He was so exasperated, he actually started the truck again, ready to follow through on his threat. He knew he was overreacting, that it was stupid to let himself get fired up by his father's pointless objections, but this was new territory for him, too, and he was acutely aware of the contradictory emotions shoving and tugging at him every second he spent in his father's presence. Pity, anger, guilt. And, as much as he hated to admit it, the echo of old fear.

Perhaps that was why he responded so easily to his father's small acts of defiance—deep inside, there was a part of him that still flinched when he saw those expressions of anger and impatience in his father's face.

Some lessons were impossible to unlearn.

"You Adamson blokes don't muck about, do you? I didn't think you'd be home until the afternoon."

It was Ally, standing on the pavement, smiling through the open window.

His father made a disgruntled sound. "Did you see what they've done to my place? Put a bunch of ugly metal all over it. Looks like an old people's home."

Ally pulled a comically concerned face. "Oh, dear. If you don't like those I don't want to be around when you see what they've done to the bathroom."

"The bathroom?" his father said.

"Oh, yes. Safety rails up the kazoo. A veritable forest of shiny chrome. You'll need sunglasses every time you go in there."

His father frowned. Tyler waited for the outburst—the angry words, the insults, the quickly raised fist. Instead, his father's mouth quirked up at the side. Then he gave a little chuckle.

"Is it that bad?" his father asked.

"Worse. And here's the best bit—it's partly my fault because I let the guy in and told him what to do." Ally made another comic face, as though she was bracing herself for the condemnation about to rain down on her.

His father chuckled again. "You're a bloody cheeky thing. Come on, help an old man out."

Tyler watched as his father let Ally support him as he slid from the pickup. It was the first time he'd seen them together and he noted the soft light in her eyes as she looked at his father, the gentle way she held his arm.

He transferred his gaze to his parent, trying to imagine what she must see when she looked at him. But it was impossible for him to remove the filter of his own experiences from his perception. He might be older, frailer, but the man making his way up the sidewalk was still the same man who had filled Tyler's childhood with fear and emptied it of certainty.

He got out and grabbed his father's bag from the truck bed.

Ally and his father were standing at the bottom of the steps when he joined them. His father stared at one of the rails for a long beat, then reached out and rested his hand on it.

"Might as well use the bloomin' things, I suppose. Since you've wasted my money on them."

Tyler bit back on the correction that rose to his lips. He'd wasted his own money making the house safe, not his father's. But this wasn't about money.

His father climbed the steps slowly, then waited while Tyler unlocked the house.

"Why don't I leave you to settle in and come back later for a cup of tea and some cake?" Ally said.

She hovered at the top of the porch steps, ready to descend.

"No, no, come in now. Tyler can make us something," his father insisted.

"Sure. I'll whip up a batch of scones, maybe a pavlova or two."

"I have some cake at my place. Why don't I grab that?" Ally suggested.

For the first time that day Tyler looked at her directly. She was wearing a knee length white skirt with red flowers printed on it and a white tank top. She looked tanned and bright and summery. Her eyes were cautiously warm as they met his. As though she wasn't sure of her reception, but was pleased to see him, anyway.

Had he been that much of a bear last night?

"That'd be great, thanks, Ally," he said.

She gave him a small smile. "I'll be back in two shakes of a lamb's tail."

As she walked away, he traced the shape of her hips and backside with his eyes before returning his attention to getting his father inside the house. He needed to stop noticing how sexy she was and start viewing her as his father's friend. Maybe that way he could keep his unruly body and imagination under control where she was concerned.

"Come on, Dad," he said, pushing the front door open. "Let's get you into bed."

"I don't want to lie down. I've been lying down all week."

"You need to take it easy. You don't want to tire yourself out."

"Plenty of time to rest when I'm dead."

His father stopped abruptly when he reached the living room.

"What have you done?" He turned to face Tyler, his eyes bright with dawning anger and outrage. "Where are all my things?"

"If you're talking about those moldering old newspapers you had piled up all over the place, I recycled them. They were a fire hazard and they made the house stink. Not to mention I found a nest of mice in one of the boxes."

"You had no right. Those were my papers. My property." His father was red in the face, the tendons showing in his neck.

"It was a bunch of useless junk. I have no idea why you were hanging on to them, anyway."

"For the crosswords."

Tyler blinked. Did his father have any idea how insane he sounded? He'd had years—*decades*—worth of newspapers stockpiled. Even if his father lived to be a hundred and fifty he'd never get around to all the crossword puzzles in those newspapers.

"Well, they're gone now. There's not much I can do about it, so you might as well get used to it."

As far as Tyler was concerned, the subject was closed. He turned away.

A hand clamped on to his forearm, the grip surprisingly strong.

"Don't you turn your back on me and walk away. Don't you dare disrespect me after all I've sacrificed for you."

His father was trembling with rage, the movement transmitted to Tyler through the grip on his arm. Spittle had formed at the corners of his father's mouth, and he had a look in his eye that Tyler recognized only too well.

Violence crackled in the air. It occurred to Tyler that if his father thought he could get away with it, he would have hit Tyler rather than simply grab him. Just like the old days.

Tyler opened his mouth to tell his father in no uncertain terms to get his hands off him.

"I've got vanilla cake, and a bit of chocolate fudge, so we can have some of both if you like."

Ally was standing inside the front door, silhouetted in the morning sunlight.

Tyler wondered how much she'd heard, what she'd seen. If she could feel the potential for violence vibrating in the air.

It took him a moment to find his voice. "Great. I'll put the kettle on."

He pushed his father's hand from his arm. It fell easily. He walked into the kitchen. He stopped in the center of the room, aware that he should be putting water in the kettle but unable to move beyond the sensation of his father's hand on his arm.

He'd come here intending to get his father settled at home, then get back to his life. But the next few days seemed to stretch before him unendingly.

Every time his father challenged him, every time he grew angry or sulky or demanding, Tyler was going to be staring down the past.

There was so much unresolved between them. So many ugly memories. So much unexpressed grief and outrage and anger.

For a split second the urge to damn duty to hell, to climb in his pickup and hit the road and leave his father to sort himself out was overwhelming. Tyler could almost taste the freedom and relief the decision would bring. He could go home, back to his life, and push all this crap into the dark corners again. Never to see the light of day.

A warm hand landed in the center of his back. Ally stood behind him, the plate of cake in hand.

"Tell me where everything is and I'll make some tea," she said quietly.

"You don't have to do that."

She didn't say anything, simply brushed past him and slid the plate onto the table. He watched as she filled the kettle and turned it on, then started rummaging in the cupboards for tea bags.

"Third cupboard on the left," he said after watching her search fruitlessly for a few seconds.

"Thanks."

He crossed the room and collected three mugs. He could smell Ally's vanilla-spice scent as he placed them in front of her.

She shot him an assessing glance. "You okay?"

"Yeah."

"You don't look okay. You look like you're about to pass out."

He frowned. "I've never fainted in my life."

For a moment the only sound in the kitchen was the sound of the kettle heating.

"You and your father really know how to push each other's buttons, huh?"

Tyler gave a small, humorless laugh. "You could say that."

He waited for her to say more, to probe, but she didn't. Instead, she sliced the cake and arranged the pieces on the plate. After a second, she put down the knife and looked at him.

"I want to say something about last night. I know this probably isn't the best time, but it's been bugging me, so I'm just going to spit it out."

"Okay." He turned to face her, leaning his hip against the counter and crossing his arms over his chest.

Her breasts lifted as she took a deep breath and launched into speech. "I meant it when I said I like you, Tyler. And I'd hate for what happened, or, more accurately, what didn't happen to stop us from being friends." Her expression was very earnest, which only made her look cuter than usual.

"Because I wanted to sleep with you and you said no?"

"Yes."

He filched a slice of cake. He took a bite, chewed and swallowed. Then he looked her in the eyes.

"I like you, too, Ally. And I'm happy to be friends. But you should probably know I'm still going to want to sleep with you." He shrugged apologetically. "It's kind of a one-way valve. Not really something I can turn on or off at the drop of a hat."

"Right." She seemed thrown by his directness. "Well, I guess I can handle that."

He ate the rest of the cake in one big bite. "Good," he said around his mouthful.

She smiled. "Nice manners."

He glanced at her curvy hips, shown to advantage by her skirt. "Nice skirt."

She slapped his hand away when he reached for another piece. "No cheating."

He knew she wasn't talking about the cake. "I'm only human."

Her gaze dropped to his chest, then his hips. "Tell me about it," she muttered, so quietly he almost didn't catch it. Then she grabbed the plate of cake. "Can you bring the tea in when it's ready?"

He watched her backside until she disappeared through the doorway to the living room.

He didn't understand her. There had been desire in her eyes when she looked at him. She wanted him, and she'd wanted him last night, too. And she'd stated boldly that she liked him. Yet she was determined to only be friends.

The kettle clicked off as it reached boiling point. He poured water into the mugs, automatically taking his father's tea bag out after a brief dunking. His father had always preferred a weak brew.

Tyler stilled when he registered what he'd done. He let out a small, heavy sigh.

A large part of him might want to drive off and leave his father to his own devices, but an even larger part seemed to be determined to do the right thing, no matter what the cost to himself or his peace of mind.

A couple of days, he reminded himself. *You can suck up almost anything for a couple of days.*

ALLY SWATTED A FLY AWAY from her face. She was
sitting on one of the twin wooden sun loungers on
Wendy's side deck, a glass of iced tea beside her, her
notepad in hand, pondering how best to respond to
Bankrupt Bridesmaid, a reader who was asking for
advice on how to deal with a friend who had morphed
into Bridezilla the moment her fiancé proposed.

Ally preferred to draft her responses to reader letters with pad and pencil, having learned long ago that
her brain communicated best with the blank page via
a pencil rather than a computer keyboard. Once she
had her responses roughed out, she polished them at
her laptop before emailing them into her editor.

Normally she loved questions like this—it gave
her a chance to sound off against the ridiculous excesses of the modern wedding. During her tenure,
Gertrude had developed a bit of a reputation for being
tough on Bridezillas and young couples who seemed
determined to start their married lives encumbered
by the huge debt of a lavish, over-the-top wedding.
Ally had handed out plenty of tough love in the form
of column inches, but today she was having trouble
concentrating.

The house next door was silent—no raised voices,
no angry words floating over the fence—yet she
couldn't forget the tension she'd witnessed between
father and son this morning.

She'd heard the thwarted fury in Bob's voice, the
shamed pride. She'd seen him grab his son's arm and,

for a heartbeat, she'd thought he was going to strike Tyler.

And the expression on Tyler's face afterward when she'd followed him into the kitchen.

He'd looked so lost and desolate. The compulsion to wrap her arms around him had been so strong she'd nearly given in to it. She'd settled for simply placing a comforting hand on his back, as if she could somehow convey her sympathy and empathy to him through that single, small contact.

She'd like to offer him more. An ear to listen. A shoulder to cry on, if that was what he needed. Someone to vent to, a sounding board. Whatever he needed—and she sensed he desperately needed something, someone, on his side. But she wasn't about to foist herself on him. In the guise of Dear Gertrude she was happy to hand out guidance, but in real life Ally was much more inclined to hang back until asked. And her gut told her that Tyler would never ask. He was too self contained, too controlled. Too used to keeping his own counsel—or, perhaps, simply sucking it up and soldiering on.

Whatever. He hadn't asked for her comfort or advice or assistance, and she'd already volunteered enough. It was none of her business.

Forcing herself to focus, she began to write.

She'd barely composed a paragraph when the sound of a screen door slamming shut made her lift her head. It was Tyler, carrying a long roll of papers and what looked like a pencil case. He seemed frustrated as he stood on the top step, scanning the rear yard as though he were looking for an escape route.

For a few seconds she allowed herself to admire the hard strength of his body. He'd felt wonderful pressed against her last night—his big arms, his even bigger chest.

She told herself to stop ogling him the same moment he glanced over and caught her staring.

"Hey," he said.

"Hey. What's up?"

"Dad's sleeping. With the radio going full bore."

Her gaze dropped to the roll of papers in his hands and she guessed his dilemma. "Finding it hard to concentrate?"

"Just a little." His gaze shifted to scan the yard again. "I was thinking of trying the shed."

Ally turned her attention to the rusted metal structure that filled the corner of Bob's yard. Not exactly the most salubrious working environment on a hot summer day.

"Plenty of iced tea and peace and quiet over here, if you like," she offered before she could stop herself. "A spare lounger, too."

Tyler looked as though she'd thrown him a lifeline instead of a casual invitation. "I wouldn't be cramping your style?"

"I have precious little to cramp. Or hadn't you noticed?"

"In that case…"

He descended the steps and she lost sight of him behind the fence. She stood, ready to let him in the front door, then she heard the thunk of a boot connecting with wood and Tyler's head and torso appeared above the fence immediately in front of her.

"Would you mind grabbing these?"

He held out the roll of papers. She took them wordlessly. He gripped the pencil case in his teeth before slinging a leg over the fence and dropping to his feet on her side.

"Nothing like a shortcut," she said.

He took the papers from her. "Thanks for this."

"No problem." She waved a hand at the other seat. "You might want to check for bird poop before you sit."

"Thanks for the warning."

She went inside to collect a glass for him. When she returned, Tyler was toeing off his shoes and shedding his socks. She watched as he settled in a crosslegged position.

"Wow. You're pretty flexible for a guy."

She tried not to stare at the way his thigh muscles strained the soft denim of his jeans.

"Yoga."

He didn't really strike her as being a yoga kind of guy. Her skepticism must have shown on her face.

"I had a bit of back trouble a few years ago and my physiotherapist suggested it," Tyler explained. "It helps get the kinks out."

"I know. It's the only thing that keeps me mobile when I've spent a whole day writing."

She sank onto her lounger and reached for her notepad and pencil. Out of the corner of her eye she watched as Tyler unrolled the papers. A rough sketch of a sideboard filled the bulk of the first page and the margins were thick with notes, as well as angle calculations and measurements.

She dragged her attention to her own work and concentrated on encouraging Bankrupt Bridesmaid to show some spine in the face of the despotic bride-to-be, but she was very aware of Tyler working quietly beside her.

She was such a hypocrite. Just this morning, she'd offered him only friendship and reprimanded him when he made a comment about her skirt. Yet she couldn't even sit beside him for five minutes without becoming ridiculously aware of everything about him.

The play of light and shadow on his face.

The flickering muscles in his forearms as he made notations on his plans.

The clean, sunshiny smell of his clothing.

Maybe inviting him to share her peace and quiet hadn't been such a great idea after all.

"Is that your column you're working on?"

She glanced up from the doodle she'd been swirling along the bottom of the page to find Tyler watching her.

"Yep. Due tomorrow at lunchtime."

"Anything good?"

"An etiquette question about texting at the dinner table, an exploited bridesmaid. And there's one about a woman who is trying to decide if she should make contact with her birth mother or not. That's the toughest one."

"What do you think she should do?"

"I haven't answered that one yet."

"But you must have an idea what you're going to say."

She did. She fiddled with her pencil while she gathered her thoughts. "I think that family is important. That it strikes at the very root of who we are and who we think we are. If this woman is plagued by questions about her birth mother and her heritage, if it's stopping her from living her life to the fullest, then I think she should take the plunge."

"And what if she makes contact and it's not what she expected? What if there are no answers to her questions?"

"Then at least she'll know she tried. She can close the door and move on. At the moment, she's in limbo, unable to commit to making contact yet also unable to put it aside and get on with her life."

Tyler shook his head. "You have a tough job."

"Sometimes. But I can't imagine doing anything else now."

"You don't feel responsible? You never worry about what might happen if you say the wrong thing? Or if you don't answer a letter from someone desperate?"

"I read everything. Sometimes there are letters written by people who are clearly in crisis. I always respond with resources for them—counselors, support groups, whatever. But most letter writers are simply looking for impartial feedback, someone to call them on their bullshit or back up their instincts. They've got friends and family dumping their opinions, muddying the water. I'm the independent arbitrator."

"You're Judge Judy." Tyler said it with a small smile.

"With better hair. I hope."

"You sound like you love it."

"I do. I feel…I don't know…*connected* to these people. Like I really am their aunt Gertrude, and they're sitting across the table from me having a cup of tea and sharing their lives. I like to think that I help them. That I make a difference."

She was very aware of Tyler's gaze on her face as she finished. She gave a self-conscious laugh. "I know what you're thinking. I need to get a life, right?"

"Nothing wrong with enjoying what you do."

His hand smoothed over the blueprints as he spoke. She wondered if he was aware of the gesture or if it was unconscious.

"You enjoy what you do, too, don't you?"

"Yeah, I do," he said slowly. "It's easy to forget

that sometimes, dealing with clients and staff and deadlines, but I do."

"I know I'm not the best judge, since I don't actually own any furniture or have a home to put it in, but the pieces I saw on your website looked great. And really, really expensive."

His grin was unabashed. "Quality costs. What can I say?"

She found herself grinning in return.

She really liked this man. She liked his quiet confidence and his slow smile. She liked the way he seemed genuinely interested in her and what she had to say. She liked the fact that he'd made the decision to help his father, even though their relationship was clearly deeply troubled. She liked the way he'd kissed her last night. The way he'd pulled her onto his lap.

She realized she was staring at Tyler's mouth, and that he was watching her, a dark, smoky look in his silver eyes.

Danger, danger, Will Robinson.

"Speaking of quality, I'd better get this sorted or I'll be pushing it to make my deadline tomorrow," she said.

"Yeah, I've got a deadline I need to make, too."

They worked together for over an hour, talking occasionally, but mostly concentrating on their individual tasks. Given how disturbing she found Tyler on many levels, Ally was surprised by how easy it was to spend time with him. It was a warm day, but the breeze was cool and the iced tea even colder and he was good company—intelligent and perceptive and wry.

She felt a pang of regret when he started rolling up his papers. "Better go check on Dad."

She could see the new tension in him as he pulled on his socks.

"Anytime you need a break, come over."

She hesitated, all her admonitions to herself about interfering loud in her ears. Then she thought about that moment she'd witnessed this morning and threw caution to the wind. "Even if you just need to talk. Okay?"

Tyler was tugging on his shoes, but he flicked a quick look at her. "Thanks."

She bit her lip to stop herself from saying any more.

Tyler stood and gathered his things. "Thanks for sharing your peace and quiet. Hope I didn't distract you too much."

"You didn't distract me. It was nice having company for a change."

Especially his company.

He took their empty glasses inside. She watched him leave them in the kitchen sink before following him to the front door.

"Good luck with the nurse tomorrow," she said.

"Yeah. I have a feeling I'm going to need it, given Dad's reaction to the safety rails."

He surprised her then by leaning in and brushing

her lips with a brief kiss. "Bye, Ally, and thanks for saving my ass again today."

He started down the steps. Ally forced herself to close the door instead of standing there like a dodo watching him walk away again.

She could still feel the warm imprint of his lips on hers as she returned to the kitchen. Which was stupid, since it had been the barest peck. Nothing like the kisses they'd shared last night.

Those kisses had been enough to make her lose her head and crawl into his lap. Those kisses had kept her awake, staring at the ceiling.

She made an impatient noise, frustrated with herself. She crossed to the fridge and pulled the carton of Nuts About Chocolate from the freezer.

When in doubt, pig out.

A tried and true solution to many of life's problems. She hoped it worked as an antidote for unrequited lust.

Although the more she got to know Tyler, the less she suspected lust was her problem where he was concerned. Lust was all about pheromones and sweaty, carnal urges, but her attraction to Tyler was about a lot more than his body.

A dangerous acknowledgment.

She grabbed a spoon from the drawer and excavated herself a huge scoop of ice cream. Maybe by the time she'd dug her way to the bottom of the tub, she'd have unearthed some common sense.

CHAPTER SIX

TYLER WOKE TO FIND HIS father standing over him. He flinched, then immediately regretted the reflex. The last thing he wanted was for his old man to think Tyler was still afraid of him.

"What are you sleeping on the couch for?"

"I don't like the bed in my old room."

"There's nothing wrong with it."

"You sleep on it, then." Tyler swung his legs to the edge of the couch and rubbed the sleep from his eyes. He glanced at the clock on the mantle. Six-fifteen.

Great.

He estimated he'd had about three hours' rest between his father getting up and down and the lumpiness of the couch cushions.

"Stupid to sleep out here. Makes the place look messy. Your mother wouldn't like it."

Tyler gave his father an incredulous look. "But she would have loved the boxes of newspapers everywhere?"

His father frowned, unable to find a suitable response.

"What do you want for breakfast? Porridge? Toast?" Tyler asked.

He reached for the T-shirt he'd thrown over the arm of the couch last night and caught his father staring at the tattoo high on his left shoulder.

"Never thought a son of mine would get himself marked up like a common criminal."

"Porridge or toast?"

"Toast. I suppose."

"My pleasure," Tyler muttered as he headed for the kitchen.

He collected butter and jam from the fridge and slid two pieces of bread into the toaster.

"I used to sleep on that bed myself when your mother was sick."

His father was in the kitchen doorway, a stubborn expression on his face.

"What's that got to do with anything?"

"You said I should sleep in it. Well, I have, and it's fine. So I don't see why you have to muck up the living room."

Tyler sighed. "Just drop it, okay?"

"It's a perfectly good bed—"

"Bloody hell, will you drop it?" The sharp crack of his voice echoed in the room.

"Don't you raise your voice at me. I asked you a perfectly legitimate question. The least you can do is answer it when you're staying under my roof."

Tyler smiled grimly. How many times had he heard that as a kid? *When you're under my roof.*

He nailed his father with a look. "You want an

answer? How about this—maybe I don't like the memories in there."

It was the closest Tyler had ever come to directly addressing the history between them. His father stiffened. For a moment they stared at each other across the kitchen.

His father was the first to break the contact, glancing away and shuffling toward the table. "I like honey on my toast."

Tyler opened his mouth to push the issue—his father was the one who'd kept on about the bloody bed, after all. Then he saw the tremor in his father's hands as he clasped them in front of him.

Being old and sick doesn't let him off the hook.

The toaster popped. Tyler closed his eyes for a long moment. Years of resentment pressed against his sternum, wanting out.

He opened his eyes and crossed to the pantry to collect the honey. He slid it onto the table and went back to grab the toast. The plate rattled as he dumped it in front of his father.

Then he strode for the door. He took the steps in two bounds. The grass was cold and dewy on his bare feet as he hit the lawn and kept walking. He didn't stop until he was standing in front of the overgrown mess that used to be his mother's vegetable patch.

He should have said something. He should go inside right now and confront that bastard. Ask why. Demand to know what kind of a man took out his petty frustrations on his own children.

Tyler didn't move.

He dropped his head, pinching the bridge of his nose.

He didn't understand what was holding him back from the confrontation. It wasn't simply his father's frailty. There was something else, something dark and heavy that stopped Tyler every time he felt the urge to lay it all out in the open.

For some reason, he thought of Ally as he stared at the ground. Remembered the way she'd placed her hand so calmly and surely on his back yesterday. That small, simple human contact had grounded him. Reminded him that there was a world outside of this childhood house of terror.

He lifted his head and looked toward her place. She'd said he should come by if he needed a break. Or if he needed to talk.

He imagined himself going next door, knocking on the door. She'd probably still be in bed, and she'd answer with her hair mussed, soft and warm. He imagined himself kissing her, taking her to her bed and making love with her until he forgot about his father and all the unhappiness of the past.

Making love with Ally would be like that, he sensed. All-consuming. Nothing else would matter.

He rubbed the back of his neck, turning away from Ally's. She'd made herself more than clear. She wanted to be friends. She'd hardly appreciate him turning up on her doorstep at six in the morning, forcing the issue.

He walked back to the house. The kitchen was empty—his father had dumped his plate in the sink. Tyler cleaned up, putting the honey and butter away, rinsing the plate. Then he went to check on his father.

He wasn't in the living room, or his bedroom. Then Tyler heard the sound of running water and swore.

Yesterday, he'd covered the rules with his father. No showers without assistance. Even with the safety rails, the shower was a dangerous place for a man in his late seventies, fresh from major surgery.

Tyler should have known that his father wouldn't listen. Robert was bloody-minded at the best of times, and it obviously chaffed him hugely to have Tyler in a position of authority over him.

Tyler stopped outside the bathroom door and knocked. "How are you doing in there?" he called.

He waited, but there was no reply.

"Dad. Are you okay?"

Again, no reply.

Tyler tried the handle and the door swung open. The bathroom was thick with steam, the mirrors foggy with condensation.

"Dad. Are you all right?"

"Go away. Can't a man shower in peace?"

The tension left Tyler's shoulders. "What's wrong with you? Couldn't you hear me calling?" He was annoyed now that he'd been worried.

"I said go away." There was a quavering note to his father's voice.

Tyler frowned. Reaching out, he slid the shower door open.

His father was sitting in the shower seat, water pummeling the wall to his left. He had a bloody gash on his shin and a red mark on his forehead and was gripping the arms of the chair like grim death.

"What happened?" Tyler asked, leaning in to turn the taps off.

"Stupid chair tripped me up. Banged my head."

His father was gray, all the color leached from his face. Blood dripped from the cut on his shin, swirling toward the drain in crimson ribbons.

Tyler looked around and saw that his father hadn't thought to bring a towel into the bathroom with him.

"Give me a second." He darted out of the bathroom and grabbed a towel from the cupboard in the hallway. Reentering the room, he saw his father hadn't moved, his grip still white knuckled on the chair. Tyler draped the towel over the wall rack and faced his father.

"Here. Put your hands on my shoulders. I'll help you stand."

Tyler bent over his father. His father's mouth worked. Tyler waited for him to object, to tell him to go to hell. But after a moment his father released his grip on the chair and leaned forward, reaching for Tyler's shoulders. Tyler waited until his father had a solid hold before wrapping both arms around his father's back.

"We'll stand on three, okay? One, two, three."

He tightened his grip and shifted his weight. He could feel his father's ribs beneath his hands, could feel the quiver of straining muscles as his father tried to stand. A few tense seconds later, his father was wavering on his feet, his breath coming in harsh gasps as he clung to Tyler's shoulders.

For a long moment they remained locked in an unintentional embrace, son supporting father. Tyler couldn't help but be profoundly, viscerally aware of his father's frailty. His nakedness, the papery thinness of his skin, the lack of substance to the body in his arms.

Despite everything, compassion stirred within him.

His father needed Tyler, and it made him ashamed and scared and vulnerable. No matter what had happened between them in the past, Tyler couldn't stop himself from responding to that vulnerability.

He'd thought he was here for himself, so he could look himself in the eye and know he'd done the right thing. Standing in this house, his father trembling in his arms, Tyler understood that his motivation was far more complex and conflicted than simple duty. There were bonds tying them together that went beyond rational words and thoughts.

He wasn't sure it was a welcome realization.

"How are you doing?" he asked.

"I can stand on my own."

"Grab the rail, then," Tyler said gruffly.

Only when his father had transferred his grip to the safety rail did Tyler release him and step backward.

"I'm okay. I can take it from here." His father's voice was shaky, but Tyler didn't doubt his determination.

"I'll be in the hall if you need me."

Tyler exited, putting a few paces between them. He pulled his phone from his pocket and called Gabby in Melbourne.

She picked up on the third ring.

"I'm going to need longer than a week," he said.

ALLY KEPT HER DISTANCE for the next few days. She left some caramel slice on the doorstep on the first day, and some new crossword-puzzle books for Bob on the third. She felt guilty about not visiting him in person, especially since she'd seen him almost every day when he was in hospital. She guessed he was probably wondering where she was, but she felt the need to put some distance between herself and Tyler after their afternoon on her deck. He was too interesting, too sexy, too compelling—and she was only human.

The two houses were so close that it was impossible for her ignore the nurse coming and going each day—once in the morning, once in the evening—and she was very aware of the fact that Tyler's pickup was still parked on the street, day after day.

Perhaps she'd gained the wrong impression, but she'd been certain that he'd planned on being in Woodend for only a few days. Already those "few days" were stretching into a week.

She was changing the bed on the afternoon of the fifth day when she caught sight of Tyler through the window. He was visible for a few seconds as he crossed the sidewalk in front of Wendy's house. She was in the middle of tucking the top sheet in, but she froze, holding her breath. Sure enough, ten seconds later she heard the low thrum of his truck starting. It flashed briefly into view as he drove down the street. Then he was gone.

She abandoned the bed on the spot, hustling into the study to grab her letter folder, then stopping in the kitchen to collect the chocolate-chip cookies she'd made that morning. She was outside and climbing the steps to Bob's place within minutes of Tyler's departure.

A plump blond woman in her early forties answered the door to Ally's knock. She wasn't in uniform, but Ally guessed she must be Bob's nurse.

"Hi, I'm Ally from next door. I was wondering if Bob was up for a visit?"

"I'm Belinda, and I think he'd be thrilled to see you. Especially with those cookies in hand."

"He does have a bit of a sweet tooth."

The other woman stepped back. Ally shot a furtive

glance to check the street was still clear of Tyler's vehicle before entering. And immediately felt foolish. So what if he came home? It wasn't as though she was going to jump his bones while his father and the nurse looked on.

Bob was sitting in the armchair in the living room when she entered, one of his puzzle books open in his lap.

"Hello, there. I thought you might like a visit and something to go with your cup of tea," she said.

Bob glanced up. "Been wondering where you'd got to."

Ally tried not to squirm with guilt. "I had a couple of tight deadlines I needed to hit," she fibbed.

Bob grunted. "That's what Tyler said it'd be."

"Can I bribe my way back into your good books with a cookie?"

"Nobody needs to bribe anybody. Just pointing out that you were missed, that's all."

It was said gruffly, with Bob scowling at his puzzle, but from a self-contained man like him it was the equivalent of a Shakespearian sonnet and Ally couldn't help but be touched.

"I'm sorry," she said sincerely. "I promise not to be a stranger, okay?"

Even if that meant seeing Tyler more often than was advisable for her sanity and peace of mind.

"Fair enough."

"So is that a yes to a cookie?"

As they snacked she helped Bob finish his

crossword puzzle before reading him a few of her letters, since he seemed to get a kick out of them.

They were debating the merits of modern versus old-fashioned manners when Ally noted Bob checking his watch for the third time in as many minutes.

"I'm not keeping you from anything, am I, Bob?"

She didn't want to mess up his routine with her impromptu visit.

"Just wondering where Tyler's gotten to. He said he was only going to be twenty minutes."

Ally tensed. She'd been visiting with Bob for almost forty minutes, which meant Tyler could return at any moment. Even though she was aware that it made her an enormous coward, she shot out of her seat and started gathering her things.

"I should really get back. Today's cleaning day, and I've got a whole bunch of rooms to dust and Mr. Whiskers needs to be brushed."

Bob blinked. "Well, okay. But I'm going to hold you to what you said—don't be a stranger."

"I won't. I promise."

She bent and kissed his cheek. Then she beat a retreat to the door. Feeling every inch the yellow-belly she was, she breathed a sigh of relief as she descended the steps.

Phew.

Then she saw a flash of red at the end of the street. Sure enough, it was Tyler's pickup.

She swallowed. Any second now he would be

parking, getting out of his truck and looking at her with those devastating silver eyes of his. And every good intention she'd formed over the past few days would dissolve like butter on a hot griddle.

She didn't stop to think, she simply scampered down the path like a frightened rabbit, bolted across the few feet of sidewalk that separated the two houses, then scampered up Wendy's path and onto her porch.

She fumbled the key, her heart thumping like a kettledrum beneath her breastbone. She heard Tyler's truck pull up, heard the engine stop. Any second now he'd be out of the truck and—

The door opened and she slipped inside and shut it behind her. She stood with her back pressed against the wood, waiting for the adrenaline to wash through her system.

What is wrong with you?

It was a damned good question. When had she gone from being content to be Tyler's friend to being afraid to spend time with him? When had she become so scared of her own feelings and impulses that she was literally barricading herself from temptation?

She didn't know. All she knew was that she wanted to be sensible where Tyler was concerned—and she was terribly afraid that she didn't have the willpower to carry it through.

She groaned, lifting the file in her hands to bang it against her forehead. She was such a mess. Not many women would be bending themselves into emotional pretzels because the sexy, available, lovely, funny, gentle guy next door was interested in them. In fact, most other women would be skipping through the day, delighted by the prospect.

But most other women had something to offer a man like Tyler, and Ally didn't. She was a guaranteed disaster, a walking, talking disappointment waiting to happen.

She walked slowly up the hall and threw her folder onto the desk in the study. Then she wandered into the living room, feeling dazed and oddly bereft, as though she'd abandoned something important and priceless. Which was nuts, given that twenty seconds ago she'd been panting with relief because she'd avoided encountering Tyler on the street.

She found herself on the deck, the sun bright overhead. She stared blankly at the garden and the deep blue sky.

Maybe she really was going nuts. Maybe she should resign as Dear Gertrude and stop perpetrating the fraud that she knew anything about anything.

The hard thwack of a screen door shutting made her start. Her head snapped around and she found herself staring at Tyler as he stood on the steps on the other side of the fence.

They looked at each other for a long, drawn out moment. Ally's heartrate picked up, the beat pounding in the pit of her belly.

"Have I done something wrong?" Tyler asked.

"No. Of course not."

"Then why are you avoiding me?"

"I'm not avoiding you," she lied.

"So why didn't you bring the caramel slice in the other day instead of leaving it on the doorstep? And why did you bolt when you saw my truck?"

Because I'm a certifiable nutbag. Because you confuse and scare and challenge the hell out of me. Because I want something that I know can only end one way—badly.

"Because."

She meant to say more, offer him some kind of face-saving lie, but the words wouldn't come. Maybe it was the way he was watching her so intently, the clear light in his eyes demanding the truth. Or maybe she was simply sick of hiding—from herself, and him.

She sighed. "Okay. I was avoiding you," she admitted.

"I thought we were going to be friends."

"We were. I mean, we are."

"You avoid your other friends like this?"

"No."

He cocked his head, considering. "I'm not sure if I should be encouraged or insulted."

There was something very…warm about the way he said it. And the way his gaze raked her body briefly before settling on her face again.

A dart of something close to panic raced down her spine. "Definitely you shouldn't feel encouraged."

"So it was an insult, then?"

She stared at him. Why was he making it so hard for her to be sensible and do the right thing?

"You know it wasn't."

"I told you I wanted to sleep with you. You said you could handle it."

"I thought I could."

"Now *that* I'm definitely taking as encouragement." Tyler started down the steps.

"What are you doing?" she squeaked, even though she already knew the answer.

"Coming over the fence."

"I don't think that's a good idea."

"I do."

She heard the thud as his boot found the first cross support. His head and shoulders appeared above the fence.

"Tyler. Stop. This is a bad idea."

"It's a great idea. The best idea I've had in weeks."

He slung his leg over the fence. Ally could feel her heart leaping around in her chest, whether from excitement or panic she had no idea. She told herself to move but her feet felt as though they were set in cement.

You want this. Don't pretend you don't.

And she did, more than anything. But Tyler had enough pain in his life right now and she didn't want to hurt him.

He landed on the deck with a thump, knees bent to absorb the shock. He straightened to his full height and took a step toward her.

She took a step backward. "I told you the other night. This is a mistake."

"Doesn't feel like a mistake." He took another step forward.

She took one backward. "We like each other too much."

His eyebrows rose. "Since when has that ever been a problem?"

He took another step. When she tried to back away again, he reached out and grabbed her shoulder.

"You just ran out of maneuvering room."

She glanced back and saw that she'd been about to collide with the French doors. She turned to look into his eyes.

"I guess that means I'm officially cornered."

"I guess it does."

He closed the final distance that separated them, pulling her close. His head lowered toward her, but at the last moment she twisted her face to the side so that his mouth found the soft skin beneath her ear instead of her lips.

A wave of need washed through her as he opened his mouth against her neck.

"If this happens, it means nothing," she said.

Tyler's tongue swirled against her skin, his mouth sucking lightly. "You don't know that."

"I do, because that's the only way this is going to happen. It has to be a one-off, a roll in the hay." She wondered if he could hear the thread of desperation beneath her words as clearly as she could. "No promises, no tomorrow. Just sex."

She clenched her hands at her sides to stop herself from grabbing him. If he agreed to her conditions, she would let herself touch him. But until then he was as off-limits as he'd always been.

"Maybe you should wait until afterward before you make any binding decisions." His words were a whisper across her skin.

"You're not listening to me. It doesn't matter how good it is or how I feel or how you feel. This can only ever be one night."

He must have heard the certainty in her tone because he pulled back a few inches to look into her face.

"You're serious, aren't you?"

"Yes. Absolutely. You think I'm playing hard to get?"

"To be honest, I don't know. But I know you want this as much as I do."

There was no point denying it, not when she was practically boneless with longing from a few simple kisses to her neck.

"Not everything we want is good for us."

She could see him sifting through their conversation, assessing her words and warnings in a new light. After a long beat, his grip loosened and he stepped away.

"I don't understand."

"I told you. I don't want to start something when

it has nowhere to go. I'm here for a few more weeks, and then I'm leaving. No matter what."

He frowned.

"So if you want to have sex, we can. As long as we both understand that it's not the beginning of something else," she said.

Tyler looked at her for a long beat. Then his gaze slid away from her to focus somewhere behind her. She knew what his answer would be. He was a man who spent hours carving a piece of wood into perfection. He didn't do things by halves.

"I want more than sex," he said.

So do I. That's the craziest thing of all. I want to wake in your arms. I want to laugh with you. I want to talk to you and learn about you. I want to ease your pain and comfort you.

"That's all that I can give you."

His gaze was intense when it returned to her. "You're the one who said this kind of thing doesn't happen every day."

"I'm trying to be smart here, Tyler. I'm trying to do the right thing."

He looked as though he wanted to say more, to ask more, but he didn't. Instead, he took a step away from her.

He had too much pride to talk her into sleeping with him. Which was just as well, because her resistance was paper-thin at best.

She smoothed her hands down the front of her thighs.

"Bob's nurse seems nice," she said brightly. "How's he getting along with her?"

It took Tyler a moment to change gears and follow her lead. "He seems to like her. And she's good at handling him."

"I noticed that. He seems stronger, too."

"Yeah. He's moving around more easily."

"I guess you'll be heading back to Melbourne soon."

"Actually, I've decided to stay on. See things through." He said the words casually, as though it wasn't a big deal. As though committing to care for his father through his final days barely merited a mention.

"That's a big change of plans," she said carefully.

"Yeah."

He didn't say any more, as usual. Not for the first time, she fought the urge to grab him by the shirtfront and shake him until some of the thoughts and feelings he held so tightly to his chest were knocked loose. But she was hardly in a position to demand anything from him, having done her damnedest to keep him at arm's length.

"If you need anything. If there's anything I can do…"

Tyler looked at her, and she knew exactly what he was thinking, what he wanted. "Thanks. I'll keep it in mind."

They were back to polite distance again. She told herself it was a good thing, even if it felt wrong.

"I told your father I'd be over more regularly. So I'll probably see you tomorrow."

Tyler nodded. He glanced toward the fence. "Suppose I'd better go start dinner."

She watched as he climbed the fence. A part of her still couldn't believe she was letting him go. But she was. And it was the right thing.

She waited until he'd disappeared inside before closing the French doors behind her and retreating to the couch. Her magazine subscriptions had arrived for the month, forwarded, as usual, with the rest of her mail by the *Herald.* She picked up *Vogue Living,* keen to anesthetize and distract herself with other people's beautiful homes.

But even as she flicked through glossy pages filled with designer decors and the latest homewares, she was cognizant of an echoing hollowness inside herself. It took her a moment to identify the feeling as loneliness.

She smiled a little grimly. *Get used to that feeling, girlfriend.*

It was better to be lonely than to hurt people. She believed that in her bones. She'd seen her mother ruin too many men—and women—to think anything else.

Most memorable was Tony, the Spaniard who'd married her mother then spent six years chasing her around the world, trying to keep her love. He'd been a wreck at the end, confused and despairing over her mother's declaration that while she loved him passionately, she would never live with him again.

Then there had been Dawn, the young artist who'd been so enamored of her mother's fire and charisma she'd put her own art aside to devote herself to being her mother's assistant—only to be cast aside when her mother inevitably grew bored with her. Dawn had attempted suicide in the aftermath of Ally's mother's abandonment, she'd been so bereft and disillusioned.

At the time, Ally had been furious with her mother for not rushing straight to Dawn's side. She'd called her mother callous and unfeeling and selfish. But that was before she'd left her own trail of wreckage in London and Sydney and Los Angeles, just as cruelly abandoning the people who loved her.

Who was she to judge her mother, after all, when she was made in the same mold?

She turned another page in the magazine.

She'd done the right thing. Definitely she had.

THAT NIGHT, TYLER SAT at the kitchen table and tried to concentrate on his design drawings instead of the racket in the living room and the one-track record in his head.

His father was watching television, the volume through the roof, as usual. And Tyler couldn't stop thinking about Ally.

It wasn't simply because she'd rejected him. Sure,

he had a healthy ego, same as the next guy, and it stung a little to be dismissed so easily. But it wasn't pique that kept her in his thoughts.

He couldn't work her out. The visits to his father, the caramel slice, the way she'd appointed herself his father's champion and confronted Tyler on his father's behalf—they were all the acts of a caring, generous, nurturing person. And yet she wasn't prepared to give the connection between them a chance to become something more than sexual attraction and a whole lot of like.

A few years ago, Tyler would have taken up her no-strings-sex offer and run with it. He would have taken her to bed and explored every inch of her body and walked away the next morning with no regrets. But he was thirty-seven years old, and he'd been around enough to know when something had the potential to be good. He didn't want a single night. He didn't want to explore only Ally's body, he wanted to explore her mind, the person who looked out at him through those warm brown eyes. He wanted to start something that had no end date. Something with a future.

Ally, on the other hand, had made it very, very clear that she wasn't interested in pursuing any connection that might develop into a relationship. She was leaving in a few weeks time. *No matter what.*

Tyler rested his elbows on the table, reflecting that if a mate came to him and told him the same story about a woman he was hooked on, Tyler would have no hesitation in labeling the woman Too Much Trouble.

Ally *was* too much trouble. She looked at him with naked desire, then held him at arm's length and told him he could have only so much and no more. She offered him friendship and comfort and understanding, but refused to consider anything else.

Like he said, too much trouble. Yet here he sat, literally unable to get her out of his thoughts.

You're officially a sad sack, buddy.

In the living room, his father's voice rose briefly above the din of the television. No doubt he was yelling at a contestant on one of the many game shows he loved to watch. There was no point asking if his father would mind reducing the volume to a more sociable level—Tyler had already tried that three times. Each time his father grudgingly reduced the sound, only for it to creep up in increments until it was once again making the windows vibrate in their frames.

He was rubbing his forehead and contemplating the purchase of a pair of really efficient noise canceling earphones when his phone rang, sending the handset buzzing across the kitchen table. The number on the screen had too many digits to be anything other than an international call.

"Jon," he said as he took the call.

There was a short pause before his brother spoke. "You psychic or something?"

"No, I have caller I.D."

"Right."

"What's up?"

"You didn't get back to me about Dad."

Tyler sat back in his chair. "You said you didn't care. Actually, you said you didn't give a shit."

"Yeah, well. Guess I'm not immune to guilt after all. How is he?"

"Improving. He's been out of hospital for six days now."

"So he's going to be okay?"

"Not in the long-term. The cancer's metastasized. It's in his liver, his kidneys. Everywhere, basically."

Silence while Jon chewed this over.

"How long have they given him?"

"Months, maybe only weeks. You know what they're like with those kinds of things. Lots of talk about how unpredictable it is."

"Right."

Tyler heard the scratch of a cigarette lighter. "You still smoking?"

"I quit three years ago."

His brother inhaled audibly on the other end of the line. Really sucking the nicotine in.

"I thought you were going to see him then bugger off?" Jon said.

"So did I. But it turns out you're not the only one who's not immune to guilt."

"So, what? You're sticking it out?"

"Yeah."

"Why?"

"Honestly? I don't know. You want to talk to him?"

"*No.*"

There was no mistaking the vehemence in his brother's tone.

"Sorry," Jon said after a moment. "I just… I don't want to talk to him." He laughed, the sound empty and hollow. "Wish I'd got a bloody letter from a solicitor or something, telling me it was all over, to be honest."

Tyler understood that sentiment only too well. "What do you want, then?"

"I don't know."

Tyler imagined his brother pacing restlessly. Jon had always found it hard to sit still for long, especially when he was agitated.

"I could keep you updated. Send you a text every now and then, let you know what's happening," Tyler offered.

His brother swore softly under his breath. Tyler knew what Jon was thinking, how he was feeling. The push and pull of guilt and anger. The desire to punish, the need for closure.

"Yeah. Okay," Jon said after a moment. "Let me know how he's doing." He sounded resigned. Pissed with himself. Another emotion Tyler was familiar with.

"Anything else you need?"

"Sure—less snow and about half a dozen more decent contractors."

"How's business?"

"Too good. Too bloody busy."

"Not a bad way to be."

"No. Listen, I gotta go."

"Okay. I'll let you know if anything changes."

"Thanks."

Tyler ended the call and picked up his pencil again but didn't immediately return to work.

Jon had always been the tough one, the hard one. So there was a strange comfort in knowing that his brother was as torn by their father's illness as he was.

Tyler turned his attention to his blueprints. The noise from the next room grew louder as his father changed channels. Tyler spent another ten minutes trying to tune it out before giving up. Standing, he gathered his things and exited the house.

He glanced briefly next door as he descended the rear steps. If things were different between him and Ally, if he hadn't misread that look in her eyes this afternoon and climbed the fence and tried to kiss her, he could go over there now and seek sanctuary.

But he had, which meant he couldn't throw himself on her mercy again.

He made his way across the yard to the shed. The double doors rattled noisily as he pushed them wide. He flicked on the overhead light. The smell of damp wood and old oil hit him as he surveyed the jumbled mess.

When he and Jon were kids, this place had been strictly off-limits unless they were accompanied by their father. Every tool had had its home on the Peg-

Board on the wall, lumber had been stored neatly in the overhead racks, and precisely labeled shelves had housed his father's many power tools.

A far cry from the shambles of today.

Tyler wondered why he was surprised—the house had been a disaster, after all—but somehow he was. This shed had always been his father's domain. His fiefdom. The place where he was most in charge of the world. And now it was a chaos of stacked boxes and grimy engine parts and old paint cans and moldy camping gear and rusty garden equipment.

Tyler almost returned to the house, but the memory of the blaring television was enough to make him stay. He needed to get some work done.

He dusted the top of a nearby carton and dumped his papers on it, then rearranged some of the junk. If he could clear the decks enough, he could use a couple of boxes as a work surface in the short-term, and in the long-term he could make a quick trip to Melbourne to grab his portable drafting table. It would be hotter than hell inside the tin shed during the day, but he figured it would cool down quickly enough at night with the doors open. Enough for him to have several hours of quiet and privacy to work in. Several very necessary hours if he was to maintain the design side of the business while taking this extended leave of absence.

He'd almost cleared a viable space when he shifted a stack of boxes and found an old table, draped with a paint-spattered sheet. It was too small to be any use to him, but something about the height and scale of the piece gave him pause.

Many years ago when he'd first finished his apprenticeship he'd made a side table for his mother. It had been a chance for him to show off his skills in marquetry and he'd spared no effort in creating an elaborate pattern in the round mahogany tabletop. He'd given it to his mother on Mother's Day with more than a little pride. She'd been flatteringly pleased with the gift, although, as always, she hadn't been able to resist one of her habitual backhanded digs. *It's beautiful, Tyler—but, of course, I have to say that. I'm your mother.*

Tyler had been too preoccupied over the past few days to register that the table had not been on display in the house. And perhaps it wasn't a huge surprise that his father had relegated it to the shed. He'd hardly welcome having a constant reminder of his estranged son cluttering his home.

Tyler tugged the sheet from the table. It had been a long time since he'd looked at any of his earlier pieces. No doubt he'd be embarrassed by how derivative the design was. If his memory served him, he'd taken many of his design cues from a classic Chippendale table. And he'd gone a little crazy with the marquetry, determined to impress his mother.

The sheet slid free. Tyler went very still.

It was his table, but in name only. The height, the shape were still the same, but the carefully polished circular top was now a scarred mess of chewed-up wood. Saw marks marred the rim in several places and nail holes pitted the surface, destroying the delicate inlay of satinwood, cherry and beech. Indentations marked where a hammer had smashed the wood, compressing the timber in regular circles. A large symmetrical gouge bit deeply into the wood on the far side. It took Tyler a few seconds to recognize it as the imprint a portable bench vise left behind when it had been clamped in place for a long time.

When he'd first started his own business, he'd taken on some restoration and insurance work to see him through the lean times. He'd seen pieces that had been left outside in the weather, mauled by pets, damaged by hot dishes and cigarettes and solvents. He'd seen scratches and gouges and breaks. But he'd never seen willful, intentional, extensive damage like this. This was...brutal.

There was no other word for it.

His father had destroyed the table. Systematically, deliberately. He'd taken a finely crafted piece of furniture—a labor of love that Tyler had offered to his mother—and turned it into a common workbench. He'd hacked at it, pounded it, scarred it. Then he'd cast it aside, his mission complete.

Tyler rested his hands on the marred surface, feeling the rough edges and pits beneath his fingers, trying to understand. Trying to get his head around the kind of vindictiveness, the malice, that it would take to do this to a once-beautiful piece of furniture.

Was it jealousy that had driven the man? Hate? Resentment that Tyler had given the table to his mother instead of his father? Anger?

But it was beyond him. Tyler simply couldn't comprehend the mind of a man who would wreak such senseless damage. Just as he'd never been unable to understand a man who would torture a family pet to punish his own child.

His father was a monster.

The thought drove him out of the shed toward the house. The door hit the wall hard as he entered. He strode straight to the living room and yanked the television plug out of the wall, silencing the deafening roar.

His father opened his mouth to protest.

Tyler took a step toward him, his hands fisted. "Why'd you do it?"

"What are you talking about? Put my show back on."

"The table. Why'd you destroy it?"

His father scowled. "The kitchen table? There's nothing wrong with it." But his gaze shifted to the side nervously.

"Don't pretend you don't know what I'm talking about, you nasty old bastard." Tyler was shaking with fury, barely able to contain himself.

"I don't have to listen to this. Not in my own home." His father started pushing himself out of his chair.

"You're not going anywhere, not until you tell me

why. Why you ruined that table and why you smacked the hell out of me and Jon when we were kids."

His father's head snapped back as though Tyler had slapped him.

"I never hit you," his father said with absolute conviction.

It was Tyler's turn to flinch. In all the years and all the times he'd envisioned this conversation, not once had he imagined his father denying the plain truth of history.

"You used to smack us around all the time. You gave Jon a bloody nose and perforated my eardrum. You beat him down the hallway with the buckle end of your belt."

"You two smashed the light on the porch with your yahooing around."

"*We were kids.* We were mucking around."

"You were out of control."

Tyler shook his head. "What about Mom? Every night you used to scream at her in the kitchen."

His father's jaw jutted angrily. "Thirty-seven and you're not even married. What would you know? All the time I spent trying to make ends meet, trying to stop you two from getting in trouble and not one single word of thanks. You've got your own business, your brother's in Canada. You're both doing well. And not one word of thanks."

Bob drew himself to his full height. In his expression was the volcanic rage of Tyler's childhood. A lifetime of memories flashed through Tyler's mind, a slide show of misery—his mother in tears, Jon cowering from their father's blows, the sound of his own fear as his father laid into him. Over and over, the memories kept coming.

"You can't rewrite history," Tyler said, his voice low and hard. "You got stuck into us every chance you got."

Something in his father's face shifted. "You don't know what you're talking about. My father used to knock me from one side of the house to the other. And you two got a couple of smacks." His father's mouth worked for a second and he swallowed noisily. *"I loved you boys."*

His father turned his back abruptly and took a shuddering breath. Tyler heard something click in his father's throat.

Then, his shoulders very square, his father walked slowly from the room, across the hallway and into his bedroom. The door swung shut between them.

Tyler was left standing alone. Adrenaline still surged through his body, but the fight was over.

And he had no idea who'd won.

CHAPTER SEVEN

ALLY KNEW THAT SOMETHING was wrong the moment she opened the door. Tension radiated off Tyler's big body in waves and his face was set like stone. Everything about him screamed wounded, angry animal.

"Tyler. What happened?"

"Can I come in? Just for a few minutes."

"Of course." She ushered him inside. "I was just about to open a bottle of wine."

She'd actually been in the middle of a yoga session, but she'd never seen a man more in need of a drink in her life.

She led him to living room, then ducked into the kitchen. She gathered two glasses and a bottle of red wine, her mind racing.

He and Bob must have had another fight. She couldn't think of any other explanation for the tight, hard expression on Tyler's face.

She added a packet of crackers to her haul, in case Tyler hadn't eaten. Then she took a deep breath and joined him.

He was standing in front of the French doors, his

gaze bouncing around as though he didn't quite know what to do with himself.

She didn't say a word, simply opened the wine and poured him a glass.

"Here. You look like you could do with this."

He glanced down, then reached out and wrapped his fingers around the bowl of the glass. "Thanks."

She watched as he tipped his head back and downed half the wine in one swallow. Another tip of his head and the glass was empty.

She sank into the cushions of the couch, her knees drawn to her chest. Waiting.

Tyler stared at his empty glass for a long moment. A muscle flickered in his jaw as though he was clenching and unclenching his teeth. The room was so silent she could hear the clock ticking and the hum of the refrigerator in the next room.

Finally, he looked at her. "He used to beat us."

She took a deep breath. Nodded. "I wondered."

It had been a dark, unvoiced possibility in the back of her mind ever since she'd witnessed that moment between father and son the morning Bob came home from hospital.

"Did you? Funny. All those years, and not a single teacher ever asked about the bruises. None of the neighbors, either."

"Some people don't want to see."

He wandered to the bookcase. She watched as he picked up and put down the small trinkets Wendy had displayed there.

"Everyone used to think he was a great guy. Good old Bob Adamson, a man you could rely on. Honest, hardworking, reliable. A regular saint." He looked across the room at her, his eyes a dark, turbulent gray. "You like him. You think he's a nice old man."

She nodded. "Yes. I did."

"He was a bastard. What he did to me and Jon…" Tyler shook his head.

She shifted to grab the bottle. "Pass me your glass."

She poured more wine then returned the glass.

"Thanks."

He drank a mouthful. Then sat on the edge of the cushion of the armchair opposite her, his elbows on his knees, both hands cradling his drink.

His posture was so tight, so protective, every instinct urged her to go wrap her arms around him. She forced herself to remain seated. As much as this man needed comfort, she sensed that the words he was slowly, painfully doling out had been sitting inside him for years. More than anything right now, he needed to talk.

"When I left here, I never wanted to see him again. I tried to stay away, but after a few years I realized I couldn't do it to Mom. So I saw them once a year, on her birthday, until she died. And then I figured I was off the hook. It was over, and I'd finally escaped."

"And then I came to see you."

"Then you came. And I told myself I didn't give a shit that he was sick, that he was dying. But I couldn't stop thinking about it, so I decided that I'd come and say my piece—all the things I'd never said to him. Get it off my chest once and for all. Then we really would be done." He shook his head in disgust.

"What happened?"

"I couldn't do it." He flicked a glance at her. "I walked into his hospital room, ready to give it to him... He looked so old. So *small*. And I couldn't do it. So I figured I'd just walk away, leave it at that. But I couldn't do that, either." He sounded so angry with himself.

"You think that's a bad thing?"

"He knocked me and Jon around every chance he got. Told me I was no good and I'd never amount to anything more times than I could count. Even when he was decent, I was scared of him, waiting for the other shoe to drop. So, yeah, I think that's a bad thing."

"I don't think compassion is ever a bad thing."

He shook his head, rejecting her words.

She abandoned her casual posture and shifted to the edge of her seat. "Something happened tonight."

"No, it didn't." He laughed, a hard, sharp sound. "All those years I imagined sticking it to him. Looking him in the eye and telling him what he was. And nothing happened."

Ally was struggling to keep up. "You finally confronted him? That's what happened tonight?"

"Yeah. I was out in the shed, trying to find quiet

to work in. I cleared away some old junk and I found a table I'd made for my mother when I finished my apprenticeship."

He took a big gulp of the wine before continuing. "He ruined it. Cut it up, nailed holes in it. Just… totally screwed it up."

Ally pressed her fingers to her lips in shock. Tyler glanced up at her, his expression tortured.

"What I don't get, what I will never get is *why*. What did I ever do to him to make him hate me so much? What did I ever do or say to earn that kind of treatment?"

It was a child's plea, issued from a man's mouth. Ally's chest ached for all the years of doubt and hurt he'd endured. This time she didn't resist the urge to go to him. She sat on the arm of his chair and slid both arms around him, pressing her cheek against the top of his head.

He remained locked in his rigid posture, unable to accept her comfort, but she didn't let him go. She couldn't.

"What did he say when you confronted him?" she asked quietly.

Tyler's shoulders lifted as he took a deep breath. "He blanked me. He said he'd never hit us, then he claimed we were out of control and he'd had to discipline us. Then he told me I didn't know what a knock was and that he loved us."

He dropped his head, fighting the emotion washing over him. The muscles beneath her hands felt as though they were carved from granite.

She'd seen him like this once before, hunched over the steering wheel of his truck. She held him more tightly.

"It's okay, Tyler," she whispered. "It's okay to be upset."

She could feel the resistance in him. Then, suddenly, he broke, turning toward her with a fierce neediness, his arms coming around her. His body shuddered and she felt the rough, choppy gusts of his breathing as he sobbed against her chest.

She splayed her hands over his back, holding him close, keeping him safe while he let out years of grief.

He made an inarticulate sound, his arms holding her so tightly it was almost painful. She smoothed her hand over his head and didn't let go.

Tears pricked her eyes but she blinked them away. Tyler did not need or want her pity.

As his breathing slowed and finally normalized, tension crept into his body in small degrees. She guessed what he was thinking, how much he must be regretting his moment of weakness. She knew without asking that he rarely, if ever, talked about his relationship with his father. That what had passed between Tyler and her was a rarity, that she was incredibly privileged to be trusted with his closely guarded truths.

She felt the honor keenly, as well as an aching

awareness that she was not what this man needed in his life. Not with her track record with personal relationships. And yet he was here, and she was holding him and now that she knew his full measure, now that she understood, she could no longer ignore the urging of her own heart.

She'd tried. She'd kept him at a distance and told herself she was doing the right thing, that it was for the best that nothing happen between them. But he'd come to her and he needed her and it was beyond her to deny him.

His arms tensed and she let him put some space between them. He used his forearm to wipe the tears from his face, not looking at her. "Sorry about that."

"Why?"

He glanced at her briefly. "I didn't come over here to dump on you, believe it or not."

She could see him pulling himself in more with every word, putting his armor on.

She dropped to her knees in front of him and caught both his hands in hers, forcing him to look at her.

"You think I pity you because of what you told me? You think that I think less of you because you cried?"

"I was wound up. I probably should have gone to the pub and gotten shit-faced."

He was so strong, so used to simply soldiering on. He couldn't conceive of a place where he could be safe. Where he could put down his burdens for a few hours and allow himself to feel and to grieve.

She acted on pure instinct, reaching out to cup his jaw in both hands, rising up to bring her face to his. She kissed him, pouring all her admiration and liking and lust into the contact, determined to prove to him that his revelations did not make him less of a man in her eyes.

After a long moment, he pulled away and she let him go.

"I don't want your pity, Ally." He sounded almost angry.

"Why did you come here tonight?"

It took him a moment to answer, and when he did he was deliberately offhand. "I don't know. I needed to get out of the house."

She shook her head, refusing to let him retreat. "You said yourself you could have gone to the pub. Or you could have left, gone back to Melbourne. You have friends there, I know. You could have done a million other things. But you came to me."

He stared at her, his gaze intent. She stared back, unflinching.

"That's why I kissed you, Tyler. For the same reason you came to me."

His gaze dropped to her mouth. "You said you weren't interested."

"I did say that." She offered him the ghost of a smile. "You should probably know that I don't have the greatest track record when it comes to making decisions in my personal life."

"Ally, I need…" He shook his head, unable to articulate what he needed, what he wanted. Why he'd come to her.

"I know. That's what I need, too."

Even though it scared the living daylights out of her.

She leaned forward and kissed him again and this time his mouth opened beneath hers and his arms encircled her. His kiss was demanding, consuming, undeniable. Which was fine with her, because she didn't want to deny him. Not anymore. She wanted to hold him close, for him to be a part of her body. She wanted to love and comfort and soothe him.

She made an approving noise and clutched at his shoulders, her fingers digging into the warm flesh of his back. Tyler answered by intensifying the kiss, scooping her body closer so that she was positioned between his open thighs, her breasts pressed against his chest.

The kiss deepened, grew more fiery. Hands began to rove, sliding beneath T-shirts, gliding over skin. Ally groaned as his hands found her breasts, his thumbs teasing her nipples. Tyler started drawing her tank top up her torso, muttering something against her lips.

"Sorry?" she said.

"I need to see you," he said, and she lifted her arms obediently as he tugged her top over her head.

His gaze fell on her breasts, hot and needy. She reached behind herself to undo the clasp on her bra. Her bra loosened, then slid down her arms. Tyler's gaze swept from one breast to the other, then his hands slid up to cup her bare flesh.

"Beautiful," he said, his voice low with desire.

She tugged at his T-shirt. "Fair's fair."

He had it off in seconds, and the next thing she knew she was on her back on the rug, Tyler on top of her. His chest was hot and hard against her breasts, the press of skin on skin satisfying and arousing all at once. She could feel his erection against her belly, could feel how ready he was, and she instinctively parted her thighs. He came to rest between them, his hard-on pressing against her through the soft fabric of her yoga pants. She shifted her hips restlessly, increasing the pressure, then he lowered his head and took a nipple into his mouth and she arched away from the floor, moaning low in her throat as sensation shot through her body.

Her fingers wove into the thickness of his hair and gripped tightly, holding him in place as he licked and sucked and tongued her breasts. She shivered, desire building on desire until the craving to have him inside her overcame every other consideration.

"Take your jeans off," she panted, reaching for the stud at his waist.

She worked it free, only to find more buttons. She groaned with frustration and tugged the buttons free from the soft denim with impatient hands. She pushed his jeans and underwear down his hips and he lifted his hips obligingly, taking his weight on his elbows while he kicked off the pants. She pressed her palm flat against his chest, then slid it boldly down the plane of his chest and belly until she encountered the thick length of his erection. Her fingers wrapped around the velvety skin, stroking, learning the length and breadth of him.

Tyler swore under his breath, then she felt a tug at her waist as he rolled away from her and started peeling her yoga pants down her legs. Within seconds she was naked and he was on top of her again, his erection nudging at the slick wetness between her legs.

Her hands found his backside, urging him closer, but he resisted.

"Condom." He started to pull away, reaching for his jeans.

She shook her head, halting his retreat. "I'm on the Pill. And I trust you."

She wrapped her legs around his waist and thrust her hips forward in silent invitation. All hesitation was gone as he slid home in one long, wet glide. Ally gave a little whimper at how perfect and hot and hard he felt.

Even though she wanted—needed—him to move inside her, even though she could feel the quivering tension in him, he remained still, buried to the hilt. He kissed her, his tongue teasing hers, his lips demanding, his arms banding tightly around her as he marked the moment indelibly in both their memories.

The first time they became one. The first moment of intimate connection.

He broke the kiss, using his elbows to take his weight as he pulled back enough to look into her eyes. He framed her face with his hands, tracing her cheekbones with his thumbs as they lay chest to chest, belly to belly, hip to hip.

"Ally."

Only then did he start to move, setting up a slow, inexorable rhythm, inviting her to join in. And all the while he stared into her eyes.

She got lost in the myriad silvers and grays of his irises, lost in the thrust and withdrawal of his body and the crazy-making friction building between them.

It didn't take long for need to overwhelm everything else. There was too much fire, too much longing, too much emotion. She started to pant, clawing at Tyler's back, making inarticulate noises as her climax swept toward her. He lowered his head and pulled her nipple into his mouth, his other hand sliding between their bodies to find the damp curls at the juncture of her thighs.

She tensed as his thumb brushed over her. Her body clenched around him. Then he caressed her again and she came, his name on her lips, her body bowing off the rug.

He murmured encouragement near her ear, riding

out her orgasm, milking the last shudder from her. Then and only then did he give himself over to the moment, his thrusts becoming wilder, more urgent. She urged him on with her hands and her body. He thrust deeply one last time, then he pressed his cheek against hers and his breath came out in a heated rush as he climaxed.

For a brief moment he was deadweight on her as he relaxed against her. Then he stirred and started to roll to one side.

"Not yet. Stay with me," she said.

He stilled, looking into her face. "I'm not exactly a lightweight."

She smiled slightly. "I like it."

His eyebrows rose, but he didn't try to withdraw. He pressed his cheek to hers again, his weight settling on her. She flattened her palms against his back and smoothed her hands over him, mapping the breadth and strength of his shoulders, tracing the long, lean muscles either side of his spine, curving her fingers over the resilient roundness of his backside. The hair on the backs of his thighs was crisp and soft, the muscles there very firm, while the skin over his hips was as smooth as silk.

He was beautiful, inside and out. Masculine to the bone, with a big, finely hewn body, his outward strength matched only by his tender, generous soul.

She rested her hand in the center of his chest, feeling the thump-thump of his heart and the rush of his blood as his body cooled. She could smell their mingled sweat and the earthy scent of sex and, beneath that, the sunshine warmth of Tyler's skin.

"I'm an idiot," she said very quietly.

He turned his head to look at her. "How so?"

"If I hadn't been so stupid, we could have done this days ago."

"Ah."

She waited for him to say more but he didn't.

"That's all you have to say? *Ah?*"

"I'm being diplomatic."

He was smiling, his eyes warm, his body relaxed and loose.

She smoothed a lock of hair from his forehead, glad that, for the moment, the shadows were gone from his eyes. He deserved a little lightness, a little happiness after the darkness of his recent past.

"You know what would make this moment perfect?" she said.

"What?"

"Ice cream."

He laughed, then slowly the smile faded from his lips. "Ally Bishop. Where have you been all my life?"

She smoothed his hair again, her chest aching with emotions she wasn't even close to being ready to acknowledge. "Waiting."

Then she nudged him gently and he rolled to the side.

"Nuts About Chocolate or raspberry ripple or

both?" she asked, her tone deliberately light as she pushed herself to her feet.

"Is that a trick question?"

She smiled and went to find the ice cream.

TYLER WOKE TO THE SCENT of vanilla and spice. A warm body curled beside him on the bed, soft and rounded in all the right places.

Ally.

They were spooned together, her back to his front, his arm around her waist. He could feel the regular rise and fall of her breathing, and for long minutes he simply lay there, enjoying the intimacy of close human contact, the comfort of skin on skin.

She'd saved his sanity tonight. He'd been half out of his mind after the fight with his father. The urge to follow his father into his room, to grab him by the throat and force him to acknowledge his own brutality had been almost overwhelming. But Tyler had never used violence to get his own way. So instead he'd found himself on the street, his keys in hand, thoughts of escaping to Melbourne and his home and his life in his mind. He'd made it into the truck, put his seat belt on—but he hadn't been able to make himself start the engine.

He'd been utterly lost then. He couldn't go, he couldn't stay. Somehow, he'd wound up on Ally's doorstep. From the moment she'd opened the door, her calm, ready acceptance had been like a balm. She'd simply waited and the words had come.

It was the first time he'd told anyone about his childhood. He wasn't sure what he'd expected, but she hadn't reeled in horror or broken down in tears or insisted on calling the police. She'd listened. She'd asked all the right questions. And when he'd lost it, she'd offered him the wordless comfort of her arms.

Humiliating to admit how much he'd needed it. He was a grown man, with a life of his own. All this stuff with his father had happened years ago. The old man should have no power over him anymore.

Yet Tyler hadn't been able to drive away.

That was the part that got him the most. The tears he could live with. Just. But for the life of him he couldn't understand why he felt compelled to stay, why, even now, lying in his lover's bed, a part of him worried that his father was in the house alone when he wasn't fully recovered from his operation.

Because Tyler was weak? Because his father still had some kind of hold over him? What kind of man took so much crap and still refused to walk away?

The tension had returned in his chest and belly. Ally stirred in her sleep and he realized he'd tightened his grip on her. Gently he eased away from her, rolling onto his back. One hand propped behind his head, he stared at the ceiling, trying to understand himself.

"Roll over and I'll rub your shoulders."

He turned his head to find Ally watching him, the

concern in her big brown eyes discernible even in the dim light.

"I didn't mean to wake you up."

"I can sleep anytime." She reached out and smoothed a hand over his chest. "It's not every day I offer ice cream *and* a free back rub. It's a pretty good deal."

He smiled faintly, catching her hand and lifting it to his mouth. He kissed her fingers. "Some other time, thanks."

He was way too wound up to relax into a massage, his brain churning.

"I know you're not big on talking, but sometimes it does help."

"Women always say that."

"Because it's true. Crying helps, too, but I know I'll never get you to concede on that one."

"No kidding."

She didn't say anything more, simply pressed her body alongside his and rested her head on his shoulder. There was nothing demanding or expectant about her silence—she was simply there, available and open. After a long few minutes Tyler took a deep breath.

"I wanted to go tonight. Wanted to get in my truck and drive and leave him to work it out for himself. But I couldn't. And I don't know why."

"Don't you?" Ally shifted so she could look him in the eye. "Do you want me to tell you?"

When he didn't say anything, she reached out and

ran a finger along the stubble on his jaw, her touch light. "Because you couldn't drive off and leave an old, sick man on his own. That's why."

He knew it was true, but he didn't like it. "I should be able to. After everything he's done. He deserves worse. He deserves to die alone."

"I'm sure he does. But you're not like him." Her eyes were depthless, soft as velvet. "You're a loving, compassionate man, Tyler Adamson. It's a miracle, given what he did to you, but you are. You're a good, good man."

There was so much warmth and emotion in her gaze. Tyler looked away, uncomfortable. Growing up, being hard had been the only value worth aspiring to, both to withstand his father's attacks and to prove to himself that he wasn't a victim. As a grown man, he'd prided himself on needing nothing and nobody and solving his own problems, righting his own wrongs.

"You think being compassionate is a sign of weakness, don't you?" Ally asked.

He shrugged noncommittally. Ally might not be a trained psychologist, but she was bloody good at putting her finger on the heart of things at times.

She pressed a kiss to his mouth. "It takes great courage and strength of character to be generous when you have every reason to be otherwise. You're the strongest man I know, Tyler. I wish I was half as strong."

He traced the delicate arch of one of her eyebrows.

What she was saying was flattering but it went against every lesson of his life. She turned her face into his hand and kissed his palm.

"I know there's nothing I can say to convince you. But I hope you believe me one day."

Because he didn't know how to respond, Tyler rolled toward her and slid a hand up her belly toward her breasts. She made a small, pleased sound as he cupped the warm weight of her in his hand.

She had a very sexy body, soft and curvy, full-breasted. Her skin was smooth and clear, her nipples a pale pink, like the blush inside a seashell. He circled them with his thumbs, watching as they hardened to arousal.

"You're setting a dangerous precedent here, you realize. Twice in one night," she said.

He smiled. Then he set himself to the task of proving to her exactly how dangerous he could be.

CHAPTER EIGHT

ALLY WOKE AT EIGHT TO find the bed empty beside her. She blinked, then a slow smile spread across her face as she remembered last night.

Tyler, making love to her. Insatiable. Intense. Gorgeous.

Then she remembered the catalyst for their encounter and her smile faded. Last night had been… incredible, but it hadn't changed the world. Bob was still next door, and he still needed care. Tyler's ordeal was far from over.

The difference, though, was that she knew now, and the days of keeping her distance were over. She would do whatever she could to ease Tyler's burden. Whatever it took.

A footfall in the hallway drew her head around. Tyler appeared in the doorway with a glass of juice and a plate of toast. She blinked in surprise. She'd assumed he'd gone next door.

"I didn't know whether you'd prefer jam or peanut butter, so I did a piece with each." He was wearing nothing except his boxer briefs and she tried not to stare too obviously.

Last night, she'd been too busy ripping his clothes

off to truly appreciate how beautifully he was put together. Now, her gaze ran over his square shoulders, well-defined pectoral muscles, flat belly and narrow hips. His thighs were muscular without being ridiculous, his calves a triumph of proportion. He was easily the sexiest, most masculine man she'd ever been with.

She swallowed a lump of pure lust.

"I like both. But you didn't have to make me breakfast."

"I was hungry. It seemed a little rude to pig out solo." He sat on the bed and passed her the juice.

She straightened and took a big mouthful. "What are your plans for the day?"

His gaze dropped to her breasts for a gratifyingly rapt second before he selected a piece of toast. "I need to check on Dad. And I promised Gabby I would get these designs to her by the end of the day."

"You can work here, if you'd like. I know you find it hard to concentrate over there." She took another gulp of juice. "And if you need me to, I'll sit with your father while you drive to Melbourne this afternoon."

He gave her a searching look and she knew he'd detected the effort she'd had to make to keep her tone neutral when she'd mentioned his father.

She reached for his hand. "He's not simply the nice old man next door for me anymore. To be frank, I'd be happy to never see him again. Or to have a chance to give him a piece of my mind. But I know that both those things put a burden on you. So I'll keep going next door and doing what I can to help. Whatever you want. But I want you to know I'm doing it for you, not for him."

She knew that for some people, Bob's illness and advanced years would be automatic grounds for a get-out-of-jail-free card for past behavior, but not for her. Tyler hadn't said much about his mother, but she understood that he'd had precious few people on his side in his lifetime. Well, Ally was on his side, and she was fiercely determined that he knew it and that all her comfort and understanding were for him. He deserved to have one champion in his life, one person who put him above anybody and everybody else.

Perhaps if Bob had sought to reconcile with Tyler in some way, she would feel differently. But he hadn't. Instead, he'd attempted to blame Tyler and twist the truth.

She couldn't see Tyler's face properly, but the grip on her hand tightened until it was almost painful.

"So do you want to work here today?" she asked again.

"If you don't mind."

"Well, I'll be honest, you're something of a distraction. But I'll suck it up."

His gaze fell to her breasts again. "I'm the distraction?"

She loved the heat in his eyes, loved the way he made her feel sexy and beautiful and desirable.

"Looks like it's going to be a long day," she said mischievously.

They showered together after they finished breakfast, then Tyler went to check on his father. Ally stood at the kitchen window, watching the house next door anxiously after he'd left. She wished there was some way she could take this burden away from him, some way she could protect him from whatever remaining ugliness his father had left in him. But even if she could, Tyler would never allow her to do so.

He climbed the fence an hour later and she went onto the deck to greet him. He had his roll of blueprints under his arm and a grim expression on his face.

"How'd it go?"

"Fine. He's alive and kicking. On his high horse, too. Told me he wanted an apology."

Ally blinked. "Wow. That's some serious denial he's got going on there."

The tightness had returned to his posture again. She grabbed his hand and laced her fingers through his and pulled him into the house.

"I've set you up in the study."

He stopped in the doorway when they arrived, surveying the empty desk and the bulletin board she'd cleared behind it.

"I thought you could hang some of your stuff up there so you could reference it easily. And I know the desk isn't as big as one of those big drawing boards you probably use, but I figure it's better than nothing."

"It's great, Ally. Perfect. But where are you going to work? I don't want to displace you."

"All I need is a chair and a pad and pen most of the time. The desk is pretty much wasted on me."

He hooked an arm around her neck and drew her close. "Thanks." He kissed her, his gaze warm and gentle.

"It was my pleasure."

And it had been. She'd enjoyed doing something for him. Something to make his life easier.

She eased out from under his arm.

"You've got work to do. And I need to start thinking about my next column."

"If you say so."

She turned for the door, only to start a little when a large hand bussed her on the butt. She gave him a dark look over her shoulder.

"That is so not going to become a habit."

"I've been wanting to do that from the moment I met you."

She stared at him, arrested. "Really?"

"You want a sworn affidavit? Or some other kind of proof?" He reached for her again.

She dodged out of the way, laughing, relieved to see him smiling again.

"Do some work. Then maybe we can talk about this proof thing."

They worked in separate rooms until lunchtime.

She made sandwiches for three and went with Tyler when he delivered one to his father. Bob was surly and taciturn and she stood in the doorway and watched as Tyler bit his tongue and didn't rise to any of his father's baits.

Amazing how differently a person's behavior could appear when viewed through a new prism. She'd always been mildly amused by Bob's gruff abruptness, but now all she could hear was the frustrated anger beneath his words. Her blood ran cold as she imagined him raising a hand to two small boys.

Bob caught her staring at him and she held his eye for a long, steady beat. She wasn't going to pretend that she didn't know what he was.

He was the first to look away.

She joined Tyler in the study when they returned to Wendy's house, curling up in the armchair with her latest letter file. It was nearly three when Tyler sat back in his chair, rubbed his neck and announced that he was done. Then he stood and plucked her file from her hands and kissed her, hard. They wound up mostly naked on the study floor, their lovemaking fierce and urgent.

Afterward, Ally watched as he dressed and rolled up his plans.

"I'll be back later tonight."

There was an unspoken question in his gaze. He wanted to know if he should come over. If she wanted him to stay the night again.

A wiser woman would say no. Things were already so intense between them.

"I'll be awake."

His slow, sweet, sexy smile was her reward. "I'll bring more ice cream."

She waved him off from the porch and then went inside. The bed was a rumpled mess so she changed the sheets. Then she sat on the freshly made bed and forced herself to face what she was doing—starting something up with Tyler Adamson, despite her promise to herself to never, ever let anyone down again.

She clenched her hands on her knees, her body tense. She didn't want to hurt him. Now, more than ever. He deserved happiness. He deserved every good thing life could throw at him.

Then, don't screw it up.

A great idea, but easier said than done. At least, it was in her experience. But it was too late to play it safe—it wasn't as though she could turn back time and change things so that she'd remained on the couch last night instead of wrapping Tyler in her arms. And she wouldn't want to, anyway, even if she could—last night had been one of the most challenging, precious, moving experiences of her life.

She stood and smoothed the quilt.

There was no point mooching around, agonizing over what might happen. After all, she'd been angsting and second-guessing herself since the moment she met Tyler and it hadn't stopped the inevitable from happening. So maybe the answer was simply to hand herself over to fate and take things one moment at a time and not get ahead of herself.

It wasn't exactly a plan, but it was *something*. And it would have to suffice.

AT SIX O'CLOCK, SHE GIRDED her loins and went next door. Bob was watching his game shows and he barely grunted when she let herself inside and said hello.

A far cry from his usual bright-eyed greeting. But he wasn't about to waste his charms on her now that Tyler had so clearly taken her into his confidence.

"Have you had your dinner yet, Bob?" she shouted over the din of the television.

When he didn't answer her, she stepped in front of the set and repeated her question.

He frowned at her and she could see him trying to work out how much rudeness he could get away with. "There's nothing to eat."

Ally knew for a fact that Tyler had prepared a plate of cold chicken and salad for his father's dinner, leaving it in the fridge. Leaving Bob to his show, she went into the kitchen to check the fridge. Sure enough, the meal was gone. On a hunch, she checked the garbage. The chicken and salad had been scraped, untouched, into the pail.

It was such a childish, spiteful act. Had Bob imagined he was making more work for Tyler? Forcing his son to do double labor in order to feed him? Punishing him in some way, as he'd punished Tyler as a child?

She stood in the doorway of the living room, watching him, trying to decide how to handle the situation.

A tuft of white hair sat up on his scalp, and the shirt he was wearing badly needed ironing. His hands moved restlessly on the arms of the chair and she was reminded of those long minutes she'd spent sitting beside him in the grass the morning he'd collapsed, holding his hand and willing him to live while she waited for the ambulance to come.

She'd felt so deeply for him then, lamented his aloneness so much. But he'd brought it on himself, and now that his son was here, helping him despite their troubled history, Bob still pushed him away and punished him.

Was he so unreachable? So set in his ways and bloody-minded that even now, when his days were numbered, he couldn't find it in himself to regret the past and try to make amends? One word, one look, of acknowledgment would mean so much to Tyler, she knew. It might even give him the closure he was so desperately looking for. It might even set him free.

The thought gave her impetus to move into the room and into Bob's line of vision.

"Bob. Can you turn the television down for a minute?"

He frowned, but he jabbed at the remote control

and the TV was muted, reduced to a flickering, distracting display in the background.

"I take it you didn't want the chicken?" she asked.

"It was off. Smelled funny."

She debated whether to call him on the lie, then decided to let it slide. She sat on the chair nearest to him and looked at him steadily.

"Is this the way you want things to be, Bob? Do you really want to spend your final days at war with your own son?"

"I don't know what lies he's been telling you, but he and his brother were always ungrateful little bastards."

"I believe him, Bob. I believe every word."

Bob's lip curled. "Think I don't know what you two are up to next door? Don't go thinking that letting him into your pants is going to get you anywhere, either. He's never been good at sticking at anything."

Ally thought of Tyler's thriving business and the way he'd put his life on hold to tend to his dying parent. She'd never met a more determined, honorable man in her life.

She stood. "Do you know what the saddest thing is? You have an incredible son. He's smart and he's kind and he's funny. And you will never, ever know him, because you're too small-minded and angry to see past your own failings. And they are your failings, Bob. Good men do not beat their children. No exceptions, no excuses."

She left the room before she said something she'd regret. Something irretrievable that would make it impossible for her to help Tyler care for Bob. She made him a sandwich, then she returned to the living room where the television was once again blaring.

She grabbed the small side table from the corner and dragged it until it was beside Bob's chair, placing the plate on it.

"If you throw this out, you'll have to make your own dinner or go hungry," she said.

Bob didn't acknowledge her. She returned to the kitchen and tidied up. Standing at the sink, her gaze fell on the shed. She turned off the tap and dried her hands and headed for the door.

There was still enough daylight left for her to open the doors and find the light switch on the inside wall. She stepped over a box of old tap fittings and the shaft of a broken trimmer and stopped in front of Tyler's table.

As he'd reported, Bob had all but destroyed it. The once-smooth wood was hacked and scarred, the delicate inlay shattered in parts, missing in others. There was one small section where the marquetry had escaped unscathed and she ran her fingers over it, feeling the smooth fineness of the work, marveling at the beauty Tyler had created.

She knew next to nothing about cabinetmaking, but she knew he'd spent hours on this table. Days. She imagined him working on it, young and eager to show his parents what he'd achieved, how far he'd come. Imagined the quiet pride he must have felt when he gave it to his mother.

A sudden conviction came over her. She gripped the edges of the table and lifted it, stepping over the boxes of junk and carrying the table out of the shed. She put it down so she could turn off the light and secure the door, then she carried the table to Wendy's house. She set it down in the living room and examined it again. The damage seemed even more profound now that it was contrasted with Wendy's delicate antique furniture.

It didn't matter. The important thing was that this was Tyler's table, and now it was safe.

"RIGHT. WE ALL SORTED?" Tyler said, shutting his diary with a snap and standing.

It was past seven, and he and Gabby had finally said goodbye to their client. The meeting had lasted almost an hour longer than he'd anticipated, but the upside was that the rush hour traffic out of the city would have cleared by the time he hit the road.

He started tossing things into his briefcase, only looking up when he registered that Gabby hadn't responded.

She was watching him, eyes narrowed, lips pursed. "What's going on?"

"What do you mean?" He slid a spare set of mechanical pencils into his briefcase.

"Why are you so keen on getting out of here? Anyone would think the building was on fire."

"Don't even joke about it."

"Seriously. What's going on? I gather from what you haven't said about your father that things have been pretty heavy going on that front?"

"Yeah. Well. Can't teach an old dog new tricks. He's determined to be an ass, and I'm determined to stick it out, so we're locked in this thing till it's over."

"You know, that's the most you've ever said about your father in all the years I've known you."

Tyler frowned. Had he really been so tight-lipped? "Probably because I hadn't seen him for ten years. He wasn't exactly at the top of my mind."

Although he'd always been there in some way.

"It's more than that. You seem…different. Lighter."

He gave her a look. "Lighter? What does that mean?"

"I'll give you an example. In the meeting just now, when that interior designer said she wanted to go with the beech on the bedside tables even though it isn't traditional, you didn't even bat an eyelid. Normally you would have gnashed your teeth and argued in favor of the cherry. But you simply made a note of it and moved on."

"She's the customer. And I've got better things to do with my time."

Gabby pointed a finger at him. "Exactly. Since

when did you have better things do to with your time than defend your designs?"

He stared at her. She stared back. Finally he shrugged.

"I've met someone."

Gabby's face lit up. "Really?"

"Yeah. Her name's Ally. She lives next door to my father."

"And you two are...you know?" Gabby made a gesture with the fingers of both hands.

"Very ladylike. You've been hanging around with the guys too long."

"I'm going to take that as a yes. Tell me about her." Gabby propped her butt on the edge of his desk.

"What do you want to know?"

"Whatever you've got. You're one of my favorite people in all the world, and I want to know who this woman is who's made you so happy."

Tyler had been about to tell her to mind her own business, but her words arrested him.

"And maybe I want to pick up a few tips for next time around. Since she seems to have succeeded where I failed."

Tyler considered her a moment, trying to read her. She'd been the one to break off their relationship, and in the two years since there had never been a hint that she still had feelings for him. But there had been a look on her face just now...

"It was a joke, Tyler." She rolled her eyes. "Get

over yourself. Now, are you going to tell me about her or not?"

"She's in her early thirties. Short. Dark hair. She writes the Dear Gertrude column in the paper."

"I love that column! Gertrude rocks."

"Ally does, too." He thought about what she'd said to him this morning.

"Oh, boy."

"What?"

"You are toast. Utterly gone. Besotted."

He shook his head.

"Don't bother denying it. You are smitten beyond the point of no return," Gabby said. "When can I meet her?"

"I don't know," he said, remembering Ally's reluctance to enter into anything with him and her insistence that she would be leaving in a few weeks time *no matter what.* "It's complicated."

"Complicated how?"

"You're a very nosey person, you know that?"

"I'm a concerned friend with a vested interest."

He sighed. There was a reason he avoided these kinds of conversations.

"Okay," Gabby said. "I'll back off. But if you like this woman as much as I think you do, you need to make sure you're both on the same page."

"Yes, Mom."

Gabby slid off his desk. "Careful, or I'll come up with a reason to delay you leaving."

"You seem to be forgetting something—I'm the boss."

She made a rude noise. "When in doubt, appeal to authority. A classic loser's move."

He grabbed his briefcase and the roll of designs and headed for the door. He tapped her on the head with the roll as he passed by. "One day that mouth of yours is going to get you in trouble."

He left her to lock up, but her words stayed with him as he drove to Woodend. Last night and today had been great, working with Ally, sharing lunch with her, making love on the study floor. Knowing he had her in his corner had made all the difference in dealing with his father. He hadn't felt so pressured, so cornered. So alone.

But there was no escaping the fact that Ally had resisted his first attempts to do something about the chemistry between them. And she'd been very clear that she had no plans to hang around once her current stint of house-sitting was up.

He'd never been the kind of man who got carried away with his lovers. There had always been a small, essential part of himself that he'd held back. But with Ally…he'd given her everything. Revealed his darkest, most vulnerable places.

His gut told him that last night had changed things for both of them, but his head wanted to nail her down, wanted to hear the words of confirmation come out of her mouth.

Too bad for his head, because he was never going

to initiate that conversation. Not only because that wasn't his style, but Ally was far too skittish, far too reluctant a recruit to their relationship for him to start asking those kinds of questions.

He would simply have to wait and hope and trust his gut.

ALLY WAS IN BED, READING the latest edition of *House and Garden* magazine when she heard Tyler's footsteps on the porch. She slid from the sheets and opened the door wearing only her tank top and a pair of panties. Tyler stilled, his gaze sliding down her body. Then he passed her a small cooler.

"You might want to put that in the freezer before I jump you."

She gasped out a laugh, but he wasn't kidding, sweeping in the door and pulling her into his arms. Her knees went weak as he kissed her with a hungry intensity.

"I missed you," he said when he finally came up for air. "And you should always dress like this. Always."

"Let me put the ice cream away," she said, slightly breathless.

"Move fast."

She found him sitting on the edge of the bed when she returned, his shirt off but his jeans still on, flicking through her *House and Garden* magazine.

"You running low on entertainment?" he asked, one eyebrow raised.

"No." She reached for the magazine.

He gave her a curious look and tweaked it out of her reach. "Is this yours?"

"Yes."

"It's *House and Garden*."

"So?"

He looked bemused. "You live out of a suitcase. You're a gypsy."

"It doesn't mean I can't read glossy magazines. I like the pretty pictures."

She yanked the magazine from his hand and slid it under the bed, tugging the skirt into place. When she turned around, Tyler was crowding her. She thought he was moving in to kiss her. Instead he dropped to one knee and lifted the skirt of the bed.

"*Tyler.* Have you ever heard of privacy?"

He ignored her, sliding a stack of glossy magazines out from beneath the bed.

"*Vogue Living, Belle Maison, House Beautiful*—flown in from the U.S., no less. *Better Homes and Gardens, Elle Decor, Country Living...*" A quizzical smile played on his lips.

Ally crossed her arms over her breasts. "What?"

"This is a bit of a dirty little secret, isn't it?"

"They're magazines. I told you, I like the glossy pictures. I find them relaxing."

"They're *home decorating* magazines. Full of glossy pictures of other people's homes."

She used the side of her foot to shove the stack

back where she'd had it. "I don't see what the big fuss is."

"You don't think there's any irony in a woman who scoffs at possessions and has no home of her own being addicted to homemaker magazines?"

Ally pressed her lips together, feeling more than a little exposed. "It's not an addiction," she muttered.

"How many do you read a month?"

She shrugged.

"Five? Ten? Twenty?" he asked.

"I don't know. Most of them come to me on subscription. I never really keep track."

"You subscribe?" He laughed incredulously.

"I really don't see what's so amusing."

She tried to march from the room but he hooked an arm around her waist and swung her toward the bed. She landed on her back and Tyler was on top of her in seconds. She tried to wrestle her way out from under him, but he just grinned down at her.

"Why are you so upset?"

"I'm not!" She heard the echo of her own strident tone and winced. She forced herself to meet his eyes. "They're just magazines."

"Okay. If you say so." But he looked very pleased about something.

Before she could question him, he ducked his head and used his teeth to pull her tank top down. When he'd exposed her left breast, he kissed his way back up the curve and pulled her nipple into his mouth.

"Did I mention that I missed you?" he said as he switched to her right breast.

After they'd messed up her nice clean sheets, she donned a robe and went to scoop some of their favorite treat.

"I meant to say, good choice on the flavors," she called.

He'd stopped at Trampoline and bought tubs of Peanut Nutter and Violet Rumble, the second being very high on her list of favorites thanks to its chunks of crunchy sponge toffee.

"I remember you saying you liked the Peanut Nutter," he said from close behind her and she nearly jumped out of her skin.

"You need a bell, like Mr. Whiskers."

"Any suggestions on where I should hang it?" He slid his arms around her waist.

"I have a few ideas."

She fed him a spoonful of ice cream over her shoulder, then concentrated on filling their bowls. He let her go so she could lead him into the living room to eat on the couch. He stopped in his tracks when he entered the room.

"I hope you don't mind, but I rescued it," she said.

He frowned, walking closer to the table. She watched as he rubbed the scarred rim with his thumb.

"I was thinking that maybe you could repair it."

She couldn't get a read on him, couldn't tell if he was upset or annoyed or grateful.

"It'd take a miracle."

She joined him beside the table. "But you could do it, couldn't you? You could make it beautiful again."

He hesitated a moment, then he put down his bowl and bent so that his eyes were on a level with the surface. He moved around the table, inspecting it closely, running his hands over the various gouges and pits. Then he crouched lower and ran his hands up and down the legs. Finally he stood and collected his ice cream. "I could do it."

"Do you want to?"

His gaze returned to the table for a beat. "Yeah. Yeah, I think I do."

She slid her arm around his waist.

"Thanks for rescuing it for me."

There was so much warmth in his eyes, it scared her. He was watching her closely, so she forced a smile.

"Better eat, it's melting." She focused on her own bowl, and after a few seconds he did the same.

Moment by moment, remember?

She joined Tyler on the couch, feeling the warmth of his body alongside hers as she sank into the cushions. He smiled at her, a little distracted, and she knew he was thinking about how he was going to fix the table. Pushing her doubts away, she rested her head on his shoulder and dug into her dessert.

This, right now, was a great moment, and she was determined to enjoy it.

THE FOLLOWING DAY, TYLER waited until Ally filed her column at midday before telling her to put on her swimsuit.

"Why?"

"There's a place on the river I want to check out. Jon and I used to go there as kids. I thought we could take a picnic."

"A picnic sounds nice."

"That's the general idea. I figured you deserved a break."

"Me? You're the one with the double workload."

"But he's my father."

She frowned but didn't say anything. He followed her to the bedroom and watched as she flipped open her suitcase.

He'd noticed before that while she'd unpacked most of her clothes, she kept a few things in the case still, things she didn't need every day. As though she was prepared to leave at the drop of a hat and wanted to ensure she had a head start on packing.

"I didn't even know there was a river around here," she said as she rummaged.

He tapped the side of his nose. "Local boy. Secret knowledge."

"So, local boy, is this a bikini kind of place or a one-piece kind of place?"

"Definitely bikini," he said without hesitation.

She gave him a dry look.

He put on his best innocent face. "What?"

"I'm not sure you're the best person to take advice from on this subject."

"With my hand on my heart, no one is going to notice what you wear except me. And I've always been a bikini man."

"I bet you have."

He was already wearing a black tank top and a pair of old jeans he'd hacked off at the knees and he leaned his shoulder against the door frame as Ally pulled a bright aqua suit from her suitcase.

"You want me to help you on with that?" he asked, pushing away from the door frame and taking a step toward her.

She laughed. "Anyone would think you hadn't gotten lucky this morning."

"It's your fault for being so sexy."

She made a face at his compliment and he closed the remaining distance between them to take her into his arms.

"You don't think you're sexy?"

"Marilyn Monroe was sexy. Monica Bellucci is sexy. I'm…cute. At best."

"You're sexy. Trust me."

He kissed her, and when things started to get interesting, she slipped from his grasp.

"We're never going to get out of this room if you don't leave me alone to change."

Tyler thought of the plans he'd made. If he had

his way, he'd consign them all to hell, but he wanted to give Ally a treat. She'd given so much to him and his father, and he wanted to give her something in return.

"I'll check on Dad," he said reluctantly.

She waved him off with a cheeky grin. The age-old tension crept into his neck and shoulders as he walked the short distance next door. Two days on from their argument, his father was still punishing him, refusing to answer his questions, behaving like a spoiled child. It reminded Tyler of the heavy silences they'd endured as children, tiptoeing around his father's moods. Frankly, Tyler wondered where his father found the energy—Tyler had never been able to sustain a bad mood for longer than a few hours. His father, however, had turned the sulk into an art form.

The house was blessedly quiet for once as he entered, the television switched off. He found his father at the kitchen table, frowning over a crossword puzzle. He looked up briefly when Tyler entered, then returned his attention to the puzzle without saying a word.

"Ally and I are heading out, but there are sandwiches for your lunch in the fridge," Tyler said.

His father ignored him. Tyler stared at him for a beat, then he crossed to the counter and wrote down his phone number. Tearing the sheet off, he dug around in the junk drawer until he found some tape and stuck the note to the side of the phone.

"Call me if you need anything, okay?"

Again, no response.

In reality, his father was so recovered from his operation that he really didn't need anyone making meals for him and supervising his showers any longer. This morning the nurse had taken Tyler aside and told him that she didn't think it was necessary for her to visit on a daily basis anymore. Between the two of them they'd decided to reduce her visits to weekly check-ups for the time being. If things changed—or, more accurately, *when* they changed—she would increase her visits again.

Essentially, they were in a holding pattern, waiting for the cancer to make the next move.

Tyler wondered how his father was dealing with this calm before the storm. If they had a different kind of relationship, he'd try to talk to him about it. But they didn't. All the same, one day soon they were going to have to sit down and talk about some things. What arrangements, if any, his father wanted made. Who he wanted to perform the service.

Not a conversation Tyler was looking forward to, on several fronts.

"I'll see you later, Dad."

When his father continued to ignore him, he headed for the door. Ally was trying to stuff two bulky beach towels into a too-small bag when he returned.

"Here, let me take care of that," he said.

She handed the towels and bag over. "This ought to be good."

He slung the bag onto the bed and draped both towels around his neck.

"I could have done that," Ally said, chagrined.

"So why didn't you?"

She poked her tongue out at him. He grabbed her by the shoulders and turned her toward the door.

"Stop trying to distract me."

"I was trying to insult you, actually."

"You're going to have to try harder. And use a different body part."

He urged her forward but she dug her heels in.

"Wait, I need sunscreen. And we should take something to drink. And what about lunch?"

"All taken care of."

"Huh."

She allowed him to usher her into his truck, and he headed into town. He stopped to collect the picnic lunch he'd ordered from the local café, then he took the freeway north until he found the turnoff he was looking for. The truck began to rock and buck as they drove onto a deeply rutted unmade roadway.

"Good grief. Where are you taking me?" she said, clinging to the armrest.

"I told you, it's a secret place."

"No kidding."

The road became increasingly rough as they neared their destination. Finally he spotted the distinctive crowns of a line of willow trees ahead and the truck entered a small clearing. He parked in the shade in deference to the hot midday sun.

"I feel like I'm in *Deliverance*," Ally said, peering through the windshield suspiciously. "Any second now we'll hear the sound of banjo music."

He got out of the truck and collected the picnic basket. "Come on, smart-ass."

She followed him up a short, well-worn dirt track, making cracks about *Deliverance* all the way. Then they emerged on the riverbank and he watched the teasing expression fade from her face as she took in the gently sloping grassy bank and the clear water of the river, all framed by swaying weeping willows, their long branches dipping in and out of the water with the breeze.

"Oh, wow. This is beautiful."

It was, although it was smaller than he'd remembered, the trees bigger, but he figured that was only natural, since it had been twenty years since he'd last been here.

"Jon and I used to hang out here every summer when we were young. All the local kids did, before they built the pool in town. There used to be an old tire swing, and we'd practice our Tarzan moves hanging out over the water."

"There still is, look." Ally pointed to the nearest willow.

It took him a moment to spot the tire propped in the fork of the two main branches. Someone had obviously stowed it out of sight for safekeeping. He put down the picnic basket and crossed to the tree. On close inspection, he discovered the tire was still firmly tied to one of the large overhead branches with a thick length of rope. He tugged the tire free and let it drop so that it swung like a pendulum.

"I've always wanted to try a rope swing. They make them look like so much fun on all those soft drink ads," Ally said, her voice muffled.

He turned to find she'd laid the towels out on the grass and was pulling off her tank top, stripping down to her bikini top and khaki hiking shorts. He watched as she bent over the picnic basket, enjoying the way her breasts pressed forward, creamy smooth and round.

"Yum. There's pasta salad. And fruit salad for dessert," she said, glancing at him.

She shook her head when she realized what he'd been staring at.

"Food first," she warned him.

He shrugged as though there had never been another thought in his head and joined her on the towels. They grazed on the selection of deli meats and salads, polishing it off with vanilla ice cream and fruit salad and a crisp, cool apple cider to wash it all down. Ally rolled onto her back afterward and closed her eyes.

"That was delicious." She cracked an eye to look at him. "This place was worth the bumpy ride, by the way."

He lay down beside her and she wriggled closer

so that she could rest her head on his shoulder, his arm around her. Tyler gazed at the blue sky, her head a heavy weight near his heart. The only sound was the rush of the river. His belly was full, and he had an incredible, generous, smart, funny woman lying next to him. He could feel the warmth of her body alongside his, could smell her unique scent.

All the things he wanted to ask her, all the things he wanted to know faded into the background. Time slowed. The world shrank.

"This is really nice," she said drowsily.

"Yeah. It is."

The kind of nice a man could get used to, he decided as he drifted toward sleep.

If he was given half a chance.

CHAPTER NINE

HE WASN'T SURE HOW LONG he dozed for, but when Tyler woke Ally was gone. He sat up and looked around, only relaxing when he saw that she was near the big willow, investigating the rope swing. He watched with growing amusement as she attempted to climb onto it, only to fail repeatedly as it rocked beneath her weight and tipped her off.

"It's a two-man job," he called.

"Then what are you waiting for?"

He stood and stretched, then walked down the slope to join her.

"Give me a boost," she said, her eyes bright with anticipation.

"First, the golden rule of river swings. Gotta check the water depth before you do anything."

He walked to the edge, stripping off his tank top. Tossing it onto the grass, he waded into the water. The river bed was soft beneath his feet, the water icy cold despite the heat of the day. He waded in up to his waist, then up to his chest. He turned back to face the bank, the current tugging at him gently.

"See where I'm standing? This is where you want to jump off, okay? Water's nice and deep."

"Okay."

He made his way back to where she waited.

"Up you get." He grabbed the rope and steadied the tire.

"Hang on a minute."

She shed her shorts, tossing them toward his tank top. She gave him an excited smile, then placed her hand on his shoulder for balance while she stepped into the hole of the tire, then climbed on top, sliding her legs either side of the rope. She gripped the rope with both hands and looked at him expectantly.

"Okay. I'm ready."

"One last thing."

He leaned forward and kissed her. She tasted like sunshine and fresh air, her mouth hot against his. She made one of the small, approving noises that drove him crazy and he angled his head to taste more of her. He tried to move closer, but the tire was a big, round impediment to greater intimacy. Ally started to giggle, finally breaking their kiss to laugh out loud.

"So much for the tire swing as a sex aid," she said.

"Yeah. I won't be rushing to the patent office with that one."

She looked so adorable that he couldn't resist dropping one last kiss onto her nose. Then he stepped away and got a good grip on the tire.

"Hold on."

He walked backward, pulling Ally with him, his

arm and leg muscles straining as he took more and more of her weight. Then he let go and shoved with all his might. She let out a whoop of delight as she swung out over the river.

"Get ready to jump!"

Ally shifted on the swing, but when the critical point came, she hesitated. "What if I fall on my face?"

"Then you fall on your face. It's part of the fun."

The tire reached its farthest point and started to swing toward shore.

"Now! Go now!" Tyler called.

But again she didn't let go. And she was coming in, fast.

Tyler glanced over his shoulder. The tree trunk was directly in her path. He'd pushed Ally with so much momentum there was a good chance she'd hit it before the tire ran out of steam.

Bracing himself, he stepped into the path of the tire.

"Tyler. Get out of the way!" Ally called as she swooped toward him.

"It's me or the tree, babe."

The swing twisted as it approached and she hit him back-first with a hard slap of skin on skin.

"I've got you," he said.

His arms wrapped around her body but the tire's momentum pushed him off his feet and knocked the air from his lungs. He waited for the impact of the tree trunk, but the swing petered out inches shy of making contact then began a more leisurely sway toward the river. He planted his feet firmly and brought the tire to a jerking halt. Ally twisted frantically to look at him.

"Tyler. Are you all right? My God. You haven't broken anything, have you?"

She was so comically concerned he couldn't help but laugh.

"I'm fine. But you need some serious coaching on tire swinging."

She scrunched her face in self-disgust. "I know. I'm a big chicken. Once I got out there, I kind of froze."

"Let me show you how it's done."

He helped her slide off, then he pulled the tire toward the tree as far as he could. He leaped onto the tire and pushed off with one smooth motion, swinging out over the river with one foot braced in the center of the tire, the other on the top. At the farthest point of the arc, he let go and performed a perfect water bomb into the middle of the river. Cold water splashed over him, rushing up his nose and covering his head.

"That was so cool. I want to learn how to do that," Ally shouted from the bank when he broke the surface.

He pushed his hair off his forehead and wiped the water off his face with his hands. "I'm sure we can work something out."

He waded toward shore, deliberately choosing to

exit where the bank was steepest. He pretended to struggle, watching Ally surreptitiously. As he'd anticipated, she immediately rushed forward to offer him her hand.

"Here," she said, bracing her legs to take his weight as she leaned toward him.

He wrapped his hand around her forearm, then he looked straight into her eyes, not even trying to hide his grin. "Too easy, Ally."

Her eyes widened with shocked understanding as he jerked her into the water. She splashed in up to her thighs, her body tensing as she registered the temperature of the water.

"Oh! It's cold!" she gasped as the water splashed her torso. "You sneak, let me go."

"Come for a swim first," he said, pulling her deeper into the water.

"It's too cold."

The water was up to her breasts now.

"No, it isn't. Not once you get used to it." He tugged her arm one last time, pulling her close and wrapping both arms around her. Her skin was warm against his in the cool water, her nipples pebbled and hard against his chest.

"How old are you? Fifteen?" she asked, but she was smiling and she closed her eyes and relaxed into his body when he kissed her.

He slid his hands to her backside, cupping her round little derriere and lifting her against him. She sucked on his tongue and pressed closer, her arms wrapped tightly around his neck.

After a few torturous moments, he broke their kiss. His heart was thundering in his ears and he was painfully hard. Any desire he'd had to swim had been well and truly superseded by another, more urgent need.

"Put your legs around my hips."

She complied readily and he got a good grip on her backside before he started walking toward the bank.

"Tyler! You'll give yourself a hernia. Put me down, I'm too heavy."

"You're small enough to fit in my pocket. Lighter than thistledown."

All the same, he was straining a little by the time he reached the towels.

"Still lighter than thistledown, am I?"

"Got you where I wanted you, didn't I?"

He tumbled her onto the towels and rolled on top of her. Her nipples were still hard from the cold water and he tugged her bikini top to one side as he lowered his head toward her. She caught his ears before he could pull her nipple into his mouth.

"Tyler. Anybody could see us." She sounded like a scandalized Sunday-school teacher.

"But they won't. We'd hear a car coming long before it got here."

He slipped free of her grasp, lowering his head and

circling her nipple with his tongue before pulling it into his mouth.

She gripped his shoulders. "Tyler." It was a half-hearted protest.

"Think of it as the ultimate form of getting back to nature."

While she was pondering that, he tugged her bikini top off and switched his attention to her other breast.

It wasn't long before Ally was fumbling at the wet waistband of his jeans, trying to gain access to his erection. The wet denim fought him every step of the way as he tugged it over his hips. When he hooked a finger into the waistband of Ally's bikini bottoms, she bit her lip and glanced up the slope toward the trail.

"Trust me. This is more private than your back-yard," he said.

She lifted her hips and he pulled her bikini bottoms down. He surveyed her, all pink and cream in the dappled light, her dark curls beckoning enticingly.

"You look good enough to eat. Strawberries and cream."

She gave a muffled protest as he started to kiss his way down her belly. He pushed her legs wide with a gentle hand, caressing her inner thigh soothingly.

"Relax. Count to ten," he said with a half-smile. "It'll be over before you know it."

She remained tense until he lowered his head and took the first long, slow taste of her. Quickly she turned to liquid in his hands, moaning and quivering and digging her fingers into his hair and shoulders until he slid up her body again and plunged deep inside her.

Her head dropped back and she closed her eyes as he started to move, her breath coming in choppy little pants. He caressed her breasts and her hips and the smooth skin of her belly, loving how soft and warm and womanly she was. Loving the feel of her around him, beneath him.

She came silently, her breath catching in her throat, her hands clutching at his backside. He let himself go, too, riding her shudders to his own completion, looking into her eyes as she dazedly came back to earth.

He rolled away afterward, breathing heavily. Ally lay languid and supine beside him for a full twenty seconds before she remembered where she was and scrambled to pull one of the towels over both of them.

"You realize we broke about ten different decency laws, don't you?"

"I counted eleven. But you might be right."

"You're a bad influence, Tyler Adamson."

"That's what my mother used to say."

She fell silent for a moment, then propped her chin on her hand. "You never talk about your mother," she said.

He could hear the unspoken questions in her voice. "Neither do you."

He had some questions, too.

"That's different."

"Is it?"

"If you don't want to talk about her, it's okay."

"I'm fine talking about my mother, but there's not much to tell, to be honest. She wasn't a very happy woman. Her and Dad used to fight a lot, especially when we were younger. She was stuck at home with two little kids all day, and he'd stay at the pub after work. I think she resented the isolation. Resented us."

He waved a fly away with his hand.

"She never did anything to stop him hitting you?"

"Never. She used to tell us it was our fault, that if we were good boys Dad would never have to lay a finger on us."

"Did he ever hit her?"

He shook his head. "They'd just go at each other verbally. One of the clearest memories of my childhood is my mother crying at the kitchen table. It was practically a nightly event."

Ally pressed a kiss to his shoulder, resting her cheek against him for a long moment in wordless sympathy.

"What about your mom?"

She stared at him as though she didn't know where to begin.

"You told me the other day she was an artist," he prompted.

"That's right."

"What sort? Painter, sculptor?"

"Painter. She worked mostly with acrylics. I guess you'd say her style was post-modernist."

"Would I know any of her work?"

"Probably not. She had a bit of success in the early seventies, but mostly she relied on friends or boyfriends to give her somewhere to live and help her get by."

"Pretty precarious way to live." Especially with a child in tow.

"Yes, but she was very charming and she never outstayed her welcome. She was always flitting around. New York, Paris, London, Sydney, Spain. She even lived in Rio for a while. She was the ultimate free spirit, really, and I think it's safe to say I was the unplanned mistake of her life."

She gave him a dry look.

"My aunt told me once that my mother was devastated when she found out she was pregnant, especially since it was far too late to do anything about it. Very typical of my mother, not even noticing she was pregnant until it was staring her in the face."

"What about your father?"

"Never knew him. Don't even know his name." She shrugged as though it made no difference to her.

She sat up and reached for her bikini bottoms, shuddering as she pulled them up her legs. "Is there anything worse than putting on a wet swimsuit?"

Tyler could think of worse things. Like being told you were a mistake, for instance, and never knowing your own father.

"I take it your mom stopped traveling when she had you?"

"She tried. But she couldn't handle it. She hated being tied down, hated 'sublurbia,' as she called it. So she left me with my grandmother when I was about six months old."

She grabbed for her bikini top and put it on.

"I don't remember Gran very much, although I always feel as though I should. She died when I was five."

"What happened then?"

"My mother came back for me and I started traveling with her."

Ally sank to the ground beside him, lying on her belly while she plucked at the grass.

"So you were an international jetsetter at five?"

"For a while. I didn't like it very much. I used to freak out at all the different places we stayed in. Sent my mother crazy." She laughed, shaking her head. "There was this one place in New York, a big old apartment in SoHo or somewhere. It took up a whole floor, but it was completely empty, utterly desolate, except for the bedroom where we stayed. I used to have nightmares about all those dark, empty rooms and wake up screaming. Then there was the place in Provence, with the scary outdoor toilet. More nightmares. And so on. Finally my mother talked her sister into looking after me."

She plucked a couple of bluebells from amongst the grass and started braiding their stems together.

"How old were you then?"

She screwed up her face, thinking. "I don't know. Six? Maybe seven. I don't remember exactly, but I hated being left behind. With a passion. Which probably explains why Aunt Phyllis was more than happy to hand me back to my mother when I was nine. I don't think I was a very grateful niece."

She shot him an amused look, inviting him to laugh at the misbehavior of her juvenile self.

"Doesn't sound as though anyone cut you much slack," Tyler said carefully.

Maybe he was misinterpreting Ally's words, putting a too-dark slant on them, but the childhood she was describing sounded far from ideal, being shunted from pillar to post, palmed off from mother to grandmother to aunt.

"Well, my mother was too self-interested to cut anyone but herself any slack. And Aunt Phyllis did her best with what she had. Which wasn't a lot, because I'm pretty sure my mother didn't send child support payments from whichever villa or loft or atelier she was crashing in."

She smoothed her thumb back and forth over the braid she'd made.

"It was better the second time around, though. I made friends with the houses we stayed in the moment we arrived, so the nightmares weren't a problem anymore."

"How do you make friends with a house?"

"It's very simple. You do a tour, and you find the door that groans and the window that rattles and the stair that creaks. Then, on the first night, when you're lying in bed and the house starts making its nightly settling noises, you tell yourself 'that's the window in the second bedroom' or 'that's the third stair from the bottom' or whatever. Works a treat. Comes in handy when you're house-sitting, too. I can get the lowdown on a new place in half an hour these days, no problems."

Her tone was light, her expression untroubled, but Tyler felt a stab of empathy for a little girl who'd been so afraid of being left behind again that she'd forced herself to stare down her fear in order to overcome it.

"How did your mother die?"

Ally's expression became sad. "She was staying at a friend's place in Spain. They were renovating, and some of the electrical work wasn't up to standard. There was a fire. The coroner said she'd been drinking, which was probably why she didn't make it out."

"How long ago was this?"

"Ten years this June. I was backpacking in America when I got the news."

She was quiet for a moment, then she threw the

bluebell braid into the long grass and pushed herself to her feet.

"Enough sad stories. Come on, rudey-nudey man, you promised you were going to teach me to jump off the tire swing properly."

She tossed him his cutoff jeans, then started across the grass toward the tire swing.

He stared after her, still processing everything she'd told him, trying to reconcile what he'd learned with what he already knew of her. He thought about the stash of home decorating magazines she had hidden under her bed and the advice column she wrote and her inexhaustible supply of pajamas. Then he remembered the way she'd warned him that first night he'd kissed her. *I'm a girl who leaves,* she'd said.

"Are you coming or not?" she called, squinting her eyes against the sun.

Tyler rose and wrapped one of the towels around his waist.

"Try and stop me," he said.

Then he went to teach Ally how to jump.

THE NEXT TWO WEEKS SLIPPED through Ally's fingers like water. Apart from three occasions when Tyler had to return to town to take care of business matters, he slept in her bed by night and worked in her study by day, occasionally disappearing into Bob's shed to work on his table. Between the two of them they cared for his father, preparing his meals and cleaning the house. Bob held on to his sullen defensiveness for longer than she would have thought possible, but eventually they all settled into a routine of sorts and she found herself exploring a new kind of happiness and contentment with Tyler by her side.

He was a wonderful lover, selfless and sensual and insatiable. He was also a wonderful conversation-alist—not chatty, by any means, because he would never be a garrulous man, but when he chose to say something, it was always smart and witty and to the point. He made her laugh a lot, and he made her think. Most of all, he made her feel complete, in a way she had never experienced before.

Quite simply, she felt as though she'd come home. Which was crazy since Tyler was only in Woodend for as long as his father needed him and she had no idea where she was going once Wendy reclaimed her home. Her life was as up in the air and temporary as it had ever been. And yet it had never felt more solid, more grounded.

Sitting in the living room on a sunny afternoon, Ally doodled on her notepad as she allowed herself to imagine what might happen next. She'd stuck staunchly to her live for the moment rule most of the time over the past weeks, but with Wendy due home soon she figured it would be smart to put some thought into her immediate future.

Normally she would have another house-sitting job lined up by now, but she hadn't so much as taken a second look at the two prospects she'd bookmarked at the beginning of the month. It felt wrong to think of moving on when Tyler still needed her.

She made a rude noise at her self-deception. She was so pitiful, so terrified of what was happening between them that she couldn't even admit it to herself.

Grow a set, Bishop.

She took a deep breath. Then she finally acknowledged the truth to herself: she'd fallen in love with Tyler. And she suspected—no, she knew, in her gut and in her heart—that he loved her, too. It had been the elephant in the room for the past week, the topic they danced around every time they lay in each other's arms or caught each other's hands when they walked down the street or simply made eye contact unexpectedly.

But she had a feeling the elephant's days were numbered. She sensed there was a conversation on the horizon—and she had no idea how she was going to handle it when it finally arrived, what she was going to say if Tyler said the things she thought he was going to say and asked the things she thought he would.

Panic tightened her chest as her mind ran over the options open to her—stay or go. She wasn't sure which terrified her more.

She heard the sound of the front door opening and put down her pad and pen, very deliberately pushing the whole mess to the back of her mind. Wendy wasn't due for two more weeks, after all. There was no reason for her to start manning the lifeboats prematurely.

"Couldn't stay away, huh?" she called down the hall.

Tyler had disappeared next door after lunch and told her not to expect him until dinnertime, a pretty common occurrence the past few days as work intensified on the table.

She waited for him to respond, but he didn't. Curious, she went in search of him. She found him in the bedroom, his back to the door as he bent over something. He was wearing his cutoff jeans again, and she spared an appreciative glance for the way the worn denim showcased his backside and thighs.

"Thought I wasn't going to see you until dinner?"

"Yeah. I finished early." He straightened, turning to face her. Then he took a step to one side and she saw what his body had been shielding.

He'd finished the table. She took a step forward.

"When…?"

"A few days ago. But it takes a few passes to get the polish right."

She reached out a hand but stopped short of touching it. The finish was too perfect, too fine.

"Tyler. It's *stunning*."

And it was. He'd replaced the ruined marquetry with a new design, a many-pointed star made up of a myriad of red-hued woods. The top tapered to a simple bevel on the rim, and he'd honed the legs and reeded them, making the table appear more delicate and refined.

"It's okay, you can touch it. It's meant to be used," he said, an amused glint in his eyes.

She ran her fingers over the central star, unsurprised to find it silky smooth beneath her hands.

"I didn't know there were so many different shades of red."

He moved closer. "This is Jarrah, and that's redgum. And this is red cedar. There's a lot of variation within each species, but I had some good off-cuts at the workshop to play with."

"Tyler, it's beautiful."

"I'm glad you like it, because it's yours."

She stilled, her gaze flying to his face. He was watching her carefully, a small, slightly nervous smile on his lips.

"You're giving this to me?" she asked, her voice rising to an incredulous squeak.

"I'd like you to have it. If you'd like it."

She lay her hand on the table. She couldn't believe he was serious. "Are you nuts? I'd love to have something so beautiful. It's…God, it's breathtaking. I don't know what to say."

She could see he was pleased that she liked his gift. She looked at him, her chest aching with emotion.

"Tyler." But she couldn't find the words to express what she was feeling and she shook her head, angry with herself for being so inarticulate.

The doorbell sounded. Ally frowned.

"I'll get it," Tyler said.

She caught his arm as he brushed past her. "Tyler. It's beautiful. I love it. I'll cherish it forever," she said.

For God's sake, say it. Tell him you love him. Tell him you're crazy about him.

But the words got caught in her throat and wouldn't come out. Tyler gazed into her eyes for a moment, then he leaned close and kissed her briefly on the mouth.

"I'm glad."

He left the room. She stared after him for a beat, angry with herself for choking.

You're a chicken, Bishop. A big old yellow-belly.

It was absolutely true.

She surveyed the table again. She hadn't owned a piece of furniture for nearly four years, and she'd never, ever owned something this precious. All her stuff had always been cheap and disposable, designed to be temporary. This piece was an heirloom. A small, perfect masterpiece that should be enjoyed for generations.

She could hear Tyler talking to whoever was at the front door. She registered that the other voice was vaguely familiar. She listened for a moment and realized it sounded like Belinda, Bob's nurse.

A trickle of unease ran down her spine. She stepped into the hall. Tyler was standing on the front porch, his face creased with concern as Belinda talked. He seemed to sense her presence and he glanced at her. She knew immediately that something was wrong and she hastened to join him.

"What's happened?"

"Nothing drastic," Belinda said. "I was just explaining to Tyler that I've noticed Bob's been using more of his painkillers lately. So I had a little chat with him, and he's been experiencing back pain."

They'd been waiting for this, so it wasn't exactly a shock. But it was still grim news.

"I think we should get him into hospital for some tests, so we know what we're dealing with and how best to make him comfortable," Belinda said.

"When?" Tyler asked.

"I can make a call now, see what's available. Tomorrow, if possible."

Tyler nodded. "If you wouldn't mind."

"That's what I'm here for."

They waited while Belinda moved off to make her call, watching the other woman pace the sidewalk as she talked and listened. Ally squeezed Tyler's hand.

"You okay?"

He shrugged. "Had to happen, right?"

"Doesn't make it any easier."

"No."

Belinda ended her call and rejoined them on the porch.

"9:30 a.m. tomorrow."

"Great. Thanks for that, we appreciate it," Tyler said.

They ate dinner with Bob that night, enduring the blare of the television to keep him company. Not that he'd requested it—he would prefer to cut his tongue out, Ally suspected—but it felt like the right thing to do.

She watched Bob eat his meal, thinking about all the things he'd denied himself with his refusal to engage with his son.

But Bob's journey wasn't over yet.

She sent a little prayer out into the universe that Bob would find a moment of truth and clarity to offer his son before it was too late. For Tyler's sake, if not his own.

THE NEXT DAY, SHE WAITED with Tyler while Bob was scanned and his blood was taken, then she waited some more when Tyler and Bob met with the oncologist to hear the results of the tests.

Tyler's expression was flat, utterly unreadable as they exited the consultant's rooms. Bob kept his gaze on the floor, but she could see he was fighting to control himself.

Later, after they'd driven home and settled Bob in his armchair with his puzzle books, she and Tyler sat on the deck next door and he told her that the doctor had confirmed that Bob's cancer had spread.

"Soon his liver function is going to drop. And then it's going to be pretty fast, the doctor said."

Ally blinked away tears. "Has Bob said anything?"

Tyler shook his head. "You know what he's like."

"Yeah, I do."

Tyler sighed. "I need to call Jon, let him know what's going on."

"Sure."

He went into the house. Her gaze moved over the fence. What must Bob be feeling right now? Was he scared? Relieved? Resigned? Angry?

She drew her knees into her chest and rested her cheek on her knees.

Over the past weeks she had found an uneasy middle ground within herself where Bob was concerned. She would never feel the same warm affection for him that she once had—she couldn't, not when she knew what he'd done to Tyler—but the initial burning outrage she'd felt had been tempered by the sheer mundanity of caring for him. It went against her nature to deny someone in need. It was as simple as that. Despite his many, many failings and cruelties, she had it in her to feel pity for Bob.

Tyler exited the house and sat beside her. She looked at him in silent question and he nodded.

"He's coming. Catching the first flight out tomorrow. I'll drive into the city and pick him up."

"When was the last time you saw him?"

"I don't know. Eight years, maybe nine."

"What's he like?"

Tyler thought for a minute. "You know, I really have no idea."

"Maybe you two can get something out of this after all."

"Maybe."

She poked him with her finger. "Don't go all silent and manly on me. This is important. You two got through your childhood by battening down the hatches and enduring. I get that, but things are different now. Take it from someone who has no one, a brother is a precious thing."

Tyler looked at her, then he reached for her hand. "You don't have no one, Ally. You have me."

Such simple words, but they made her chest expand with warmth and love.

This man. This incredible, loving man.

She reached out to cup his face, but once again the words in her heart failed to make it out of her mouth. To cover the moment, she leaned forward and pressed a kiss to his lips, holding him close, trying to tell him with her body what she wasn't able to verbalize yet.

Soon, she told him silently, deepening the kiss. *Soon.*

Following his lead as he pulled her down onto the deck, she tried to ignore the little flutter of apprehension in the pit of her stomach.

TYLER GOT UP EARLY TWO days later to make the drive into the city to pick up his brother. Ally stirred briefly when he got out of bed, then again when he dropped a kiss on her cheek on the way out the door.

"Drive carefully," she murmured before burrowing into the pillow.

He stared at her for a moment, thinking about the conversation that was looming between them. Wendy was coming home soon. Which meant it would be time for Ally to move on—if she wanted to. If she was prepared to walk away from what they'd built between them.

On a good day, he knew, absolutely that she would stay. Knew that she loved him, and that the intense connection he felt with her was a shared and mutual thing.

But there was always that half-packed suitcase in the corner to remind him that Ally had a long, long history of not putting down roots.

There's a first time for everything.

He bloody hoped so, anyway, because he loved her with everything he had, and he didn't want to even think about a future that didn't include her. A concession indeed from a man who'd once prided himself on needing no one and nothing.

He left the house quietly, pausing for a moment in the quiet of predawn. The forecast was for another hot day. The last time Tyler had checked, it had been below freezing in Toronto—Jon was in for a rude awakening.

He let himself into his father's house to check that all was well before he took off. He expected his father to be asleep, but when he ducked his head in the door of his father's bedroom he saw the bed was empty. The living room was empty, too, and the kitchen. He checked the toilet and bathroom, then headed out to the yard, only to pull up short when he spotted his father sitting at the bottom of the steps.

"Dad. You gave me a scare."

His father shifted his head slightly but didn't fully turn around. "You're up early."

"I'm going to pick up Jon. Remember?"

His father nodded. Tyler descended a few steps.

"Are you okay? You're not in pain?"

"Only so many tablets a man can take."

"We can talk to Belinda if you need more."

"I'm fine."

Tyler stared at the back of his father's head. Ally had given his hair a trim last week and his hairline was military straight. The lines on his neck were deeply scored, the skin loose with age.

"Dad. If there's anything you want to talk about, anything you want to say, now's the time," Tyler said quietly.

He waited, his body tense.

His father didn't say anything.

Well. It had been a long shot, anyway.

"I'll see you when I'm back with Jon."

He was about to slip back into the house when his father spoke.

"Don't put your foot down, those coppers are everywhere with their radar guns. Cost you a bomb if you get caught."

"I'll be careful."

His father grunted and Tyler walked through the house to the front door.

They were on the home stretch now, whether they liked it or not. All they could do now was hang on and endure.

ALLY WOKE AGAIN AT EIGHT and showered and made herself breakfast before she went next door to see if Bob needed anything. She could hear the television as she walked up the path. Bob had started early today. Usually he liked to do his crosswords in the morning and save the television for when his game shows started in the afternoon.

She rang the doorbell to let him know she was there, then let herself in the front door.

"It's only me, Bob."

There was no response, but that was hardly surprising, given the racket of the television.

She walked into the living room. Sure enough, Bob was in his usual chair, his crossword puzzle book on his knee.

"Good morning. Have you had breakfast yet or would you like me to make you some?"

When Bob didn't respond, she stepped into his line

of vision, which was when she saw that his glasses had slipped slightly down his face and that his eyes were closed.

"Bob."

She rushed forward, grabbing his hand to find his pulse. To her relief she felt the faint, weak flutter of Bob's heartbeat against her fingertips.

He was alive. But something was wrong. She checked his airways were clear, then went into the kitchen to call an ambulance. She gave the address and what information she had, then hung up and bit her lip. She thought about calling Tyler, then decided to wait until the ambulance arrived so she could give him more information. He would be at the airport by now, waiting for his brother's plane to land. There was nothing he could do from so far away.

Déjà vu swept over her as she knelt beside Bob's chair, holding his hand while she waited for the ambulance. It had barely been a month since she'd last done this. How the world had changed.

The ambulance arrived within five minutes and she stood to one side while the attendants checked Bob over. He remained unconscious and she felt a growing dread as they took his vital signs.

"He has cancer," she explained. "It's in his liver, kidneys… And he's on medication."

"Do you know what kind?" the female attendant asked.

Ally went to collect the bottles.

"What do you think is wrong?" she asked when she returned.

"Looks as though he's had a heart attack. Pretty big one, judging by his heart trace." The woman gave Ally a sympathetic look. "Might be a blessing, given what you told us."

"I need to make a call."

She moved into the kitchen, her hands icy as she dialed Tyler's number. She pressed her fingers against her closed eyelids, willing herself not to cry. They'd all known this was coming, that Bob was dying. As the woman had said, a heart attack was a blessing, given his circumstances.

The call connected.

"Tyler, it's Ally. You're not driving, are you?"

"I'm at international arrivals. Jon's flight has been delayed by half an hour. What's wrong?"

"Your father has had a heart attack. He's still alive, but the ambulance crew seem to think it's pretty serious."

There was a profound silence at the other end of the phone. She imagined Tyler in the middle of the busy airport, trying to think.

"Where are they taking him?" he finally asked.

"Kyneton again. I'll go with him."

"Thanks, Ally."

"I'll see you soon, okay? And I'll keep you updated."

Tyler said something, but the sound was muffled.

"Sorry, I missed that."

"I just saw Jon."

"Okay, I'll let you go. Be safe."

"I will."

He ended the call.

She returned to the living room as the attendants were strapping Bob into the stretcher.

"I need to grab my phone and purse from next door, then I'll come with you," she said.

A tense ambulance ride later, Bob was rushed into the emergency department. Ally was asked to wait in the waiting area and she wrapped her arms around herself and paced anxiously.

She didn't know what she was hoping for. It seemed cruel to will Bob to live simply so Tyler could say his final goodbye. As for Jon... She could only imagine how he was feeling right now.

"It's Ally, isn't it?"

She glanced up to see Bob's oncologist standing in the doorway of the waiting area.

"Yes, that's right. I'm Bob's neighbor."

"Tyler's not around?"

"He's picking up his brother from the airport."

"That's unfortunate. I don't suppose you know if he and his father ever discussed a D.N.R.?"

"I'm sorry, I don't know what that is," Ally said.

"Sorry—doctor speak. It's shorthand for Do Not Resuscitate. If something happens, we need to know whether Bob would want us to keep him alive."

God.

"I don't know. Tyler never mentioned it. Bob wasn't big on talking."

"I noticed. Last of the stoics."

"I'll call Tyler."

She pulled her phone out. The call had barely connected when it was picked up.

"Tyler's phone," a deep voice said.

For a moment Ally was thrown, then she realized it must be Jon.

"It's Ally. Is Tyler there?"

"He's driving."

"Jon, I'm sorry to do this, but can you ask him if he and Bob ever discussed a Do Not Resuscitate order? The doctor needs to know."

"Right."

She heard muffled conversation, then Jon came back on the line.

"Tyler says no."

Ally caught the oncologist's eye and shook her head.

"Can I talk to him?" the doctor asked.

"It's Jon, Tyler's brother," she explained.

Quickly she introduced the doctor before passing him the phone. A short, terse conversation later, the doctor handed back the phone, gave her a nod of thanks and left.

"Where are you?" Ally asked.

She'd overhead enough of the conversation to know what Tyler and his brother had told the doctor.

If Bob became critical, they'd agreed it was kindest to let him go.

"We're passing the turnoff for Macedon," Jon said.

Which meant they were only half an hour away.

"We'll see you soon." She slid her phone into her bag. She'd seen a coffee machine in the hallway. Something warm would be welcome right now.

She was taking her first sip when the oncologist returned. "Bob's awake, if you'd like to see him."

"Oh. Yes," she said, abandoning her cup on the nearest flat surface.

She followed the oncologist into the busy emergency department, stepping under his arm as he held back the curtains around one of the cubicles for her.

Bob lay flat on the bed, his bare chest covered with leads. Oxygen prongs pinched his nostrils and a monitor tracked his heart rate with audible beeps. She moved to his bedside and touched his arm and his eyes opened. It took him a moment to focus on her and she guessed they'd given him some sort of pain relief.

"Bob. It's Ally," she said.

Bob closed his eyes again. "Ally. You're a good girl," he said weakly.

She tried to think of something to say, something comforting that wouldn't require an outright lie.

"Tyler and Jon are on their way. They'll be here any minute."

Bob's hand moved on the bed. She reached for it and he gripped her fingers with surprising strength. He opened his eyes and looked at her.

"Don't want to die." He sounded frightened, like a child. Ally swallowed a lump of emotion. She didn't know what to say to him. They both knew he *was* dying. That if this wasn't the end, it was damn close to it.

She glanced surreptitiously at her watch, willing Tyler to arrive. Only ten minutes had passed since she'd ended the call, which meant they were still at least twenty minutes away.

"Thought the cancer would get me. But my bloody ticker gave out." He closed his eyes again and his grip slackened on her hand.

The monitor made a different sort of beep and Ally's gaze flashed to it. A series of uneven rhythms spiked on the screen. She glanced over her shoulder fearfully.

"Help! I think something's happening."

The curtain whipped back and two nurses and a doctor rushed in as Bob's monitor sounded an alarm.

"We need you to wait outside, please," one of the nurses said and Ally was suddenly on the other side of the barrier.

She stood there, arms wrapped around herself, listening to the hospital staff talking shorthand to one another for what felt like a long time. The alarm kept up a continuous whine.

Then, suddenly, there was silence.

Ally pressed her fingers to her mouth. A tear slid down her cheek. A few minutes later, one of the nurses slipped through the curtains.

"I'm sorry," she said simply.

Ally nodded, unable to speak for the moment.

"Would you like to sit with him?"

"Yes." Ally choked on the word.

It seemed wrong that Bob should be left on his own so soon. And Tyler and Jon would want to see him when they arrived.

"I need to make a call first," she said, her heart heavy.

"You'll have to go out to the waiting area to do that, I'm afraid."

Ally made her way out of the emergency department, pulling her phone from her bag. She found a quiet corner and dialed Tyler's number.

"Ally." It was Jon again.

She took a shuddering breath, forcing the words out. "I'm really sorry. Bob had another attack. He's gone."

A moment of silence. She could hear Tyler's brother breathing on the other end of the line.

"He's gone," Jon repeated, and she knew he was talking to Tyler and not to her.

The sound of fumbling, then Tyler's voice came down the line.

"Are you okay?" he asked.

She closed her eyes. Only Tyler could ask that five seconds after he'd learned his father had died.

"I'm fine. I'm so sorry."

"It's okay. We're ten minutes away. Hang in there, okay?"

She returned to Bob's cubicle to wait for his sons to arrive. They'd removed the prongs from his nose and the leads from his chest, and the heart monitor was now blank and silent. His arms were by his sides, resting on the bed.

Ally sat beside him and took one of his hands in hers and waited.

CHAPTER TEN

THE PICK-UP HAD BARELY stopped before Jon was out and racing across the parking lot toward the emergency entrance of the hospital. Tyler followed more slowly, understanding his brother's misplaced urgency. He, too, felt the need to make haste, in case there had been some kind of mistake, a last-minute reprieve.

There wouldn't be, of course. His father was dead. And it wasn't as though seeing him one last time would change anything. Everything that was ever going to be said between them had been said. Tyler knew that in his bones.

Jon had no such certainty, though. He'd flown halfway around the world and arrived twenty minutes too late. He hadn't said a word after Ally's phone call, but Tyler had felt the tension radiating off him in waves.

He'd been shocked by his brother's appearance when Jon had exited customs at the airport. His brother was unshaven, his eyes bloodshot. Understandable, perhaps, after a long flight, but he was also very lean, as though he'd lost a lot of weight recently. He looked like a man on the edge, a man in crisis.

Ally was hovering outside a closed cubicle when he arrived in the emergency department.

"Tyler," she said, opening her arms.

He walked into her embrace and held her close, inhaling the smell of her, feeling the warmth of her cheek against his own.

She sniffed and he pulled back a little so he could look into her face.

"You okay?" he asked.

"Stop asking me that. He's your father. How are you?"

He glanced toward the curtain. "I'm okay."

She studied him, a small frown pleating her forehead. "I'm so sorry you weren't here."

"It doesn't matter."

She frowned again but didn't say anything. He nodded toward the curtain.

"Is Jon in there?"

"Yes. I figured he'd probably want some privacy…"

Typical Ally, always thinking of others, always doing the right thing. He pressed a kiss to her forehead, then he released her and turned toward the cubicle.

"I'll wait here," Ally said.

Jon was standing near the head of the bed, arms crossed tightly over his chest, hands buried beneath his armpits. He was frowning fiercely as he stared at their father's body, his lips pressed into a tight, thin line as he fought to suppress strong emotion.

Tyler stopped beside him, taking in his father's stillness, the gray cast to his skin, the sunken boniness of his face. The cancer had stripped more weight from him in the past weeks, despite the fact that Tyler had been doing his best to provide hearty, nutritious meals.

Beside him, Jon made a choked sound.

"I know you probably had some things you wanted to say to him. Things you wanted to hear from him," Tyler said, carefully not looking at his brother. "If it's any consolation, even if we'd gotten here in time, he wouldn't have said anything. I don't think he could."

"He was an old prick. A sadist. He—" Jon used his forearm to take a swipe at his eyes.

"Mate." Tyler could feel his brother's anguish and fury, all the unresolved feelings clamoring for out. He laid a hand on his brother's shoulder.

Jon's face twisted as his emotions got the better of him, then he jerked away from Tyler's touch and pushed past him, disappearing through the curtain in a flurry of fabric.

Tyler let him go. He was willing to bet his brother had never cried in front of anyone in his life.

He returned his attention to the bed. A strand of his father's hair was sticking up and Tyler reached out to smooth it into place. He let his hand rest on his father's skull, aware that a few short weeks ago, the thought of touching his father with anything approaching gentleness would have been unimaginable to him. Proximity had burned out most of Tyler's anger, and Ally had done the rest. Her patience and understanding and love.

He studied his father's face one last time. For good or for ill, the man who had once lived in this body had been the biggest influence in his life. He'd shaped Tyler in a thousand different ways. He'd been cruel, violent, selfish. And he'd also been scared and small and isolated.

Not much of a life, when it came down to it.

"Rest in peace," he said quietly.

He turned away from the bed. There would be arrangements to make, papers to sign.

His father was dead. It was over. Finally.

SIX HOURS LATER, TYLER made the short walk from his father's house to Ally's. He and Jon had been busy making arrangements all afternoon. Ally had quietly bowed out after lunch, leaving the two of them to work through it together. He knew what she was doing: giving them room to become the kind of brothers she thought they could be.

It was a nice idea, but there was something closed off and hard about the man his brother had become. It would take a hell of a lot to break through all those barriers.

He could hear Ally clattering around in the kitchen when he entered.

"Hi," she called out. "I bought some beer. I figured you guys might need a drink."

Tyler stopped in the kitchen doorway. Ally was standing at the counter wearing her Shrek pajama pants tossing a salad, and he could see she'd made kebabs for dinner.

"Jon's not coming."

Her face creased with concern. "What's he going to do for dinner?"

"He'll probably get hammered and pass out."

"You Adamson men. Would it kill you to talk once in a while?"

"I talk."

"Sometimes."

He moved closer and hooked his finger into the waistband of her pajamas. "What do you want to talk about?" He tugged her closer.

She came willingly into his arms but her eyes were worried as she looked at him.

"I know you must be feeling cheated. You came here and put your life on hold so you could get some kind of closure with your father—and he died before you could clear the air."

Tyler caught her earlobe between his thumb and forefinger, caressing it lightly. She was so soft, every part of her warm and welcoming.

"We were never going to clear the air."

"I know he blanked you that time you fought, but I thought that once he'd had a chance to process the news he'd had this week that he'd change his mind."

He slid his hand around to the back of her neck, shaping his hand to her nape. "No."

"You sound so certain."

"I didn't get a chance to tell you, but I found him sitting on the back steps this morning before I left for the airport."

"Really? What was he doing?"

"Waiting for the sun to come up, maybe. I really don't know. But he was so quiet. It was the most reflective I've ever seen him. So I asked him if there was anything he wanted to say, anything he wanted to get off his chest."

"What did he say?"

"Nothing."

He watched understanding dawn in Ally's eyes. "God, he was such a stubborn old bastard."

"He was. Till the end."

She lay her head on his chest. He smoothed his hand over her hair.

"I hate that you didn't get what you needed from him."

"It's okay."

"No, it isn't. The least he owed you was acknowledgment. To look you in the eye and own his own actions."

"I know what happened. I don't need him to acknowledge it."

She lifted her head to look at him. "You're really okay with this?"

He thought about it for a moment. "Yeah, I am.

I came because I couldn't live with myself if I did anything else. I did my best by him. I can live with that."

Her gaze searched his face, then she stood on tiptoes and pressed a kiss to his lips. "You're a beautiful man, Tyler Adamson. I love you."

He stilled.

Finally—*finally*—she'd said it. He'd been waiting, taking his cues from her, biding his time. But she'd said it. At last.

"Does that mean you're not going to take off when Wendy comes back next weekend?"

There was a short pause before she answered. "I haven't got another house-sitting job lined up yet."

It wasn't really an answer, but he hadn't really asked the question he wanted to ask, either, had he?

"Ally. I love you. More than I ever thought it was possible to love anyone. Will you come to Melbourne with me, move into my place? Live with me?"

He heard her suck in a quick breath, but he knew his question wasn't a surprise. They'd been leading up to this since the moment they first met.

She gripped her hands together as though she was bracing herself for something. His gut tightened. He had no idea what he was going to say or do if she said no.

"Yes."

Relief made him stupid. He blinked. "Yes?"

"Yes."

He closed the distance that separated them and embraced her.

"God, I love you, Ally Bishop."

"I love you, too."

He kissed her. Despite the heaviness of the day, he felt a little giddy. She'd said yes. After all his caution, all his concern about stifling her and overwhelming her, she'd said yes.

"Let's go to bed," he said.

She glanced toward the counter. "What about dinner?"

"It can wait."

He waited while she stowed the salad in the fridge, then he pressed her against the wall and kissed her until she was pliant and breathless. They barely made it to the bedroom. He peppered her body with kisses, telling her he loved her, how much she meant to him. All the things he'd been holding inside for too long.

If today had taught him anything, it was the value of speaking and sharing and connecting.

Afterward, she dozed with her head on his chest. He stroked her arm, mentally making space for her in his closet, clearing out the spare room, rearranging the house so that she could make it her own.

Much easier to do that than to think about that small, telling moment when she'd clasped her hands together and braced herself before giving him her answer. As though she was forcing herself to the point.

He knew she had issues around settling. Hell, until he'd given her the table, she hadn't owned a single stick of furniture. She saw herself as a born nomad, a dyed-in-the-wool gypsy. But things were good between them. The past few weeks had proved that beyond a doubt. And she loved him. Surely that would be enough.

They would make it work. Somehow. He wasn't giving her up. Not when it had taken him thirty-seven years to find her.

TEN DAYS LATER, ALLY did one last quick survey of Wendy's house.

There was probably something she was forgetting. Normally when she house-sat she was very disciplined about where she left her things. This time, she'd gotten sloppy. She'd infiltrated every room of the house, and no doubt her friend would be finding traces of Ally's presence for months to come.

"I can't see anything obvious," she finally said.

Wendy looked up from where she was scratching Mr. Whiskers's belly.

"I can forward anything to you. Or come visit. I'm in Melbourne all the time."

Ally nodded. There was a tight feeling in her chest and she told herself she was simply being sentimental. A lot of good things had happened during the three months she'd lived here. It was only natural that she'd be sad about leaving.

Except the feeling in her chest didn't feel like sadness. It felt more like anxiety. Verging on panic.

Stop being such a drama queen. You want this. You love Tyler. There's nothing to freak out over.

She knew it was true, but she was still incredibly wary about moving into Tyler's home. When he'd asked her, she'd known that they'd reached a point of no return. The elephant had finally been named, and Tyler was asking her to make a decision about her future. Their future.

In all honesty, she'd expected it to be harder than it had been. But as she'd stood there looking at him, his declaration ringing in her ears, she'd tried to imagine life without him, all the mornings she'd have to wake up without him beside her if she stuck to the promise she'd made to herself five years ago and walked away.

It had been impossible. Literally unimaginable. So she'd said yes, and it had been both easier and harder than she'd thought. Easier, because she loved Tyler desperately, and harder because she'd immediately felt the burden of what she'd committed to.

It wasn't that she didn't want to live with Tyler. She did. More than anything she wanted to move in with him and started weaving the strands of her life with his. It was simply that she'd been here before. Not this exact same place, true—because she'd never felt as connected as she felt with Tyler—but close enough. She'd made promises. Put down roots. And then she'd started to get itchy feet and the walls had closed in and she'd had to get out of there—but not before she'd hurt someone. Daniel in London, Jacob in L.A., Bailey in Sydney.

It will be different this time. Tyler is different. He's the one. The man who will make staying in one spot doable. Bearable.

God, she hoped so. With every fiber of her being.

"I still can't believe Bob's gone. And so quickly," Wendy said, pushing herself to her feet. "I was away for only twelve weeks."

"The world can change in twelve weeks."

"I guess."

She'd notified Wendy about the funeral, and her friend had flown home to pay her last respects to her elderly neighbor. It had been a short service, and Ally had stood between Tyler and his brother at their father's graveside and grieved for both of them, as well as herself.

Bob had not been a perfect human being. In fact, he'd been a very flawed, angry, narrow-minded human being a lot of the time. But he'd produced two good men, and he'd not been without his small moments of humanity.

"You want a hand carrying your table out to the car?" Wendy was standing beside the table, admiring Tyler's craftsmanship again, the gleam of avarice in her eye.

Ally gave her a mock-steely look. "Hands off. I've already told you you can't have it."

"But it looks so good in my house."

"Then you'll have to commission one of your own."

"It wouldn't be the same as this."

Ally lay her hand on the table, thinking about all the work that had gone into it, the history behind it. "No, it wouldn't."

She let Wendy help her carry it outside, worried about bumping it against the door frame. They were about to descend the steps when a voice called out.

"I'll do that." Jon bounded up the path, ready to intervene.

"We can manage."

"All the same," Jon said. "I told Tyler I'd help you pack when he left yesterday."

Ally threw up her hands and stepped back. She'd already learned it was useless to argue with him. Tyler's brother had some very old-fashioned ideas where women were concerned.

She and Wendy watched as he picked up the table easily and strode down the path with it.

"Who would have thought there could be two in one family?" Wendy murmured out of the side of her mouth, her eyes glued to Jon's backside.

It was true—Jon was as good-looking as Tyler. They shared the same big build and dark hair, and they had the same square jaw. Jon's eyes were more gray than silver, however, darker and stormier, and his face more angular. He looked as though he'd lived a harder life than Tyler, too, the lines around his mouth etched deeply, his hair touched with gray at the temples.

"How long did he say he was hanging around for, clearing out the house?" Wendy asked.

Ally nudged her with an elbow. "It's open-ended. And you have a perfectly lovely boyfriend, remember?"

"I do, it's true. Which is probably just as well. Jon might be lovely to look at, but I have a feeling he'd be hell to house-train."

Ally studied Jon as he bent to the task of fitting the table into her already crowded car. Knowing what she did about Tyler and Jon's upbringing, she suspected he had more than his fair share of monkeys on his back.

"Yes. Some lucky woman's got her work cut out for her, that's for sure."

She returned inside to collect her handbag, then rejoined Wendy.

"Thanks for everything, Ally. It was a load off, knowing you were keeping the home fires burning," Wendy said. "Keep me posted, okay? I'm waiting for the next big announcement with baited breath."

Ally gave her a confused look and Wendy started humming the wedding march.

"No. We're not getting married," Ally said adamantly.

It was enough that she was moving in with Tyler. *More* than enough.

"Then maybe this, then." Wendy mimed a big

baby belly and held her back in the classic pose of pregnant women everywhere.

"No." Ally shook her head. She hoped her friend couldn't hear the thread of panic in her voice. "We're taking this one step at a time."

"Maybe you are, but Tyler's practically building nursery furniture and planning your retirement home. That man is crazy about you."

"I should get going," Ally said abruptly. "I want to make it to Tyler's place before it gets dark."

She kissed Wendy goodbye, then did the same with Jon, thanking him for his help. Then she slid behind the wheel, started the car and pulled away from the curb.

I can do this. I can move in with Tyler and love him and not make a mess of it. I can.

She gripped the wheel tightly and told herself the same thing over and over as she turned onto the freeway to Melbourne.

She knew she was making a mountain out of a molehill. Knew that the moment she saw Tyler again, all the doubts would fade. What they had together was right. The best thing that had ever happened to her. This time it was going to be different.

That's what Mom said with Tony, remember? Then she left him after nine months.

"It's not the same," she said out loud.

She heard her voice echo around the car and reached to punch on the stereo. She needed to stop thinking and simply let things happen. That's what she'd been doing all along with Tyler, and things had worked out fine. Just fine.

She got lost twice trying to find Tyler's house and finally had to pull over and call him for directions. He guided her the last few streets. When she turned the final corner, she saw him standing on the sidewalk, phone to his ear.

He was wearing his most raggedy, faded jeans and an old, worn T-shirt with a surfer logo on it, and he looked utterly precious and dear and familiar to her as she parked at the curb and cut the engine. Her heart gave a painful little squeeze and she practically fell out of the car, craving the reassurance and certainty she always felt when she was in his arms.

He met her halfway, scooping her into an embrace, and she kissed him with everything she had in her, holding him tightly, fiercely, her arms trembling with the force of her emotion.

He broke the kiss after a moment and laughed. "Miss me, babe?"

"Yes." She pressed her head against his chest, waiting for his steady presence to still the tumult inside her.

"How was the drive down?"

"Fine. No problems."

His hand caressed her back, but she could feel his distraction. He wanted to unpack the car and show her his home. Her home.

She let him pull away, even though every instinct told her not to let him go.

"You ready for this?" he asked, his eyes dancing with silver light.

"Of course."

He took her hand and she turned to face his house. It was exactly as she'd imagined—and also a million times better. A double-fronted Victorian, it had a central door with windows on either side. A bull-nose veranda shaded the front of the house. The smooth stucco finish on the facade had been painted a soft vintage white while the trim on the windows and veranda was glossy black. A neat box hedge lined the redbrick path, and the veranda was covered with earth-hued heritage tiles in a traditional tessellated pattern. A graceful bench sat to one side of the veranda, and matching cumquat trees were placed either side of the door in big stone pots. The lights were on in both the front rooms, giving the house an internal golden glow in the deepening dusk.

"It's lovely."

"Come inside."

She could see his pride, his excitement as he led her up the path and through the door. He wanted her to love his place as much as he did.

"Our bedroom is on the right, the guest on the left," he said as their footsteps echoed on the wide, worn planks of the floor in the generous hallway.

She stopped in the doorway of his bedroom— their bedroom—and looked at his big king-size bed and his beautiful wooden bed frame and nightstands. White plantation shutters were folded on either side of the front window and a dark chocolate-colored carpet covered the floor.

"I like your colors."

"We can change them if you like. None of it's set in stone."

"No, it's all lovely."

He gestured for her to explore further and she crossed the plush carpet and ducked her head into the doorway to the en suite. A gleaming antique washstand with a white marble counter and shiny chrome taps dominated the space. A freestanding claw-foot bath was situated in an alcove, a double shower next to it.

"Wow."

In a daze, she followed Tyler into the hall and beneath a decorative archway.

"This used to be the third bedroom," he said, throwing the door open.

She stared at the desk he'd set up in the corner and the cushioned window seat beneath the bow window. The walls were a buttery soft yellow, the trim a crisp white. The floor was covered with a faded antique rug in shades of umber, gold and brown. A carved bookshelf sat empty on one wall, waiting to be filled with books.

"I thought you could use this as your office."

He was watching her closely but for the life of her she couldn't think of anything to say.

The room was…perfect. From the color of the walls to the window seat with its fat, colorful cushions to the gleaming desk with its leather inlay. Just like a page in one of the magazines she spent hours poring over.

"I've always loved window seats."

She felt as though she'd fallen down the rabbit hole. She'd expected Tyler's house to be nice—the man was a meticulous craftsman, after all, and she'd already deduced that he was a bit of a neat freak—but this house was more than nice. It was mellow and worn in all the right places, it had charming quirks and modern finishes, and, most of all, it was filled with Tyler's warmth.

It wasn't simply a house, it was a home. A home with heart and warmth, a place to settle and be comfortable and put down roots.

She crossed to the desk, imagining herself working there, gazing out the window as she pondered an answer to one of her letters. She'd keep a big vase of fresh flowers in the corner at all times, and a fluffy throw blanket on the window seat in case she wanted to curl up with a book. And when Tyler was working from home, she could give him the desk to lay out his designs and she could write from the window seat...

"Come and see the kitchen."

It was as charming as the rest of the house—white country-style doors with wood countertops and an old-fashioned porcelain farmhouse sink. The living room boasted a huge fireplace and opened to a paved entertaining area and a stretch of grass bordered by trees.

"It's a bit bare out here," Tyler said, flicking on a light so she could see. "I'm not much of a gardener."

Ally shook her head, blown away. Utterly overwhelmed. "It's amazing. All of it. I feel as though I should ask you to pinch me."

Tyler smiled. "No pinching. Not yet, anyway."

He dropped a kiss onto her forehead. "I'm going to start unpacking your car before it gets too dark."

"Okay."

She followed him as he walked toward the front of the house, stopping in the doorway of the study again.

She was still standing there when Tyler returned with her table.

"You okay?"

"This is surreal," she said without thinking. "I feel as though I'm in a dream."

He frowned. "Is that a good thing or a bad thing?"

She forced a smile. "It's a good thing, of course."

He gestured toward the table. "In here or in the bedroom?"

"Um. Here, I guess."

He carried the table into the study and placed it near the window seat.

They made multiple trips to her car. She frowned as she realized how much she'd accumulated over the past few months. Normally it would take her only two trips to unpack her car, but somehow she'd collected a bunch of stuff while she was at Wendy's. For starters, she'd brought all her magazines with her, something she never did. Usually she donated them to a nearby women's shelter or left them for the owner of the house to enjoy. But not this time. She'd bought a few cookbooks, also another no-no, since books were hard to carry around. And somehow she'd bought more clothes than her suitcase could accommodate.

"I don't know how that happened," she murmured as Tyler lay the excess clothes on the bed.

"What?"

"I don't remember buying so many clothes."

"There's lots of storage, don't worry."

He crossed to the built-ins and opened the first set of doors.

"I've cleared out a space for you."

He left to collect the final items. She stared at the empty rails in front of her. She could see Tyler's clothes at the far end, pushed aside to make room for hers. She heard footsteps in the hall and Tyler appeared in the bedroom doorway.

"That's it, all done. I bought chicken for dinner. I'll put it on while you unpack."

"Sure. Great."

He disappeared. Ally turned to her suitcase, reaching for the zip to open it. The hand she stretched out was trembling violently. She stared at it for a moment—then she gave in to the panic battering at her from all sides and sank to her knees.

She pressed her forehead against the rough canvas of her suitcase, trying to get a grip on herself, trying to hold it together. She clenched her hands, pressed them tightly against her belly. Tried to breath through her nose, slowly and deeply.

Nothing helped. Everything in her still wanted to run screaming for the exit. Which was crazy. This place—this home—was beautiful and warm and welcoming. She could imagine herself cooking dinner in the kitchen, then lounging up on the couch with Tyler afterward, watching TV. She could imagine herself sleeping in on Sunday mornings, then getting muddy in the garden. God help her, she could even imagine little feet running up the corridor and the skitter of claws as the family pet followed their child.

And it was too much. Too big, too all encompassing. Too real. Too possible.

"Ally. What's wrong?"

Tyler's hand landed on her shoulder, warm and steady.

She shook her head, unable to articulate the realization crystallizing inside her.

"Ally. Talk to me. What's going on?" He tried to draw her into his arms but she stiffened and pushed him away.

"You're shaking."

"It'll pass. It's just a panic attack," she said.

He crouched beside her, his eyes dark with worry. "I didn't know you had panic attacks."

"I don't. Not full-scale ones like this. Not since I was a kid."

"Can I do anything?"

Ally stared at the carpet in front of her for a long moment. Then she slowly raised her head until she was looking him in the eyes. "You can let me go," she said.

There was a beat of silence before he responded. "You want to leave?" He sounded very calm. Almost as though he'd been expecting something like this.

"I can't stay."

"Are you sure about that?"

She held out her hand so he could see how much she was shaking. "A part of me wants this. But the other part of me knows it's not right. I told you from the start, I can't settle. Your house...your house is beautiful, Tyler. I want to believe I can live here with you and make it work, because I love you so much. But I can't even unpack my case."

"Right. The gypsy gene."

She started to cry. "I told you. I'm a screw-up. I've screwed up every relationship I've ever had. And now I'm going to mess things up with you and hurt you and I don't want to. I love you so much and I don't want to hurt you."

She started to sob, her body jerking with the power of her grief and misery. Tyler tried to pull her into his arms again but she resisted him.

"No. I don't deserve your comfort. I've led you on and made promises I can't keep. I tried so hard not to be like her, to keep my distance and not hurt anyone else, but I have. I have—" She broke off, unable to continue, curling in on herself.

Tyler pulled her into his arms despite her wordless protests, pressing her close and holding the back of her head in his hand as though she was incredibly precious to him. It only made her cry more.

"I don't deserve you. I don't deserve you," she said over and over.

"Jesus, Ally." There was a ragged break in his voice. "Stop saying that. It's not true, and it's killing me."

She shook her head.

"You don't believe me? You don't believe you have a right to be happy?"

"This isn't about happiness. This is about knowing yourself. I should never have let this happen between us. Not when I knew this would happen."

"What is *this,* Ally? Explain it to me."

"You know what it is. I told you. I have to go. I can't stay here. If I try to settle, it'll only be worse in the long run. Harder. Messier."

"Why can't you settle?"

She pushed away from his chest. "Because that's what I do. I leave. I'm my mother's daughter. A faithless, feckless gypsy who can't stick."

"You're the least faithless person I know. As for being a gypsy, I've never met a person who wanted a home more in my life."

Ally stared at him. He lifted a hand and started counting off points.

"Your favorite pastime is reading decorator magazines, looking at other people's homes."

"I like the pictures."

"No, Ally. You like the *homes.* You're a Peeping Tom, a voyeur, looking through the window at what you want."

"That's not true."

"Then there's Dear Gertrude. You think it's an accident that you get so much out of helping other people? That you feel 'connected' to them and like the fact that you help them? You need them every bit as much as they need you, Ally. They're the family you've never allowed yourself to have."

It was like a slap. She flinched.

"*Allowed* myself to have? As though I had a choice, when my mother didn't want me and my grandmother died on me and my aunt resented me. As though I *chose* any of those things."

Tyler didn't say a word. It took a second for her own words to sink in. She pushed herself farther away from him.

"No. This has nothing to do with my family."

"This has everything to do with your family, Ally. This has everything to do with a little kid who learned early on never to get comfortable and never to trust anyone. A lesson you learned so well you've spent your entire adult life rejecting people before they could reject you."

She stood. "You don't know what you're talking about."

Tyler remained on his knees, looking up at her. "I'm not going anywhere, Ally. I love you, and that's never going to change. I'll take any vow, sign any contract, climb any mountain it takes to prove it to you. I love you, and I will never let you down, and I will never stop loving you."

"This isn't about love. I know you love me. It's not about that."

"What's it about, then?"

"I told you. I'm my mother's daughter."

"No, you're not. You're not a selfish, self-involved woman who takes what she wants and then moves on. You're the kind of woman who appoints herself champion for an old man facing his own mortality. You're the kind of woman who doesn't think twice about helping others. You're the kind of woman who cares and loves deeply. And I am not letting you go without a fight, Ally Bishop. I believe in us and I believe in you and I know this is right."

Ally stared at him, utterly caught by his words. Wanting to believe him, so badly.

She closed her eyes and scrubbed her face with her hands. "You don't know what you're talking about."

"I do. I know you. But I don't think you do."

"I have to go."

She left the room blindly, coming to a halt in

the hallway. She looked left, then right, then faced Tyler.

"I need my car keys."

He looked at her for a long moment. "They're on the hook near the phone in the kitchen."

She swiveled and walked to the kitchen. Her keys were hanging next to Tyler's. She grabbed them, then headed for the door.

She half expected Tyler to say something, to try to stop her again, but he didn't. She saw him out of the corner of her eye as she walked past the bedroom, sitting on the bed, looking at his hands.

She made herself keep walking, telling herself that she'd done the hard part. She simply had to leave now, and Tyler could get on with his life without her.

The door swung shut behind her and she stepped out onto the veranda.

He'd be better off without her. He'd see that soon. Once he'd stop being angry with her, he'd see that she'd done the right thing, pulling out before they became so entwined in each others lives that it would be impossible to separate him from her. It was far better that she leave now rather than later, when he would have invested so much more in her.

She carefully didn't think about *her* feelings, about what she would be losing and all that she'd invested in him. The important thing right now was to escape. To remove herself from the temptation that Tyler and his beautiful home and the future he offered represented.

She strode to her car, pressing the remote to un-lock it.

I've never met a person who wanted a home more in my life.

She paused, shaken all over again as his words echoed in her mind. No. She slid into the driver's seat. Tyler didn't understand. He was simply seeing things he wanted to see. Trying to hold on to something that was never meant to be.

You're a Peeping Tom, a voyeur, looking through the window at what you want.

She started the car and pulled away from the curb. She liked the pretty pictures in those magazines. That was all. She liked imagining the families who lived in those glossily depicted homes and the parties they had in their perfect yards and the meals they'd cook in their state-of-the-art kitchens—

Her foot eased on the accelerator as it hit her that what she'd just described to herself was, indeed, a form of voyeurism.

So perhaps Tyler had been right about that one thing. But was it so crazy that a woman with no fixed address might fantasize about how the other half lived?

The moment she acknowledged the doubt in her own mind, the rest of Tyler's words rushed her.

This has everything to do with a little kid who learned early on never to get comfortable and never to trust anyone. A lesson you learned so well you've

*spent your entire adult life rejecting people before
they can reject you.*

She was shaking so badly she had to stop the car.
She felt sick, as though she might throw up. She told
herself over and over that Tyler didn't know her, that
he didn't know her personal history. But his words
struck a deep, resonate chord inside her, a true note
on the tuning fork of her emotions.

Things had been good with Daniel before she'd
ruined them by chipping away at their happiness and
finally leaving. She'd told herself that it was because
she was a gypsy, her mother's daughter, that being
unable to settle was in her blood. But what if Tyler
was right? What if she'd simply hit the emergency
button and abandoned the relationship because she'd
been afraid that Daniel would abandon her first?
What if she'd bailed because she was afraid to trust
another person with her happiness?

She wrapped her arms around her torso, her head
bowed as she tried to understand herself. She remembered that day by the river and the story she'd told
Tyler about her nightmares. She hadn't told him that
they'd been worse when her mother had brought her
home, that for the first six months she'd lived with
her aunt she'd woken with night sweats on a weekly,
if not daily, basis. She used to lie in bed trembling in
the aftermath, then she used to climb out and creep
into her aunt's room to make sure she was still there,
that she hadn't been abandoned again. Then, because
it was the only way she could calm herself, she would

drag her pillow and quilt to her aunt's doorway and sleep across the threshold for the remainder of the night. She'd told herself it was because she wanted the comfort of being close to her aunt, but in a belated flash of insight Ally saw it for what it really was— her childish attempt to prevent her aunt from going anywhere without taking her.

The way her mother had. And her grandmother before her.

Ally pressed her hands to her face, but it didn't stop the tears. All these years she'd been roaming, telling herself it was in her blood—and all the time she'd been running from her childhood fear of being abandoned.

It made her feel small and weak and utterly defenseless. What woman got to the ripe old age of thirty-three before she learned these things about herself?

The kind of person who learned early that pretending fear didn't exist was the only way to survive. The kind of person who was taught through bitter experience that people were unreliable and that love means nothing.

The answer came from the pit of her belly. Visceral. Instinctive. She'd learned early that insecurities and neediness and dependence would not be tolerated. And she'd trained herself to move on whenever she'd felt herself putting down roots and connecting deeply with someone. Neediness equaled rejection.

And the only way to avoid becoming dependent on someone was to leave.

Tyler had been right. About everything. He'd seen the truth of her before she had.

And he still loved her.

The knowledge made her gasp. The ache in her chest expanded.

Tyler loved her. He'd said it a million different ways, with his hands and his eyes and his body and his mouth. He knew her, and he loved her, and he understood her—better, perhaps, than she understood herself.

He said all that—but he didn't try to stop me from leaving. He said he'd fight for me, that he wouldn't give me up—but he let me go.

The voice in her head spoke with a child's fear, trembled with a child's uncertainty.

Then Ally remembered the almost last thing Tyler had said. *I believe in us. I believe in you.*

She reached for the gearshift. Didn't think. Didn't second-guess herself. She put the car in gear and pulled into the street. She'd turned one corner since leaving Tyler's house, so she simply drove in a circle until she'd completed the block and once again turned onto Tyler's street.

She saw his house, lit up with warm golden light. And she saw him, sitting on the bench out the front of his house.

Waiting.

He looked up when he heard her car. Pushed

himself to his feet. She stopped and got out. She walked across the sidewalk and up the path, her heart banging a nervous tattoo against her ribs, her stomach cramping with uncertainty.

What she was about to do was utterly new to her. Revolutionary. She was about to trust another human being. Completely. She was about to hand over her happiness and her safety and her love to another person and trust that he would never grow tired of her or resent her or stop loving her.

She stopped at the bottom of the single step to the veranda. Tyler looked at her, and she could see the pain and doubt in his eyes. But she could also see the hope. The belief.

For a moment the old fear choked her. She closed her eyes for a long second, then opened them again. "I don't know how to do this."

It was true. All her experience was with leaving and running. She didn't know how to stay.

"It's easy. As easy as falling off a tire swing into the river," Tyler said.

He stepped forward and she was in his arms, being held tightly, fiercely, possessively.

"I've got you," he said, and she remembered the other time he'd said those words to her, when he'd stepped between her and a tree.

This man—this amazing man—had protected her with his body. He'd stood by his abusive father with compassion and love until the end, despite great provocation, despite never hearing the words he needed to hear to lay his own ghosts to rest. He'd let her go and waited for her to return. He was all heart.

And he was hers.

If she wanted him. If she had the courage to want him.

"I love you," she said.

"I know. I love you, too, Ally. And I'm not going anywhere."

"Neither am I."

Tyler stilled. Then he pulled back a few inches so he could look into her face. "I'm going to hold you to that."

"Good."

She held his gaze, wanting him to know he could trust her, too. That they were in this thing together.

"I'm sorry for freaking out. So sorry. You must have been—"

He lowered his head and kissed her, cutting off the rest of her words. She kissed him back, meeting his passion with her own. After a few minutes Tyler kissed his way to her ear.

"Let's try this again," he said.

He stepped backward and took her hand, then he led her inside his home. This time, he took her straight to the bedroom.

They moved onto the bed together, needing the confirmation and reassurance of skin on skin. They made love slowly, murmuring praise and encouragement to each other, savoring the closeness. Ally didn't look away from his eyes as she came, baring herself to him utterly. Then she watched as he lost himself, and afterward she curled against him on the bed and listened to the steady, reassuring thump of his heartbeat beneath her ear.

She lifted her head after a few minutes as a thought occurred.

"You were waiting for me out front, weren't you?"

"Of course."

"But what if I hadn't come back?"

"I knew you would. I know you."

She stared at him, stunned by his utter confidence in her. He smiled and reached out to brush her hair from her forehead.

"You once told me that I was the strongest person you knew. Well, you're the strongest person I know, Ally Bishop. You're honest and you're brave and I knew that you'd choose to face your fears rather than run from them."

"I don't deserve you."

"Yes, you do. We deserve each other. If the past few months have taught me anything, it's taught me that. We deserve to be happy, Ally. And we're going to be."

There was so much love and certainty in his face. She touched his cheek, then pressed a kiss to his mouth. Then she settled her head on his chest, over his heart.

"Okay," she said.

"That's it? *Okay?*"

"I trust you."

And she did. With her happiness. With her heart. With her future.

EPILOGUE

One year later

"JUST A LITTLE FARTHER to the left. No, too far. Back a little more to the right. Yes! That's it, perfect," Ally said.

Her husband released his grip on their bulky three-seater sofa and stood, rubbing his back, while his brother did the same at the other end of the sofa.

"You're sure now? You don't want to try it on the other wall?" Tyler asked. "Again."

Ally bit her lip guiltily. "You're sick of me moving the furniture around, aren't you?"

She'd reorganized the house four times in the past twelve months. Couldn't help herself. After years of having no home, she was like a child with a dollhouse, determined to explore and enjoy and savor the experience to the full.

Tyler dusted his hands on the seat of his jeans before crossing the room to her side. They'd been married a little more than six months, but the sight of him walking toward her still made her mouth dry. She was beginning to suspect it always would.

He kissed her, then he caught her earlobe between

his thumb and forefinger and caressed it fondly as he smiled into her face.

"Babe, you can mess with the furniture all you like. Whatever tickles your fancy. But we do have guests arriving in about twenty minutes, and I figured you might want to change before they get here."

Ally looked down at herself. She'd been in the yard, planting out the annuals she'd bought to give the garden a bit of extra color for their delayed Christmas party for Tyler's staff. The workshop had been so overwhelmed with orders prior to the festive season that they'd opted to do a late celebration after Christmas when everyone was more able to enjoy it.

"You really think your staff are going to notice if I'm wearing gumboots and have a little mud on my shorts?" she asked.

"They'll be crushed. You know they have a very high opinion of Gertrude." He patted her on the backside. "Why don't you slip into the shower and I'll join you in a minute?"

There was a light in his eyes that Ally recognized only too well. She smiled, her gaze dropping to the swathe of tanned skin visible at his neckline.

Jon made a disbelieving noise in the background. "Seriously, guys. The honeymoon was over months ago."

Tyler didn't bother turning around as he ushered Ally toward the hallway.

"Shut up. Make yourself useful and warm up the barbecue."

"Sure. But what should I tell everyone when they get here and you two are missing?" Jon said.

"We won't be missing," Ally said.

Tyler gave her a knowing look. Her heart gave an excited little leap.

"Improvise," he said over his shoulder.

Then he hustled Ally into the en suite bathroom before she could say anything else.

"We can't be late for our own party," she said as Tyler slid his hands beneath her grubby T-shirt.

"Have I ever mentioned how much I love a woman in gumboots?" he said as he walked her backward until she was pressed against the tiled wall.

"No."

"Well, I do. Especially when that woman is you."

He kissed her and the protest she'd been about to voice died in her throat.

"You really don't mind that I keep rearranging the house?" she said as he pushed her top up and started working on the clasp for her bra.

"I'd say if I did," he said, his hungry gaze roaming over her breasts.

"I'm pretty sure I'll grow out of it."

Tyler caught her chin so she had to look into his eyes. "I don't care, Ally."

She relaxed. "Good."

"You know what would be even better? If you weren't wearing these shorts," Tyler said, frowning at the bulky knot in the drawstring at her waist.

"Huh. How did that happen?"

They bent their heads together as they tried to unravel the knot. After a few seconds, the absurdity of the situation hit Ally. She glanced up into her husband's face and found a smile curling the corners of his mouth.

Their shared sense of humor was one of many joys in their relationship. Over the past twelve months, she'd discovered so many things about both herself and the man she'd married. She'd learned that trust was possible, that fears were bearable and that love was not a static thing. Instead, it deepened and broadened and grew richer with every day.

"Scissors?" she suggested.

"Definitely."

He pulled away to go find them, but she caught his shoulder.

"I love you, Tyler Adamson."

"I love you, too, Mrs. Adamson."

She let him go and settled against the wall to wait.

He wouldn't be gone long.

And she wasn't going anywhere.

* * * * *

A sneaky peek at next month...

Cherish™

ROMANCE TO MELT THE HEART EVERY TIME

My wish list for next month's titles...

In stores from 16th March 2012:

❏ The Last First Kiss – Marie Ferrarella

& The Husband Recipe – Linda Winstead Jones

❏ The Daddy Dance – Mindy Klasky

& Made for Marriage – Helen Lacey

In stores from 6th April 2012:

❏ One Good Reason – Sarah Mayberry

& The Mummy Miracle – Lilian Darcy

❏ Fortune's Proposal – Allison Leigh

& Healing Dr. Fortune – Judy Duarte

Available at WHSmith, Tesco, Asda, Eason, Amazon and Apple

Just can't wait?

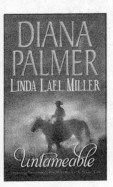

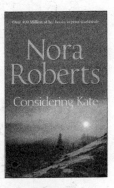

The World of Mills & Boon®

There's a Mills & Boon® series that's perfect for you. We publish ten series and with new titles every month, you never have to wait long for your favourite to come along.

Blaze®
Scorching hot, sexy reads

By Request
Relive the romance with the best of the best

Cherish™
Romance to melt the heart every time

Desire™
Passionate and dramatic love stories

Have Your Say

*You've just finished your book.
So what did you think?*

We'd love to hear your thoughts on our
'Have your say' online panel
www.millsandboon.co.uk/haveyoursay

- Easy to use
- Short questionnaire
- Chance to win Mills & Boon® goodies

Visit us Online

Tell us what you thought of this book now at
www.millsandboon.co.uk/haveyoursay

YOUR_SAY